LOVER'S CARESS

Boone frowned. "Hatred is a hard taskmaster. It can enslave you, if you let it, and then you can say goodbye to any hope for salvation."

Staring into his eyes, Jude felt again that loneliness in him, and her own aching need to banish it. All at once, she could no longer fight the pull between them, no longer wanted to. "Save me now, then," she said on a sigh, reaching up to pull his head down to her own.

With his lips on hers, Jude felt a shot of ice-cold heat rocket through her body. His arms closed around her, pulling her to his chest, and she lost all sense of the world around her. All that existed was the here and now, and Boone's capable hands caressing her heated body.

Leaving her dizzy with pleasure, Boone pulled back. Staring at her, smiling, he returned to her mouth. Kissing her deeply, he ripped away the covers separating them, then stretched out beside her, his hot, bare chest meeting her own, sparking yet another white-hot wave of passion. She sidled closer, wanting every bit of them touching. Her hands traveled over him, exploring each long, lean inch she'd watched so long from afar. She savored it all—his lush golden hair, the strong planes of his chest and muscled arms, the rough denim clasping his thighs.

He responded by sliding his hands up under her shift, finding all the intimate places, before slipping it over her head. Tossing it to the floor, he paused a moment to gaze down at her. The fire in his gaze as he smiled at her, the reverent way he touched her, made her feel she was the most desirable woman in the world. . . .

Books by Barbara Benedict

A TASTE OF HEAVEN

DESTINY

ALWAYS

ENCHANTRESS

EVERY DREAM COME TRUE

Published by Zebra Books

Every Dream Come True

Barbara Benedict

Zebra Books
Kensington Publishing Corp.
http://www.zebrabooks.com

ZEBRA BOOKS are published by

Kensington Publishing Corp.
850 Third Avenue
New York, NY 10022

Copyright © 1997 by Barbara Benedict

All rights reserved. No part of this book may be reproduced in any form or by any means without the prior written consent of the Publisher, excepting brief quotes used in reviews.

If you purchased this book without a cover you should be aware that this book is stolen property. It was reported as "unsold and destroyed" to the Publisher and neither the Author nor the Publisher has received any payment for this "stripped book."

Zebra and the Z logo Reg. U.S. Pat. & TM Off.

First Printing: December, 1997
10 9 8 7 6 5 4 3 2 1

Printed in the United States of America

*To my two guys, Scott and Jon,
for always being there when I need you most*

One

This was their man?

With dismay, Jude watched the long, lean form of Tucker Boone edge Lilah Matlock, the notorious madam of this saloon, up against the far wall. This . . . this leering wolf was the man Uncle Ham sent them to find?

Hiding next to her in a niche under the stairs, her brother wore the same stiff frown. They weren't prudes, neither she nor Christopher, but they'd seen enough of what drinking and womanizing could do to a man's resolution to feel dismay. They needed a tracker with a clear head and razor-sharp wits—not some sloppy drunk with an itch in his trousers.

Not that Boone seemed the least bit sloppy, she conceded, in either his appearance or pursuit. He had to be inebriated, considering all the whiskey they'd watched him knock back, yet he approached Lilah like a tiger stalking his prey, every muscle tensed and ready. Since he'd kept his back to her this past hour, Jude had yet to see his face, but she could well imagine his tightened jaw and intent gaze, for she could see his hunger mirrored in Lilah's features. Her world-weary expression vanished completely into tight, hard need as Boone backed her up against the wall.

At the impact Jude gasped.

Hazily she realized her brother had turned to gape at her, but her attention remained riveted on Boone. Around them the din went on—the tinny strains of a poorly tuned piano, the less harmonious wailing of the female accompanying it, the clatter of coins being plunked down on the tables—yet all Jude heard was the pounding of her heart as she watched Boone rest his hands on either side of Lilah's blond head, pinning her there. He and Lilah gazed so intently at each other, the rest of the world might as well have ceased existing.

Unable to look away, Jude watched Boone's hands slide down the gaudy purple satin, gliding over Lilah's wasplike waist to her rear. Squeezing, cupping the soft flesh of her buttocks, he pulled her against him, rubbing her hips against his groin. With the same fluid motion, he slanted his lips over hers, taking her mouth with slow, sensuous determination, while Lilah's avid hands twined through his thick, blond hair.

Jude was no stranger to desire. She must have seen Rafe and Guin kiss a thousand times, but surely this animal lust was a travesty of the love her adoptive parents shared. She tried to tell herself that she must look away, that it meant nothing to her what these degenerates did in the shadowed corner of some seedy bar, but her body throbbed more as Lilah pressed closer, gyrating her ample hips against his lean ones, boldly taking his hands to cover her generous cleavage.

Lewd, shameful, immoral, Jude recited silently, but she feared the words were the Reverend Byers's, not her own. Try as she might, she could not avert her gaze, mesmerized by the powerful intensity linking these two—a primitive force that at twenty-one years of age, she'd yet to experience herself.

Oh, she'd been chased and sought after enough, but while most girls her age were married and having babies, she'd yet to find a man to even remotely stir her senses, nothing like Lilah's weak-in-the-knees melting against the wall, letting demanding hands roam over her body.

Her childhood had taught her to be wary of men, but

surely she should have outgrown those painful memories by now, cocooned by the loving care of Rafe and Guin's family. When she'd asked her oldest brother if there was something wrong with her, Patrick had told her in his quiet, thoughtful way that there would be something wrong if she *wasn't* wary, after what she'd been through with their real father, Jacques Morteau.

Besides, Patrick had insisted, after playing the tomboy so long, Jude knew more about the male species than most men themselves, and it would take a rare breed indeed to impress her. Why not relax and stop worrying, and wait for the right man to come along?

Trouble was, patience had never been Jude's strong suit. If it were, she wouldn't be here now, once again posing as a boy, waiting for a chance to get this hard-drinking Romeo alone, so she could convince him to help them.

As if none too patient himself, Boone suddenly swept Lilah into his arms, purple satin cascading about his arms as he strode in Jude's direction. For a frozen instant, she was convinced that he'd seen her and Christopher and was coming to roust them from their hiding hole. But then Boone marched past up the stairs, his intense gaze locked on the female he held in his arms.

"He's younger than I expected," Christopher whispered next to her.

That he was, Jude thought. Worse, he was what Mrs. Tibbs, their elderly neighbor and guardian angel, would have called one handsome devil. Something happened in Jude's midsection when she'd gazed at Boone's bronzed features, something that had nothing whatsoever to do with being discovered before she was ready to present her case properly. His fair good looks hadn't caught her unawares; they made her suddenly *all too aware* of where he was going and what he'd be doing.

"So," her brother whispered beside her, snapping her back to the here and now, "what do we do now?"

She ran a hand through her recently cropped hair, daunted by the fact that she'd been lost in her thoughts. She mustn't forget what was at stake here. Binding her breasts and snipping off her long black tresses wasn't enough—she had to stay in focus. Mooning over a man like Boone could only spell trouble, which was something her family didn't need any more of at the moment.

If she had any sense, she'd march out of this saloon and return to Louisiana where Uncle Ham could find them someone older and far less attractive to help them with their mission.

The thought of home brought on a wave of yearning. What she wouldn't give to hug Guin and Rafe and all seven of her brothers and sisters. But that wasn't going to happen, not until she and Christopher accomplished what they'd set out to do.

"I said," Christopher repeated, "what do we do now?"

Stifling a shiver, she fought the sense of time running out. It would be all right, she told herself fiercely. She would make it all right.

"We follow him," she answered, before edging out of the niche to melt into the shadows. "And then wait till he's alone."

Hearing the distant crow of a rooster, Tucker Boone came instantly awake and found himself staring into the double barrels of a shotgun. He froze, having seen what such a weapon could do at close range and having no wish to see his insides scattered on Lilah's purple and gold striped wallpaper.

"You Tucker Boone?" Soft, quiet, and obviously young, the voice drew his glance up past the gun's barrels to a pair of dark, deep, and disturbing brown eyes.

Trouble, Tucker thought instantly.

Fighting off the grogginess of last night's whiskey, he

studied the boy, taking in details. Dusty and travel worn, the ill-fitting shirt and pants had seen better days. Castoffs, he judged. Cotton might be scarce, even with the war over, but only those dependent on the charity of others would wear the gray wool of the Confederate army in July. It didn't seem the poor kid got much to eat either, for he stood barely a shade over five feet, with not a spare ounce of flesh on that fragile frame.

On the surface Tucker found little in the boy to alarm him, but he hadn't survived thus far by ignoring his instincts. Trouble, his initial reaction had warned, and a cough to the right reaffirmed this. One scrawny youth might not pose much threat, but two, attacking from opposite directions, could prove a different story.

Quickly he sized up both assailants. Same dark hair and youthful features, but the second stood a good six inches taller and had peach fuzz sprouting on his chin, while the one with the shotgun had cheeks as smooth as the day he'd been born. The first boy must be younger, yet the weapon implied a certain authority. He had to be the brains, if not the brawn, of this duo. Get the shotgun, subdue the first one, and Tucker would be in control.

His gaze shot to the corner where his Colt revolver—and clothing—lay in the heap where he'd shed them. Reaching with one cautious hand to pat the cold mattress, he realized that Lilah, having gotten what she wanted, had long since quit the room. He was on his own.

Nothing new there. Most of his life he'd been scrambling through one scrape after another, depending on none but his own wits to get out of them.

"Christopher, get his gun," the first kid snapped, nodding at the corner, "and kick his clothes out of reach. This being Sunday morning, maybe he'll think twice about running off with nothing but the suit God gave him."

That Tucker would, indeed. The powerful matrons of Salvation, Missouri, would rather see a man rob a bank than cavort naked about the streets on the day Our Lord set aside for rest, church, and holy meditation. Leave Lilah's saloon as he was, and he'd find himself locked behind bars before most folks sat down to their Sunday dinner.

Clever kids, he thought with grudging respect. They weren't locals, for they spoke with a drawl—Louisiana Bayou, he guessed, catching the slight Cajun twang. But why come so far north to find him?

"You Tucker Boone or not?" the first boy repeated, nudging him with the weapon.

"I'm Boone," he said cautiously, his voice sounding like coarse gravel. He rose to a sitting position, intending to leave the bed.

"You stay right where you are," the second kid growled. "And you keep yourself covered with that sheet."

Tucker thought such modesty odd, having relinquished all pretense at it himself, but something about these two, something wide-eyed and innocent, had him tucking the sheet at his waist. From their darting gazes and trembling grips on the weapons, they were out of their depths here, and all three of them knew it.

"Me and my brother need your help. To find a man." Tucker heard a sharper edge to the voice now, to go with the glint in those intense brown eyes.

"Try three doors down," he said wearily, his pounding head reminding him just how many whiskeys he'd downed last evening. "Buck Llewellyn isn't so particular about who he takes money from. Me, I tend to steer clear of children."

The pair exchanged dubious glances. "He's right, Jude," the one called Christopher said uncertainly. "Look at him. He isn't what we need."

Now that stung. It was one thing to bow out gracefully, but Tucker didn't enjoy being dismissed out of hand.

"Hush, Christopher," Jude snapped, confirming the suspicion that he was the ringleader. He turned back to Tucker, his dark gaze unfathomable. "Word has it that you'll take on most any job for the right amount of cash."

Hiring on to take care of other folk's dirty business wasn't an occupation Tucker held much pride in, but too often a man's empty belly chose his life's work, and his had been empty for too long a time now. Clear down to his soul. "And what's your idea of the right amount?" he asked.

"We hear you were a scout in the war," Jude went on, ignoring his question. "If you have half the talent they say at tracking a man down, we've come to the right place. Help us and we'll make it worth your while. Say, twice the going rate?"

Faced with such a sum, Tucker was sorely tempted. He could sure use the money. "What if you're wasting my time?" he asked, eyeing their rough woolen clothing and road-beaten shoes. "Where would you kids come up with that kind of cash?"

"We have it." Glaring at him, Christopher dug into a pocket. "And there's plenty more where this came from," he said, holding out a few bills for inspection.

"Christopher!"

Tucker couldn't blame Jude for hissing. "If I were you, I wouldn't go flashing money in front of Buck or anyone else you approach. You could find yourself shorter of cash, if not flat on the floor with a hole in your skull."

"Think we're dumb enough to be carrying all our money?" Jude continued to frown at Christopher, as if willing him to keep his mouth shut. "What we're offering is a retainer. You get the rest when the job is done."

A retainer? Somewhere along the line, the kid must have been talking to lawyers, and that implied a certain degree of financial comfort. Taking a sharper look at Jude, Tucker noticed details he'd overlooked before. The skin wasn't soft just on his face—Jude's hands were white and smooth, too. No street urchin he knew ever had clean fingernails.

Maybe these kids *did* have money.

Sorting through the implications behind that, he felt the pounding in his head return with a vengeance. His well-deserved hangover clouded his brain, kept him from fingering just what it was he was missing. Instinct insisted that there was some clue he'd overlooked, which in the end could prove his undoing.

That same instinct was all but screaming at him to run, to get far away as fast as possible. Gazing up at Jude, who kept vigil with the shotgun trained at his chest, Tucker weighed his chances. He could probably wrestle the weapon away—the boy would be no match for his experience and strength. And Christopher's lax grip on the Colt suggested the boy had little experience at holding a man with a pistol. The trick would be to keep Jude between them, of course. No matter how good or poor a shot Christopher was, the boy wouldn't risk shooting if it meant hurting his brother.

"This man you want me to find," Tucker asked, taking the sheets with him as he eased to the other side of the bed. "What did he do to you that you're so willing to part with so much money?"

"We're not paying you to ask questions," Christopher snarled. Jude tightened his grip on the shotgun, eyeing Tucker warily, but did nothing to stop him from rising on the other side of the bed.

But then maybe that was because Tucker did so none too steadily.

"Never could handle Lilah's rotgut," he muttered aloud as he staggered to his feet. Holding the sheet—a purple satin that had seen better days—to his waist, he met Jude at the foot of the bed, keeping the boy between him and the Colt, just in case Christopher got trigger-happy. Both boys eyed the sheet—Christopher with a scowl, Jude with a surprising redness in his cheeks.

Interesting, Tucker thought, wondering if he could use

their modesty to his advantage. "As I see it," he drawled lazily, "I'm not accountable to your rules since I haven't agreed to work for you yet. Which I'm not likely to without a few answers. You don't blame me for having reservations, do you, Jude?"

"Stay back," Christopher growled. "Least until you get dressed."

"And how do I do that? You've taken my clothes." Tucker spared a glance at Christopher, whose grip on the gun now seemed less casual. Returning his attention to Jude, he tucked the sheet in at his waist and held up his hands in a gesture of surrender. "Besides, what can I do? You two have both weapons."

Jude's knuckles showed white around the trigger. "Leave him be, Christopher. Let him ask his questions."

Broadening his smile, Tucker took a step closer. He felt ridiculous in the sheet, and his head felt like stampeding buffaloes, but somehow or another, he had to get control of that gun.

Stopping mere inches away, he became acutely aware of the difference in their sizes, how small and fragile Jude seemed next to his own six-foot, trail-honed frame. Chin out and jaw rigid, the kid struggled to hide the tempest of emotions waging inside him, but someone should warn Jude how his expressive features gave him away. Too obviously he was desperate and scared, and Tucker's mere presence was making things worse.

Staring at the young, vulnerable features, Tucker felt a flash of regret. Too well he could remember a time when he'd been that innocent—when he, too, believed that if he fought long and hard enough, he could still make a difference. He didn't like thinking that such blind faith would be lost, or that he'd play a part in its destruction. These kids needed a protector, not some battle-weary cynic wrestling their gun—and with it, their hopes—away.

Annoyed by his reaction, Tucker told himself the sooner

he got the shotgun and sent the two packing, the better. For them all.

Keeping his mind on self-preservation, he moved closer. Jude edged backward, a strange glint in his eyes. Tucker struggled to focus, but his brain felt like unbaled cotton. Cursing last night's debauchery, he hoped he had it in him to do this without getting them all killed.

Jude's back met the wall with a thud. Ten paces to the right, hearing his brother's soft grunt, Christopher cried out, "Get back, Boone. I swear, I'll shoot."

Again raising his hands in surrender, Tucker tried to ease to the left, putting Jude between him and Christopher, but the damn satin slipped its knot. The sheet fell, tangling around his ankles and tripping him up. In the attempt to right himself, Tucker stumbled forward.

He fell against the side of the shotgun barrel, and he had the rare treat of experiencing its metallic chill before the gun exploded with searing heat, discharging its buckshot into the far wall. Hearing the shattering of disintegrating plaster, he glanced back at what was left of Lilah's prized statue of Venus.

He had no time to assess further damages, for the Colt gave an answering report behind him, its bullet glancing his shoulder. Reacting defensively Tucker went down on top of a kicking, fighting Jude.

His shoulder stung like the devil, but Tucker had his hands full with the ball of fury beneath him. He managed to grab the shotgun and toss it aside, but Jude was out to prove that he didn't need a weapon to inflict damage. Bloodied grooves appeared in Tucker's chest; quick thinking alone prevented the little monster from sinking sharp teeth into his uninjured arm.

Conscious of the boy's knee, so near to that most private and precious part of him, Tucker nearly backed off, but the kid's expressive face warned that his brother was creeping up behind them. The Colt had no bullets left, but the cold steel of its butt could still inflict harm to Tucker's whiskey-bruised skull.

As he glanced back at Christopher, Jude stretched for the shotgun, fallen in their struggles. Reaching for his arm, Tucker got shirt instead. With a telltale rip, gray wool came away in his hands, and a shrieking Jude began pummeling furious fists into his chest. He straddled the boy, snatching those flailing arms and pinning them to the floor, only to feel the Colt press against the side of his head.

Whatever threat Christopher might have uttered was drowned out by Lilah. Bursting into the room, she shouted, "What in tarnation is going on here?"

Panting heavily, Tucker stared down at his captive, his gaze drawn straight to Jude's chest. Though not large, the tear in the gray wool was strategically placed. From Tucker's vantage point above, it was hard to miss the cotton strips, unraveling in their struggle, that were meant to hide Jude's secret.

He now knew what his senses had been screaming, those little clues he'd been missing. This was no boy writhing beneath his naked body. Jude, of the disturbing brown eyes, was a furious woman.

Oh, yes, he'd found trouble indeed.

Two

Jude could tell the exact moment Boone's perception of her changed. In one breath he manhandled her like an opponent in a barroom brawl; in the next his grip loosened, then softened as he stared down in astonishment.

Following his gaze, she noticed the tear in her shirt, underneath which the cotton strips had begun to unravel, no doubt in their struggle for the gun. The rip wasn't large, nor did it expose any more chest than a ballroom gown would, but it certainly revealed that she was no boy. From the scowl on his face, she guessed Boone was none too pleased with the discovery.

His gaze bored into her, bold and intensely physical. Trapped by the thighs straddling her, the strong grip pinning her arms to the floor, Jude felt frightened and vulnerable. Up close Tucker Boone was so intensely masculine he could well be one of those Greek marble statues she'd once seen in a New Orleans exhibit, a powerful god come to life, as powerful—and as naked—as the day he'd been born. Even with the coarse gray wool of her clothes between them, she could feel his sun-bronzed skin pressed against her, gleaming everywhere they touched. Arms, chest—everything about him seemed knotted with muscle. Up close she could see the sprouting stubble of his beard, the soft vee of hair on his chest narrowing down to . . .

Her reaction shifted to panic, and a sudden sharp need to get away from him. A quick glance warned that Christopher would be of little help. At Lilah's entrance, he'd turned to gape at the madam, lowering the gun in his astonishment.

Noticing that Boone's attention had also been snared by Lilah, who was now charging into the room like an avenging angel, Jude tried to struggle free of Boone's grasp, but he held her in place with little apparent effort.

Barely covered in a feather-trimmed wrapper, her face nearly as purple as her garment, Lilah marched across her bedroom, green eyes flashing as she assessed the disaster. "My wallpaper," she cried as she paraded about the room. "My carpet . . . oh, my lovely Venus!"

Jude felt Boone stiffen. She expected him to pop up and start stammering excuses, but he merely tightened his grip. "I'll survive, Lilah, but thanks for asking," he said, shifting slightly to keep Jude's exposed bindings from view. "Had a bit of a tussle here with these . . . boys. I think we've come to an understanding, though. Haven't we, Jude?"

It unsettled her, that probing gaze of his, and he darned well knew it. "Maybe," she told him angrily, "if you get your dead weight off me."

He cast a quick glance at her chest, warning her to cover up the best she could, before lifting himself up to go find his clothes without a backward glance.

He was shrugging into his trousers when Lilah strolled up to him, her painted mouth curved into a smile. "How charming," she said, laying a possessive hand on his arm. "Pray tell, what was this misunderstanding?"

Yanking the pieces of wool together, Jude clasped her shirt with one hand as she scrambled to her feet. Christopher tightened his grip on the Colt as if just now remembering he held it and stepped up to stand between her and Boone.

The boy was barely sixteen, she thought with a frown. He should be home with the other kids in their family, not stuck in some sleazy bordello, standing guard over a sister who could take care of herself.

All evidence to the contrary.

"I guess no one ever warned these kids not to wake a man with the wrong end of a shotgun," Boone told Lilah dryly. "Not unless they're prepared to use it."

Knowing he'd meant that for her, Jude scowled at him. "We were ready," she countered. "Or am I the only one not overlooking that hole in your shoulder?"

His surprised glance had her wishing she'd kept her mouth shut. She didn't want him thinking she cared that he might be injured.

"Still doesn't explain why they felt a need to wreck the room," Lilah said, drawing his attention back to her. "Who are these urchins, darlin', and why do they feel such animosity toward you?"

"Urchins—"

Boone silenced Jude with a look. "It's a long story that can wait until later," he said, keeping his scowl trained on her. "They're just leaving anyway."

Irked by his haste to hustle her and Christopher away, she frowned at the pale hand locked on his tanned arm, the voluptuous body all but attached to his side. "If you want to be alone with your . . . your friend here," she said, "why not let that wait until later?"

Boone turned to Lilah with a shrug as if to say, *See what I mean?*

Lilah smiled unconvincingly. "You boys must be hungry. Go on down to the kitchen, and Bertha can rustle you up some breakfast while Tucker and I talk."

The way the woman pawed Boone, she could be a fat, purring cat anxious to sink her claws into a fresh, prized catch. "Right neighborly of you, ma'am," Jude said sarcastically. "But we'll stay right here until Boone hears us out."

Ignoring her, Boone linked gazes with Lilah's. "A saloon's no place for boys to be eating breakfast. They can go down the street to Myrna's Cafe."

"I said we're not leaving," Jude repeated through gritted teeth.

Christopher, ever her protector, did his best to stem her rising temper. "I sure am hungry, Jude. Let's wait for him at this cafe."

Boone turned to her then, his gaze holding her as effectively as the hand he reached out with, his eyes as blue and open as the vast prairie sky. "I'll meet you there," he told her solemnly. "I swear it."

"Yeah." She didn't want to keep looking at him, didn't want this confusing, conflicting reaction to a man she barely knew.

"I said I'd be there," he said sharply. "And I never go back on my word."

Jude could remember her uncle uttering those same words. Rafe Latour had promised to take care of her and her brothers, to make them a family, and even when things looked their worst, he'd kept his word to the letter.

Yet wasn't it stretching logic to think this stranger could be cut from the same mold? In Jude's experience honor and nobility were ideals most men talked about more than they practiced, and nothing in Boone's behavior indicated that he could be trusted.

But what was her choice? Boone didn't seem likely to talk in front of Lilah, and she needed him to help keep her own promise. Before she'd left home, her mother and Patrick had made her swear to hire a professional and stay with him, not go off half-cocked trying to find Rafe on her own. "I'm taking you at your word then," she told Boone gruffly. "But I warn you. If there's one thing I can't abide, it's lying."

His gaze didn't waver.

"C'mon." Christopher tugged her arm. "Let's go wait at Myrna's."

Jude met Boone stare for stare. "If I were you, I wouldn't waste time here. I'd be off to the doctor, seeing to that wound."

Boone raised a brow. "Thanks for the concern—I think—but as long as I'm not bleeding on the rug, I might better tend to business." He nodded at Lilah.

With a low, throaty chuckle, the woman grabbed his arm, no doubt to prevent him from detaining Jude with it. "And it's adult business," she said, catching his gaze and holding it. "No kids allowed."

Ignoring the woman, Jude instructed Christopher to give Boone back his gun, then led the way to the door. Lilah could have Boone, she thought irritably. All Jude needed him for was to serve as a glorified chaperon to keep her family happy. At this late date, she didn't have time to go searching for a replacement.

He'd better be a man of his word, she thought angrily as she hurried down the back stairs. Or Lilah or not, she'd be coming back for him.

Watching Jude leave, Tucker fought a strange sense of confusion, almost bemusement. That had to have been the strangest encounter he'd ever had, and the look in Jude's eyes had promised it would be far from the last of it. What in the name of all good sense had possessed him to suggest meeting at Myrna's?

"All right, lover." Lilah gazed up at him with deceptive softness. "Why don't you tell me the real reason those two were here."

Real reason? He probably knew less than she. "They came looking to hire me," he said with a shrug.

"For what? Forgive my skepticism, darlin', but you've never struck me as the type to play nanny."

"They want me to find someone," he added, knowing

Lilah would probe until she got what she sought. "We never got around to discussing particulars."

"And I suppose the shotgun was to convince you that you could work just as well without pay?"

Her sarcasm had begun to annoy him. "I assume they meant to get my attention, but things got a little out of hand. While I was showing Jude I don't take kindly to threats, Christopher winged my shoulder."

"With your own revolver?" She raised a brow, a smile playing at the corners of her full red lips. "How droll."

"Yeah, a real hoot." He reached back to inspect his wound with his fingers. It stung, but it wasn't deep and had already stopped bleeding. "Too bad all my mornings can't be so entertaining."

She ran a soothing hand up his arm. "Poor darlin'. I'd think you'd want to avoid them, not meet them later."

Owner of half the businesses in town, Lilah hadn't gotten where she was by being dim-witted, and the fact that she now watched him so shrewdly made him distinctly uneasy. "Let's just say I'm curious," he said offhandedly, pulling away to gather up his belongings. "They did offer twice the going rate."

The dollar signs all but danced in her eyes. "Twice the usual? My, my, but that should just about cover what you owe me."

Tucker had been in the process of bending down for his shirt, but at her words he snapped to attention. "What are you talking about? I know better than to get in debt to you."

She merely smiled as she gestured about the room. "Look at this place. I have to get Lloyd in here to patch up the wall, and look at the blood on the rug. Someone's got to pay for the damages." Her gaze came to rest on the shattered remains of the statue. "Sorry, lover, but my Venus didn't come cheap."

Tucker had been there when she bought it, so he knew

exactly how little the plaster imitation had cost, but he also knew better than to argue. Nobody came out ahead when talking money with Lilah. "Let me guess," he said dryly. "You've already calculated the bill."

She made a great show of scanning the room. "I can't see how it can be any less than one fifty."

"One fifty?" He choked back the protest, figuring she'd only up the ante. "Why come at me?" he asked instead. "The kids did the shooting."

"A bird in the hand, lover." Sidling up to him, she ran her palm across his bare chest. Obviously she'd seen the rags on the kids and gone instantly for the viable source. Annoyed, he flung her wrist away. "Good luck, then. We both know milking money from me is like bleeding a stone."

She chuckled. "Tucker, sweet thing, you forget whose bank is guarding that tidy sum you've been squirreling away."

He neither needed nor wanted the reminder. He'd had his misgivings about entrusting his savings to her institution, but he wanted to keep his money in a neutral site like Salvation, and Lilah owned the only bank here. Behind the scenes of course. Business boomed, she'd once told him, if the town's sanctimonious citizens thought her manager, Tom Riley, ran the show.

"Nobody's touching that money," he told her, stabbing his arms into the sleeves of his shirt. "The sole reason I put it in your damned bank was so I couldn't spend it. You know that."

"Maybe." She looked up at him, tilting her head. "But I still don't know why. I do love a man of mystery, sugar, but all this secrecy is wearing thin. Can't you tell me what the money is for? Aren't we friends?"

No. Lilah might be the closest he had to one, but in truth all they had between them were sporadic bouts of heavy drinking and nights of hot, hard sex. Hardly a reason for sharing confidences.

And he had an almost superstitious reluctance to reveal his current plans. He wouldn't risk anything going wrong now, not when he was so close to achieving his goal.

He could feel Lilah's gaze on him, her frown deepening with the silence between them. "You're not gonna tell me, are you?" she asked with a mock pout.

"No, ma'am, I'm not." Facing her, he tucked in his shirt and strapped on his holster. "You said it yourself. Business and pleasure don't mix."

"How right you are." She went suddenly hard—her gaze, her voice, even her posture. "Speaking of which, when will you be paying for these damages?"

Tucker longed to tell her to fix her own damned room, but along with her other properties here in Salvation, Lilah owned the sheriff and circuit judge. "Relax," he told her curtly. "You'll get your money, sooner or later."

She shook her head. "I'll be setting a bad example if I let you slide on this. 'Old Lilah's getting soft,' they'll be whispering. Why, I'll be needing to hire extra muscle just to keep the gentlemen paying their tabs."

She did so love to prove who was boss. Too often he'd watched her flex her financial muscles with other men, but he'd never before been one of them. "Get it through your head, Lilah, I'm not touching that money."

"You don't have to—I will. I need but give the word, and my good friend, Judge Rankin, will slap a lien on your account. Sugar, I can have my hands on your money before the month is out."

Fingers tightening on the pistol, Tucker fought an insane urge to use it. "I don't take kindly to being backed into a corner."

"Going to the corner is your choice, lover. You have other options. You can always come work for me."

They'd been down this road before, her offer always ending with his refusal. Lilah was managing enough as a lover—as his boss, she'd be unbearable. "Thanks for the offer, but I think I'll pass."

"Ah, yes, the infamous Boone law of ethics. He can steal a man's fortune at the gaming tables, but all bets are off when it comes to working in a bordello."

"Lay off, Lilah."

"And aren't you inconsistent with your morals." She sashayed over, making great business of straightening his shirt. "As I recall, it was the wee hours of the Lord's day of rest when you backed me into the barroom wall last night. Are you saying it's all right to take what you want from me, where and when you want it, but any wages I might pay are tainted because I'm not one of your precious ladies?"

"Cut the melodrama. I didn't take anything you didn't want to give."

She tossed back her head with a chuckle. "Yeah, there's nothing I enjoy more than squeezing your tight little ass, sugar—unless it's tallying up my money—but you see, that's the difference between me and the dainty females you tiptoe around. I know the difference between business and pleasure."

"And how to get the most out of both."

She smiled, clearly pleased with the assessment. "At least I'm honest about it. And that being the case," she said, gripping the front of his shirt, "I won't beat around any bush. I want my money, and I aim to get it."

"Where do you think I'm going to rustle up that kind of cash? We both know I wouldn't be in Salvation if I had hope of employment elsewhere."

"Take the job those brats offered. Charge them extra for expenses, since they got you into this mess. Frankly, lover, I don't care how you get the cash. Just make sure all two hundred is in my hands by the end of the month or I—and my good friend, Judge Rankin—will be taking it out of your account."

That gave him just a little under three weeks. "You can be a real bitch, you know that?"

"Yeah," she drawled, smiling up at him. "Don't you just love it?"

No, he did not. "You'll have your money," he ground out, pulling away roughly. If he had to scrub dishes or muck out stables, he'd pay her every penny. And the day he did would be his last visit to Lilah's saloon.

Reaching out, she tugged at his sleeve. "You hurry back, lover." She nodded toward the bed. "You and I have unfinished business."

"I don't think so, darlin'," he said, yanking free and heading for the door. "No sense mixing business with pleasure at this late date."

He didn't wait for her comeback. Having burned his bridge, he meant to leave Salvation and the sooner the better.

Intent upon where he'd go next, and how to earn the most money in the least amount of time, he stomped out of the saloon, forgetting all about the pair he'd left waiting down the street.

Three

"What are we going to do?" Jude muttered as much to herself as to Christopher as they headed to Myrna's Cafe. "How can we depend on a man who thinks less with his head and more with . . ." She let her voice trail off, having no wish to name, much less think one more second about, that particular part of the man's anatomy.

Besides, being male, Christopher didn't need her to elaborate. "Can't say I blame him," he said with a grin. "That Lilah sure is nice to look at."

"Nice?" Jude stopped in her tracks, turning to gape at her brother. "Nice has to be the last word I'd use to describe that fat cow."

Chuckling again, Christopher continued walking. "As I recall, you once called Guin a cow, and look how you regretted that snap judgment."

He was right. The first time she'd met Rafe's future wife, all Jude had seen was a spoiled Southern belle who'd disrupt their lives, yet it hadn't taken long before Guinevere McCloud proved herself equal to the task of keeping their family together. These days, the word Jude used to describe Guin was mother, a tribute to the woman who had so patiently taught her the value of true love and trust.

Indeed, it was for Guin that Jude had come seeking Tucker Boone's help.

Falling into step beside her brother, she cast a glance over her shoulder at the saloon. Maybe Christopher was right and her assessment of Lilah was too quick to be valid, guided less by logic and more by inner demons. Then again, Guin had never worn the steely glint she'd seen in Lilah Matlock's hard green eyes. The madam's cold gaze seemed to consume Boone, as if he were a delicacy to be gobbled up, a gift placed on this earth for her sole personal pleasure.

Opening her mouth to explain this to Christopher, Jude caught his boyish grin. "Why, you little brat," she said, wanting to throttle him. "You don't think much of Lilah, either. You just couldn't resist the chance to tease me."

No real surprise, since all her brothers thought it their duty to provoke her and never passed up an opportunity. Lately they'd even been bringing in the younger ones, Guin and Rafe's three natural children, to participate in their practical jokes on their sister. Christopher could tease with the best of them, but like Patrick, was quick to quit if he saw it bothered her. "I was just hoping to make you laugh," he said, sobering. "I didn't think now was the time to let your temper get the best of you."

"I know, but you have to admit Lilah was awful. I swear, she showed more concern about her dumb broken statue than the hole we put in Boone's shoulder."

"If you ask me, he didn't act all that concerned, either. In fact, you're the only one it seems to be worrying. What's it to you if Boone got injured?"

What indeed? "Maybe I'm just not in the habit of wounding a man," she blustered.

Christopher frowned, and she knew he was thinking of the time she'd wielded a gun to protect him from their father. "And all else aside," she added quickly, "Boone won't be much help if he's down with a fever."

"Yeah, well, I've been thinking about that." Christopher pursed his lips before going on. "I'm not sure hiring him is such a great idea. What say we just ride off and pretend we never met him? He's liable to cause more trouble than he's worth."

Stunned by his vehemence, Jude stopped to stare at her brother. "Now who's making snap judgments?"

"This is different, and you know it."

"Is it? I told you my reasons for mistrusting Lilah, so how about explaining yours. What is it, Christopher? What do you have against Tucker Boone?"

He shrugged, clearly uncomfortable with the question. "It's nothing definite, more a feeling. Men like him, they're different from you and me, Jude. Life's made them harder and colder, and set them seeking things we can't even imagine. No matter how I look at it, I see only trouble."

His words caused a chill in her chest, but she instantly denied it. "He can still do the job, and we can't afford to be picky." She was anxious to be on the road, looking for Rafe, and could see no reason to waste time looking for another candidate. As far as she was concerned, one chaperon was as good as another. "We have to keep personal feelings out of this," she added primly.

"I will if you will."

"And what's that supposed to mean?" she demanded.

Turning away, he gazed down the street. "Don't you be taken in by those good looks of his. Remember what happened when Guin made the mistake of trusting Lance Buford."

Jude shook her head, remembering only too well how that evil man had teamed with their father to burn down their home and threaten their lives. "Buford thought that the world owed him a fortune. He told himself it was all right to lie and cheat and steal to get what he wanted."

"And you're so certain Boone isn't cast from the same mold?"

Was she? Lance Buford had taught her how easily startling good looks and easy charm could hide a monster.

"All I'm saying is we both need to keep our wits," Chris-

EVERY DREAM COME TRUE 31

topher pressed. "Sorry, Jude, but it's as clear as day that man has you rattled."

"I can handle Boone," she insisted.

Christopher saw right through her bravado. "The only reason Patrick went along with this scheme of yours was because no one's supposed to know you're a girl," he reminded. "He didn't want me fending off brutes who think you're a woman of easy virtue, something Boone is bound to do, seeing you roam about with the ease and freedom of a man."

For Jude it had long been a sore point that her brothers, just because they were males, could do far more than she. "That's so unfair—"

"Maybe, but that's how life *is,* and you can't change the world overnight just because you wish it." He shook his head in exasperation. "You're so stubborn and headstrong, and Boone . . . well, you saw him back there with Lilah. I just don't see how it's gonna work out."

Uneasily she saw his point. Not that Boone would ever feel the same uncontrolled lust for her that he showed for Lilah, but she didn't want him thinking he could take liberties. "Don't worry," she assured Christopher. "From now on, I'll give Boone no reason to remember I'm anything but your brother. After all, I spent most of my childhood acting and thinking like a boy."

"You can't really expect him to forget what happened back there," Christopher pointed out. "He'll have that hole in his shoulder to remind him."

"So he knows I'm a girl," she said flippantly. "He couldn't be any less interested. You saw Lilah. That's how Boone likes his women, all filled out and knowledgeable about men. All I'll ever be to him is a thorn in his side."

"You so sure of that?"

"I'll make it work, Christopher, just see if I don't. Besides, what's our choice? Going back home to Uncle Ham will take time, something we can't afford to waste right now. Boone's our best hope, and we have to take it. Trust me, little brother. I can handle him."

"I don't like this," he repeated stubbornly.

"I don't much enjoy it, either, but like you said, life doesn't always turn out the way we want it. Besides, what's the sense arguing over this when he hasn't even agreed to take the job? You go on over to the cafe, find us a table, and start thinking of how we'll talk Boone into helping us." She nodded at the white clapboard house before them. "I'm gonna pop in and visit the doctor."

Christopher frowned. "He can't possibly be there yet. You know Boone's with Lilah."

"I'm not chasing him," she said in exasperation. She pointed to the tear in her shirt. "If I want to pose as a boy, I'd better sew up this shirt. Since none of the shops are open yet, I need to get the needle and thread from the doctor. Go on, I'll meet you at Myrna's in a couple of minutes."

It was plain Christopher didn't like her plan, but he was no match for the aroma of fresh-baked blueberry muffins. Visibly torn, he soon gave in to the growlings in his stomach and started for the cafe.

Watching him go, Jude felt a pang. Christopher relied on her to be strong, all of her family did, and she'd rather roast in hell than disappoint them. Was she making a mistake, as he implied, by pinning their hopes on Boone?

Pushing open the white picket gate, she relived the moment in which Boone had made his promise. It happened rarely in this life, that instant linking, but something had hit her hard when she stared into his deep blue eyes. It didn't make sense, knowing so little about him, but in that instant, she'd felt a bone-deep conviction that here was a man she could trust. Not in all things—she wasn't that naive—but if Boone said he'd meet them at Myrna's, then she fully expected to see him there.

Crossing her fingers tightly, she stepped inside the doctor's office.

Making his way to the livery stable, Boone cursed under his breath. This had been far from his best visit to Salvation, and he was eager to leave town. His shoulder ached like the devil, his head kept pounding, and his pride stung more than he thought possible. Left a bad taste in his mouth, Lilah's jab about his morals.

As did his memory of last night, the careless way he'd all but taken her right there on the barroom floor. Maybe she had egged him on with her innuendoes, the constant strokes and caresses, but Tucker had never before been so far gone to proper public behavior. What had happened to the fine, upstanding citizen his mama had raised him to be?

War had happened, he thought bitterly.

Hard times had forced him to take on jobs he might otherwise have looked down his nose at, to mingle with folks he might more wisely avoid. Bit by bit, circumstance had whittled away at him, stripping off the gentlemanly veneer until all he could now legitimately lay claim to was being a man of his word.

Stopping where he stood, he belatedly remembered the promise he'd made to Jude and her brother.

Another string of oaths erupted from his mouth. Maybe she'd forgotten, he tried to tell himself. Or, given the fiasco in Lilah's bedroom, Jude had realized that hiring him wasn't such a good idea, and right at this moment, she and her brother were riding off in the other direction.

But deep down Tucker knew better, even before he turned to look down the street to see Jude striding into Myrna's Cafe.

He could still leave, pretend he never saw her. All his instincts screamed at him to get on a horse and start riding fast, but to do that, he'd have to ignore that small scrap of decency withering daily in his hard-bitten, cynical body.

Go on, escape, the devil inside him coaxed. When fate dealt a losing hand, the wise man folded—and getting involved with Jude was a losing proposition from the get-go. It wouldn't be dishonorable, leaving her and her brother waiting—he might better call it survival. If anyone took issue with that, hell, what could they expect? Tucker Boone was what life made him.

For the longest time, he stood there, debating between the wise—and the right—thing to do. In his mind he kept seeing Jude's soft brown eyes pleading with him, urging him to do what was decent, not convenient, and before he was aware of it, he found himself closing the distance to Myrna's.

He paused outside the cafe, giving himself time to plan out what to say. He'd be gentle, yet firm, in his refusal. He'd give it five minutes, ten at most, before making his way south to Texas. Jim Hackett, down in Amarillo, was always looking for extra hands. True, Hackett paid slave wages and was neither kind nor honest in his dealings with his neighbors, but it had to be smarter than hooking up with Jude and her brother.

Slipping in the back door, hoping to call as little attention to himself as possible, he found Jude immediately. She sat at a front table opposite her brother. Watching her lean over the table as she talked, Tucker could feel the heat of her again, all that coiled energy, as if she still writhed beneath him.

Coming here was a big mistake, he decided. He needed simplicity, peace of mind, and this girl was a complication he might better avoid.

Yet he wound his way to their table, eyes locked on Jude as she spoke urgently to her brother. At first he couldn't hear what she was saying. The cafe was packed with men from Lilah's, late-night stragglers drawn by the aroma of

EVERY DREAM COME TRUE 35

fresh-baked muffins—and still juiced from the night's festivities, they made a far from quiet bunch. Tucker was nearly at Jude and Christopher's table before he could make out their conversation.

"I say we leave," Christopher growled. "It's obvious he isn't coming."

"He said he'd be here."

Her stubborn, matter-of-fact tone implied a belief in him that Tucker hadn't expected. Oddly it meant more to him than he was prepared for.

Christopher put it in clearer perspective. "You can't possibly trust him . . . that hard-drinking, womanizing, gun-for-hire?"

Shaking her head, Jude brought Tucker down another peg. "He might be all those things, but Uncle Ham says he's the best tracker hereabouts, so I'm willing to wait all day if I have to. Don't worry. If Boone goes back on his word, I'll track *him* down. He shouldn't be that hard to find. Come dark, he'll be in some saloon, looking for cheap whiskey and the first available skirt."

Tucker didn't know what irked him more, her worldly view or her low assessment of his character. His mama had been right about that, too—eavesdropping wasn't the most pleasant way to hear what folks really thought about you.

"Hey, Myrna," he called to the matronly female emerging from the kitchen. "Quite a crowd. Gotten so a regular customer can't find a seat."

Beaming, Myrna rushed up to fuss over him, insisting that she'd always have room for Tucker Boone. It was a running argument between them, she claiming he was responsible for her success by bringing over the night crowd from Lilah's, while he maintained, quite rightly, that all credit lay with her muffins.

It was a good thing he'd come, Myrna insisted, for he needed filling out, and she had some freshly ground sausage.

Shooing him off, she promised to be right back with a pile of them, as well as a plate heaped with eggs and potatoes.

Reaching Jude's table, Boone found the girl glaring at him again. "Must you flirt with everyone?" she snapped as he pulled out a chair.

Tucker sat slowly, more convinced than ever that he shouldn't be here. "Listen, Miss—"

"It's Jude. Just Jude," she whispered, glancing swiftly about the room. "I'm a boy, remember?"

He couldn't help it—his gaze went straight to her chest.

"I mended it," she said defensively. "More or less, given the time I had. If you want, I can also stitch up that shoulder."

He nearly blurted out *God forbid*, but the offer had been an earnest one, and he saw no need to rile her. "Thanks, but I'll take care of it myself."

She frowned. "Don't be so stubborn. Obviously you had no time to stop in to see Doc Richards, and I can't imagine that Lilah doing much in the way of nursing." She nodded at the bundle at her feet. "I've got ointment and bandages, but it might be best if we step outside. The less these folks know about our business, the better."

"Only business I have is the breakfast Myrna will soon be serving."

The frown deepened. "You can come back to it, just as soon as I've dressed your wound."

"She always boss everyone around this way?" he asked Christopher.

"If you're smart, you'll call her a 'he.' " The boy almost grinned. "And yeah, our Jude's a regular tyrant when *he* wants something done."

Jude rose abruptly, lifting the bundle. "We're wasting time. You coming, Boone?" With no further ceremony, she headed for the back door, Christopher at her heels, neither one glancing back to see if he followed.

He'd done what he had to, Tucker told himself irritably.

He'd come here and met them, and no one could expect him to do more.

Yet before Myrna could set his food on the table, he was rising to his feet. Telling the woman that he'd be back to eat in a moment, he strode to the door and burst out into the bright, morning sunlight.

Jude and Christopher waited for him in the yard. Years ago, when Salvation had still been a stopping point for folks heading west, wagons would pull into this area to fill up on goods from the nearby shops. Most of the town had since turned to farming, with the pioneer traffic drying up during the war, but while the supply stores had since gone out of business, the wagon yard, with its railed hitching posts, still remained.

Christopher sat motionless on one rail, with Jude perched on another, rummaging through the bundle in her hands.

Eyeing the girl, indistinct in her bulky gray wool, Boone felt better about not recognizing her gender. With that close-cropped hair, her dirt-streaked face, and belligerent attitude, anyone could be forgiven for thinking her a boy. Wasn't much there to get a man's pulse jumping.

Except maybe for the eyes.

Uneasily he realized it kept coming back to that, the way he felt when she gazed up at him. He supposed he should be grateful that she was now so focused on the stuff she held in her hands.

"Sit over here," she told him abruptly, not bothering to look up. It got his goat, the way she expected him to so docilely follow, as if it never even occurred to her that he might have a mind of his own. Sauntering over to the rail, standing with legs apart and arms crossed at his chest, he decided it was time to show her that he was in charge of this interview.

Still digging through the bag, she spoke almost offhandedly. "Take off your shirt."

"Isn't it a tad early in our relationship to be undressing?" he drawled. "Especially out here in public?"

Her cheeks turned a gratifying pink, the only outward indication that she'd heard his taunt. "Then again," he pressed, "it won't be a first for you, seeing me without clothes. Though last time, as I recall, you held a gun to my head."

"Shut up," Christopher snarled.

Tucker ignored him, keeping his gaze on Jude's averted, reddened face. "Mind telling me what you hoped to accomplish by waking me so rudely? Surely there was an easier way to get my attention."

"The gun was my idea," the boy volunteered. "Jude got tired of waiting for you to finish with that . . . that Lilah, and I was afraid where her impatience might lead. No offense, Boone, but we don't know you from Adam, and I wasn't about to take the chance my sister could get hurt."

"That's enough, Christopher." Setting down the bundle in a businesslike manner, Jude held up bandages and some noxious-smelling salve. "I might feel duty bound to tend to the wound we inadvertently inflicted, Boone, but we have much better things to do with our time than to stand here chatting. Do you want me to stop that bleeding or not?"

"It stopped bleeding an hour ago," he felt compelled to point out.

She ignored that, too, gesturing him to remove his shirt.

"You might as well let her dress the wound," Christopher said dryly. "She's nothing short of stubborn."

Realizing that he was being fairly mule-headed himself, Tucker yanked off his shirt and plopped down on the rail beside her.

With surprisingly gentle fingers, Jude probed at the groove in his shoulder. "It's just a graze." Holding out a cup, she directed her brother to fill it from the cafe's water barrel. "Doesn't need stitching. Just some washing, then the ointment and bandages. We can talk while I work."

"You mean I actually get to speak? Ouch. Take it easy, will you?"

Her touch instantly gentled, as did her tone. "I suppose we didn't get off to a good start, but that's as much your fault as mine. You haven't exactly gone out of your way to be pleasant."

"Am I supposed to be happy about waking with a raging hangover and a shotgun shoved in my face?"

"We had to get your attention. Yours, and yours alone."

He couldn't help but catch the defensive note in her tone, nor did he miss the urgency. "I don't like secrecy."

She looked from him to Christopher, now returning with the water. "It's not secrecy. It's discretion. We don't need folks knowing our business."

"Not knowing makes it hard for a man to do the job. Why don't you just tell me what this is all about?"

Christopher made a noise, but she held up a hand to silence him. "We're trying to locate a prisoner of war."

She didn't look at him as she said this, and he found her tone suddenly evasive. "The war's been over months now," he said, watching her face. "Most prisoners have been released, and those that haven't can be found through official channels."

"It will take months to get through the red tape and confusion, and we need to find him now. Besides, we've been having trouble tracking down this particular prisoner. He vanished some months ago."

Tucker didn't know why, but what she was saying—or, more accurately, wasn't saying—made him uncomfortable. "This vanishing, did it take place in a Confederate prison, or Union?"

He watched Jude and her brother exchange glances. Christopher scowled as he shook his head, clearly not wanting her to volunteer more.

"Confederate soldier, Union transport," Jude said stubbornly. "The Federals were moving him from St. Louis to

Chicago when the train went off the rails. Rumor has it that the derailment was no accident, that the train was ambushed for the sole purpose of freeing the prisoner. Folks say the Gray Ghost Riders are behind the escape."

Tucker's unease deepened. He knew more than a few members of that gang, having ridden with them himself, and they were some of the toughest, meanest, and most bitter Johnny Rebs to ride the plains. Cutting their teeth on the border wars with Kansas, these Missouri bushwhackers had been happy to step into the breach when the rebel forces were routed from the state, sabotaging and harassing Union troops and sympathizers while waiting for a Southern invasion. Unfortunately the Confederate army didn't return in force to Missouri until near the end of the war, too late to make a difference. Left to the harsh, bitter retribution of the victorious North, and faced with long prison terms at best, many of those guerrilla outfits had chosen to band together, surviving by doing what they did best—raiding and looting the plains like modern-day pirates.

Chances were, Tucker knew the man Jude sought. "Why not tell me what this is really about?" he asked, reaching out for her arm. "Who is this man you want me to find?"

She didn't answer at first, just stared at him with those wide, brown eyes. Under his grip, he could feel the delicate bones of her wrist, the soft, throbbing acceleration of her pulse, a sensation that left him with conflicting desires—to stand and protect her . . . and to run for his life.

"His name is Rafe Latour," she said quietly, holding his gaze.

He let go of her arm. A splash of cold water would have been as effective as the shock of hearing that name. At first Tucker thought it a tasteless joke, some sick clown's need to watch him squirm, but nothing in Jude's steady expression gave cause to assume she wanted anything more than what she said. To find the one man Tucker hated most on this earth.

EVERY DREAM COME TRUE 41

"What did Latour do to you?" he ground out, not trusting himself to say more.

"Don't tell him anything." Christopher edged closer to his sister. "It's none of his business anyway."

Apparently she didn't listen to her brother much, either. "Let's just say it's important to us," she told Tucker. "You don't need to know more than that."

She was wrong there. Glancing from her to Christopher, eyeing their troubled faces, Tucker was painfully aware that there was a *great* deal more he needed to know.

Rafe Latour, he thought bitterly. How many ways could one name crop up to haunt him?

Tucker stared at Jude and Christopher with new eyes. Funny that they should show up now, offering good money to find the man with whom he had a score to settle. It was almost as if the fates, after knocking him around, wanted to offer this consolation. Only an ungrateful fool could refuse, he told himself, and he'd been raised to be neither rude nor stupid.

"If I take this job," he said slowly as Jude finished dressing his wound, "I'll need money up front for expenses. Fifty now and two hundred when I hand Latour over."

"Two fifty?" Christopher gasped. "Forget it, Jude. We can't—"

She silenced him with a look, then turned her attention to gathering up her supplies, her agitation betrayed by how roughly she tossed the ointment and bandages into the bag. "You have to understand, Mr. Boone. Your demands are steeper than we bargained on."

"You did offer twice the going rate."

"Yes, but—"

He saw the desperation in her features, but he willed himself to ignore it. "That's my price," he said stubbornly. "You can take it or leave it, Miss . . ."

"McCloud."

She said it too quickly. Combine that with the surprised

glance from her brother, and Tucker had to believe the name an assumed one.

"And it's Master McCloud, if you please," she added sternly. "I shouldn't have to warn you how important it is that folks continue to consider me a boy, especially out there on the trail."

"Whoa, now. What trail?"

She eyed him as if he were the village idiot. "We'll be traveling through some rough territory, tracking down the Gray Ghosts. You'll have worries enough without the distraction of constantly protecting my honor."

"There won't be any distractions." Tucker rose to his feet to face her, his expression stern. "I have no intention of taking you with me, *Master* McCloud. You both can wait for me here."

She drew herself up to all five foot two of her. "We're paying you good money to take us to . . . to Latour, and we're not about to sit here twiddling our thumbs while you gallivant around the countryside. Apparently, Boone, I didn't make myself clear. I *need* to be there when you find him."

He took a few steps closer until he towered over her. "Let's get this straight. The two fifty gets you Latour, not leave to tell me how and when to do my job. The last thing I need is some managing female and her wet-behind-the-ears brother getting in my way and risking all our necks."

"Managing female?" she sputtered.

"Wet behind the ears?" Christopher echoed with a wounded expression.

"Tucker Boone works alone," he told them firmly. "Always has and always will."

"But—"

"Those are my terms," he said coldly. "Take 'em or leave 'em."

She looked ready to spit sparks, but to her credit, she had the good sense to know when arguing would get her nowhere. Looking away, gripping the bag, she spoke in a tone so tight, each word had its own punctuation. "I suppose if you leave us no choice . . ."

"No, ma'am, I don't."

She sucked in a breath, then turned back to him with her hand extended. "Then I guess we'll have to accept your terms."

"Jude!" Christopher looked none too pleased, but again it took only a look from his sister to silence him.

Leaning down for his shirt, Tucker found it poetic justice, that this pair would inadvertently pay for the damages they'd inflicted, but from what he'd seen of Jude so far, he thought it prudent not to mention where her money would be going. She was just liable to hire someone else for the job.

"We hear you have contacts with the Gray Ghosts," Jude said quietly. "I suppose you'll go to their camp first."

Tucker tensed, wondering how she'd known about his connection to the gang. He'd known their lieutenant, Billy Cochran, since they were kids, had even served with him during the war, but Tucker had shed that part of his past like a rattler did a skin. No one should know it existed.

"How far away is this camp?" she added offhandedly.

"Three days' ride, maybe. Why?"

She looked away, avoiding his gaze. "We'll need a general idea of where you'll be headed and when you'll be back. We can't stay here waiting forever, you know."

"Why would you wait here? Go on home where you belong."

"We need to be close, so you can send for us. I told you, Boone, I mean to be there when you find him."

It seemed a strange request, but nothing about this job was normal. He began to wonder if she had some vendetta of her own against the man. Lord knew, he understood the driving force behind a need for vengeance. "There's a Western Union office down the street," he told her, relenting a bit. "I'll send word when I learn something. In the meantime you can stay at Myrna's. The rooms she rents are clean and reasonable, and the food in her cafe is the best."

He expected another protest, but Jude merely nodded. Christopher, Tucker couldn't help but notice, watched his sister as if she'd grown a second head. Probably wasn't used to seeing her so agreeable.

Tucker eased his injured arm into the sleeve. "If I'm not back by the end of next week, head home," he added as he buttoned his shirt. "You can leave word with Myrna where you'll be, and I'll hook up with you later. About that retainer . . ."

Watching her slowly and deliberately peel each bill from the wad, Tucker recognized the look in her eyes. He felt a twinge as he remembered her telling him she couldn't abide lying. He wasn't precisely telling an untruth, he insisted to himself. Not admitting his true reason for taking this job was more the sin of omission than prevarication.

"Don't you dally none, Boone," she said, as one by one she deposited each crumpled bill in his palm. "We'll be waiting to hear from you."

Closing his fist over the bills, Tucker nodded and turned to go. Better that he take her money anyway, than some other unscrupulous bastard. At least Tucker Boone would do his best to earn what she paid him.

And if he had a hidden agenda, well, that was his own business. Chances were, he wouldn't be seeing much more of Jude McCloud in the future anyway, so what did he care what she thought of him?

What indeed?

Hands at her waist, Jude watched Boone stride into the cafe, no doubt eager to gobble up the huge breakfast he'd ordered, when he should be taking to the trail. "Men!" she muttered. "Can't ever trust them to do the job right."

Christopher turned to her, his eyes dark with confusion. "What in blazes was that all about? I can't believe you agreed to his terms like that."

She gave an unladylike snort. "Don't be silly. I only said it to get rid of him."

"I should have known." Christopher seemed almost comical in his relief. "But did you have to waste fifty dollars? We're going to need it to hire the next name on Uncle Ham's list."

"We won't be riding home just yet," Jude said with a secretive smile. "You and I, dear brother, have unfinished business with Mr. Boone."

"We're gonna go get our fifty back?"

"Not exactly."

His grin faded, the wariness returning to his eyes. "Ah, Jude, what are you cooking in that devious brain of yours now?"

"While he eats his breakfast, we'll get our horses." She smiled again, this time with undisguised determination. "He doesn't know it, little brother, but you and me are gonna dog his footsteps, every inch of the way."

Four

Swamps, Tucker thought with distaste as he urged his mount deeper into the marshy area near the Mississippi River. No one could track a man better in the clean fresh air of the forests, or the dry sweeping vista of the plains, but here in the bogs and reeds of Missouri's swampland, he invariably felt out of his element.

It had been the same during the war, when his vastly outnumbered unit had to beat a hasty retreat from hostile Federal forces. Jem Bailey, a crafty old coot who'd spent most of his life on the river, had led them to a clearing where he swore they'd never be found. Nor had they been, though some nights, Tucker found himself wishing for the noise and confusion of the Union prison camps. Billy Cochoran, on the other hand, had thrived here, and from what he'd heard, continued running raids from the very same spot long after Tucker cut himself loose from the war. Knowing his old buddy, Tucker considered it a safe bet that Billy and his Gray Ghost Riders would be operating out of the same camp now.

Unfortunately the terrain had changed drastically in his three-year absence. Nudging the horse down a narrow path to his left, Tucker fought a growing disorientation. Sounds were different in the swamp, muffled and distorted by the slap of water against a log, the wind whistling through the reeds. He found it hard to get a feel for the terrain when so much of it sat under water and when even the dry land seemed to shift beneath his feet. How was he to find his way in an area littered with paths and streams that managed to all look the same?

He kept looking for his landmark, a small stand of oaks guarding the path leading into the camp. Bordered on three sides by water—two sizeable streams and a cove leading out to the river—Jem's hideaway had been a clearing nestled within a tall bed of reeds. Back then, sentries had been posted in the oak trees, and at the first sign of an intruder, each gave a birdcall. Woe to the uninvited, for more often than not, it was a case of shoot first and ask questions later.

Granted, this was not wartime, with vengeful Federals breathing down their necks, but most of the Gray Ghosts carried prices on their heads and Billy, for all his flamboyance, had never been one to ignore precautions. Tucker might better wait until nightfall, when dark would cover his movements, and the gang would be passing the inevitable whiskey jug around. With them preoccupied, he'd stand a better chance of sneaking up on Latour and spiriting him away. He'd need at least a two-hour advantage before the Gray Ghosts discovered the abduction, he figured, especially with his handicap in finding his way around the swamps.

Given that Latour was there at the camp.

Tucker frowned, for he'd yet to figure out what role, if any, Latour had played in that train wreck. Had the Gray Ghosts been rescuing, or abducting, him? For all he knew, Latour could be out on a raid with them now, or he might have gone home to visit kinfolk. Then again, he could be dead, a victim of vengeance, and for Tucker this little foray back to the swamps would be time wasted.

Swatting at a mosquito, he imagined the night ahead—frogs chirping at all hours, snakes slithering past his bedroll, the constant sting and itch of insects buzzing about his head—and wished he'd paid more attention to dressing his shoulder. Having lived through a war, he knew it was less often the wound itself that killed a man, and more the infection that set in afterward.

He thought of Jude and her ointments, the sure yet gentle manner with which she'd bandaged his shoulder. Odd the way she'd gone out of her way to nurse him. Had she thought she could change his mind with kindness?

Annoyed that his thoughts kept straying back to that woman, he sat straighter in the saddle. He was on a job that needed his powers of concentration, and all he could think about was a female's tender, healing touch?

But he couldn't let go of it, couldn't stop wondering about her motivation, her background. *I did some nursing during the war,* she'd said, a service normally done by refined women, ladies who would never in their wildest dreams consider sneaking into a whorehouse and rousing a naked man from his sleep at gunpoint. Not unless they had a thirst for revenge to rival his own.

It would take a powerful need for vengeance to go to such lengths, cutting off her hair and roaming the countryside, posing as a boy—but where were her menfolk that they would allow it?

Tucker tried telling himself that it was none of his affair. Jude had paid him to do a job, and that should be the end of it. Yet every time he thought he'd banished her from his thoughts, he'd relive how it felt to have her warm, delicate body trapped beneath him.

He shook his head vehemently. This was crazy. He favored lush, ripe women like Lilah—sensible, amenable types who posed few questions and even fewer complications. Jude offered both in abundance, a walking contradiction with her tough words and soft touch, her proud, military stance and deep, soulful eyes. If Tucker didn't take care, she'd soon have him obsessed with all the whys and wherefores that had brought her into his life.

Look at what she already had him doing, traipsing

through this god-awful corner of the world he'd sworn never again to visit, opening old wounds he'd hoped to leave fester. No wonder he'd taken one look at her and seen nothing but trouble.

As if to punctuate that thought, he heard a sudden sound in the rushes behind him.

He reined in his horse, cursing inwardly. An amateur's mistake, losing track of his surroundings. Paying heed now, frozen in place, he heard the buzz of insects, a gentle rustling in the undergrowth. Only the breeze, he thought, feeling the air stir about him. Nothing to be alarmed about.

Still no sense taking chances. Pushing on cautiously, he kept one ear cocked, his brain focused on the task ahead. No wasting time—or concentration—on things he could do nothing about, on someone he was better off avoiding.

He had his own survival to think about, thanks all the same. The last thing he needed was to be taking on any more lost causes. Jude McCloud, or whatever her name really was, would just have to fend for herself.

Fending quite well, in her opinion, Jude ducked lower in their hiding place in the reeds, warning Christopher with gestures not to move or make a sound. After coming all this way, she didn't want Boone discovering how close they were behind him.

She didn't need to see her brother's disdainful expression to know what he thought of Boone's abilities. He'd wasted no time pointing out that Boone should have detected their presence miles ago, and the fact that he hadn't had Christopher renewing his campaign to find a replacement.

Her brother didn't understand that this gave them a distinct advantage. Having spent their childhood hiding in the Louisiana bayous, she and Christopher could find their way around blindfolded, which was why she'd opted to travel on foot. On horseback they'd have less mobility in the streams and reeds, and like Boone, less ability to get a feel for their surroundings.

Clearly the man was far from at home in the swamps and disliking the experience immensely. His expression of distrust and wariness reminded Jude of Guin's first few weeks with her and her brothers, when they'd reluctantly showed their new mother the hidden beauty of the bayou.

Thinking back to those days, Jude touched the locket dangling at her neck. A family heirloom handed down through the generations, Guin had called it a symbol, a means of linking two people together, reminding them of the love and support no separation could extinguish. Over the years Jude had clutched Guin's gift to her heart through many a dark, lonely hour. It was her talisman, her proof that if she tried hard enough, any dream could come true.

She hadn't always felt that way, she thought, stifling a shudder as she thought of those nightmare years with her real father. An awful man, and an even worse parent, Jacques Morteau's sole legacy to his children was a memory of pain and guilt and betrayal. It still had the power to hurt, the way he'd so callously left them to the mercy of the evil Lance Buford. To her grave, Jude would be haunted by the part she'd played in that drama, but she'd do it again in a heartbeat if it meant keeping that monster from hurting her family.

After all, protecting her family was why she was here. Her fingers closing tight over the locket, Jude knew Guin understood why she'd had to undertake this mission. Female or not, Jude was still the best tracker, the best shot, and the most accurate in sizing up a man's character.

And no one knew better why it was vital to find Uncle Rafe. Not only for his own safety—though fear for him gnawed at her constantly—but to save his dream. If the taxes on the family's plantation weren't paid by summer's end, Rafe's hard work and sacrifice would fall by the wayside.

All that stood between them and absolute ruin was a

healthy bequest left by dear old Eleanor Tibbs. Trouble was, Mrs. Tibbs had left the money to Rafe, never guessing he wouldn't be there to claim it. Shaking their gray heads, the lawyers had explained that it was a bad time for Rafe to come up missing. Until he was found, or declared legally dead, no one could touch a dime of his inheritance.

Jude had to find Rafe. If it turned out her instincts were wrong, if Boone *couldn't* be trusted, then it would be her fault if her family suffered.

Hearing his horse continue down the path, she released the locket, looking around her with the dazed awareness of the freshly awakened. Something had changed in the swamps while she'd been woolgathering. Nothing she could quite put a finger on, but she felt a shift in the air nonetheless.

Uneasy, no longer feeling the least bit cocky, she motioned her brother to follow as she started off in cautious pursuit. The fact that Christopher fell into step without even a silent protest screwed up her apprehension another notch.

Hearing a mournful hoot, she froze. No self-respecting owl would be out hunting in the full light of day, she knew, suggesting that this threat might be more the human kind.

Gesturing for Christopher to wait in the reeds, she crept forward to a lonely oak, hefting herself up to a low, overhanging branch. Climbing up from there, she positioned herself so she could see down the path where Boone was headed.

She nearly gasped aloud as a tall lanky man with hair the color of weathered straw stepped from the reeds to aim a rifle at Boone's chest.

"Well, well . . . will you look at what we have here," the newcomer said to the half dozen men emerging with him from the undergrowth. From their shining new rifles, to their hard, driven expressions, it was plain these men hadn't come to offer a neighborly welcome.

She glanced back at the reeds, weighing her chances of

getting to the shotgun in time to make a difference, but she should have anticipated that her brother would have ignored her instructions to stay put. Already shimmying up the oak to join her, he wore the shotgun strapped to his shoulder.

Taking the weapon from him, she set herself in position to aim it, to be ready for any possibility. She heard the leader's soft chuckle, carrying all the way to where they sat. "Look boys," he called out to his ragtag companions, "and tell me it ain't our old pal, Jesse Holland."

Jude looked to Christopher in confusion, only to see his smug I-told-you-so expression. *Jesse Holland,* they'd called him, not Tucker Boone. So much for her being a good judge of character. Even his name was a lie.

Maybe Christopher was right—maybe she *hadn't* been thinking straight since meeting the man. Why even now she had the embarrassingly insane urge to go rushing down there, demanding that those desperate-looking men lay down their weapons and slink quietly back into the holes they'd crawled out of.

"Hi, Billy," Boone said, his tone conversational. "Looks like time hasn't mellowed you none."

The man he'd called Billy chuckled again as he gazed at Boone with apparent affection. "Gotta say, sure have missed bandying words with you. How is it we got to be fighting on opposite sides?"

Boone shook his head. "I've got no fight with you, Billy. I'm just here to ask a few questions. Hear me out, and I'll be on my way."

Billy studied Boone for the longest moment, then broke into a grin. "Tie him up," he barked at the man next to him. "Hate to act unneighborly, Jesse old pal, but these days can't be taking chances. No offense meant by it."

"None taken." To Jude's eyes, Boone seemed amazingly calm about having his wrists tied behind his back and being forced at gunpoint. This was his friend? Billy seemed the sort that usually found himself on the wrong end of a rope.

Billy continued on in a conversational tone as they ambled away, but Jude could no longer make out the words. Once they'd vanished from sight, she motioned Christopher down the tree, his face mirroring her confusion. "What do we do now?" he whispered. "Go after him?"

Sheer suicide, of course, but it was more than their generous supply of guns that made her hesitant. She'd never seen a meaner group, except maybe for Jacques Morteau's drinking cronies, and if she'd ever had doubts of the evil some men could do, her birth father had swiftly dispelled them. She had a feeling that if she and Christopher wanted to live to find Rafe, they'd better make good and sure those men never learned they'd strayed anywhere near their encampment.

"Forget Boone," she snapped, shaking her head. "We have to concentrate on finding Rafe."

Christopher nodded, but his expression remained pensive as he gazed down the path. "Yeah, but Jude, didn't you notice what those men were wearing?"

"Yeah, so?"

He stared at her funny, as if wondering how she could be so dense. "They had on Confederate uniforms, Jude. *Gray* uniforms."

She spun her head back in their direction, even though the men were long gone. That Boone had her so flustered, she'd been blind to the fact that he'd led them, whether unwittingly or not, straight to the Gray Ghost Riders.

Guin McCloud Latour paced through the dark, empty rooms of Camelot, her Louisiana plantation home. Unable to sleep, she traced the steps of happier days, yearning for the laugher that had once filled these halls. The front parlor reminded her of the many times they'd gathered there to exchange gifts and affection during the holidays, the study brought back thoughts of solemn family discussions about finances. But it was the memories in the dining room that most effectively pierced her heart. The war was over, she couldn't help thinking, so why wasn't her family once again gathered around her? How could she ever sleep peacefully again until they were all gathered together safely under this roof?

Gliding over to the dining table, she touched each chair, missing the noisy, raucous mob that once convened here, the children shouting and vying for the chance to relate their version of the day's events. Soft-spoken, sensitive Patrick, the rock she had clung to these past four years, had gone down to New Orleans to conduct business, and to collect his twin brothers, Peter and Paul, recently released from eastern Yankee prisons—a process he'd warned could take over a week. The three youngest—John, Amanda, and Jeanie—had gone for their summer visit to Roseland, to spend time with Guin's cousin, Edith Ann, and her children. Christopher had left with Jude of course. . . .

Guin paused at the next chair, tears welling in her eyes as she realized that of all the children, she missed Jude most of all. Years ago they'd stood together fighting off the evil Lance Buford and the children's real father, Jacques Morteau, and to this day, she and Jude had a bond that could never be broken. With a brief smile, Guin thought of the locket she'd once given the girl, hoping it would indeed serve as the talisman to keep Jude safe.

How ironic that only one month ago in this very room, Guin had expressed her worry that Jude was devoting too much time to the running of Camelot and not enough to her own future. Guin had tried to encourage her to visit New Orleans, to see more of the world than their family plantation, not guessing the girl would take it into her head to go charging off to Missouri instead. Dressed as a boy, no less.

Running her hand along the chair's cypress wood frame, Guin relived the heated arguments they'd had in this room, Jude so adamant that she, not Patrick, should be the one to go. Grudgingly she'd agreed to take Christopher. Even more reluctantly Jude had promised to hire a professional tracker and stay with him to the end. Not because it was the sensible thing to do, but because she knew it was the only way her family would let her leave the house.

Sighing, swamped with worry, Guin said a silent prayer that the headstrong Jude would be all right. Most people thought her prickly, mainly because Jude wanted them to, but Guin was well aware that hard experience, and not her true nature, made the girl act so tough and independent. Deep down she was as soft and vulnerable as they came, and easy prey for the hard-hearted. Guin could only hope that the tracker she hired would understand that about Jude, and not take advantage of her loving nature.

Stubborn, fiercely loyal Jude. "Have faith," she'd told Guin as she left, throwing her own words back at her as if Guin were the child who now needed reassuring. And in truth there was no one on this earth she trusted more. If Jude couldn't find Rafe . . .

Guin bit her lip, refusing to finish that thought. Jude *would* find Rafe, and soon they'd all be gathered together here at this table, laughing and shouting and ignoring her requests to behave. And there, across the table, Rafe would grin back at his wife, understanding how very proud Guin was of all their children. And how, even after all these years, she remained so very deeply in love with him.

She went to his chair, stroking the hard wood surface, trying to absorb the essence of the man she had chosen to spend her life with, missing him with all her heart. She'd understood his reasons for enlisting, knowing that Rafe was a man of honor—but, oh, how she resented the war that had taken him away from her. Rafe was her strength, her reason for living, and without him she felt lost and alone.

Each day she worked from dawn to dusk to keep their dream alive for the children, but it grew harder with each week Rafe didn't return.

Guin understood why Jude was so anxious to go after him. It was hell, sitting here waiting, doing nothing, dying a bit more inside as each day passed with no word.

Have faith, Jude had told her in parting. Gripping the wood, Guin clung to that thought as tightly as she grasped Rafe's chair.

Five

Tucker knew exactly who these men were as he followed behind Billy. They went way back, he and Billy, to the days before the war started, when both had been kids killing time while their mothers worked at the Paradise Saloon outside Independence, Missouri. Shunned by "decent" folk, sneered at by the other children, he and Billy had formed a bond born more of loneliness than kindred spirits. A transplant of city streets, Billy's mother had neither the education nor patience to teach her son the rules of good behavior that Sarah Holland drilled into hers, but running free in the woods, Tucker and Billy had found adventure enough to overcome the differences in their mothers' expectations.

It wasn't until they'd joined Quantrill's Army, the run-and-gun bushwhacker unit under Bloody Bill Anderson, that the contrasts between them became clear. Where Billy Cochoran had found a thrill, a sense of long-awaited power in those murderous raids, Tucker had merely been sickened.

To Tucker the massacre at Lawrence, Kansas, had been the last straw. Transferring to a regular unit in the Confederate army, he'd regretted leaving his old friend behind. Over the years he'd come to feel responsible for Billy, as if he were a younger brother he had to keep out of trouble. He'd asked Billy to leave the bushwhackers with him, but with his lopsided grin, his friend had said no—that he'd always known that someday they'd choose a different path to follow.

Well, they were on the same path now, Tucker thought wryly as they made their way to the three oaks guarding the camp. All things considered, he couldn't hope that a shared past would make a difference—tying his wrists and holding him at gunpoint made for a mighty cold welcome.

Billy gave a sudden shout, the bloodcurdling rebel yell bushwhackers used on their raids. As they entered the clearing, Tucker watched others from their old brigade step up, their reception no warmer. Though he'd once saved Renny Claiborne's life, the man glared at him with blatant hostility. Nor did Brady Watkins or the two dozen or so warily watching seem any happier to see him.

Stopping suddenly in the middle of the clearing, grinning without any real humor, Billy nodded at the gun at Tucker's waist, waiting while Brady relieved him of it. "I'd have to guess this visit of yours ain't social," he said, twirling his own pistol on his shooting finger.

Tucker smiled back, saying nothing.

Billy widened his grin. "Good ol' Jesse, always the deep one. Tell you what. You and me, we'll sit over there in the shade and share a jug for old times' sake, and you can ask these questions of yours."

Tucker hadn't meant to be "deep" by not talking, he'd merely been mindful of saving his neck. He could hardly tell Billy that he'd come to snag Latour, and unable to think of a story his friend would swallow, he'd elected to keep his mouth shut. No one would believe he now wanted to join up with them, not after his bitter departure from the group during the war.

Striding toward the wooden table set up inside a thatched-roof lean-to, Billy called to a scrawny-looking man with gray hair and whiskers. "Bones, go fetch us up that rotgut of yours. Jesse and me need to have us a heart-to-heart."

Tucker followed Billy to the table. Heads turned as he passed by, scowls radiating anger in Tucker's direction.

Garbed in tattered Confederate gray, all bore the stamp of hard luck and harder circumstance. Forgotten soldiers, weathered by suffering, these men had been honed to a supreme indifference of another's misfortunes.

Some Tucker recognized from his days with Anderson, but nowhere in this ragtag group of twenty or so did he find signs of Latour. Again he wondered if the man could be out on a raid with the others or like himself being held prisoner, perhaps in one of the ramshackle huts lining the clearing.

At the table Billy gestured for him to sit, then reached for the earthenware jug the old man offered. Brady and Renny stood a discreet but convenient distance away, their rifles at the ready.

"Old Bones," Billy said, grinning at the wizened man, "is a prime example what them Federals can do to a man. Had a bright future, poor old Bones did, a farm, wife and kids, but did that matter one whit to them Yankee devils? Just like that, they mowed the place down, burnt the house with his family inside . . . and why? General Order Eleven is why—their legal excuse to maim and murder."

Though Tucker had his own reasons for resenting the military ordinance giving Union troops the excuse to seize or burn any property belonging to known rebels or Southern sympathizers, he doubted this was the time to express it.

"Not a day over forty," Billy added quietly as the man hobbled off, "though you'd never know it to look at him."

"I'd hazard the guess that every man here has his story."

"That he does, Jesse boy." Billy nodded sadly before focusing his gaze on Tucker's face. "Yourself included."

Refusing to dig up his past, Tucker redirected the conversation. "Not Jesse. Nowadays, I go by the name of Tucker Boone."

"Sorry, old habits die hard. Speaking of which, you do still swig down the hard stuff?" Billy held out the jug.

Tucker tried not to grimace. He didn't need alcohol fogging his brain, but sharing a drink was part of the ritual, and the one sure way to make Billy part with information. "Sorry," he said, nodding at his hands, "but I'm tied up right now."

Billy laughed. "Renny, you come on over here and undo your handiwork so poor old Jesse . . . I mean, Tucker, can slake his thirst."

The haste with which Renny hustled to untie his wrists, coupled with the speed with which the man returned to his post, made it seem less a request and more an order. Clearly Billy was flexing his muscles and enjoying himself immensely.

For the time being, Tucker was content to let him, so long as his hands were free. He rubbed his wrists, grateful to feel the blood flowing through them again. Renny Claiborne was famous for his knots. When he secured a prisoner, there was no escaping.

Sitting in the chair opposite him, Billy smiled broadly as he tilted the jug to his mouth. "Whoo-eee," he whistled when he was done. "Old Bones sure knows how to clean out the system. This stuff'll burn a path clear through your innards."

Reluctantly taking the jug, Tucker drank more cautiously, determined to keep a clear head. Things might seem relaxed, but he could taste tension in the air. He'd been through too much with him not to know when Billy was up to something. Playing for time, sipping while his friend took long, hard pulls from the jug, Tucker listened as Billy waxed nostalgic about their childhood at the Paradise Saloon.

In Tucker's mind, no amount of time—or whiskey— could glamorize those days, but Billy always did have a knack for glossing over the unpleasant. Before long he had even Tucker chuckling over their forays to the upstairs bedrooms of the saloons, reliving the fun of catching the local gentry with their pants down.

Eventually talk drifted to the war, to their days serving

together under Bloody Anderson. "Ah, it was grand while it lasted, wasn't it, Jesse?" Billy asked wistfully, leaning back in his chair to rest on the two rear legs.

"I'm not sure grand is how I'd describe it."

"Ah, but we were important then. The power we had, riding victorious through each border town we liberated. The respect. They revered us, glorified us. Hell, we were regular gods of the battlefield."

"A lot of innocent people died."

Billy eyed him curiously. "You're starting to sound like them sniveling politicians. No struggle is worth draining their purses, they decide, and just like that, we're supposed to give up all we stand for and go begging for forgiveness they ain't never gonna grant. Them Federals and their loyalty oath," he said, spitting on the ground. "That and a bucket of beans will buy you salvation."

He was right. Missouri had been a battlefield far too long, and far too many of Quantrill's guerrillas had gone to the gallows for any bushwhacker to hope he'd be given a fair hearing.

"You were smart, Jesse, getting out when you did," Billy added in a thoughtful tone. "The rest of us have got a price on our heads. Don't give us much of a choice, way I see it. If we're gonna hang anyway, why not get the most out of life beforehand?"

Tucker could see his point. Jayhawkers from Kansas had committed equal atrocities, but history was written by the victors. Those men would die heroes, while Billy and his ilk would be branded murderous villains. "You could always head west, or lose yourself in Indian territory," Tucker suggested.

Billy shook his head. "And do what? Heck, all I know is war. Fighting's in my blood now. It's all I'm trained to do. It's what people expect of me."

Again Tucker feared he was right, but for the sake of friendship, he tried to convince him otherwise. "America's a huge place. A man can lose his past in the mountains or wandering over its vast plains. You need to change your identity."

"Like you?" Coming down on all four legs of the chair, Billy pinned him with his gaze. His brown eyes held glints of gold that could sharpen sometimes, giving him a hardened edge. "Don't sit well with me, Jesse, the idea of deserting. Wouldn't have thought it would suit you, either."

Tucker resisted the urge to flinch. "It wouldn't suit Jesse Holland," he told Billy in an emotionless tone, "but he's dead and buried—and, like I said before, I go by the name of Tucker Boone now."

"Mind telling me why?

Tucker did mind, but despite the drink they'd shared, he was still Billy's prisoner, and the man wouldn't relent until he had his answer. Grabbing the jug, Tucker took more of the rotgut than his stomach expected. "I had to walk away, start over. I'd had all I could take of officers, worrying more about pleasing the politicians than winning the war." He handed the jug back, hoping Billy hadn't noticed the bitterness in his tone.

"Yeah, well, if you're talking about Captain Latour, I can assure you that the man has no friends here, either," Billy muttered.

Hard to hide his surprise. He'd have thought a man like that would have won the admiration of these men. "Strange," he said, feeling his way. "I'd heard the man's running with you now."

Lowering the jug, Billy eyed him warily. "And what gives you that idea?"

Careful, Tucker cautioned himself. "Rumors circulate. Word has it the Gray Ghosts waylaid a train to liberate Latour from his Union transport."

"Well, word is wrong." With an unexpected burst of energy, Billy sprang from the chair to pace before him. "If we went after Latour, it sure wouldn't be to free him. I'm not saying we did, mind you—but if we had, we were doomed from the start. That Latour always was one lucky bastard."

Tucker had many epithets for the man, but to date lucky hadn't been one of them.

"He wasn't on that train." Billy sat back down with a huff. "Made me look damned stupid, let me tell you. It was my operation, my chance to look good, but some damned Yankee fool must have gotten wind of our plans. I sure don't know why else they would hold him in St. Louis."

"St. Louis?" Tucker knew he showed too much interest, but it struck him that he was wasting time sitting here drinking with Billy if Latour was in some Federal prison upriver.

"He was scheduled to be released," Billy went on bitterly. "But at the last minute, they shipped him back to the Jefferson Barracks. All we got from the raid was three ancient rifles and one busted knife. You know how bad it was, trying to explain the results to a commanding officer hell-bent on revenge?"

Tucker had met his captain, and nothing in Bud Jackson's devil-may-care manner indicated such driving passion. "I thought Jackson and Latour were pals."

"Jackson got overreckless there at the end and got himself hanged by the Federals. We got a new man running things now, and Cap'n wants Latour's blood spilled all over Missouri. He'll get it, too. Cap'n has got this way of stirring folks up, of getting them wanting what he wants."

"Which is?"

Billy gave a cold, humorless laugh. "Exacting revenge on anyone who stands in the way of the South regaining its power. Way he sees it, Latour paved the way for Federal occupation by proving too soft."

In Tucker's experience Latour hadn't been soft . . . he'd been the most vicious of them all.

"What's your interest in the man?" Billy asked suddenly, training a wary glance on him. "That why you're here? Looking for that traitor?"

No use lying. When Billy got that look in his eye, he poked and probed until you spilled your guts. "I've been hired to track him down," Tucker said with a shrug. "By some kids with a thirst for vengeance."

"They got names, these kids?"

Tucker cast about in his mind for a name. "McCloud," he offered, reasoning that it couldn't hurt if it wasn't their real name anyway.

Billy's skeptical look deepened. "What are they to you, these McClouds?"

"Nothing. No one. Hell, Billy, it's just a job, what I do. I deliver the prize, and they pay me the money."

"Don't sound like you, taking money from children."

The man knew him too well. "Times change, and the wise adjust to them," Tucker said, keeping his voice and manner as offhand as possible. "You of all people should understand that."

Billy leaned across the table, pointing a finger at Tucker's face. "Well, you can tell those kids that revenge belongs to the Gray Ghosts. Warn them McClouds to stand out of the way, 'cause we don't brook no interference."

"Fair enough," Tucker said, recognizing Billy's pontificating phase, a clear sign that he was well on his way to the bottom of the jug. "I'll leave right now and relay the message."

Billy's fist hit the table. "Sit back down, Jesse boy. Think I'll risk your running off to report to him? The trusty old scout warning Latour that the Gray Ghosts are breathing down his neck?"

"For pete's sake, Billy, you know there's no love lost between me and that man."

"Time was, I thought I knew you," Billy said wistfully, rising slowly to his feet. "But you've got this new life.

Hell, you got a whole new identity. If I trust you and it doesn't pan out, I end up with another black mark on my record."

Tucker met him look for look. "I've always been square with you."

Billy studied his face. "First you quit the brigade to serve with Shelby, then abandon the Cause altogether. Sorry, Jesse, but all my men know or care about is that you're a traitor, and treason is a crime they can't abide. I let you go and they start looking at *me* as the traitor."

Snatching up the jug, taking another swig, Billy spun on a heel to face Brady and Renny. "Tie him up again," he said gruffly, refusing to meet Tucker's gaze. "Over there, to the tree. And if he gives you any trouble, just shoot him."

"Jeez, Billy—"

He turned to glare at Tucker. "Yeah, we have a past between us, and I'd sure hate to be the one to bury you, but I'm a soldier, don't forget, trained to carry out orders. Bones, Preacher, get your scrawny carcasses over here and start rustling up dinner. All this jawing has stoked up a powerful hunger."

"You're just going to leave me tied to this tree?" Tucker shouted at Billy as the two goons began weaving their ropes around his wrists. The question was purely rhetorical, since it was painfully obvious what he meant to do.

Billy seemed almost sad as he faced him. "You've been sitting on the fence too long, Jesse boy. You take this time to figure out what you mean to do. Sign that oath for the Federals or stick with us, fighting for the Cause."

"C'mon Billy, the war is over."

"Not for us, it ain't." Voice going hard, Billy seemed all the more a stranger. "Every last man of us took a vow to stand firm for the Confederacy. You're with us, Jesse, or against us. Can't have it both ways."

Tucker felt a strong pounding in his head as the ropes

tightened on his wrist and ankles. "Do I get time to make this decision, or will I be marched out and shot at daybreak?"

Tucker had meant it sarcastically, but Billy's solemn expression was all too serious. "Cap'n should return by sunup," he said coldly as he turned away, "so you'd better decide, old buddy. Either you're with us, or you're going six feet under."

Six

Cursing Renny Claiborne and his skill with knots, Tucker studied his surroundings. The sun had long since set, but little else had changed in the hours he'd been struggling to loosen his ropes. Billy still held court at the table, dealing the cards for a game of poker, a new jug added on a regular basis. He must be winning big, Tucker supposed, if his hollering were anything to go by.

No surprise there—poker had been part of their education at the Paradise Saloon. When they weren't upstairs spying on "gentlemen callers," he and Billy had been watching the betting tables, honing their skills, learning how to spot the cheaters. Billy had taken it a step farther, of course. He often boasted that he could beat any man living, save maybe his pal Jesse, never bothering to explain that Jesse knew to look for every ace he'd stuck up his sleeve.

When the cards first appeared at the table, Tucker had tried talking them into letting him play, an all-or-nothing bid for his freedom. Once Billy would have jumped at the challenge, but today he ignored it. Like those seated around him, he took his orders from an unknown quantity now, and until the arrival of his Cap'n, he'd leave Tucker alone with his fate.

Eyeing his captors' backs, all turned to him as if he didn't exist, Tucker had to wonder about this Cap'n and how he could command such loyalty. He must have a heap of charisma to coax this gang of hardened veterans into following a cause the rest of the South had abandoned. The question was, why go to the trouble? The war *was* over—and better so, for both sides—so what could anyone gain by prolonging an issue long since dead and buried?

A question Tucker would prefer to ponder from a safe distance. Having no desire to be here when this Cap'n made his appearance, he tugged and pulled the ropes at his wrists, planning out what he'd do next. Escape, obviously, but then in the first town he came to, he'd hop a riverboat for St. Louis.

He paused in his struggles, realizing how the change in plans might affect his employer. All too well he could picture Jude pacing the floor, waiting none too patiently for word as he made his way upriver. If too much time passed, there was no telling what she might take in her head to do. He should probably let her know his plans, but he couldn't contact her in Salvation. If and when he escaped, it would be the first place the Gray Ghosts would look.

Uneasily he remembered telling Billy about working for Jude. Hell, he'd even given him her name.

An *assumed* one, he corrected, but the thought nonetheless chilled him. He yanked at his bindings, anxious to be free. He had to get to the nearest Western Union office and wire a message to Christopher and Jude. Wait at home, he'd tell them, and he'd meet up with them there later.

A good plan, except he hadn't the least idea where they lived. Nor was it smart for them to go blabbing to anyone about their destination. If Tucker could find them, so could Billy and his Cap'n.

Slow down, he told himself, and stop imagining mountains where there might only be molehills. So far all he posed to these men was a nuisance, so why would they go to such lengths to track him down? Besides, Billy didn't know Jude was female. As long as she stayed a boy, she should be safe enough.

EVERY DREAM COME TRUE 69

Over at the table, Billy slammed down his cards with a laugh of triumph, a raw, almost maniacal sound. Another icy chill snaked down Tucker's spine.

"For pity's sake, Boone," a voice whispered suddenly at his ear. "How do you expect me to cut through these ropes the way you're wriggling?"

Tucker went deathly still. He knew that voice, the touch, the very scent of her—Jude McCloud in the flesh.

A sea of sensations washed over him. First relief at seeing her safe and sound, then confusion as he wondered how she got here, and finally fury as he realized she must have been following him all along.

"What in blazes do you think you're doing?" he hissed back.

"I thought I was rescuing you." None too gently she grabbed his wrists. "Of course if you'd rather I left . . ." She let the whisper trail off, both of them knowing he wanted no such thing.

"Just cut the damned rope." The instant they were safely away, he vowed, he'd let her know what a mistake she'd made in disregarding his orders.

As if aware of this intention, she gave the rope a vicious slash, nicking him slightly on the left hand.

"Hey, watch—"

"Hush," she whispered in warning. "Your pals are so liquored up, they're liable to shoot at their shadows. If I'm going to help you hobble out of here, I don't want to be caught in the cross fire."

"I don't hobble," he muttered, resenting that she was right. He'd been tied to the tree so long, he'd lost all feeling in his limbs. "Give me the knife," he said through gritted teeth, shaking his hands to restore circulation. "I've got to cut the rope at my ankles."

Her only answer was a soft, muttered "Damn!" as she moved back into the shadows.

"What's that, Jesse?" Billy called out suddenly, his hand

going to the pistol at his waist, his wiry body poised for action.

Tucker froze, holding his arms behind him as if they were still tied to the tree. He prayed Jude had managed to duck out of sight in time.

"Who you talking to?" Billy pressed, squinting as he peered into the shadows. "You seeing ghosts in the dark?"

Tucker suffered through the inevitable round of laughter. "I'd rather it be ghosts," he called back. "They don't bite like these blasted mosquitoes."

Chuckling, Billy visibly relaxed, his hand coming up to slap his own neck. "Reckon you'll get used to it in time. By morning you'll be so full of welts, you won't even notice anymore when they bite you."

Sharing another hearty laugh, the group passed the jug around as they settled down to the card game. Tucker took a deep breath, mentally willing Jude to stay hidden. Billy, he knew from experience, was too cagey to let it go at that.

True to form, Billy did glance back now and then, but each time Tucker was ready. Drooping his head, keeping his arms wrapped around the tree behind him, he feigned sleep while Jude continued to stay out of sight.

As the moments wore on, and she didn't emerge from the shadows, Tucker decided she must have taken a good look at the situation and fled. With his hands free, he could untie his own ankles, so she had no real need to stay. It certainly made things less complicated. Tucker had enough on his plate without having to look out for another. A female, no less.

He gave another quick glance to the table, where drink and a winning hand claimed Billy's attention. Now or never, Tucker figured, and was just about to reach down and wrestle with the rope at his feet when he felt the cool, reassuring weight of a knife being dropped in his palm.

He should have known Jude couldn't let anything stay less complicated.

Reaching down to saw at the rope, he kept one eye on the compound, weighing the chances of reaching his horse. Not good, he saw instantly, finding it locked in a corral with the gang's livestock. Nor were his hopes of retrieving his gun—sitting on the table in front of Billy—much better.

Jude grabbed his shoulder. Involuntarily he flinched from her touch.

"Sorry, I forgot your wound," she whispered. "I'll dress it later, but really we've got to get going."

Needing no further prompting, Tucker rose to his feet. Jude had vanished into the bushes, apparently expecting him to follow, but the pins and needles shooting through his legs all but crippled him. Muttering oaths as he limped in her wake, he swore that at first opportunity, he'd be giving Miss McCloud the talking-to she richly deserved. Somebody had to let her know she was looking for trouble, traipsing around at night by herself.

A wiser man would head off in the other direction and leave the reckless female to her own devices, but with no horse, gun, or even viable plan of his own, he had to rely on her and pray that she wouldn't lead him into disaster.

He held his tongue as they pushed through the thick undergrowth, skirting the rim of the cove, reserving comment until she came to a sudden stop at the bank of the river. Looking about them, trying to keep his voice low and his misgivings hidden, he asked where in blazes she'd left her horse.

He hadn't been happy about the prospect of riding double behind this female to the nearest town, but he liked even less how she now avoided his gaze. "No horse," she whispered softly, her profile pale and appearing frightened in the moonlight. "We have to go by river."

He eyed the dark, churning surface of the water skeptically. "It won't be easy, steering a boat in that current. Where is it anyway?"

"No boat." She turned to him with a tight smile. "We'll swim."

"Of all the lame-brained . . ." Belatedly realizing whose brain must have concocted the scheme, he tried a different approach. "You expect us to swim in these heavy boots? And how long do you think it will take them to pick up our trail and figure out where we're headed? They'll be waiting for us at the first stop downriver."

A faint smile spread across her lips. "I hope so. We're heading north."

"Against the current?"

The smile vanished. "We haven't a trainload of options. And we're wasting valuable time, standing here arguing. Like it or not, Boone, we've got to go."

Hearing the hoot of laughter in the distance, Tucker knew she was right. It was just a matter of time before Billy looked up and noticed him missing.

Not that Jude left room for argument. "Put your boots in the sack," she said, yanking off her own and dumping them inside. "I'll carry it on my shoulder."

For efficiency's sake, Tucker removed his own boots, but he drew the line at her swimming with the sack. Wrenching it out of her grasp, he glowered down at her when she opened her mouth to protest. "I'll carry it," he stated firmly.

She gave him a dubious look. Nor could he blame her, given his sore shoulder. He'd have enough difficulty swimming without adding extra weight, but he'd have to be paralyzed from the neck down before he'd let a female assume the burden. "Let's go," he said gruffly, nodding toward the river.

She bit her lip, looking suddenly uncomfortable. Bracing himself for the argument, he folded his arms at his chest.

"Could you turn around?" she asked in a small voice, surprising him yet again. "I, er, have to loosen my, er, disguise. I can't swim if I can't breathe," she added brusquely, as if he'd been the one trying to argue.

Prickly Jude, he thought, stifling a grin.

Happy to give her privacy while she fiddled with her bindings, Tucker strode past to the river. He stepped into the water, daunted by how cold it felt. Not much relishing the prospect of plunging his entire body into it, he was about to suggest wading along the banks when he heard a shout from the camp. The rebel yell, he thought uneasily. Someone must have discovered him missing.

"C'mon, let's get out of here," Jude hissed behind him, running past to plunge into the water. Diving right in, showing none of the hesitancy he'd expect from a woman, she began making her way upstream with an efficient breaststroke. As was fast becoming her habit, she didn't wait to see if he followed.

Behind him, Tucker could hear the shouts intensify, as if every raider had joined the search. Left with few options, he moved deeper into the water, slinging the sack over his good shoulder. He had to fight both the shock of cold water and the throbbing of his wound as he, too, started upriver, silently trailing in Jude's wake. It went against the grain to take the rear position, but the need for stealth took precedence over male pride for the moment. He could overtake her once they were out of earshot.

Or so he thought before he saw how adeptly Jude moved through the water. Watching her transition to smooth, even overhand strokes fifteen minutes later, he realized he'd never swim past her, not with the weight of the sack and the ache in his shoulder.

Although the Gray Ghosts could no longer hear them, they continued on silently, both understanding their energy could better be spent in battling the capricious current. Jude avoided the main flow wherever possible, but even near the banks, the eddies and swirls were unpredictable. The ache in his shoulder intensified. He could feel the weight of the sack increase with every stroke.

He'd begun to despise his boots enough to drop them

and say the hell with covering feet he could no longer feel anyway, when Jude surprised him by heading for the shore. "We've been swimming long enough," she called back over her shoulder. "It should be safe to travel by land from now on."

Had the sack felt one ounce lighter, or had the agony in his shoulder burned one degree less, Tucker would have swum past her, but even in his present mood, he knew it would be a clear case of what his mama termed, "biting his nose to spite his face." Instead, muttering to himself, he dragged himself to dry ground, careful not to betray how grateful he was for the rest. From now on, he'd tell her, he'd be the one calling the shots. Just as soon as he caught his breath.

Jude plopped down on a nearby log, her legs sprawled out in front of her. Happy to see her equally winded, Tucker let the sack drop at his feet. With her wet hair and dripping clothes, she looked almost as miserable as he felt.

Determined to gain the upper hand, Tucker remained standing, gazing down on her like an irate parent. "Mind telling me what you thought you were doing back there?" he asked with a fierce scowl.

She blinked up at him. "I beg your pardon?"

"Correct me if I'm wrong, but I believe you hired *me* to find Latour. I left Salvation under the impression that you were content to let me do my job."

Hard to tell in the moonlight, but it sure looked like she was blushing. The thought strengthened both his resolve and his sense of satisfaction.

"I know," she said hesitantly, "but I thought—"

"No, Miss McCloud," he said, "you didn't think. That's exactly my point."

If indeed she'd been flushed, the cause was no longer embarrassment. Dark eyes flashing with indignation, she popped up from the log, five feet two of fury standing before him. "Just you wait a minute, Boone—"

EVERY DREAM COME TRUE 75

"Not until I'm finished," he growled back, not about to let her get started. "What female in her right mind would come traipsing across the countryside after a man and then go charging into that den of cutthroats—"

"I neither traipsed nor charged." The words were clipped, as if she struggled to contain her temper. "Those men still haven't the slightest idea I was even there." Chin held up, she wrapped her arms defiantly across her chest.

He wondered if she knew that the action thrust her breasts upward, or if she realized how much of her anatomy was revealed by the threadbare wet wool. He hoped not, for in that case, she must be equally aware of his heated reaction.

She seemed almost otherworldly in the pale moonlight, her dark hair slicked back to reveal each delicate feature as if it had been etched in marble. The wide eyes, the high cheekbones, and lush lips all added up to classic beauty, a far cry from the ragtag boy he'd grown used to. "The point remains," he said, not one whit pleased by his observation, "it was a dumb fool thing to do."

"Your gratitude overwhelms me."

He bristled at her sarcastic tone. "Damnit, Jude, I told you to stay put for a reason. The roads aren't safe for a female."

"I'm dressed as a boy, remember?"

He couldn't stop the quick glance at her breasts. No wonder she'd stopped to take off the bindings, he found himself thinking. She must have been wrapped tighter than a mummy to keep those lush, firm mounds hidden.

"No man's gonna take notice of me," she finished off defiantly.

"Unless they catch you like this, at an unguarded moment," he said roughly, as angry at himself as at her. "Billy and his gang are just a sample of a whole horde wandering the roads these days, men made desperate by war: thieves and killers who wouldn't hesitate to gun down their own granny if she got in the way."

"Nice company you keep."

He locked his own arms at his chest, matching her glare for glare. "I don't keep any company. I work alone, remember?"

"Maybe you should reevaluate your policy." She smiled nastily. "Wouldn't appear to me that you've been getting along too well on your own."

She was like a burr stuck under his saddle, he decided, bent on rubbing him the wrong way. "I might not know where Latour is," he countered, "but I did manage to find out where he is not. I have a new trail to follow, which I aim to set off on the instant we reach the next town. Alone."

"Get off the high horse, Boone. You know you need me."

"No, ma'am, I do not." Even as he uttered the words, Boone saw the absurdity of them bickering like kids, exchanging dares.

Well, maybe not kids, he thought, as his gaze once again drifted to her breasts. Erect and firm, the peaked nipples strained against the wet shirt. Her reaction could be caused by the cold, yet just as easily be a result of arousal. Jude might talk and act like a boy, but underneath that gray wool, she was all too obviously a woman.

Frowning at the thought, he uncrossed his arms and lowered his tone. "Go home to your family, Jude. You and your brother . . ." For the first time, he noticed the boy was no longer with her. "What happened to Christopher?"

"He's waiting at the next town." Her glare faded, became defensive. "I did take precautions, you know. I told him to wait until tomorrow noon, and if I still didn't show up, he should bring the law down to the swamp."

Impressed in spite of himself, Tucker silently agreed that she'd shown remarkably good sense for a female.

He didn't much like the realization that he'd underestimated her yet again.

"Besides," she added defiantly, "I figure we're gonna need dry clothes, not to mention footwear. I don't know about you, but I've got a hankering for a warm, dry bed right about now."

The image swam before him—Jude stripped of the threadbare wool, those luscious breasts freed of all constraints. His hands itched to touch them, stroke them, caress them. "Is that an invitation, Miss McCloud?" he asked, his voice going husky.

She took an instinctive step backward. "A what?"

He closed the distance between them, deciding it was time he taught her a lesson. "The way you've been pushing those breasts forward, what am I to think but that you're itching to share that warm, dry bed with me?"

Her eyes widened, first in alarm and then in dismay, as she stared down at her chest. Hastily unwrapping her arms, she held her fists clenched at her sides. "I didn't mean to . . . that is, I meant . . ." Her gaze narrowed as she took in his expression. "Are you laughing at me, you—you . . ."

"Cad?" he supplied for her.

"Scoundrel!" she snapped back.

"Lucky for you, I'm neither. Sorry to disappoint, but I only meant to point out how easily you can get into trouble. Count your blessings I was raised a gentleman, or you'd have been on your back in the bushes long before this."

Her nostrils flared, giving him ample warning, so he was able to grab her arms before she could haul off and slap his face. He'd meant to protect himself, and perhaps steady her until she regained her temper, but something earthy and primitive crept over his resolve as he stood staring down into her deep brown eyes. He didn't want to act like a gentleman, didn't want to release the frail, panting female he held in his arms. Every inch of him ached to pull her closer.

As if caught by the same primitive force, she didn't struggle to wrench out of his grasp, nor even try to break their gaze. Mesmerized, like the snared rabbit, she seemed to grasp that she was the prey, and Tucker the hunter, and all that was left was for nature to have its way.

He was leaning down, drawn against his better judgment to her soft, full lips, when the strains of music and laughter erupted into the still night air.

Jolted back to his senses, he dropped her arms and moved a safe distance away. Of all the ridiculous mistakes to make, kissing the boss—especially a female boss the likes of Jude McCloud—had to be the worst of them. Just how many ways did he want to mess up his life?

"That must be the riverboat headed for St. Louis," he said brusquely, reaching for the sack. "If we hurry, maybe I can make it to town before it sails off again."

"St. Louis?" she asked. "Is that where you're planning to go?"

Cursing to himself, Tucker remembered too late that he had to watch what he said around this female. Chalk that up to yet another reason to put distance between them.

Digging the boots out of the sack, he tossed Jude's to her and donned his own. "My destination can hardly matter to you. We're heading in opposite directions."

"But—"

"You're going home, Jude, as soon as I can arrange transportation," he told her sharply as he yanked the sodden leather over his swollen feet. "Just keep quiet and follow my trail, because I'm not listening to any more arguments." He grabbed the now empty sack and turned for the riverbank.

"But Boone—"

"Button your lip," he growled, none too pleased to find the bank littered with debris and cave-ins. "I warn you, I'm fast losing patience."

"Fine, throw the biggest fit in the world if you've a mind

to, but let me warn *you,* I won't be around to listen. I plan on taking the road."

If she'd been wearing skirts, they'd have made a decisive swish as she marched off into the darkness. Once more Tucker was left staring after her, with the definite impression that yet again, she'd managed to get the upper hand.

Pride demanded that he take the riverbank, but pride wasn't always expedient. Between the soggy clothing and stiff shoe leather, not to mention his physical exhaustion, he wouldn't last ten minutes, much less the night. If Jude knew a way to the road, he'd punish no one but himself by refusing to take it.

Grumbling as he followed in her wake, he swore that he'd put a stop to her outguessing him, manipulating him to do what she wanted. She was too shrewd by half, and too prone to getting in his way.

Come what may, Jude McCloud was going home—and that was that.

Seven

Late the next day, Jude stared at the steamboat bound for St. Louis, making her own plans about what to do next—none of which included sailing home to the family plantation. Boone was far too full of himself, not to mention blind, if he thought she'd meekly board the New Orleans packet just because he ordered her to. She didn't care if he'd paid for her passage out of his own pocket. She was going with him to St. Louis, and *that* was that.

Scanning the decks, she looked for sign of him. She knew he was aboard—she'd watched him march up the gangplank a good half hour ago, but she'd yet to see him in the crowd milling about the decks. Knowing Boone, he was probably off charming the ladies or engaged in a game of cards. She hoped so. It would suit her plans better if he stayed out of sight.

She eyed the main deck, where roustabouts were busy stacking wood and tossing ropes. From their actions, she reasoned she had fifteen minutes to a half hour before the boat pushed off from the dock. Timing, that was the key. She had to wait until the very last moment.

"Well, I'm back, and I still can't believe you mean to go through with this."

Jude spun to face Christopher. "Did you get what I asked?" she pounced, her mind focused less on details and more on the task ahead.

Frowning, he held up a carpetbag. "It's all in here. I'm

telling you, this is your craziest stunt yet. Patrick will have my head for letting you talk me into it."

"He told me that I have to stay with the tracker, and that's what I mean to do." She snatched the bag and began riffling through it. "Did you get everything I asked for?"

Christopher shrugged. "I handed your list to the shop owner. She told me she followed it to the letter. I don't know about the dress, though. It's . . . well, you'll see what I mean when you put it on."

Too harried to heed his warning, she hurried to an abandoned lean-to she'd spotted earlier. "Stand guard for me," she told her brother as she slipped inside the shed.

Already unbuttoning her shirt, she shut the door, paying even less heed to her brother's protests. It wasn't as if he'd anything new to offer—he'd been playing the same tired song since she and Boone straggled into town late last night. In summary, Christopher expected her to start thinking with her brains instead of her emotions, to get far away from the unreliable Tucker Boone, and for them both to leave at once for Louisiana.

Well, he was about to get his wish on one count, she thought, as she donned her new undergarments. Come tomorrow Christopher would be heading back home, but she had no intention of going with him.

Lifting the dress out of the carpetbag, she drew in a sharp breath. She'd asked for widow's wear, something demure, but the shop woman had been far too imaginative. Holding it in her hands, she could pinpoint nothing outright racy about the stylishly elegant burgundy merino, but on her body, its simple cut—cinched in at the waist and belled out at the hips—would cling to her every curve. Add on the lace-trimmed décolletage playing peekaboo at her breasts, and it would stir even the most preoccupied man's imagination.

A tiny grin curled her lips. Lord help her, but she couldn't wait to see Boone's face when she strolled up to him.

It would serve him right to be disconcerted, she thought, as she pulled the dress over her head. She'd grown mighty weary of watching him charm every female they encountered, those looks of his turning female shop clerks and cafe owners into absolute mush. He didn't even seem aware of his effect on women, acting as if flirting was his sole means of communication. With everyone *but* Jude.

"I still don't see why I can't come with you," Christopher continued to gripe outside the door.

Hastily slipping into the soft kid shoes from the bag, she spoke from what had become rote. "I've explained a good dozen times that it'll be hard enough for one of us to slip onto that boat unnoticed. Dressed like this, I stand a chance of getting past Boone, but he'd spot your height and dark hair in an instant."

"I could wear a disguise, too."

Funny how dressing like a female had become her disguise, instead of the other way around. "There's no time," she said, digging in the carpetbag. She found a nightgown and more undergarments, but not what she sought. "Where's the bonnet?" she asked, stepping outside to join her brother. "Christopher, I can't possibly pull this off if I don't cover my sawed-off hair."

He held a straw poke bonnet by its strings, a half smile forming on his lips. "What say we make a trade? This for my passage."

Behind them the steamboat gave its first warning blast, a loud, mournful hoot from its whistle. "Christopher Allen Latour, this is no time for teasing. I swear, I'll never forgive you if you make me miss that boat."

Taking in her appearance, he sobered instantly. "Criminy, Jude, you can't seriously expect me to let you go anywhere in that dress. Not on your own."

She wished now that she had a handkerchief to stuff in the bodice. "I'm not on my own," she answered defensively. "I'll be with Boone."

EVERY DREAM COME TRUE 83

His snort made it clear what he thought about using Boone as a safety net. "And what do you think will happen when he finds out you've tricked him again? He's liable to toss you out at the next stop. What then?"

The thought had occurred to her, but Jude pushed it aside. "Then I'll come home to Camelot," she said brightly, her attention sliding to the dock where the roustabouts busily untied the ropes. "I have to do this. Don't you see?"

Apparently he did not. "He's trouble, Jude. You can't trust him."

Against her will her thoughts returned to the night before, when she'd stood mere inches away from a very intense Tucker Boone, convinced he meant to kiss her. Trouble? Her brother didn't know the half of it—and she wasn't about to tell him. "This has nothing to do with Boone. It's about Rafe and finding him before it's too late. I'm going on that steamboat because it's the right thing to do, the only thing. I feel it, here."

As she laid her hand over her heart, she felt the coolness of silver. "I'll be fine," she added with a smile, lifting up the locket. "I have my good-luck charm."

He tried to smile. Of all her brothers, Christopher best understood how often Jude had clung to that locket for strength and courage. "All well and good for you," he said with mock bitterness. "But what do I have to protect me when I get home? I'm gonna have to face Patrick. And Guin. What can I say to them that won't have me sent to bed without supper for the rest of my life?"

She had to grin. "Why not tell the truth? You tried to make me see reason but as always, I proved too headstrong. They'll understand. They've too often tried to talk sense into me, too."

She said that to cheer him up, but in her heart, Jude knew Guin would accept her decision. From the start her adoptive mother had always had faith in her abilities, sometimes more than Jude had in herself.

She smiled reassuringly. "Look at it this way. Someone has to report what we've learned so far. Guin needs to know that Rafe is alive."

"Or so we hope. Remember, we have only Boone's word to go on. It could be a hoax to soak us for more and more money."

It was her turn to frown. She was enough of a cynic herself without her brother shoving more doubts in her face. "Tell her he's alive, anyway," she insisted. "It's time Guin heard some good news for a change. Besides, until I find cause otherwise, I'm believing Boone. I have to, Christopher. He's all we have."

"Maybe, but don't take that trust too far." Christopher took her hands, his stern expression more fatherly than little brother. "Don't tell him anything more about us, Jude. He doesn't need to know where we come from or who Rafe is to us. I'm not saying he's evil, mind you—but a man like that might be tempted to take unfair advantage if he guessed somewhere, there was money in it for him."

Behind them the steamboat gave a second warning blast. "I've got to go," she said, torn by the urgency to get on the boat and the fear of leaving her brother—and with him, her last link with home—behind.

"Promise me you'll keep quiet," Christopher repeated stubbornly, holding fast to her hands, "or I swear, I won't let you go."

"Very well, I won't tell him anything." The words came out in a rush, and she regretted it the instant she uttered them. Skirting the truth was one thing, but this could require outright lying. Lies, she'd found, had a way of getting bigger and less manageable the more you tried to maintain them.

Christopher released her hands, his young face softening as he realized what he'd asked her to do. He knew that lying didn't come easy to his sister, that Jude would rather shoot her own foot than go back on her word.

"Tell everybody I love and miss them," she told him as she jammed the bonnet on her head. "And first chance I get, I'll wire a message letting you know how I'm getting on."

"You'd best."

She smiled, then reached out to hug him close. "I'll miss you." Hearing the catch in her voice, knowing this was no time to give way to emotion, she pushed away and snatched up the carpetbag. "Actually, what I'd *best* do is run like the devil to catch that boat before it sails off without me."

"Sure you won't change your mind and let me come along?"

"No. You stay right here, out of sight. Boone's liable to be watching."

As she turned to go, he gently touched her arm. "You take care, y'hear?"

She nodded, holding up her locket. "Don't worry, I'll find a way to make everything come out all right. Don't I always?"

He grinned, every inch her trusting little brother once more. Giving the locket an extra squeeze, she prayed she would not let him down.

She left Christopher at the shed, racing to the gangplank just as they were about to withdraw it. Painfully aware that she was calling too much attention to herself, she kept her head lowered as she presented her papers and followed the steward aboard. He led her up to the next deck, to a cramped, windowless cabin tucked in among the stacks and far too near the boilers. Economy had been her objective in attaining accommodations, not comfort. All she truly needed was a place to hide from Boone.

As the door closed behind the steward, though, she found herself missing the breeze-gifted deck. Removing her bonnet and undoing the top button of her dress, she sat on the lumpy bunk—the only furnishing in the cabin—wishing for a little more quiet and a lot less heat. With the boilers clanking and steadily building steam, she wondered if she'd survive even an hour's isolation.

She cast a longing glance at the door. Only a fool would risk going out on deck, she told herself. She had to wait until they docked in St. Louis and it was too late for Boone to stop her.

An hour later, reduced to fanning herself with her shoes as she sprawled on the uncomfortable bunk, she nearly missed the knock on the door. She couldn't tell which pounded more, the engines or her aching head, and the banging at the door could as well have been another mechanical protest from the boilers.

Rising slowly, taking care not to crash her knees into the wall opposite, she silently mouthed what she meant to say to the steward, a speech she'd practiced as she lay there waiting. She wanted a bigger cabin, she'd tell him, and the devil with the cost. Indeed, she was so intent upon delivering her request and saying goodbye to this prison cell, it took a moment to register that it was no steward standing on the other side of her door. All words froze in her throat as she recognized Boone.

And he was not one whit pleased to see her, either.

To call Boone displeased was an understatement. Furious, maybe, even ready to explode, but he'd gone way past *displeased* the moment he saw Jude glide so audaciously past him. It had taken all his powers of persuasion, a healthy chunk of cash, and the better part of an hour to convince the steward that some riffraff with main deck passage could have any business with a passenger from the staterooms above.

Not that this cabin could claim much in the way of exclusiveness, he thought as he scornfully scanned the five-by-six cubicle. Aside from the bunk, he couldn't see where

Jude's accommodations outranked the main deck. At least there, he could breathe in fresh air.

Then again, air wouldn't have been her priority. He knew Jude had paid the extra sum because she wanted to hide. From him.

Angered anew, he glared down at her, resisting the urge to push her before him into the room. It was no gentlemanly instinct that stopped such action, but the relative danger of touching her anywhere while she wore that revealing dress.

Oh, he'd had warning enough—the wet, clinging shirt, the tight trousers—but nothing prepared him for how he'd feel faced with such blatant femininity. Bit by bit he'd begun to realize how incredibly lovely Jude was, but what he hadn't realized—hadn't let himself realize—was that she was also damned sexy.

He could hardly deny it now, though, with her creamy breasts pushing so seductively out of that delicate lace. Even her hair, which he'd done his best to make fun of, seemed far from boyish now the way it curled around her face, framing and softening her features, drawing his gaze to her full, red lips. Standing there, gaping at her, it was all he could do not to tumble them both to the bed.

He had to get rid of her, send her home where she belonged, but he wasn't going to deliver his ultimatum in such close quarters. Getting too near this female was a mistake he had no intention repeating. "We have to talk," he barked at her.

At his words her jaw snapped shut. As if she'd just now recovered her senses, she tried to slam the door in his face, but anticipating this—someone should warn her about her expressive eyes—Tucker wedged his boot in the frame.

"Move your foot," she told him angrily, shoving with all her might on the other side of the door. "If you don't leave this instant, I'll scream for the steward and have you thrown overboard."

"You can try," he said smoothly. "But I paid the man a goodly sum to look the other way while I hashed things out with my estranged wife, so you might be wasting your breath. Actually you might better save your energy for your explanation. As I recall, I left you waiting for the packet to Louisiana."

His calm tone didn't fool her. Her widened gaze told him she knew full well how angry she'd made him.

And being Jude, she wasn't about to back down an inch. Pushing her shoulder to the wood, she told him again to go away.

Losing patience, he gave a heave of his own. Both door, and Jude, went flying backward. The door slammed against the foot of the bunk, Jude onto the mattress.

Stepping inside the claustrophobic cabin, he found little room to move or even breathe. The sight of Jude spread out before him, her creamy breasts all but spilled out of that dress, made his inner demons all the louder in their urgings.

He had to say his piece and get out of here, provided Jude—and those blasted boilers—stopped sputtering.

"We'll be putting in to Cairo soon," he said over the din, wondering how she could stand it. "If you know what's good for you, you won't be on this boat when it pulls out again."

She sat up, all woman with her heaving breasts and heated words, yet equal part little girl in her defiance. "I just might happen to know better what is or is not good for me."

"Get off the damned boat, Jude. Or I'll make sure you wish that you had."

He turned—no easy feat in that cabin—and stomped off before she could make him angrier.

Lord help him, but the mere thought of joining her on that bed sent the blood pounding to his groin.

Lengthening his stride, determined to put distance between them, he fought to regain both his temper and good sense. He didn't much like the direction his thoughts were taking. No matter how angry she made him, he could never justify forcing a woman against her will.

But that was the trouble. That light in her eyes just now, the softening in her posture last night, all told him how little it would take to convince her she didn't need forcing. He'd seen how easily he could take advantage of her wide-eyed innocence, and with equal conviction, he knew they'd both hate him afterward if he did.

Reaching the lower deck, he went to the rail, breathing deeply of the fresh, reviving air. It wasn't sane, being this furious. It wasn't like him, at all. Even Lilah at her most irritating had inspired little more than disdain.

It was that damned dress, he decided, seizing on the most convenient culprit. Jude as a boy was one thing, but to be faced with all those womanly charms so prominently displayed, was it any wonder he felt this overwhelming urge to touch her, taste her, feel her warmth pressed against his own?

"How did you know?" she asked, materializing beside him.

For a disoriented moment, he thought he might have asked the question aloud. "Beg your pardon?" he asked, focusing on her face. She'd taken the time to button up her dress, he noticed with relief, and she'd covered her mussed-up curls with a bonnet.

Clearly uneasy under his scrutiny, she looked out over the river. "It's just . . . well, I can't figure how you knew. I changed my clothes, wore a hat, and kept my face averted. How on earth did you recognize me?"

Good question. It hadn't been through sight or logic—the recognition had sprung from something deep in his gut. Watching from the shadows, seeing the "young widow" hurry up the gangplank, he'd known only an irresistible urge to move closer. It wasn't until Jude brushed past him, and he'd caught a whiff of her distinctive scent, that the realization struck full force.

After that it was easy—the way she walked, how she tilted her head as she listened to the steward's directions—well, he'd caught on then, but too late to prevent her from escaping to the deck overhead.

"I'm paid to notice things," he said gruffly, choosing the half-truth instead. "You're not nearly as clever as you think."

That shut her up, a fact for which he was both grateful and sorry. If he hoped to have any peace, he needed to get the upper hand, yet he'd hate to be the one to make this little spitfire so uncharacteristically quiet and forlorn.

"Could be you're not so clever yourself," she said after a time. "You'd still be tied to that tree if it weren't for me."

He should have known better than to think her forlorn. It had just been a lull while she gathered her strength for her next attack.

"I've managed things quite well, if you ask me," she went on. "Without my intervention, you wouldn't be on this boat to order me off it. Of course," she added darkly, "you're hardly out of the woods yet. I've been thinking it over, and the way I see it, the Gray Ghosts might come after you, not wanting to risk your telling someone about their location. They'll want to recruit you . . . or kill you."

For a female she had remarkable powers of deduction, but she didn't have all the facts, and he saw no reason to supply them. He could just imagine her reaction if he admitted that he'd once been part of that gang.

"Most likely they'll look for you in Salvation," she continued, "but sooner or later, they'll remember you asking about Ra- . . . about Latour, and they'll come looking for you in St. Louis. As a man alone, you're bound to stand out, but the Gray Ghosts won't be looking for anyone traveling with his missus."

"No!" The word all but exploded from his mouth. "No way. No how."

"Why not travel together? I aim to go to St. Louis anyway." She turned, smiling coyly. "At least if I'm with you, I'll have protection. A *gentleman's* protection."

"You're not doing it right," he said cynically. "To charm me into doing what you want, you need to swish your fan and bat your lashes."

"Why, of all the conceited—"

"Unfortunately for you, I've been flirted with by the best in the business, and I'm now immune to it."

She took a deep breath. "I'm going to ignore your deliberate rudeness. Something I suppose I'll have to learn to do often in the future."

"Are you deliberately obtuse? Or haven't you been listening?"

No coyness now, only spit and fire. "I'm listening just fine," she told him, her full breasts heaving. "You're the one not paying attention. If you weren't so danged stubborn, you'd admit that I'm not a burden. That I've proven to everyone's satisfaction I can pull my own weight."

"That's not the point."

"Well then, here is the point." She stepped in front of him, mere inches away, to stab a finger into his chest. "I'm not asking your permission to tag along. I'm *telling* you that I'm going wherever you go, with or without your consent. Now we can work together, pooling brains and resources, or you can keep trying to elude me. But by telling me nothing of your plans, you risk me stumbling into the middle of them. You'll have no one but yourself to blame if I mess them up out of ignorance."

He grabbed her finger, scowling down at her. "That's your idea of a threat?"

"I could have left you there at the camp," she said softly, extricating her hand and lowering her arm awkwardly. "Heavens knows, it would have been the smart thing to do. But when you hired on, Boone, you became one of us, and I couldn't leave you in the lurch. I should have, to save us the cash. Let's face it, now that I know where Latour is, Christopher and I could have struck out for St. Louis on our own."

"Why didn't you?"

"Because we made a deal, and I, too, keep my word." She met him gaze for gaze. "You can trust me, Boone. I swear, I won't do anything stupid. All I ask in return is that I can be there when you find Latour."

"Why?" he felt compelled to ask. "What makes you so determined to track down this man?"

"He's . . ." She blinked, her gaze sliding off and away as she turned back to the rail. "Let's put it this way. Have you ever had a dream?"

Tucker felt sidetracked by the question, and suddenly wary. "A dream?"

She stared out over the river, her mind a thousand miles away. "Not the sleeping kind, but a great, shining hope you pursue while you're awake. A dream you follow against all odds, and not just for yourself, but for those you love."

"Dreaming's for children," he said dismissively, refusing to even think about the past. "And maybe for fools."

"I doubt you'd understand about Latour then," she said on a sigh. She turned back, facing him with a sad expression. "If we're going to work together, maybe it's better we don't poke into each other's private affairs. You keep to yourself, and I'll show you the same regard."

Studying her, her posture stiff and unrelenting as she faced him, he realized it might be smarter to let her tag along. By fair means or foul, she'd stick like a burr to his coattails until their mission was finished anyway. At least if he knew where she was, he could keep an eye on her.

It might not be so bad. Look how she'd tracked him down, then around, until he was free from his ropes. That was a pretty neat escape she'd planned, too. She had indeed proved he could count on her.

Trouble was, Tucker wasn't used to relying on anyone. Before he could take a headstrong woman like Jude anywhere, he had to know he could control her. "If I let you tag along, you have to understand, I call the shots."

She studied his face as if considering this. "You're the expert, of course, but you might discover I have ideas of my own worth exploring. Surely you wouldn't want to limit your possibilities by arbitrarily dismissing my suggestions."

"I'll keep that in mind." He leaned back against the rail, trying not to be amused by her. "This is the deal, Miss McCloud. I'm willing to try this, er, alliance, but any disagreement over how things are to be done, and we part ways, with you heading back to Louisiana."

"Isn't that a tad harsh?"

"Life's a tad harsh, and you'd best get used to it. Do we have a deal, or not?"

Biting her lip, she studied his face again, no doubt sifting through the pros and cons of his offer. Apparently deciding that the benefits outweighed the drawbacks, she broke into a sudden, dazzling smile. "Two minds are better than one," she said cryptically, extending her hand. "All and all, I think we shall deal quite satisfactorily together, Mr. Boone."

He felt a sudden strange reluctance to shake her hand, as if by thus sealing their agreement, he'd be sealing his fate.

Not that she'd let him avoid it. As she reached for and clasped his hand, he was struck how small hers felt in his, yet how warm and sure. No limp-wristed grip for Jude McCloud. No, she shook hands with the firm, direct grasp of a man.

Yet he found nothing masculine in the look she gave him, or the soft, floral scent surrounding her like a cloud. For the briefest instant, he let himself imagine how it would feel to throw caution to the winds, to let himself know this woman, in every sense of the word.

Alarmed by the strength of the temptation, he dropped her hand and took a step back. It was his turn to watch the river. "You still have your uniform?" he asked, his tone harsher than he'd intended.

He heard the surprise in hers. "Yes, why?"

"Change into it. Now. You'll be safer traveling as a boy, and a little brother is just as good a decoy as a wife."

"Yes, but—"

So it started, he thought irritably. Not five minutes into their alliance and already she was bucking him. "I thought we agreed to do things my way."

"Actually I thought we agreed to discuss things before you made your tyrannical decisions."

Hearing the odd note in her voice, he risked a glance at her. Her anger he was ready to deal with, but not the gentle grin.

"Stop trying to be such a bully, Boone," she said, tilting her head to study him. "My brothers are masters at it, so this is something I'm quite immune to."

Unaccustomed to women throwing his words back at him it, Tucker was momentarily robbed of speech.

Not Jude. Never Jude. "Relax, I'm not trying to undermine your authority," she went on. "You would know best. Confederate gray it will be, then."

"Thank you."

He couldn't keep the sarcasm out of his voice, any more than she could prevent her annoyance from stealing across her expressive face. "Finding Latour is very important to me, Boone. If you mess it up—"

"Just go change, Miss McCloud."

"If I'm supposed to be your little brother on this little adventure, don't you think you ought to be calling me Jude?"

It was all he could do to keep his voice even. "Go change your clothes, *Jude.*"

"Aye, aye, Captain." Giving him a mock salute, she flounced off.

Tucker frowned as he watched her glide up the stairs, uneasiness wriggling through his gut. He didn't like the way that female kept getting under his skin. *If you mess it up,* she'd said. He liked even less how much that rankled.

No doubt about it, she'd put him in an impossible position. His instincts screamed at him to run, yet he needed the money to pay off his debt. Lilah represented his rock and Jude the proverbial hard place. Not for one minute did he doubt her intention of following him—from her words, deeds, and expressive brown eyes, Jude made it plain that no one could be more stubborn.

Unless it was Tucker Boone. Maybe he had agreed to let her tag along, but he'd never said he'd make the going easy. No more casual conversation, no accommodating his longer stride to hers . . . hell, from now on she could carry her own luggage.

All in all, he thought, her dislike should be simpler to handle than that soft, brief moment she'd smiled at him.

Lord help them both if she smiled at him like that again.

Eight

Trudging along behind Boone into the St. Louis hospital, Jude itched with frustration. He had to know these doctors weren't going to tell them any more than that stiff-necked colonel at the Jefferson Barracks had, certainly not without official clearance. No Federal was going to volunteer information—she and Boone had to be imaginative, if not outright sly.

Being crafty was what led them to this hospital. Back at the Jefferson Barracks, tired of Boone's questions and the colonel's evasive answers, she'd slipped off to a dark office filled with official files. She'd found it harrowing, knowing she could be caught at any moment while sifting through the information, but better that than sitting through the colonel's oration, an hour-long diatribe on the steps to atonement each Southerner must take before being accepted back into the Union.

Huffing, shifting her carpetbag to the other hand, she wondered how Boone had stomached the man's preaching. The fat, pampered colonel couldn't have seen much fighting himself, so what gave him the right to act like Peter guarding the gates of heaven? If his precious Union had been such a paradise, she'd wanted to ask the pompous fool, why had so many folks wanted out of it?

But conscious of her mission, and already having the name of this hospital tucked in her brain, she'd pretended to get violently ill. Five minutes later they'd been escorted out the door.

But did Boone thank her for the rescue or congratulate her on unearthing the information? No, he'd all but ignored her. With barely a grunt—and not even in her direction—he'd bulldogged ahead, expecting her to trot at his heels like some obedient puppy while he confided nothing of his plans on their hell-bent dash from the barracks back to the city.

"You know, I really should change into my dress," she said to him now, trying to keep her tone polite and pleasant. "A grieving widow should have more luck gaining sympathy—and information—from military doctors."

He turned to face her, clearly exasperated. "Who in his right mind will believe you're Latour's widow?"

She dropped the carpetbag, which by now felt like a thousand tons, to face him squarely. "I happen to be a very fine actress."

"You're too young. Unless the man married you when you were a baby."

"Very well, I can be his daughter then."

He fixed her with his stoniest glare. "Latour was a planter. His daughter would be a lady. How do you plan to explain that hacked-off head of hair?"

Trying not to wince, she looked away, her hand slipping up to touch the travesty she'd made of her once glorious mane. Boone should have seen her before the war started, when a parade of young beaus had hailed her as the belle of the parish. "My bonnet will cover my head."

"No!" His scowl punctuated the command. "I said no dress, and I mean it. It's too near nightfall for you to be wandering around dressed as a female."

She wanted to scream at him for being so stubborn, but knowing it would get her nowhere, she summoned the last of her poise and patience. "I won't be alone. I'll be with you."

Her only reward for such marvelous self-control was a sneer so insulting, she'd have boxed his ears if he hadn't marched away in the other direction. "I swear to you," he growled over his shoulder, "if I see you in that dress, I'll leave you to fend for yourself."

Hands on hips, she watched him march off. The devil take him and his stubbornness. He could show a little less skepticism when it came to her ability to play the sweet, grieving lady. Why, once she put her mind to it, no doctor, not even the most war-hardened Federal, could prove immune to the tears brimming at her eyes. She'd charm that information out of the man in ten minutes flat.

But no, Boone was determined to do this his way, man to man, no females permitted. Why, the way he acted, you'd think he was afraid of her as a woman.

She paused, considering that possibility. He'd certainly been ill at ease, standing beside her on the deck. He had no trouble ordering a boy around, she realized, but he lost all composure when she put on her dress. If she batted her lashes and fluttered a fan as he'd teased, could she charm Boone into doing what was best for them? One would think so. He was a man, wasn't he?

She remembered that night by the river, how her body had trembled with far more than the cold, how they'd both been only too aware of the difference in their sexes. Reliving that moment, she knew a piercing thrill of fear. Don the dress now, and she could well be playing with fire.

She bit her lip, weighing the risks, already glancing about her for a place to change. After all, she told herself, the real issue was finding Rafe. Results, that's what they needed, and if it meant getting burned by Boone's fury, then it was a risk she'd have to take.

Spying an empty storage closet, she ducked inside and began digging through the carpetbag. No time to dally. She had mere minutes to change before Boone turned around and discovered her missing.

EVERY DREAM COME TRUE

* * *

Tucker had too much on his mind to notice whether Jude followed or not. Ushered into a cramped, book-lined office while the nurse fetched Dr. Briggs, he wrinkled his nose in distaste. The smell, the sounds, the walls that seemed to close in on him—all brought back memories he'd prefer to keep buried. He'd seen too many soldiers go into death traps like this and never come out again. No wonder he was in such a foul mood. It wasn't always a good thing, surviving. Left you with all sorts of incomplete feelings, ugly ones like loss, regret, and guilt.

Rubbing his shoulder, grateful that it was healing quite nicely, he thought of Jude and how she'd nursed him. Maybe he'd been a little hard on her, he conceded. Turning around to see if she were still scowling at him, he discovered for the first time that he was alone in the room.

But not for long. Before he could entertain notions of how he'd throttle Jude's lovely neck, a tall, thin man in a white cotton frock coat strode into the room. "Samuel Briggs, physician on duty," the man announced as he marched to the desk. "I have five minutes to spare. I suggest you make the most of them."

"Tucker Boone." Risking a glance over his shoulder before turning back to Briggs, Tucker told himself he should be glad Jude hadn't joined them. Nothing went as predicted with her around.

Taking the seat Briggs offered, Tucker studied him as the man perched on the edge of his sturdy oak desk. From his crisp gray hair to his well-polished shoes, the man exuded a self-confidence that bordered on arrogance. His body poised for immediate action, he made it clear that he was used to having his orders obeyed, his time protected, and as such would not suffer fools gladly.

He met Tucker's appraisal with his own probing gaze, taking him in, weighing what he saw, and reaching an instant decision. One could practically see the shutters close over his deep-set, intelligent eyes.

"I've just come from the Jefferson Barracks," Tucker stated bluntly, determined to say his piece before Briggs had him ushered from the room. "A certain rebel prisoner was transferred here for treatment some months ago. With an infected leg wound. Can you tell me if he's still in this hospital?"

Standing abruptly, Briggs spared a tight smile. "Forgive me, but I'm not at liberty to discuss private medical records." He gestured at the waning light outside the window. "The hour grows late, and you're wasting your time and mine, Mr. Boone. I must get on with my evening rounds."

Tucker reached for his arm as the man tried to brush past. "Can you at least tell me if he's alive or dead?"

Briggs frowned at his hand, which Tucker grudgingly withdrew. "That is privileged information," Briggs said curtly. "Given out only to immediate family."

"Oh, but he is," Jude drawled behind them. "Or at least, as near as."

Both men turned to face her, Tucker with outraged astonishment, Briggs with a slow, spreading smile. Tucker could almost see the hostility ooze out the man's body as Jude glided up to them, so lovely and demure, if slightly disheveled and flushed. She was wearing the dress, Tucker saw, and once again she looked too damned good in it.

"Darling, didn't you tell Dr. Briggs you were my fiancé?" she asked sweetly, wrapping a possessive arm around Tucker's. "You'll have to forgive him. Such a sweetie-pie, trying to protect me from what we fear most. . . ." She bit her lip, took a gulp, before plunging on valiantly, "Tell me, is it bad news?"

As much as Tucker might want to strangle her for disregarding his order, he could see Briggs responding to her little performance. Only a fool would ignore her cue. Slipping an arm around her back, noticing the sudden rigidity of her spine, he realized he could kill two birds with one stone. By playing the concerned suitor, not only could he convince the unyielding Briggs to part with the necessary information, but he could derive great satisfaction from watching the defiant Miss McCloud squirm under his far too solicitous attentions.

"But, precious, I asked you to wait downstairs for me," he said in the same syrupy tone, even while running a soothing hand up and down her arm. "We can't have all this illness and suffering distressing you." He finished off by gripping her firmly at her waist, an intimate gesture meant to mark possession. It proved a two-edged sword. He'd made his point to Jude, but he couldn't help but notice how tiny her waist was, how satisfyingly the soft curve fit in his grasp.

"I'm not some delicate flower," she snapped, before remembering the role she played. "As you no doubt recall, it was while nursing your own injury," she added more gently, her smile drenched in honey as she edged away from him, "that you and I got to know each other better."

"As if I could ever forget." He'd meant to sound like her devoted swain, but Jude's glance at his shoulder assured that she'd caught his true message, that there would have been no need for nursing—or even getting to know him—had she and her brother not shot him in the first place.

"I need to hear for myself, darling," she told him firmly before turning a pleading gaze to their audience. "I'm in a fever to have news of my daddy, Dr. Briggs. Please, can't you tell us anything?" She sucked in her bottom lip, as if to keep it from trembling, and Tucker was hard-pressed to tear his gaze away.

"I'd be happy to help," Briggs told her, "if I knew who your father is."

"But of course." She gave a nervous giggle. "His name is Rafe Latour. He served in the cavalry under General Jo Shelby."

Briggs shifted uneasily, looking from Jude to Tucker. "I'm afraid I can't help you after all. You see, he's . . ."

Briggs paused, choosing his words with care, and Tucker saw the tension seize Jude's body. Without thinking, he again grasped her waist, this time reassuringly.

"I can take whatever news you have to tell me," she said with a proud tilt to her chin. "I've come all the way from Louisiana just to learn the truth, and I'm not about to turn away now. Please, I need to know if he's alive or dead."

Seeing the soft pools of moisture spilling from her huge brown eyes, Boone had to remind himself that this was just a pose. Lord help him, but he longed to comfort her, to kiss away the tears on her delicate cheeks.

Without the benefit of prior experience with this female, poor Briggs melted like the last snow of April. "Miss Latour, I'm sorry," he began awkwardly, looking everywhere but at her face. "I'd bring him to you this instant if I could, but the fact of the matter is, your father is no longer with us."

Instinctively Tucker reached up to clasp her shoulder and offer his support.

"Poor Mama," she said with an unmistakable catch in her voice. "Rafe Latour was her sole reason for living. Never, not even in my darkest moments, have I ever believed he could truly be dead."

"Good heavens, no," Briggs blurted out. "You misunderstood. I meant that your father is no longer here, at this particular hospital. We received orders to transfer him to a prison camp west of here."

"He's alive?"

Watching her, Tucker couldn't help but be impressed by her acting ability. Between the breathiness in her voice and the eagerness shining in her eyes, even he would be convinced that this was Latour's grieving daughter, had he not spent the last few days with her.

He dropped his arm, realizing he'd been offering concern

and support where none was needed. Jude took instant advantage by sidestepping away, wandering to the window to plot out her next move. Tucker found himself trailing behind her. To keep an eye on her and keep her out of trouble, he insisted to himself, though that didn't explain the urge to wrap his arm once more around her waist.

"This is wonderful news," Jude told the doctor, pausing before the window to dab at her eyes. The smile she flashed at him could have lit the dark, airless room. "I don't suppose y'all can tell me exactly where my daddy was sent?"

"Normally no. With so many patients, it's impossible to keep track of everyone, but we struck up a brief friendship, your father and I, discussing our views on the evils of war. I want you to know, Miss Latour, that I did my best to block his transfer. The detention center in Jefferson City is hardly the most pleasant of places, nor was I satisfied with the condition of your father's injury. It was my opinion that he required more healing time. Unfortunately, as my superiors pointed out, the conditions of war make the rules, not us physicians."

She sighed along with him. "Yes, but the war is now over. Isn't it time for us all to heal our wounds?"

"Amen to that," Tucker muttered under his breath as he moved beside her. He tried to take her arm, thinking to use her role-playing to hold her next to him, but with a neat little movement, she danced free to go gliding over to Briggs.

Annoyed, his first impulse was to march after her, to force the infuriating female to stop playing her games, but he happened to glance out the window.

His gaze drawn to the scene below, he took in the six heavily armed men carefully considering the front door of the hospital. With a quick shot of alarm, Tucker recognized the blond hair and wiry frame of Billy Cochoran. How in blazes had the Gray Ghosts found him so soon?

He watched Billy motion to his men. One headed to the

front door, four to the back, no doubt to guard the rear two exits. He and Jude had to leave now, this instant, or they'd be trapped inside the hospital.

Jude had gone to the other side of the desk and was now taking the doctor's hands in her own. "I can't thank you enough for your help," she gushed. "With what you've told us, I hope to end my daddy's own personal war. I'm bound and determined to find him and bring him home where he belongs."

What happened to the evening rounds you were so anxious to make? Tucker thought in annoyance as he noticed the man's fatuous grin. Briggs looked as if he'd be happy to stand there holding her hands all night. Swearing inwardly, Tucker strode across the room to snatch Jude away and out the back door.

"Please write when you get him home and settled," Briggs was saying in his deep, fatherly tone. "I'd appreciate word of your father's safe return. In this line of work, I find happy endings are few and far between."

Tucker grabbed at her arm, wrenching her away. "We've got to get back to our search," he told her firmly.

"In a moment, darling," she said, her tone tight as she in turn yanked free of Tucker's grasp. "I want to thank the kind doctor for his help."

"You did that. Let's go."

"In a minute." Hard to believe those dark brown eyes could flash so much fire. "We don't want Dr. Briggs thinking we're rude, do we?"

Tucker imagined the goons, inching ever closer to the door. "I'm sure he'll excuse us. It's getting dark and we have miles to travel."

Stubbornly Jude held tight to the doctor's hands, bestowing her warmest smile on the man. "I promise to write at first opportunity. I'm certain my father will want to contact you as well. One other thing, though—"

"We've got to go," Tucker barked at her, losing all patience.

"I'm not leaving without thanking Dr. Briggs, *darling*." Jude looked decidedly rebellious and inclined to make a scene. Cursing inwardly, Tucker knew he might as well kiss the back exit goodbye. With all the time that had elapsed, and Jude proving so difficult, he'd need to come up with an alternate plan. But for that he needed someplace quiet and undisturbed where he could think. Eluding the Gray Ghosts was unlikely, but he might yet devise a way to confront them and still come out unharmed. "We are in your debt," he told Briggs, while grabbing Jude's arm firmly. "But we've interrupted your schedule too long as it is." Leaving no room for protest, he dragged her to the door.

"I look forward to hearing from *you*," Briggs called after them, obviously limiting his goodwill to Jude, but Tucker was too busy overcoming her resistance to pay him heed. "You will come with me, and you'll come now," he whispered between gritted teeth, "or I swear, I'll leave you here without looking back."

"Go ahead," she hissed, yanking her hand free the instant they turned the corner into a quieter, gaslit corridor. Once out of sight and earshot of the good doctor, her voice rose accordingly. "You're not much use to me anyway, the way you're acting."

Tucker stopped where he stood to glare at her. "And what's that supposed to mean?"

"It's one thing to ignore my every suggestion, no matter how plausible or well conceived, but to play caveman, to drag me off when we had that doctor willing to supply the information we needed was sheer pigheaded folly. What can I think but that you're intent upon sabotaging all my efforts?"

Her militant pose and clipped tones might have been more impressive had Tucker not been battling a fury of his own. "We had the information we needed," he told her coldly. "You were wasting precious moments. It was time to leave, not to be flirting and holding hands with a man old enough to be your father."

Her brown eyes bored into him. "I wasn't flirting. I was trying to get a name. Things will go smoother in Jefferson City if we have a specific person to contact, but no, you had to barge right over my tactful questioning with your deplorable lack of manners. Was it any wonder Dr. Briggs felt disinclined to impart any information to you? I'm even beginning to feel sympathy for the colonel at the Jefferson Barracks."

That stung, though Tucker would never admit it to her. He'd have to be blind not to notice how easily she'd extracted the information in comparison to his own attempts, but he nonetheless resented the hell out of her pointing it out to him. "Go on, dance around all proud and cocky, but you might want to consider what danger you've put us in by parading around as a woman."

"Danger?" She eyed him with scorn. "From whom? Dr. Briggs? One of the poor patients? Do you fear one of them will knock me down with a crutch?"

She had him so angry, he nearly blurted out that the Gray Ghosts were outside, but he made the mistake of considering what truly did frighten him. The fact that he feared more for Jude's safety than his own stopped him cold.

Gazing down at her, he felt the rage seep out of his body. Jude, with her misplaced loyalty and misguided bravado, would insist upon standing beside him as he confronted the Gray Ghosts. She might infuriate the hell out of him, but with stark, cold clarity, he knew he could never do anything to risk this woman's life.

"I can't help feeling that speed is crucial," he told her, thinking ahead to how he'd might best keep her from harm. "What if Latour isn't in Jefferson City, and we have many more stops before we find him? Don't you think the sooner we start off, the better?"

"Maybe, but—"

"I had no right to stop you from thanking Briggs, I realize that now. Why don't you go back and apologize, get what information you can, while I go make travel arrangements?"

She tilted her head to study him, clearly caught off guard by his change in tone. "Mr. Boone, if you're trying to apologize, why not just come right out and say you're sorry?"

"Don't press your luck." He ignored her grin. "Time's awasting, Jude. Hurry and talk to Briggs, then change back into your uniform. I'll meet you out in front." He had to look away, having no intention of being anywhere near the hospital when she stepped out the door. With any luck, by that time he'd have diverted Billy to a new location, as far away as humanly possible from Jude.

He frowned as he pictured her, standing alone on the steps in the dark. She'd be wondering what had become of him, unable to believe he could strand her in a strange, unwelcoming city with no friends and little money. Still she'd given him no alternative. Alone, and dressed as a boy, she'd fare far better than if she fell into the hands of the Gray Ghosts and Billy.

"Do you think we'll find him this time?" she asked, her voice quiet, her gaze searching.

It took Tucker some moments to realize she meant Latour, struck as he suddenly was by the realization that he'd likely never see her again. It didn't help that the gaslight framed her dark hair with a golden glow, that her features—even her posture—had softened, bringing each into a clear, poignant focus. He was going to miss this woman, he realized, and on the heels of that thought, he had a strong, mad urge to pull her close and keep her there.

"I'll find him," he told her instead, "or I'll die trying."

She smiled, not knowing how literal his words were

likely to be. "I like it so much better when you're not raging at me."

So did he, Tucker realized. Too bad he had to figure that out so late in the game. "Go—go get changed," he said, chucking her gently on the chin. "Before you get me riled again."

He turned away, willing himself to walk down the hall. He'd have liked to watch Jude glide off—she moved with surprising poise and grace in that dress—but he knew Billy's impatience, and he didn't want him storming into the hospital. The last thing they needed was for Billy to get an eye on Jude in that outfit.

Stifling a shudder, Tucker made his way to the front door. Given his upbringing, perhaps it wasn't surprising that Billy wasn't particularly kind to the opposite sex, but it had caused more than one nasty argument between them. The prospect of Jude in Billy's hands, and Tucker powerless to stop him . . .

He stopped that thought before it could take hold. If he meant to keep the two apart, he must begin at once, if the shouting in the lobby were anything to go by. Hurrying to the source of the noise, he found Billy yelling at the poor harried female manning the entrance desk.

"I believe he's looking for me," Tucker told the nurse, grabbing Billy and leading him toward the door. "Ignore him, ma'am. He tends to lose all sense of polite behavior if he waits too long between meals. We'll go eat supper now," he growled at Billy as he dragged him through the front entrance.

Outside Billy broke free with his disarming grin. "Well, if it don't feel like old times, Jesse boy, you covering up for me again." Still grinning, he scratched his head. "Though I can't recollect it being a punishable crime, a lack of manners. S'pose it's just one more law heaped upon us by them Northern prim-noses."

This was no time to be getting in a political discussion,

not outside a Union hospital. "How did you find me?" he asked curtly.

Billy tossed back his head with a good, long laugh. "Ah, we have our ways, Jesse. Don't you worry none about that."

"Fine. *Why* are you here then? You didn't come all the way to St. Louis on a whim."

"Nope, I didn't. I'm here because you and me need to discuss some serious business."

Now that had an ominous ring. Risking a glance at the door, Tucker was only too aware of the minutes ticking by. "Let's talk over drinks. I know a tavern down by the docks."

"Why go all the way to the river?" Billy nodded to the right. "Mulligan's is right down the street."

Tucker glanced again at the hospital. *Down the street* wasn't as far away as he'd like, but while he stood here arguing with Billy, Jude could come barging out that door. "Fine, Mulligan's it is then."

With a grin Billy turned toward the bar, making no attempt to collect the five men who'd been with him.

"What about the others?" Tucker asked. "You wouldn't come here alone."

Billy chuckled. "Hell, I sent them off to find their own beer. You've ridden with us—you know what happens when we hit a town like this. It's every man for himself, until business needs to be done."

And just what *was* their business? Tucker wondered with a frown. At first glance he'd assumed they'd come for him, but then Billy should be holding a pistol to his head, not strolling beside him to a bar for a discussion over drinks. Had he'd misread the scene he'd witnessed from the window? Instead of sending his men to guard the entrances, had Billy merely been dispersing them to seek their various amusements?

Not that it mattered. Either way Tucker had to get Billy away from the hospital before Jude came through that door.

Every instinct he owned insisted that he keep those two from colliding.

With a last glance at the door, and the faint, futile hope that she'd come to understand that he'd left her to protect her, Tucker fell into step behind Billy.

Nine

Jude squeezed her eyes shut, hoping against hope that this time when she opened them, she'd find they were playing tricks on her. Be on the floor where I left you, she chanted softly. Everything she owned was in that carpetbag. Easing her eyes open, she told herself that it had to be there.

It wasn't, though.

Panic mushroomed in her chest. What would she do without her disguise, the bindings, the small fortune she kept hidden in those bindings?

Sick with desperation, she scanned the tiny room again, making sure this was indeed the right closet, that she hadn't mistaken it for another, but no such miracle occurred. This was the right closet, and all too obviously, someone had taken her carpetbag out of it.

Swallowing hard, willing the panic away, she told herself not to jump to conclusions. Someone might have picked it up by mistake—the bag could have been given to one of the nurses for safekeeping. Holding tight to that hope, Jude asked every staff member in sight, but too harried to notice anything but their own heavy workload, no one could remember seeing the bag.

Standing alone, watching nurses bustle past to care for their patients, Jude blinked back tears of frustration and fear. Her belongings were gone and with them all hope for finding Rafe. How on earth could they get to Jefferson

City without funds? Boone might have money, but only a naive fool would expect him to stick around when she couldn't pay his wages.

Boone. With a sick dread, she imagined his reaction. "Naive fool" would be the least he would call her. If he'd been angry before, just think how he'd rage at her for being stupid enough to leave her belongings unguarded in that closet. He'd consider it proof that she was too young, and too female, to serve any real use on this quest.

Overwhelmed by the unfairness of it all, she felt the anger rise up inside her. It was Boone's fault that she'd lost her things. If he hadn't been in such a foul mood, or so stubborn about letting her wear the dress, she wouldn't have felt so rushed about getting back to him. In hindsight it was obvious that she'd made a mistake in leaving the carpetbag behind, but then all she could think of was getting dressed before Boone had another conniption fit and sent her home.

The spurt of resentment, fortifying while it lasted, drained away as she realized what little weight her excuses would hold for Boone. She could picture his scowl as he reminded her that he'd expressly forbidden her to wear the dress in the first place. He'd probably accuse her of losing the bag on purpose.

And now, because of her willfulness and negligence, she was stuck in the dress forever, no longer able to retreat into the safety of her disguise. Of course he'd leave her to her own devices. Protecting her virtue, he'd made more than clear, was not why she'd hired him.

No doubt about it, facing Boone would be far from pleasant.

Wincing, she glanced behind her, weighing her chances of escaping out the back door. She could go to Dr. Briggs, appeal to him for help. If she explained her situation, surely the kindly doctor would loan her money to get to Jefferson

City. Once she found Rafe, she wouldn't need Boone and his autocratic bullying.

Yet before she could take a step, her conscience reared its insistent head. She'd promised Guin and Patrick that she would stay with the man she hired and not go off on her own. Worse, she realized belatedly, she couldn't leave Boone with no apology or explanation. She could hear Guin's soft tones, sternly reminding that Jude had been raised better than that.

Wincing, she imagined Boone waiting alone, slowly realizing that she wasn't going to join him, that she'd let him down by running away. It might be easier if his last words to her had been angry ones, but he'd been subdued, almost tender as he chucked her on the chin, giving her a brief glimpse at the innate gentleness he rarely let others see. How could she turn her back on that?

Sucking in a deep breath, she made her way downstairs, determined to do the right thing, the decent thing, no matter how he might rage at her. At the front door, she took hold of the knob, bracing herself against his fury, feeling as if she were being marched to the guillotine.

Once outside, though, she found little stirring but the cool, evening air. Looking about her in bewilderment, she felt rather as if she were back in the closet again, looking for her carpetbag. She knew Boone should be here, yet search though she might, she could find neither hair nor hide of him.

Her dread of facing him threaded into anxiety. Where was he? What could have happened?

Yet as moment slipped into moment, doubt and suspicion began to breed. All that worry about letting *him* down, while he'd been busy executing his own escape. No wonder he'd been so surprisingly nice. Why hide his tender streak when he had no intention of seeing her again?

Yet as much as she wanted to blame him for all the worst possible motives, her logical mind could make no sense of his actions. What could he possibly gain by deserting her now? His job wasn't finished, he hadn't been paid. Jude still owed him money, a sum he so obviously needed, so why would he leave before he collected? Unless . . .

No, she thought with a sudden cold pang. She wouldn't believe Boone had stolen her carpetbag. She couldn't.

Hugging herself for warmth, she faced the obvious. He could have guessed she'd left the carpetbag somewhere, then sent her to Briggs to give himself time to snatch it. And when she finally emerged from the hospital, scared and worried about his reaction, he wouldn't have to face her. Not Mr. I-Work-Alone Boone. Oh, no, he'd be long gone with her money.

Not Boone, a little voice in her cried, while the more practical Jude began glancing about for her luggage. If he only wanted the money, he'd toss the bag to the side of the road, not caring if she found it.

It proved fortunate that she was looking to the right, for she did indeed spot her carpetbag, though not discarded on the road. A young, rather grimy-faced boy was sneaking out of the side door of the hospital with it, both hands clasped tight around his prize.

"You there!" she called out without thinking, taking a step in his direction. "Wait, that bag is mine."

The boy responded the only way he could. He bolted.

Jude did her best to catch the little urchin, but hampered by her skirts, she couldn't gain ground on him. But if she kept following, she hoped, the weight of the carpetbag would eventually slow the boy down.

All well and good, had she been left to her chase, but it was nightfall in a strange city, so it was inevitable that the street thugs would come along.

"Now, now—look what we have here," one of them growled in her ear as he grabbed her from behind. "I reckon Billy will be pleased as punch with this."

* * *

Seated across the scarred wood table, Tucker studied his surprisingly quiet friend, trying to figure out what Billy was up to now. It was unlike him to pick such an empty saloon, much less choose a spot in its darkest, most shadowed corner. The Billy he knew favored loud music and boisterous women. This brooding man, pensively sipping his beer, could be a complete stranger.

"Out with it," Tucker said impatiently. If this were a trap, he'd rather Billy just sprang it. After the last few days, Tucker was in no mood to play cat and mouse. "Just why are we here?"

"Fate brought us here, Jesse boy. You can't fight destiny."

"What in blazes are you talking about?"

"Ever wonder why things happen like they do? How you can be going along, not a care in the world, and then one thing happens—one tiny, seemingly unimportant event—and before you know it, your world's spun out of control. . . ."

Tucker didn't answer. For one thing it seemed a rhetorical question, and he doubted Billy expected a comment—but more, it took him aback, this new side of his friend. Billy Cochoran, the philosopher? No wonder he knew about this place. From the sound of things, he must have been drinking here all afternoon.

"Way I see it," Billy said on a sigh, "life is a great, powerful tide, sweeping us along, taking us where it wants. Ain't no such thing as free will. What we are, what we become, is set out before we're even born."

Definitely drunk, Tucker thought. "C'mon, Billy, you don't believe that."

Billy focused on Tucker's face. "Look at us, Jesse. Remember the plans we once had? You were gonna farm that big spread your mama hankered after, and me, well, I'd aimed to see the world."

"We're young yet. Our lives are far from over."

Billy snorted. "Always said your mama did you a disservice, putting notions in your head. Urging you to dream, letting you think you could fight your fate."

Tucker had long since accepted the cold, hard logic behind Billy's words. Habit made him argue, not conviction. "What if I don't like my fate?" he asked, aware that old habits did indeed die hard. "I'm supposed to just lie back and take it?"

"It would've been easier on your mama had she just accepted her lot in life. I mean, where did all her struggling ever get her? Where will it get you? In the end we all end up right back where we belong."

"What's your point?" Tucker snapped, the memory of his mother's death burning in his heart. "I assume you're going somewhere with this?"

With a sigh, Billy straightened in his chair. "I'm here to help you find your way, to fulfill your destiny."

"Silly me. And here I thought you meant to drag me back to face your captain's wrath."

Billy actually seemed surprised by the suggestion. "Hell, Jesse, we're friends. If that's what I was here for, I'da said so right out."

"Why are you here then? And cut the destiny crap."

Grinning, Billy settled back to savor his beer. "We had your trial without you. I must admit, some of the boys wanted you roasted on an open spit, but I argued them into giving you a second chance."

"That's mighty generous of you. A second chance at what?"

Tilting his head, Billy frowned, as if Tucker had somehow disappointed him. "Why, to serve the Confederacy of course."

Tucker should have seen it coming. Nothing worse than

a reformed ne'er-do-well with a cause. "Seems to me we already had this argument."

Billy's frown went hard, as if carved from granite. "It's what you were born for, Jesse. What we were all born for. And this time," he added, his tone just as unyielding, "you'd best not let us down."

Tucker might wonder *or what?* but knew better than to vocalize it. "I suppose you have a mission in mind," he said instead. "Specific orders passed down from this Cap'n of yours."

Billy nodded grimly. "Could have come from the Cap'n, or maybe the man he works for. All I know is when I told Cap'n who you were tracking, he saw you in a whole new light. Find the traitor for us, Cap'n says, and we'll pay a year's wages."

Tucker gripped his mug, determined not to betray how the offer both surprised and tempted him. "I told you, Billy, I've already been hired for this."

"Tell the McCloud kid to take a walk. Or don't tell him anything at all. Hell, Jesse, we don't care if you get paid twice, so long as you know where your loyalty lies. When all is said and done, you just make good and sure you bring Latour to the Gray Ghosts for justice."

Billy made it sound easy. Tucker merely had to do what he meant to do anyway, and he could earn more money than he'd ever dreamed possible. Trouble was, life never worked out that easy. There had to be a catch.

"For such a likeable guy," he said slowly, "Latour made a lot of people angry. Mind telling me what he did to the Gray Ghosts that you'd be so eager to part with such a sum?"

"Me?" Billy said, betraying his puzzlement. "I got no bone to pick with the man. I just follow orders. It's Cap'n, or maybe this Morteau he works for, that wants him so bad. That's how I convinced him you were the man for the job."

"Appreciate the vote of confidence, but," Tucker said, testing what would happen should he refuse, "I've been having the devil's own time locating the man. Maybe you should hire Jimbo Hackett, or Buck Llewellyn. They haven't got half the distractions I have."

Billy reached into his pocket and pulled out a wad of bills, all of them twenties. "Maybe this will help you forget your distractions."

Every base urge in Tucker yearned to snatch up those bills. The sight of all that cash made his head swim. "Jude won't be easy to fool," he said, as much to himself as Billy.

"Find a way. Hell, he's just a kid, ain't he? We both know you can talk rings around anyone once you set your mind to it." Features darkening, Billy leaned across the table. "You'd be smart to take this job, Jesse. Cap'n don't take kindly to disappointment."

"Few do. Just how unkind do you reckon he'll be?"

No grin now. Billy couldn't be any more serious as he stared into Tucker's eyes. "Let's just say he's a hard man and a determined one. Won't be an inch on this continent you'll find safe to sleep in."

Tucker wasn't fool enough to take the threat lightly. Too well, he could remember the ruthlessness with which desperate men could kill. He'd take the job in a heartbeat—he needed the money, and what better revenge against Latour than handing him over to the Gray Ghosts—but a pair of soulful brown eyes gave him pause. Jude wouldn't like him working for somebody else, he sensed. She'd resent what she'd call a conflict of interests.

Yet looking at Billy's hard, unrelenting face, Tucker knew his sole interest at the moment should be his own survival. He reached for the cash, smiling tightly. "Since you put it that way, I reckon I am the man for the job."

No one said Jude had to know anyway, he thought, tucking the cash in his chest pocket. He wasn't about to tell her, and as long as she never talked to Billy, Tucker could collect from both employers—a sum, incidentally, which would take care of all of his problems. "I'll need my Colt back," he told Billy, rising to his feet. "Back in the swamp, you took it from me, remember?"

With a sheepish grin, Billy dug it out of his saddlebag and handed it over. "We'll expect to hear from you regularly," he said, leaning back in his chair. "Cap'n will want to know what progress you're making."

"Fair enough." Savoring the feel of his Colt resting again in its holster, Tucker offered to telegraph his reports to Salvation. "The Western Union operator is a rebel sympathizer, so you—or whoever collects the messages—should be safe enough. You'll like the town. Lilah has one of the finest saloons in Missouri."

Billy flashed his boyish grin. "She got girls?"

"Long, leggy, and lovely, just the way you like them."

Watching the grin turn wolfish, Tucker thought of Jude and how Billy would react to her dress. No matter how he looked at it, the encounter could not end well. Jude was proud and tough and stubborn, and Billy, well, he would know only one way to deal with a headstrong woman.

Walk away from it, his instincts screamed. *Take the damned money and run.*

The wad of bills pressed against his chest as he thought of Jude, alone and unprotected on the streets where Gray Ghosts roamed free. Forcing a smile, doing his best to appear casual, he decided he could at least go check on her. "Best get back on the trail," he told Billy. "The sooner I find Latour, the sooner we make your Cap'n happy, and I get paid my wages."

"You never were one to let the moss grow on your feet." Drawing contentedly from his mug, Billy made no move to even shake Tucker's hand in farewell. "But then I guess that's how you were meant to be."

"Meant to be?"

"Fate, Jesse, my man." Billy wore that faraway look

again. "You and me, we're what life's made us. Loners. Always were, always will be."

Loner. Up to now he'd accepted that he would make his way alone—hell, he'd embraced the idea—but hearing Billy put it in words made it sound suddenly like a lifelong sentence.

"Yeah, well, this loner's got to get going," he said, shrugging off the uneasiness as he turned for the door.

"Good luck to you then," Billy called out to him.

Tucker heard the odd, almost wistful note in his voice, but he ignored it, anxious to get away from the doubts his friend had fired up. Stepping outside, he told himself that going to Jude had nothing to do with loneliness. His conscience propelled him forward, his mama's soft voice still urging him to do the honorable thing. Jude had hired him to deliver her safely to Latour, a feat he could hardly accomplish by stranding her in a strange city.

His sense of duty made him go to her, he insisted as he made his way to the hospital, but it didn't explain his stunned disappointment at finding Jude nowhere in sight.

He felt suddenly foolish for expecting to find her waiting. Why should she hang around? She no longer needed him—she had her information. Probably two minutes after he'd gone, she was already on her way to Jefferson City. He couldn't blame her, not when he'd been so tempted to do the same himself.

He shrugged, jamming his hands into his pockets. It was no loss for him if she'd bolted. She'd done him a favor. His conscience was eased, he could leave unencumbered. No more arguments, no more defiance. As far as having no help in finding Latour, who needed it? As Billy pointed out, Tucker Boone operated best when working alone.

Life would be far simpler without Jude in tow, he continued to insist as he turned down the street toward the docks. He could go right now and wire the sum he owed Lilah and with her off his back, he'd be free of distractions.

He'd find Latour, bring him to the Gray Ghosts, and collect the bounty Billy promised. He'd have his revenge and all the money he needed.

All for the best. All neat and tidy. So why in hell did he feel so empty?

He heard the shouts before their significance registered. It was a woman—a very angry woman, by her guttural oaths—arguing with a group of males. Being in this part of town, she must be a prostitute collecting her wages. Considering the proficiency with which she swore, she sounded capable of taking care of herself.

All before recognition set in and he realized it was no prostitute. Those unladylike shrieks came from Jude!

Tucker was off and running, turning the corner before his survival instincts could kick in. Had he thought first, he'd have counted the male voices and known, even before coming upon the group of raucous, drunken louts shoving Jude from one to the other, that he'd be facing five to his one.

One definite disadvantage of being a loner.

It didn't stop him from charging, though. Something came over him at the sight of her being manhandled by those thugs, something wild and ferocious. For all her bravado and colorful language, he could hear her fear. He could almost taste it, and it made him fit to kill.

He grabbed for the one currently holding Jude, yanking so hard, the man lost his grip and Jude went flying, landing on her rear in the middle of the street. Before her attacker could recover, Tucker rammed a right hook into his jaw. The man went staggering backward.

Unfortunately his pals weren't as stunned by the attack. Snarling like dogs, they came at him. Backing up, Tucker went for his gun. Even more unfortunately someone got to his holster before him.

"Not so fast," Billy drawled behind him, holding the revolver to Tucker's head. "This is just getting interesting."

Ten

Rooster O'Leary stood in the alley, trying to catch his breath. Usually when he pinched another's belongings, he escaped with none the wiser. He should have known, the minute he saw that woman-dressed-as-a-boy that nothing connected with her would ever be normal.

He'd sensed at the time that it was folly to take that bag, but he'd been hungry and not thinking straight, or he'd have snatched what he could off the top and left the rest where it was. Greedy, that's what he'd been, and there was always someone somewhere only too happy to make him pay for it.

Tonight it was the screaming banshee behind him.

Indeed she'd had him so flustered, he'd been tempted to toss her bag at her and run for his life until those five big brutes grabbed her. Rooster's first impulse was to flee, his own safety being his primary precaution, but while circumstance might have made him a thief and occasional liar, he still had a code of ethics that wouldn't let him stand by and abide such rough treatment of a lady.

To his relief, just as he'd been gritting his teeth and bracing himself to go join the fray, along came this guy like a runaway meat wagon, charging at the bullies and knocking one off his feet. That was one lucky lady, Rooster had thought as he watched in awe, if she had a prime fighter like that in her corner.

Counting his own lucky stars that the man's presence made

his own unnecessary, Rooster decided to take the opportunity to return to the abandoned shed he now called home.

Tonight, he thought with a smile as he headed toward the docks with the carpetbag, he'd be having himself a fine dinner.

Around the corner Tucker was cursing the fates Billy seemed suddenly so fond of, wondering why his destiny always seemed to put him on the wrong side of a gun. Damn, but Billy had been light on his feet. Though in all the excitement, Tucker couldn't be blamed for not hearing his approach.

Sure left him in an untenable position though.

Now that he had time to focus on Jude's attackers, Tucker saw what he should have seen from the start, had he not been consumed by animal rage. Gray Ghosts, all of them, from Clem Farley, spitting out blood on the street, to Preacher Morton and the three awaiting Billy's next order, all of them ogling Jude.

That damned dress, he swore under his breath.

"Good ol' Jesse, ever the knight in shining armor. Come to rescue the damsel in distress?"

"Jesse," Jude said pointedly as she rose to her feet, "sure took his own sweet time getting here."

Tucker groaned inwardly. Bad enough she'd now be pestering him with questions about his name, but she'd drawn undue attention to herself from Billy. *Stay quiet,* Tucker mentally coached her. *Don't help him guess the connection between us.*

"Sure is a feisty one, gotta grant you that." Billy gave a low-throated chuckle. "But it ain't like you, Jesse, to be brawling over a woman. Not to the extent of dislocating poor old Clem's jaw. Just what is this female to you?"

"My name is Jude McCloud," Jude said stiffly, offering a hand as she stepped in their direction. "I—"

"She's my woman," Tucker interrupted, pulling her tight against his side. Gun to his head or not, he wouldn't let her say one word more.

Studying her, Billy lowered the weapon. "Pleased to meet you, ma'am. You sure are one fine-looking lady, though if you don't mind my saying, I can't rightly remember ever seeing a hairdo like that."

Distracted, she reached for the bonnet that had fallen to her shoulders in her struggles. Tucker took the opportunity to speak for her. "She had a fever recently. Had to cut off her hair."

Jude's frown betrayed her confusion. Billy just nodded. "Them curls suit her. Must say, I admire your taste," he said to Tucker, while doffing his hat in Jude's direction. "Reckon I'd feel she was worth risking my neck to protect, too."

Tucker's flesh crawled as he watched Billy's appreciative gaze travel up and down her body. Tightening his grip at her waist, Tucker glanced down to see how she took the appraisal, but she seemed unaware of Billy, her eyes searching his own. He saw her hesitation, her fear, but most of all, her bewilderment.

"Play along," he whispered in her ear as he leaned down to brush her cheek with his lips. "Just trust me on this."

He heard her sharp intake of breath and braced himself for her protest, but yet again, she surprised him. She reached up to touch his face like a woman would caress her lover. The gentle gesture affected him more than it should, certainly more than was safe, given their current circumstances.

"She has her charms," he said aloud to Billy, setting her firmly at his side. "And you know I've never been one for sharing. The next man to touch her will have more than a bloody nose." Tucker kept his tone even. He had to stake his claim in terms these men would understand to have any hope of protecting her. "And if you don't mind, I'd like my gun back."

Grinning, all too aware of how recently they conducted this same ritual, Billy made great ceremony of returning the Colt. "Not much for polite conversation, is he?" he asked, turning to Jude. "You ever get tired of him, you come calling on Billy Cochoran. I'm twice the man Jesse is beneath the sheets—"

"Jeez, Billy," Tucker interrupted before she could blurt out the truth. "Is that any way to be talking to a lady?"

For a long moment, Billy stared at Tucker, trying to glean every thought in his brain before turning once more to doff his hat in Jude's direction. "Begging your pardon, ma'am. Reckon I've been too long out on the trail. Maybe Jes . . . er, Tucker . . . will bring you round again and you can learn me some manners."

"We've got to get going," Tucker said sharply, anxious to get Jude away before Billy tried something, or blurted out anything about their prior conversation.

"I meant what I said," Billy pressed. "Love him like a brother, I do, but ol' Jesse ain't known for being reliable and is apt to leave you alone and stranded. That happens, you just send word to the Western Union office in Salvation, and I'll show you he ain't the only one who comes charging to the rescue."

Tucker started to protest, but Jude's hand gripped his arm. "I appreciate the offer," she told Billy sweetly, the perfect Southern belle once more, "but it won't be necessary. The Jesse you once knew is not the man I know now." She raised her face, her gaze pinning Tucker. "Tucker Boone is a man of his word."

It did something to him, hearing her say those words. Logically he might know she was as skilled at play-acting as a circuit-weary ham, but gazing down at this woman, he knew a sudden deep need to hear her say those words again with conviction, and more, to prove them right.

"But if y'all will excuse us," she said, pulling her gaze away, "we have a train to catch. You did make the travel arrangements, didn't you, darling?"

So much for proving himself trustworthy. How did he expect to explain away the half hour or so he'd wasted? Say *oh, I was just plotting with Billy about working for him behind your back?* "I made them," he told her, lying through his teeth. "Shall we?"

Offering his arm to her, nodding goodbye to Billy, he led Jude off in the direction of the depot, though he had no intention of taking a train. He'd let Billy—and Jude—think that was what he meant to do, but the instant the Gray Ghosts could no longer see them, Tucker planned to double back and head for the docks.

"Forget the train," Jude whispered as they turned the corner. "I think we should take a steamboat."

He wondered if she would ever cease to amaze him.

"Whatever you say," he told her, grabbing her hand to race for the river. "You're the boss."

"Yeah," she said dryly. "I noticed that."

Catching a glimpse at her stiff profile, Tucker knew that she was just waiting to let him have it. Fine, he thought, as he dragged her behind him at a run. He had issues of his own to settle. Right now they had to put distance between them and the Gray Ghosts, but the instant things calmed down a notch, he meant to let her know what he thought of her going against his orders. She could be real glib about him keeping his word, but earning and keeping trust, he'd point out, was a two-way street. So far she hadn't done much for her own credibility by not being where he'd told her to wait.

And for that matter, what had she thought she was doing, wandering around in that outfit? Against his will, he remembered how it felt to hold her, how hard it had been to pull away. How could he blame those men for lusting after

EVERY DREAM COME TRUE 127

Jude when she looked and smelled and felt every inch a desirable woman?

It was that dress, he thought, as he quickened their pace. The gray uniform hadn't inspired such crazy notions. She'd have been safe from Billy's bunch in her boys' clothes and pose less threat to him, too. To his safety *or* peace of mind.

Reaching the docks, eyeing the row of steamboats waiting on the river, he came to a decision. Before Jude went with him to Jefferson City, or anywhere else for that matter, that dress would have to go.

Billy watched Tucker stroll away with his lady, feeling a spike of envy. Did things to a man when she looked at him, that young filly did. If she could stir up such unwanted feelings in an old reprobate like himself, Lord only knew what she could do to a hopeless case like Jesse. Hard choices, that's what a woman like that would force his old buddy to, and sadly enough Billy could no longer rely on Jesse to make the right ones.

"Follow him," he barked out at Preacher. "And don't let them out of your sight."

Jude stumbled along beside Boone, bemoaning the loss of her uniform. Pants were sure easier to get around in than these bulky skirts, especially when the man yanking you along didn't care if your feet were tripping over them. Some bug seemed to have bitten Boone, something more than that encounter with Billy, and it had him more preoccupied than ever. In the past hour or so, he'd gone from calm and gentle when he'd left her in the hospital, to raging bull when he punched the thug in the jaw, then matter-of-fact as he'd introduced her to Billy. Lord, but the man was as unpredictable as the weather.

He stopped suddenly. She noticed they'd reached the

docks, but she found herself staring more at Boone than at the impressive row of vessels lined up along the river. What was it about him that kept drawing her gaze? He was handsome, yes—but she'd been surrounded by good-looking men all her life, none of whom inspired more than a passing glance. And why the strange thrill when he'd called her "his woman"? She knew he'd said it only to protect her.

Remembering the feel of his lips on her face, she reached up to touch her cheek as gently as he had. Lord help her, but she'd been swept up into the moment until it had seemed the most natural thing in the world to play along as he'd asked, to trust him, to believe Tucker Boone was indeed a man of his word.

But then he'd swept her off, dashing through the night as if the devil were hot on their heels, uttering absolutely no words at all.

And in the wake of his silence, she couldn't stop the questions from multiplying. Just who was this Billy? Why did he call Boone Jesse, and for that matter, why had he come to St. Louis? Given the way they'd left the gang's camp, she'd expect Billy to cart Boone off strapped to the back of a horse, not make small talk with him in the middle of some dark, forsaken city street. Billy called himself a friend, yet he couldn't be much of one, to her way of thinking, if he could be bad-mouthing Boone to "his woman," right there in his face.

And what was behind her own sudden fierce compulsion to defend Boone? Lord knew, she had issues enough of her own to take up with the man.

Primary of which was his autocratic habit of yanking her here and there without her consent. She deserved some answers, she decided, and she was not taking another step until she got them. Pulling free of his grip, she told him so.

He gazed down at her with blatant exasperation. *"You* have questions? How about explaining why I found you wandering the streets of St. Louis when I told you to wait on the hospital steps? And what in hell are you doing still dressed in . . . in that?"

He scowled at her dress with such revulsion, it could have suddenly sprouted snakes. She wanted to defend herself, but she knew the reason she'd been in that alley. If Boone were angry now, it wouldn't make him any happier to learn about the missing carpetbag.

When trapped in an indefensible position, she'd learned, attack from a different angle. "I *did* wait," she told him curtly. "You didn't come."

He looked away. His sudden evasiveness told her she'd struck a nerve, that he had no real right to outrage, but she gained no satisfaction from it. "You never did go to the depot, did you?" she pressed, knowing she should get everything out in the open, yet having no heart for it. "You never meant to take me to Jefferson City. You were going to leave me behind."

"It was for your own good, damnit."

Dumb to hope he'd deny it. *"My* good. Tell me, if you will be so kind, just how is it in my best interests for you to take off for Jefferson City without me?"

At least he had the grace to look guilty. "I figured you'd be okay until I got back. You would have been, had you been wearing your uniform like I told you."

Apparently he knew the rule about the indefensible argument, too. "I didn't disobey you, if that's what has you barking at me," she said, holding up her chin. "You might think me a ninny, but even I can see the sense in wearing boys' clothes down by the docks. For your information, Boone, I'd have changed long ago had I the choice."

Eyeing her dress, he raised a skeptical brow.

"For heaven's sake," she blurted out, "you think I did it on purpose? This isn't about defying you. Sorry to prick your vanity, but it has nothing to do with you at all. The sole reason I'm not wearing the uniform is because I no longer have it."

"Beg your pardon?"

Her and her temper. Probably she'd never find a good way to admit her mistake, not without seeming the fool he thought her, but this had to be the worst opening possible. "It's gone," she stated baldly. "My uniform, money, everything. Some kid stole my carpetbag while we were with Briggs. That's why I was in the alley when those brutes grabbed me. Chasing the little thief."

She braced herself, waiting for him to rant on about her stupidity at leaving the bag unprotected, but he merely watched her more closely. "I thought you'd taken off," he said quietly as though talking to himself. "When you weren't there, I thought *you* had run away."

"Wait a minute. You returned to the hospital?" Silly heart, did it have to leap at the thought? "You came back for me?"

Grimacing, he rubbed his knuckles. "And got more than I bargained on."

Thinking back, she remembered how relieved she'd felt when she'd seen him charging her attackers, his face so ferocious, his actions so in control. Her initial thought had been *now I am safe*.

Jude, unaccustomed to leaning on any man, found herself breaching the few steps between them. More than anything, she wanted to just lay her head against his sturdy chest. "Your shoulder," she said softly. "I should bandage it again. Damnit," she swore, remembering. "My supplies were in the carpetbag."

He shrugged. "Forget it, I'm fine. But this changes everything." He sighed as he turned to face the river. "Got no choice now but to send you home."

"Home?" He could have slapped her face, the words came as such a shock. "How many times are we going to have this argument, Boone? We've been through this already. I'm going with you to Jefferson City."

His features tightened, the soft moment between them a

thing of the past. "Lord, woman, haven't you got the good sense God gave a post? You can't go traipsing around in that dress. What does it take for you to learn your lesson?"

"Get this clear, Tucker Boone, or Jesse Holland, or whatever your name really is." She had the brief satisfaction of seeing his frown. "Finding Rafe Latour is vital to me, and with or without you, I'm going to Jefferson City."

"With what? You lost all your money."

She fought the urge to pummel his chest with her fists. Not out of any fear that she'd hurt him, but because she knew her effort would be wasted. More than ever, she regretted promising that she wouldn't go after Rafe alone. She had to convince Boone to take her along—he was her only option. "I wouldn't advise you to thwart me in this," she said, striving for a menacing tone. "If you do, I swear to you, I won't rest until I've made you regret it."

He merely seemed more exasperated than ever. "Damnit, Jude, those men could have raped you. Or worse."

She shuddered, knowing only too well what a close call it had been. "And who's to say I won't have similar troubles, traveling home alone?"

A master stroke, she thought, as she saw his tightening features. She only wished she'd thought of it sooner.

But if she'd hoped he'd relent easily, she hadn't been paying attention. "I'll hire a companion," he said coldly.

"With what? Hiring servants costs money, or do you think your looks and charm can get you anything?"

"I have money," he said with a wry grin as he patted his chest pocket. "Though I'm not averse to using the looks and charm if it will save me some."

"Damnit, Boone—"

"Such language, Miss McCloud."

It made her uneasy, each time he used Guin's maiden name, but now was not the time to correct him. "I'm asking—no, I'm begging—a favor. Please take me along. I'll pay back every penny. If the dress bothers you that much, we can get boys' clothes somehow. Just give me a chance."

"Jude—"

"You have to admit I was good today, getting information." Brightening, she remembered her trump card. "And I have our contact in Jefferson City. Dr. Briggs gave me a name when I went back to say goodbye."

"And obviously you have no intention of giving it to me."

"Would you, in my place? C'mon, Boone, you said you'd take me to Latour. Doesn't your word mean anything?"

He paused a long moment, gazing down at her face, his own features troubled as if he fought inner demons. "Fine," he said at last. "You win."

She couldn't stop the wide, ever-broadening grin.

He did not match it. "You really should be more careful about backing folks into a corner," he said, his tone now menacing. "One of these days, one of your victims is liable to strike back."

"Not you." She felt almost giddy with relief. "Like it or not, Boone, you've got this streak of decency that won't let you hurt a fly."

He gave an ugly laugh. "Don't let the looks and charm deceive you."

"No." Staring at him, she'd never felt more certain of anything. "Maybe I don't know you so well, but deep down, hidden under all that bitterness, hides a good man. You've got your past, and I'm not going to probe into it, but I believe what I told Billy. Whatever else you've done, you're still a man of your word."

She saw the strain in his eyes as his hand reached up to brush her face. "Could be you're too trusting. Don't forget, I left you stranded on those steps."

"I remember." Her voice was barely above a whisper. "But then, too, you came back for me."

She watched his eyes darken, grow intense, and for a dizzying moment, she thought, even hoped, he would kiss her.

But with a low muttered oath, Boone moved away. "Yeah, I came back," he said roughly. "And it was a mistake."

He turned toward the docks. Confused, Jude reached out to grab his arm. "You can't mean that."

"Can't I? Don't get taken in by your own playacting, sweetheart. We both know it's all make-believe. You, in that dress. Me, charging to the rescue."

"All of it?" She hated herself for the tremor in her voice.

He wouldn't meet her gaze. "You and me, Jude—where we've been, where we're going—we're worlds apart. I'm a loner, always will be, while you, well, it's clear you've got others to worry after. This is nothing more than some big, long dream from which we'll both eventually have to wake up. Me, I'd just as soon open my eyes now."

"Who's stopping you?" she ground out.

He nodded as if she'd said the wisest thing. "Just so you know. No sense harboring unreal expectations. The minute we dock in Jefferson City, we'll buy pants and a shirt, and you'll stay in boys' clothes until you're safe back at home."

He strode off, and this time she let him go. How could he sound so bitter, so hard, while she stood here alone, still so soft and aching?

She should be angry. She wanted to be angry, deserved to be, yet all she felt was foolish. For a moment there, she hadn't seen it his way at all. Kissing Boone—touching him and reaching down into the heart of him—had seemed only too real. More real than anything else in her life.

Trouble was, it didn't feel so good now with him walking off, his stride so sure and swift. In that much he was right. She'd be making a big mistake, spinning dreams about a man so eager to be quit of her.

So be it, she thought, as she made her way after him to the docks. She'd suffered emotional setbacks before—she knew how to deal with them. Heck, her own father had taught her early on how to recognize those who would deal her nothing but pain, and how not to waste her feelings on them.

And in truth this made matters simpler. Boone was her partner on a quest, nothing more. And should she feel a twinge of remorse, or worse, yearning, she knew how to squelch it. No man had gotten the best of her—and Tucker Boone, for all his dazzling grin, would not be an exception.

Too much rode on her finding Rafe. She couldn't afford to be giving her true self away to anyone. Better to stay in her boys' clothes, hiding her identity and emotions behind a wall of indifference. It would be safer.

Too bad she still felt that pang in her heart.

Lance Buford stared at the docks, fighting the urge to reach out and grab Jude Latour. How like her uncle she looked: all that dark hair, the proud tilt of her chin. He wanted to rush at her, to make his presence known, but he had to stay hidden in the shadows until he'd set his trap. Soon, he promised himself, he'd have the sublime pleasure of watching Latour and his family beg for mercy. But until that time, Lance had to content himself with watching the girl from afar.

Ten years ago Lance had been engaged to Guin McCloud, but Latour had wormed his way into her heart, cutting Lance out of any hope of ever running her daddy's grand plantation. Desperate to win her back, Lance had allied himself with the conscienceless Jacques Morteau, Jude's actual father.

He reached down and rubbed the scar on his arm, that legacy of Guin's betrayal. She'd sworn in court later that she'd jabbed him with scissors to save her family, but Lance maintained that Latour must have bewitched her. The Guin he'd known would never have turned on her own kind like that. He and Guin were landed aristocracy.

Perhaps he and Morteau had been a mite overzealous in bending some laws, but what had gone wrong with Southern justice that it could put a gentleman in jail, letting a nobody like Latour live the life Lance had been meant to savor? If not for the Civil War, Lance could still be rotting in that dank Louisiana prison. The sadly depleted rebel army had needed warm bodies, and Henri Morteau had been sitting in the right position to expedite the transfer from jail to battlefield.

Clever Henri. Unlike his brother, Jacques, who'd died a drunken pauper, Henri had the financial craftiness to amass a small fortune, which he put to work influencing the local political machine to his own advantage. A veritable chameleon, he'd managed to emerge from the war without a Confederate taint, and unlike many of his erstwhile competitors, conducted a booming business with the Federals, who now ran the state.

Maybe he should try to contact Henri again, Lance thought. Money, power—could he ask for a better ally? He need only dangle the name Latour, who Henri still blamed for the death of his brother. To a Morteau, blood was thicker than money, and no risk was too great if it brought the much-longed-for vengeance.

Yes, Lance thought, as he watched Boone and the girl embark. Henri Morteau, with all his connections, could move faster than Boone ever could. And once he'd located Latour . . .

"Cap'n, the men want to go drinking. Can I dismiss them?"

Lance spun to face his lieutenant, Billy Cochran, a boy after his own heart. Loyal, eager, and with a crafty intelligence, Billy could be trusted so long as he saw profit in it for himself. "Yes, yes," Lance told him, making a dismissive gesture with his hands. "Let them all go. We don't need them anymore anyway. Not now that Boone and the girl are boarding the steamboat."

As the others marched off, Billy stared at where Lance pointed. "Looks to be heading upriver. Want me to find out where?"

Lance nodded. "Of course. I know you think highly of Boone, but I have no reason to trust him. I'd hate, for your sake and mine, to learn too late that he means to double-cross us."

"He won't," Billy said with undeniable conviction. "He needs the money we've offered."

"Be that as it may, we need to know where he's going. I expect efficiency from you, Lieutenant. Don't make me regret leaving you in charge."

"Me, in charge? But where will you be, sir?"

Lance nearly didn't tell him, distrust being one of the hazards of having a price on your head, but that would run contrary to his own best interests. Until he made contact with Morteau, Billy would be his eyes and ears in finding Latour, so they had to stay in contact. "I'm too visible in St. Louis," he told his lieutenant. "Maybe I'll head over to this town of his, this Salvation, to intercept any messages he might relay. You can contact me there."

Billy frowned. "The girl, she could cause trouble. What do I do if she gets in the way?"

Lance thought about Jude Latour, and how difficult she'd made life for him in the past. "You're a clever boy, Lieutenant," he told him with a cold smile. "Be creative."

Eleven

Tucker leaned on the rail as he stared out over the Missouri River, seeing nothing in the night despite the bright party lights glittering behind him on the steamboat. Music blared from the decks above, chatter and laughter drifted down from the gaming rooms, but he remained too absorbed by his thoughts to notice.

Shifting his weight, he leaned on his other arm, trying hard to ignore Jude, sitting behind him, her back against a sack of grain as she stared off into her own particular hell. Taking his cue, she'd kept to herself, not speaking more than a dozen words since their awkward confrontation on the dock.

Maybe he'd been too rough on her. His accusations had been far from fair, considering he'd been just as guilty of spinning dreams. When he thought how close he'd come to kissing her . . .

Forget it, he told himself, pushing back from the rail. It was over and done and would never happen again. The way Jude ignored him now, he could count himself fortunate if she even glanced at him in the future.

Which was the way he wanted it. He didn't need her disarming honesty, those resolve-melting gazes, that walking temptation in burgundy merino. The instant they docked, he was buying pants and a shirt. The sooner he got her out of that dress . . .

It swept over him, the image of slipping it down her soft shoulders, her tiny waist, slim hips.

Latour had better be in Jefferson City, he thought, unable to banish the erotic image from his brain.

Against his will, he glanced at Jude, half expecting to find her glaring at his back. Instead she stared intently at a spot to her left, her brows gathered in consternation, giving every appearance of being unaware that he even existed. Head cocked to the side, she seemed to be listening.

He watched her rise slowly, her expression confused and concerned. Inching forward, she moved like a cat who'd just cornered her first mouse.

Ignore her, logic insisted, yet there he was, taking steps in her direction. She's a babe in the woods, he insisted to himself. Someone had to protect her.

She edged in amid the sacks and crates bound for upriver and dropped to her knees. Startled by the movement, he rushed up behind her, verifying what his ears had suggested. Jude hadn't been shot or in any way injured. With unerring instinct, she'd found the real wounded party and now meant to nurse him.

Gazing down, Tucker studied the still form she so gently inspected. A boy from the looks of him, no more than twelve, though he sported the cuts and bruises of a fighting man three times his age. The dirt and rents in his clothes could have been caused by the scuffle he'd been in, but the gaping holes in his shoes were the true badge of his poverty.

Tucker shook his head. Unaccustomed to much of life's bounty, the boy wouldn't know how to respond to kindness. When and if he came around, he'd as likely slit Jude's throat as thank her. "Leave him be," Tucker tried to warn. "Helping him can only bring trouble."

"But he's hurt bad." She moved gentle fingers over the boy's bruises, probing for injury. "Whoever did this didn't expect him to get up and walk away."

"Crawl away, you mean. Something you should let him continue doing. You could be put ashore if you're caught harboring a stowaway."

"You can't know that he is."

"A paid passenger wouldn't be holed up in the cargo. And where would a wharf rat get the money to sail on a boat like this?"

"From me."

She spoke so softly, he almost didn't catch it. "I beg your pardon?"

"It's him. The boy who stole my carpetbag." She didn't look at Tucker as she said this, as if fearing the scorn she'd see there.

Only he wasn't feeling scorn. Confusion, maybe, and certainly dismay that she had every intention of feeding the mouth that bit her. "I don't get it. The kid stole from you, but you'll risk being set ashore to help him?"

She looked at Tucker then, her gaze probing into him. "What's the alternative? Leave him here so anyone can finish the job those thugs started?"

"Helping him won't get your money back."

"No, I don't reckon it will." She returned to her explorations. "But then he won't get it, either. Whoever attacked him must be long gone, back there in St. Louis. When you think about it, this poor boy is worse off than I am."

"That's one way of looking at it."

She sighed. "You've made your point. You want to view life cynically, and I can't stop you, but all I see is an injured boy who needs my help. Turn around," she ordered, gesturing imperiously as she rose to her feet.

"No, ma'am. Every time I let you out of my sight, I live to regret it."

She eyed him impatiently. "For pity's sake, Boone, I need to rip strips off my petticoat to make bandages. Given your speech on the dock, I assumed my ankles were the last thing you wanted to see, but if you're so determined to be difficult, be my guest."

She reached down to yank up her skirt. It would serve her right if he stared, Tucker thought. Damned infuriating female. She was making him halfwitted, with her combination of naivete and earthbound practicality. How was a man to react, when she kept wavering between hard-edged woman and little girl lost?

And how was he to think straight when he could so vividly imagine the rest of her creamy white leg?

"You'll need water," he snapped, daunted by the lurid turn of his thoughts. "You rip while I fetch it. Be careful, though, of where you flash those ankles. Our fellow deck passengers are a far cry from the gentlemen you're used to. Once they wander down from the bar, you'll find they're a lot less sensitive than I."

Her withering glare showed how much she doubted that possibility.

Annoyed, Tucker strode off to the water barrel at the rear of the boat, his thoughts chugging in time with the huge paddle wheel sluicing through the river. His mind hadn't been his own since encountering that woman. Round and round Jude took him, out of one predicament and into another, always arguing, coaxing him to run counter to his common sense. Bad enough he must be saddled with Miss I'll-Do-It-My-Way McCloud, but now she had to add this juvenile highwayman to the package. Just what in blazes did she expect him to do with the kid? Drag him around like yet another albatross draped on his neck?

I work alone, he insisted to himself.

Picking up the cup beside the barrel, he dipped his hand in the water, letting the liquid cool more than his fingers. Taking one deep breath after another, he conceded that it wasn't so much this business with the boy that had him riled, though Lord knew, it was provocation enough. No, he didn't enjoy the prospect of watching her play angel of mercy, so tender and caring to that urchin, while she got colder and colder toward him. The way things stood now, you wouldn't find any more distance between them than had she moved to a different planet.

It had to be this way, he reminded himself. If he must be saddled with Jude on this trip, they had to stay separate, keep to themselves. Only . . . did she have to behave as if he were somehow beyond her notice? *Beneath* her notice?

Foolish question. Of course she did. It was how females manipulated the men in their lives. All too often he'd watched wilier women than Jude pull the stunt with far less reaction on his part. She was an actress, he mustn't forget, used to getting her own way, and her way was to . . .

Her way was to risk her neck to stand by him, to nurse him, and take care of this stranger.

Taking another deep breath, feeling the anger seep out of him, he thought rationally about what Jude had been doing. Offering kindness for kindness sake was far from the action of a selfish, conniving woman. He had to face facts. Jude wasn't anything like other females, not any of his acquaintance.

Her sole crime had been to get under his skin. Put plain and simple, she scared him, left him wary of what she was making him think and feel and be. And that, in a nutshell, was the source of the problem.

One way or another, he had to put a stop to it.

The only solution, as far as he could see, was to send her away.

Knowing he had to head back to her, he took in another deep breath, filling his lungs, mind, and body with resolve as he strode down the deck. Whether or not they found Latour in Jefferson City, he was sending Jude home. If she wanted a companion, she could take this boy she'd adopted, but come tomorrow evening, Tucker's responsibility to her—not to mention the threat she posed to his peace of mind—would be over.

All he need do was get through tonight.

Jude stared at the battered child before her. What sort of monster could do this to a kid? She had few illusions about her patient's innocence—after all he had stolen her carpetbag—but he was nonetheless just a boy. A very young and skinny boy, to whom, by the looks of him, life had dealt hardships enough.

She wished Boone would hurry back with that water. The knife wound on the boy's arm had stopped bleeding, but the sooner she cleaned him up, the better. Given their present surroundings, and having lost the ointments from her carpetbag, his risk of infection increased with each moment the cut stayed exposed. Maybe she should just wrap him up and clean it out later. She could do a better job of it anyway with the right supplies and proper lighting.

Just then the boy's eyes fluttered open. With a guttural whimper more animal than human, he tried to back away from her. Unfortunately a sack of grain stood in his way.

"Hush, don't be afraid," she crooned to him. "I'm trying to help you."

"I ain't afraid," he snapped, still trying to edge backward. "Not o' you. Not o' anything."

"Good, that will make my work easier," she told him matter-of-factly.

"Work?"

She had to smile at his skeptical expression. "You have a nasty slice on your upper arm. Unless you want it to fester, I need to clean and wrap the wound. It's going to smart, I fear, so I'm glad you're not afraid of a little pain."

"You ain't touching me." He tried to sit up, only to fall back with a groan.

"Please, trust me," she soothed. "I'm only trying to help."

"Yeah, I bet. You think I'm so stupid, I don't know you're the banshee?"

Jude cocked her head, afraid for a moment that he'd grown delusional.

"The screamer," he explained impatiently. "The lady who chased me."

"With good cause." She might resent the image, but she supposed she must have seemed like a banshee, as intent as she'd been on retrieving her belongings. "You stole my carpetbag."

"Even so—and I ain't saying I did—why would you help the likes of me?"

Jude sat back on her heels, giving him the distance he needed. Clearly it had been some time since the boy had been shown any kindness. Was it any wonder that he found it hard to trust a stranger? "Look at it this way," she said. "Had I wanted to hurt you, I should have done it while you were unconscious. It's too late, now that you can defend yourself."

He frowned as he thought this over.

Jude pressed her point. "Besides, I've got nothing to gain by hurting you. Not unless you still have my money."

She said it half hopefully, but his snort put that optimism to bed. "I don't have it no more. I wouldn't be here talking to you if I did."

"He took it, didn't he? The man who did this to you?"

"Wasn't one man." He puffed up his skinny chest. "Takes more than one to stop Rooster O'Leary. Lily-livered cowards," he added with another snort. "Grabbed me from behind, too."

"Rooster? That's your name?"

He shrugged. "My folks baptized me Michael Thomas, but out there on the wharves, you need a name with some bite. The others, they call me Rooster. First up in the morning, that's me, and the last to sleep at night."

Jude could hear the fierce pride in his claim, yet she could sense the misery behind it. As a kid she'd been a lot like young Michael Thomas O'Leary. She, too, had stayed up to keep watch, long after the rest of the world lay tucked in their beds, all too aware of how bad things caught up to you when you weren't awake to see them coming.

"Well, Rooster, my name is Jude," she told him curtly, knowing from her own past that he would neither welcome nor trust any attempt at sympathy. Like a wild animal, he'd have to be soothed and wooed into friendship, much like Rafe and Guin had gradually won her over. "I may not look it now, but I spent many a day nursing soldiers during the war, and I learned that wounds must be dressed to keep them from festering. We can do this now, or we can wait until the man I'm with returns with the water, but you'll find he's not nearly as patient as I."

She watched Rooster's eyes go wide with something close to awe, before sensing the presence behind her.

"I'm already here," Boone growled. "Best do as she says, son, or trust me, she has this way of making you sorry."

"Don't I know it."

"His name is Rooster O'Leary," Jude said stiffly. Growing up with four brothers, she'd learned to resent the male habit of talking about her as if she weren't there. "Rooster, this autocratic bully goes by the name of Tucker Boone."

"Here's the water." Boone thrust the cup into her hands. "Now that we're done with the pleasantries, let's get to the bottom of things. What lopsided logic makes you both think we can overlook your stealing the lady's carpetbag?"

"I didn't steal nothing." Rooster actually looked hurt before reverting back to belligerence. "I don't have to answer nothing, neither."

"No, you don't," Boone said calmly enough. "But then no one has to help you. Jude might think you're worth saving—but me, I'd just as soon throw you overboard for the fish to eat."

"Boone!" Jude turned to gape at him.

Giving her a quick glare, he hunkered down before the boy. "Let's get this straight, Rooster. I mean to be honest with you, but I expect no less in return. The lady has a soft heart, so you can get away with lying to her, but don't for a second suppose I share her affliction. Tell one more untruth and the instant we dock, I'll hand you over to the sheriff and you can explain this to him instead."

Rooster pursed his lips. He was trapped, and clearly he knew it.

"Really Boone," Jude said, dipping the cloth in the water. "Can't this confession wait until I've bandaged him up?"

Boone flashed her a look that might have withered anyone who'd never seen his gentler side, but she saw how he'd glanced from the boy's arm to the cloth she was holding. He meant to use the questions to distract the boy while she cleaned his wound, she realized. Though being Boone, he'd never admit it.

"I never meant to keep the dumb bag," Rooster said, apparently uneasy with the silence. "I was going to return the clothes and stuff," he said, wincing as Jude applied the cloth to the wound. "All I wanted was the money."

"A hospital seems an odd place to get cash."

"I go there most days because the nurses, they're real nice about saving me scraps from the food trays."

Jude noticed how quickly Rooster responded to the question, as if he, too, saw the value in being distracted. She tried to be gentle, but the cut was more a tear, as if whoever had sliced the boy had struck out viciously. Hearing his talk about begging scraps, seeing this proof of the danger he must face daily, she grew determined to see that he never returned to those docks.

"Sometimes," Rooster went on, wincing every so often as Jude probed with her cloth, "I get lucky and find a visitor who ain't paying attention. Though I gotta say, ever since the war ended, them marks keep getting harder to find."

"Marks?"

"Victims," Boone explained, though he didn't bother glancing at Jude. "Young Rooster, I'm assuming, is a pickpocket by trade."

"The best in St. Louis." Sad, the things Rooster chose to be proud about. "This one here," he said, nodding at Jude, "she was the perfect mark. Not at first, not in them pants and shirt, but when I seen her coming out of that closet dressed as a lady, all distracted and worried and no longer carrying her bag, I figure, hey, ain't this my lucky day. So I go right in there, snatch it up to race downstairs, but wouldn't you know, Jed Perkins comes on duty just as I'm trying to skip out." He paused, grimacing as Jude's cloth reached a particularly jagged spot.

"Jed Perkins?" Boone asked gently.

"Jed's the night guard." Rooster inhaled deeply before going on. "We talk now and then, so he knows I got no business with this bag. And before I can get to the door, he plops down with the desk nurse—he has this thing for her—and they make small talk for ages while I'm stuck in the corner. When he finally strolls off, and I'm thinking I can, too, in comes that loud-mouthed friend of yours. Old Jed spins around, this close to drawing his pistol. Good thing for your buddy that you came along and ushered him out. Wasn't Boone he called you though. As I recall, he kept saying Jesse."

Startled, Jude looked at Boone, but as was becoming his habit, he ignored her completely. Only one man used that name as far as she knew. What had Billy been doing at the hospital? And why had Boone gone off with him?

"Go on," Boone prompted, clearly not wanting to dwell on this.

"Well, just as I'm recovering and ready to make my

move, she marches by looking real worried." He spared a nod in Jude's direction. "Jed's moved on by now, but not her. No, she keeps pacing up and down the steps, and I can't slip by, not with her bag in my hands. Finally she looks down the street, and I figure it's now or never, but wouldn't you know she'd come after me screaming like a banshee. I'm lucky she didn't bring down the cops on me, instead of those hooligans. Ouch. Hey, lady, you trying to kill me?"

"I warned you it would hurt," Jude snapped, then felt contrite. Rooster's portrayal of her actions had been unflattering, especially in front of Boone, but no nurse should ever take her personal feelings out on her patient. "That's it, I'm finished cleaning," she said briskly, laying down the cloth. "Go on with your story while I wrap up your arm."

Rooster was watching her, looking somewhat contrite himself. "Hey, I don't blame you for screaming. What I did, taking your bag and all—well, it wasn't right. I can see now that it was real important to you, but then I wasn't thinking of nothing but my empty belly. You might wanna know though. I wouldn't have left you to face them thugs alone if he hadn't come along." He pointed behind her at Boone. "When I saw him charging, I figured you didn't need me anymore."

Jude looked up at Boone, remembering the relief and gratitude she'd felt when he'd rushed to her rescue. How like him, one minute risking his life for her, the next behaving as if she no longer existed. Would she ever figure him out?

"After that," Rooster went on, "I dashed home to inspect my loot. Darned near had a cow when I saw all that cash."

"I suppose it's too much to hope that you still have it?" Boone asked dryly.

Rooster shook his head. "I was just stuffing it in my pocket when them thugs ambushed me. Let me tell you, I gave as good as I got, but I know when the numbers are stacked agin me, and I could see no reason for sticking around when they was itching to use their knives. Not finding anywhere better, I crawled onto this boat to hide. I guess I, er, must have fallen asleep."

Passed out, more likely, Jude thought, but respecting Rooster's pride, kept that observation to herself "What happened to my carpetbag?" she asked instead, wishing she could at least have her uniform back.

"I reckon it's on the street where I left it. Sorry," he said, no doubt seeing her disappointment. "I didn't really mean to cause you no hardship."

Why blame Rooster? she thought as she rose to her feet. From the minute she'd started this quest, when had anything gone as she'd planned? "You'll have ample opportunity to prove your regrets once we reach Jefferson City," she told him sternly. "I'm going to need you to run some errands for me."

"Whoa, hold up a minute." Boone also stood. "Treating his injuries is one thing, but we've got worries enough without dragging this juvenile cutthroat around with us."

"Hey, I didn't cut nobody's throat," Rooster protested.

Frowning, Jude pulled Boone over to where the boy couldn't hear. "For pete's sake, where's your sensitivity? That poor boy has been through hell. We can't just abandon him, too?"

"That 'poor boy' is a thief, not to mention an invalid." He grabbed her by the arms. "Jeez, Jude, for once think with your brains, not your heart."

Funny, it was pretty much what Christopher had said, but he'd been warning her not to trust Boone. "I am thinking logically," she said, yanking free of his grasp. "And I don't see any invalid. Rooster's banged up, but none of his bones were broken. He might have a headache in the morning, but he'll be able to walk on his own two feet."

"Good, then let him walk back to the hole he crawled

out of. I don't need another burden. Looking out for you is hard enough."

She was proud that she didn't flinch. "I've been taking adequate care of myself, thanks all the same."

"Really? Those brutes back in St. Louis didn't think so."

Had she been any less of a lady, she'd have hauled off and slapped him. Self-control, Guin had taught, was the cornerstone of civilized behavior. "Those brutes," she said calmly, "are all the more reason why we can't leave Rooster to the mercy of the streets. Look at him, forced to act so mean and tough, when in reality he's still just a kid."

"You think so? That kid has seen—and probably participated in—more of life's ugliness than most adults. More than you can ever imagine."

Jude shuddered, thinking about her father's drunken rages, her mama's cries for help. "Don't be so sure of that," she told him with far more coolness than she felt. "Could be there's a lot about *me* you can never imagine."

He stared at her a long moment, forcing her to remember the yearning she'd felt for him such a short while ago. This time she made sure it was she who looked away first. "Don't worry, we won't be a burden much longer. Just as soon as we find Rafe Latour, you needn't be bothered by us again."

"Just what did the man do to you?" he asked sharply. "Why this fever to get at him?"

"We're not discussing me," she said evasively. "We're talking about Rooster now, and our responsibility to see him safe."

"Responsibility? Jude, pay attention. The kid stole from you. He owes you, not the other way around."

Touching the locket at her neck, she remembered her own attempt to steal, and how Guin had looked past the crime to the need underneath. She'd sensed that Jude had taken the locket because it reminded her of her dead mother, not out of any malice. "Rooster didn't mean me harm," Jude tried to explain, feeling a kinship with the boy. "He was surviving the only way he knows how."

"Maybe, but he'll keep trying to survive, and what happens to those who get in his way?"

"Come on, Boone, in all your checkered past, wasn't there ever a time you wished someone would reach out to help you?"

An odd look passed over his face, but he masked it immediately with his gruffest tone. "I didn't hire on to play nursemaid."

"You don't have to. I'll watch out for Rooster, and I'll even pay his way." She remembered the missing carpetbag. "That is, I'll pay you back when I get the money from home." Which wouldn't be until they found Rafe, but she saw no reason to mention it. As Christopher advised, she'd tell Boone only what she needed him to know.

"You're not going to let go of this, are you?" His face still looked fierce, but a softening in his eyes implied he might be relenting. Being Boone, though, he did it none too graciously. "Fine, but I warn you, Jude, the boy is your responsibility. Every morsel he eats, every penny he costs me, I'm keeping an account."

"That's understandable."

He shook his head, clearly not understanding any of it. "What is it with you?" he asked, staring at her face, sounding bemused. "Life isn't complicated enough, you have to take on more and more?"

She touched his sleeve, wanting him to understand. "Sometimes all it takes is a little kindness to help even the most desperate cutthroat find salvation."

He stared at his sleeve as if her fingers had burned through it, then looked up to stare deeply into her eyes. "Face it, Jude, some folks aren't meant to be saved," he said in a tone so empty and dead, she knew they were no longer discussing Rooster. "Damnit, can't you see you're courting disaster?"

She wanted to protest, to take his face in her hands and show him the tenderness he'd so clearly been lacking in life, but as if to score his point, the steamboat ground to a halt, sending Tucker, with Jude on top of him, crashing to the deck.

Twelve

Let that be a lesson to you, Tucker thought, feeling Jude's warm, tempting body so near his own. Every time he let himself dream that maybe this time things could be different, life had a way of splashing cold water in his face. This latest reminder, however, had been more dramatic than most.

"What happened?" Jude asked breathlessly, her face mere inches away.

Another man might read the situation differently, see it as more an opportunity than a slap to the face, but that lucky devil didn't have Tucker's experience. Reluctantly easing Jude up and off him, he took special care not to focus on her soft, trembling lips. "My guess is we've hit a snag," he told her as he stood, leaning down to offer his hand.

She grasped it firmly, giving him another uncomfortable moment as they stood face to face. Eyes widening, she turned suddenly to where they'd last seen the boy. "Rooster?" she called out tremulously.

"I'm okay," he said, peeking out from behind the cargo. "What's a snag?"

For living on the docks, the kid didn't know much about the river. "A log, submerged in the water," Tucker answered. "Boats get caught in them often, especially if the crew's been partying with the passengers." All hands must be sobering up now, he thought, hearing shouts and running footsteps on the deck above. The music and laughter had long since stopped.

"Are we in danger?" Jude asked, gazing up with a troubled expression.

"Are we okay?" Rooster echoed.

"We'll be fine," he told the boy. "Lie down and get some rest. We won't be going anywhere until morning." Tucker turned to reassure Jude. "It's a matter of breaking free, though in the dark, and with this current, I doubt it will be soon."

The crew would need help, he realized. Ordinarily Tucker wouldn't think twice about volunteering his services, but tonight he had more than himself to consider. Back in St. Louis, conscious of the need for a hasty departure, he'd settled for the more economical passage, overlooking the undesirables that soon would be making their way down to sleep on the lower deck. He should have remembered, for years back, he'd tried using his luck at cards to make a living on the riverboats. He'd soon learned that the best games, and therefore the prized purses, were reserved for those who could afford the more luxurious staterooms. Those who slept down below, he'd discovered, were those who traveled without hope, inveterate gamblers and hard-core sots, lost souls long removed from the niceties of polite society. Aware of the rough language and brawling that could occur here in the wee hours, he wished now that he'd splurged for a cabin. He certainly couldn't leave Jude—or the boy—alone and unprotected.

"Tomorrow could be another rough day," he told Jude, nodding over at the now quiet Rooster. "I think we should take his example and get some sleep."

"Here? Out in the open?" She couldn't have looked more appalled than if he'd suggested jumping into the water and swimming for shore.

"We can move closer to Rooster and the privacy of those

sacks." He reached for her arm, thinking to lead her, but she deftly spun out of his grasp.

"I-I'm not tired."

"Well, I am, after the day we've had." And because of it, in danger of losing his patience. "What's the matter, Jude? Afraid we'll discover that you snore?"

"I do not snore!" Her indignation faded, disappearing as quickly as it had come on. "It's just that I . . . well, sometimes . . . I have these nightmares. I can be"—she looked away, plainly uncomfortable—"I can be a bit loud."

It pricked him, her reluctant confession, as did the subsequent lifting of her shoulders. In ways unknown to him, she must have been bruised as badly as Rooster, though being Jude, she'd rather die than let it show.

"A few shouts won't bother me," he told her teasingly as he again took her arm to lead her over to the dozing boy. "Here, lean up against the sacks and close your eyes. I'll keep the ruffians at bay. Knowing you, I'll need the practice. No doubt you'll be causing yet another fracas in Jefferson City."

Rather than offer the expected protest, she gave him a sheepish grin as she let him settle her amid the cargo "Poor Boone. I don't set out to make your life miserable, you know. Lately trouble just seems to follow me around."

"I noticed." Charmed in spite of himself, he sat down opposite her. "You're liable to be the death of me yet. You have any idea how much a kid like him can eat?"

"Have some faith, Boone," she said, closing her eyes. "Don't you know the good Lord looks out for children?"

"And fools," he muttered under his breath. Staring at her, fighting the urge to gather her in his arms, he knew he might as well count himself in their number.

Foolish was the last thing Jude considered Boone as she lay there watching him doze off. Staring at his far too hand-

EVERY DREAM COME TRUE 155

some face, she kept thinking of the moment before the crash. His words kept coming back to haunt her.

Some folks just aren't mean to be saved.

She knew he'd been referring to himself, but she couldn't help making the comparison to her own past. Everyone else seemed inclined to overlook what had happened with her father, but all this time, she'd been unable to forgive herself.

Which was undoubtedly why she still had the nightmares.

She hadn't wanted to tell him the true nature of those dreams. Having seen his weariness, she had no wish to burden him further, but her true motive was sheer utter cowardice. She couldn't bear to see that look in his eye, that withdrawing. It took trust to unburden one's soul and expect understanding, a broad leap of faith no man had yet been able to inspire.

Only here she was, alone in the dead of night and the middle of nowhere, wishing this unlikely drifter would somehow prove her salvation.

Boone, she thought, with self-derision. Had she heard nothing of her brother's warning? Hadn't she decided to forget him? He might be nice to talk to, and nicer to look at, but Boone was a self-proclaimed loner. When push came to shove, his kind always took off without looking back.

A girl would have to be the biggest kind of fool to care about him. Give her heart to Boone, and she was begging to have it shattered to bits.

She could see the wisdom in every harsh realization, but she kept thinking back to how he'd come charging to her rescue, how relieved she'd felt, how safe. And more than anything, she longed to feel his warmth again.

Who would it hurt if she now moved closer, near enough to hear his steady breathing, she thought, inching closer. Surely she, too, could doze off if she listened to his slow, soothing cadence.

Propping herself up against the sack next to his, their sides nearly touching, she closed her eyes. Yes, she thought with a smile. Now she could sleep, too.

Which was the exact opposite of Tucker's reaction, opening his eyes the next morning to face the dawning sun. Disoriented, unsure of his surroundings, he remembered only that he shouldn't have fallen asleep.

Gradually aware of a pleasant warmth, he glanced down to find Jude snuggled against him, her head resting peacefully on his shoulder. Still in a dazed state, he savored the sensation of how good she felt there, how natural, as if he were meant to wake every morning with this woman nestled close to his side.

For a few peaceful moments, he let himself stay as they were, enjoying the scent and feel of her, keeping the demons at bay. Life was always its best in the early morning hours, he thought lazily. Before reality, and all its implications, could rear its ugly head.

This morning reality appeared in the person of one Rooster O'Leary.

Standing over them, a scowl on his face, the boy looked a bit more chipper but no less ragged. The sour expression, Tucker thought cynically, must be disappointment. Rooster had probably hoped to pick their pockets and zip off unmolested, only Tucker had foiled his efforts by being awake.

He'd have to watch this one carefully.

"Going somewhere, Rooster?" he drawled lazily, carefully extricating his arm from beneath Jude's head.

She stirred, opening her eyes, her expressive face betraying fear. Popping up, scrambling away from him, she couldn't have been more unflattering in her haste to get away. "I was—" She broke off awkwardly, her face going red. "I had trouble getting to sleep," she finished off. "Sorry, I must have—"

"Forget it," he snapped, rising to his feet. Did she have to feel that much regret for crawling into his arms? "I already have."

She looked away, the blush deepening, for some reason making him feel as if he had slapped her. "I should see about getting us some food," he said to change the subject. "And maybe find out just how long we'll be stuck here."

"I could come with you," Rooster said eagerly. "I sure am hungry."

Tucker shook his head. "Stay here with Jude." He nodded at the degenerates sprawled on the deck around them. "She needs a protector."

Puffing out his chest, Rooster made it clear he would take the job seriously. As much as Tucker hated to admit it, the kid did have his moments.

"While you're up there, you will see about paying his passage?" Jude asked quietly.

It had been Tucker's intention, but her reminder irritated him unduly. "The good Lord gave me a conscience," he told her. "I don't need you acting as one."

"I'm sorry, I didn't mean—"

"Lord, woman, you aim to apologize for breathing next?" Seeing her startled expression, he realized he was being unreasonable, but he couldn't seem to stop himself. He didn't much like reality, he discovered. He'd far rather be lying back on the deck with Jude tucked trustingly in his arms.

An unlikely occurrence, as evidenced by her straight spine and stiffer expression. "While you're up there, see what you can do about rustling up some clean bandages, too," she told him coldly. "I need to rewrap Rooster's arm and at the rate I'm going, I'll soon run out of petticoat." She gave him a smile that would freeze a stone. "I ripped my skirt in that melee last night and am already in too great a danger of exposing my ankles."

He glanced down at the tear, running halfway up her left

calf. "We'll get you new clothes in Jefferson City. Male clothes."

"Yes, sir! Do I at least get to pick out the color?"

He was about to snap back at her, but he realized how it heated his blood, arguing with the woman, and all things considered, the sight of her long, creamy leg had him heated too much already.

Turning on a heel, he thought it better if he just walked away.

"What's gotten into him?" Rooster asked an hour later, watching Boone once again stomp away from them. After dropping off food and medical supplies, he'd taken off again. He'd muttered some nonsense about helping the crew, but as far as Jude was concerned, it was merely an excuse to flee.

Busy tending to the boy's arm, she didn't bother to answer, embarrassed to admit that she was the source of the man's ill temper. What had possessed her to snuggle up to him? Of course such a man would shake her off and go running for his life. She must have scared the bejeezus out of him, clinging to him like that.

In her defense, she'd made the move in her sleep—she'd never be that bold when conscious and alert—but try explaining it to Rooster or Boone himself. No, all things considered, the less said, the better.

"He sure is angry," the boy persisted. "I hope I didn't do nothing to make him that way."

Sparing her own feelings was one thing, but how could she let Rooster think it was his fault? If she wasn't mistaken, the poor kid had the beginnings of a powerful hero worship, and she didn't want him unnecessarily hurt. "It's not you," she said brusquely, pulling off last night's bandage to inspect his wound. "It's me he's angry at."

Rooster studied her face, plainly curious. "What did you do?"

"If you must know, I stepped over the line." The cut was oozing some, she noticed, but it looked clean enough. "A little water and some of that salve," she told Rooster, "and you'll be as right as rain."

"What's this line you stepped over?"

She pursed her lips. She shouldn't have let that slip, but she'd forgotten what a bulldog kids his age could be—probably because Rooster rarely acted like a twelve-year-old. "People have this imaginary fence they put around themselves," she explained as she worked. "Boone, well, his is denser than most."

"Yeah," Rooster agreed. "He likes to go it alone."

"That he does." Sighing, she spread the ointment on his arm. "He needs space, you can't crowd him. You might want to keep that in mind for the future."

"You really think he'll let me tag along with you?"

He tried to hide it, but she could hear the eagerness in his voice. "It's not his choice to make," she told Rooster firmly as she wrapped his arm. "Right now he's working for me. If I say you're part of the team, he has to accept it."

She spoke with far more confidence than she felt—and trust Rooster to call her on it. "He didn't seem so accepting."

"He'll come around." Securing the last of the bandages, she decided she should advise the boy not to expect a long-term commitment from Boone. Or perhaps she just felt a need to repeat the warning to herself. "It's only until we find the man I'm seeking. Once the job is done, Boone will run off, and we'll likely never see him again."

Studying her, Rooster frowned. "We?"

She gathered up the supplies and set everything back in the box. "I don't want you going back to the docks," she told him. "In fact, I was hoping you might consider coming home with me."

He gaped at her as if she were missing her head. "I got a home," he blustered. "I don't need no one's charity."

"It's a far cry from charity. My family has a plantation in Louisiana, and now that the war is over, we'll need a lot of hands keeping it going. All I'm offering is hard work for meager wages, at least until we get back on our feet. And of course, a clean bed and plenty enough good food to keep you going."

"You don't know nothing about me."

"You know even less about me. For heaven's sake, Rooster, somebody has to start taking down these fences. Isn't the world lonely enough?"

For an instant he looked as hurt and vulnerable as if she'd struck him, before retreating back into his devil-may-care shell. "Thanks for the offer, ma'am, but I got other fish to fry."

She'd just bet he did. "Well, the offer still stands. At least think it over. You can give me your answer when our search is done."

"Yeah, sure," he said, moving off to sit by himself.

Apparently here was another line she'd crossed over. If she didn't take care, soon no one would be talking to her.

Walking over to the rail, she wished she could have the last twenty-four hours to do over. She'd meant well in everything she'd done, but she'd only made matters steadily worse. Had she not lost her carpetbag, they'd probably be in Jefferson City by now, not stranded in the middle of the Missouri River.

Looking over the side of the boat, she saw why they called it the Big Muddy. And up ahead in the middle of that brown, churning water struggled a bare-chested Tucker Boone.

The rope tied around his waist helped him hold his own against the current, but she could see by his straining muscles what the effort cost. She couldn't help worrying about his shoulder, wishing she'd checked it last night when she'd bandaged Rooster.

Though she wouldn't know he'd been shot from the way

he moved. Six other men worked with him, roustabouts from the looks of them, trying to secure lines to a second boat, now approaching from upstream.

She didn't know how long she watched him, fascinated by his strength and efficiency, not to mention the play of his muscles on that broad, powerful back. Against her will, she relived the first time she'd seen him, carrying Lilah upstairs to her gaudy bedroom. And then later his naked body holding her down, stirring feelings she'd long since given up on. Did strange things to her insides, imagining how it would feel to touch him tenderly, to soothe his aching muscles at the end of the day.

It wasn't until he glanced back and saw her watching that she had the good sense to return to her position by Rooster. She prayed Boone hadn't noticed her yearning, her hunger, for if he had, especially after last night's folly, he'd have been fleeing with the wind.

Boone had seen Jude watching him, but it wasn't escape he thought of early the next day. Standing on the deck, facing the shoreline as they made their way upriver, he wondered what would happen if he gave in to the urge her gaze had inspired.

But that was stupid. He knew exactly what would happen. He'd take what she so unwittingly offered and regret it for the rest of his life. Jude wasn't the kind for casual mating. Giving her body meant giving her heart, he sensed, and in the end, all he could offer in return was heartbreak.

"Hey, Boone, mind if I ask you a question?"

He looked down to find Rooster beside him, seeming ten times healthier than he had when they'd found him. He'd likely wear that shiner for a week or so, but he had good color in his cheeks and the bruise on his chin was fast subsiding. "What's troubling you?" Tucker asked the boy.

"Her." Grunting, the boy pointed at Jude.

That made two of them, but then Jude was a troubling woman.

"What is it with her?" Rooster went on. "She looking to get splattered?"

"Beg your pardon?"

"It's what happens to the good eggs. You know, the nice ones, the ones who help others and hurt nobody. They never seem to see it coming, not like you and me, but all the same, that great wall of pain comes crashing down and the next thing you know, *splat!* Nice-person omelet."

Hearing such cynicism from the mouth of a twelve-year-old kid made Tucker uneasy. "Don't you worry about Jude," he told the boy. "She sees a lot more than you'd think."

Rooster glanced back at her, tilting his head as if trying to figure her out. "Well, I don't get it. What's her angle? Why is she being so nice, and what are these errands she wants me to run?"

Tucker shrugged. He had to be the last person on earth who could explain, or even guess at Jude's *angle,* but maybe it was time to question Rooster's own motives. "What she wants is between you and her, but I should warn, I'm here to keep her from being hurt. She seems to think there's something in you worth valuing, and I won't stand by and watch you disappoint her."

Rooster gaped at him as if he'd grown another head. "Are you guys some kind of church folk, out to save the world?"

"Not me. At the moment I'm a glorified bounty hunter Jude's hired on."

"Bounty hunter?" Eyes wide, Rooster now gaped at the Colt on his hip. "You mean, you really can use that thing? Can you draw?"

"I can wing your butt at fifty paces, which is all you really need to know."

EVERY DREAM COME TRUE 163

Rooster nodded solemnly, eyeing the gun with a covetous expression. "Jude says you're after a man. She's asked me to help."

So she was determined to bring Rooster. "Since she's the boss, I have to go along with her decision—but if you ask me, she's far too trusting." Smiling grimly, he reached down to stroke the Colt. "Con the rest of the world, but I expect you to treat Jude with the honor and respect you'd give to your mother."

"My mama is dead."

Though he'd suspected this, the boy's flat tone caused an unexpected pang. Tucker knew more than anyone how it hurt to lose a mother. "Then all the more reason to value Jude," he said gruffly. "I mean it. I won't tolerate your nonsense around her. Do what you must in your own time, but around Jude, you'll act every bit the saint she thinks you."

"And what about you? I ain't noticed you acting so saintly. You about bit off her head back there."

Touché. "I'm just the hired help, boy. Nobody's holding a gun to my head. Or butt, in your case."

"You wouldn't shoot me."

"No?" The kid spoke with enough bravado, but Tucker could see the doubt in his eyes. "You could test me of course. We'd see then."

"See what?" Jude said, coming up behind them.

Both males spun to face her, no doubt dual pictures of guilt. "Man talk," Tucker said, recovering first. "Don't let it concern you."

"I hate it when you males do that," she said quietly. "Man talk. As if what you talk about is so deep and intellectual, silly little me could never understand it."

Oh, she'd understand their conversation, all right, and she'd start yelling at Tucker for interfering. "Rooster and I were mapping out plans. We'll be docking in Jefferson City soon, so we need to know what to do first. Food, probably, then head to the dry goods store to rustle you both up some new clothes. We'll need to present a more upstanding image if we hope to get far at the prison."

"This is man talk?" Jude asked, her dark eyes questioning him.

"I'm laying out ground rules." Evading her probing gaze, Tucker turned to Rooster. "I told him that from now on, there'll be no lying, no cheating, and no stealing. Toe the line, and he gets a bed at night and three square meals a day."

"And you emphasized this with your pistol?"

Her suspicious tone had him wondering just how much she'd heard of their conversation. "Rooster understands me."

The boy nodded, flashing a conspiratorial grin.

"But the way I see it," Tucker said, turning to Jude, "he's having trouble understanding *you*. He's a bit unclear on these errands you want him to run."

Jude's annoyed expression proved what Tucker suspected: that she had no real errands . . . she'd made them up to make the boy feel useful.

To her credit, she now did her best to think up chores for him—scouting out the town, finding a hotel and eating establishment—the conversation keeping them both occupied as the boat pulled into the Jefferson City landing.

Remaining uninvolved in the exchange, Tucker watched Jude as she spoke, struck anew by how quick she was at thinking on her feet, how adept she was at making a person feel valued and useful. Had she been a man, she'd have made one fine officer on the field of battle.

But she wasn't a man, and that of course was the problem.

When they docked, Tucker accompanied the pair to the gangplank and off the boat, determined to find Latour and get this fiasco over and done with. The sooner things could return to normal, the better for them all.

Jefferson City was booming, crowded with citizens and

merchants scurrying to do business or book passage up-river. Tucker could find no overt threat in the bustling, and the balmy weather couldn't have been finer—yet looking about, he couldn't shake the sensation that he should be watching their backs.

As if sensing it, too, Jude eyed him with a worried expression. "I know Rooster's hungry, but can we postpone eating until after we visit the prison? It probably sounds silly, but I have a feeling we should go there without delay."

Tucker nodded, for once in agreement. "I'll ask directions." Noticing a group of three men gathered by the ticket office, he stepped forward. "Beg your pardon," he called out as he neared, finding something disturbingly familiar about the one with his back to him. "Can you direct me to the prison camp?"

"Funny, we was just asking the same," a too-familiar voice answered, the man turning to face him. "Maybe we can all go together?"

Billy, Tucker thought with a lurch.

Thirteen

Bouncing along in the stagecoach bound for Independence, Missouri, Jude thought about the past day and night, marveling at how quickly life could take an unexpected and unwelcome detour. Instead of heading home to Camelot with Rafe, here she was dashing off to yet another unknown part of Missouri with Boone, Rooster, and the three strangers on the seat opposite.

Billy she recognized from their last encounter, but she'd never before seen the two men napping on either side of him. She didn't like that his "buddies" hadn't been among the five who'd accosted her in St. Louis. Just how many Gray Ghosts were there, and more importantly why this compulsion to follow Boone?

He didn't seem to know, either, or if he did, he wasn't saying. Right away Billy had drawn him aside, and though both had glanced often in her direction, neither seemed about to enlighten her.

Nor had Boone been inclined to listen to her protests when he'd announced Billy would be joining them. Jude didn't want the man tagging along, and she'd swear Boone didn't, either—yet there Billy sat with his two goons beside him, as they followed yet another frustrating lead in their quest to find Rafe.

He hadn't been at the prison camp. Five days after he'd reached Jefferson City, they'd been told, Rafe was transferred to Independence, to the post nearest his capture. There he should have been processed, discharged, and sent home.

Only Rafe hadn't gone to Camelot. Any doubts about this were answered by a quick wire to Louisiana, to which Patrick promptly replied to the negative. He had to be in Independence, Jude had decided, and they had no choice but to make the trek westward.

She hadn't expected Billy to volunteer to accompany them, any more than she'd anticipated Boone letting his friend take charge of arrangements. Appalled to learn they'd be taking the stage, she'd questioned Billy's decision, but Boone had looked the other way while Billy answered. Cozied up inside, he'd told her with a boyish grin, they'd stand a better chance of getting to know each other.

Not likely, Jude thought irritably. Even if she felt inclined to chat, Billy was lost in his own world, and his two friends were dozing. To her left Boone stared out the window in preoccupied silence, and Rooster was intent upon watching the three men opposite. He seemed fascinated by the guns they wore on both hips, what to Jude seemed an excessive amount of firepower for a cramped little coach.

Riding by stage had to be the most despicable mode of travel, she decided as they hit yet another rut in the road. She couldn't go careening into Rooster's bruised body, but then she didn't want to bang into Boone's shoulder, either. In truth she'd prefer to avoid all close physical contact with the man. The strength and warmth of his thigh pressed against her own served as too vivid a reminder of how easily she could make a fool of herself, something she could ill afford to do in front of Billy. His gold-tinted eyes had a way of darting between her and Boone that left her feeling distinctly uneasy.

Looking up with a frown, she discovered Billy's gaze on her now, his face breaking into a smile as color flooded her cheeks. He seemed to enjoy her discomfiture. He certainly did his best to make her blush.

His appraisal passed over her pink-flowered cotton dress, the replacement for the torn burgundy merino he'd insisted she buy in the dry goods store back in Jefferson City. Odd how Boone had so adamantly pressured her to wear pants and a shirt, yet never once had he mentioned he wanted her dressed as a boy to his friend.

"Hey, Jesse," Billy said suddenly, prodding Boone with his boot, yet keeping his gaze trained on Jude. "What's it been, a year or more since you've been back this way? Reckon you must be feeling a mite tentative about this visit. Gotta have a heap of ghosts haunting you."

"Cut it out, Billy," Boone said sharply. "Nobody's interested."

How very wrong he was. Jude couldn't have been more curious, and the suddenly alert Rooster seemed just as eager to learn about Boone's past.

"I gotta say, the Jesse I knew would never be scared of a few memories," Billy pressed. "He'd be near busting at the seams to get home."

"Home?" Jude asked, startled. "You two grew up in Independence?"

"In the general area." Billy's smile seemed pleasant enough on the surface, but his eyes held a sly quality. "Stayed there most our lives, until we signed on to serve the Confederacy. Oh, the stories I could tell you about Jesse as a kid."

"Some of us are tired," Boone growled, nodding at the dozing pair flanking his friend. "Shut up so we can sleep, too."

"I'd like to hear more," Rooster said eagerly, sounding more his age than his usual world-weary adult. "Was he skinny like me?"

Almost reluctantly Billy dragged his gaze from Jude to focus on Rooster. "Jesse? Nah, I was the skinny one. Jesse was always bigger, stronger, and smarter than any kid in town. Back then you couldn't find anyone faster at the draw or surer with his fists. And when it came to brawling, nobody dared touch him. Or me for that matter, so long as Jesse was there to keep them at bay."

"And brawling was a favored pastime." Too well, Jude could picture their younger versions, strutting about town, terrorizing the local youthful population.

"I fought only when I had to," Boone said dryly. "Though I often wondered if Billy picked fights on purpose, just to see if I could win."

"Jesse, you wound me. You and me, we were like brothers. Nobody sang your praises more than I."

Billy frowned, the picture of hurt feelings, but Jude sensed Boone was right. Brothers or no, more than mere friendship colored Billy's praise—she also heard envy.

The stagecoach grew quiet, the only sound being an occasional light snore from the men beside Billy. It was hardly a restful silence for Jude, not with the way he kept smiling as he glanced from her to Boone. She had a feeling he was plotting out how best to embarrass him next.

Oblivious, Rooster pursued his quest to learn all he could about his new hero. "Why do you keep calling him Jesse? Jude calls him Boone."

Once again Billy didn't look at the person who asked the question, but rather at the subject of his reply. "Back when I knew him, he *was* Jesse. Jesse Holland. He changed his name during the war."

"Why?"

Tilting his head, Billy grinned at Boone. "Good question. Ask him to tell you why, since I don't rightly understand myself." He turned to Rooster. "But I can tell you why he picked that particular name. You want to hear?"

Boone glared at him, but Rooster nodded eagerly.

"Took me a while to figure out," Billy went on, ignoring Boone. "His last name was easy enough. As kids, we used to pretend to be trailblazers. I had to be the Indian scout, while he got to be Dan'l Boone. Outright handy with a knife, Jesse was, so it didn't do me much good to argue. Yup, the Boone part was simple to figure, but I had to search through my memories to recall why he'd pick that first name. He ever tell you about our dog?"

"For pete's sake," Boone snapped. "You've bored us all enough with your chatter. Let it rest."

Billy merely grinned. "No, now I think the boy and your lady friend will be mighty interested in this one. Reckon you'd just love a peek at old Jesse's true character, wouldn't you, ma'am?"

Boone looked ready to spit, but Billy was right—she was dying to hear his story. Not that she'd give him the satisfaction of knowing it. "Somehow I don't believe my interest, or lack of it, much matters to you, Mr. Cochoran. I do believe you intend to proceed no matter what I say."

Billy chuckled. "Don't you just love the way she talks? Such a lah-di-dah lady. Can't help wondering what she's doing with the likes of you, Jesse."

Intercepting the look they exchanged, Jude wondered if this was at the root of Billy's curiosity: a need to know the true nature of their relationship. "Stop teasing," she told him in her best schoolmarm tone, "and just tell your story."

Billy turned to her then, his expression making it plain that he not only knew the reason for her interruption, he was amused by it. "As you wish. Now where was I? Ah, yes, the dog. Only pet either one of us ever had."

Lips tight, Boone turned to stare out the window.

"We weren't normal kids, you gotta understand. No grand old house or farm for us to go home to at night, not even a father. We lived on the wrong end of town at the Paradise Saloon, our mamas being hardworking women, for all that they plied their trade in the wee hours on their backs."

The glare Tucker trained on Billy could have seared through his brain.

EVERY DREAM COME TRUE   171

"Living in the local bordello, me and Jesse were pretty much shunned by the good citizens and their children. Pair that with mamas too harried to pay us much heed—"

"My mother gave three hours a day to our schooling," Boone corrected as if the words were wrenched from his lips. "It's not her fault you chose to skip lessons."

Jude wasn't sure which surprised her more—Boone's stern defense of his mother or Billy's sudden sheepishness.

"Heck, you know I adored your mama," he told Boone with what seemed like sincerity. "All I meant to say was that me and Jesse were left pretty much on our own. All we had was each other and our little adventures."

"Adventures?" Eyes shining, Rooster leaned forward.

"Like I said, we liked to play out there in the woods. Each day we'd cut a new trail, Jesse hacking away at the undergrowth with his big Bowie knife and me listening for sounds of pursuit. Never did encounter much in the way of danger, least nothing outside our imaginations, but one day we did come upon this stray."

Billy paused, eyeing Boone. "Should have seen Jesse when he found that mangy mutt. All of a sudden, he goes still as a post, clasping his knife and looking angrier than I'd ever before seen him. Dog couldn't walk—could barely breathe after the beating it took—so Jesse lifts up its battered carcass and carries all fifty pounds of bleeding, smelly fur back to town. Doesn't say a word, mind you—but me, I know him, so I recognized his fury. Had they been anywhere close, Jesse would have turned his knife on them that abused that animal."

"Did the dog live?" Jude found herself asking.

Billy turned his grin on her. "More or less, thanks to Jesse. He nursed it back to health—no easy feat, considering the saloon's strict rules against keeping animals. He had to muck out stalls just to use a corner of the stables—"

"Don't sell yourself short," Boone interrupted. "You forgot to mention who charmed the scraps from the cook in the saloon kitchen."

"Yeah, well, never could tell you no." Billy frowned, clearly not liking when the talk focused on himself. "But back to the dog," he went on, directing their attention elsewhere. "Got so it could move around, but it never did fully recover. Old when we found it, and battered by life, it hadn't a prayer of keeping up with two young boys. Tried hard enough, and Jesse slowed his pace to accommodate it, but by the end of every day, the mutt got plumb tuckered out. That's what we ended up naming it. Tuckered Out. Only mostly we called it plain Tucker."

Jude glanced at Boone. His gaze bored through the window as he tried to distance himself from them, but he couldn't quite manage it, any more than he'd been able to bury his past. That decent streak in him couldn't quite let go of the heartfelt moments, as evidenced by the name he'd chosen. What had happened, she wondered, that he, too, would feel so "tuckered out"?

"One day the dog got shot," Billy went on casually, as if the event had the emotional impact of a discussion on the day's weather. "Dumb mutt chose to sprawl on the saloon steps one morning, waiting for me and Jesse to come out and play—only instead this drunk comes stumbling out. Made the man mad, tripping over that dog, and the drink made him reckless, so the rest took barely a minute. We heard the yelp, then the gunshot and god-awful howl, but by the time we got there, ol' Tucker was reduced to whimpering. Never heard such a pathetic sound, nor saw such a pitiful sight, as that dumb dog looking up at Jesse as he cradled it in his arms. There I was, watching and feeling powerless, when Jesse stands and yanks the gun from the drunkard's hand. Sure was eerie, let me tell you, the silence after Jesse pumped that slug into that dying dog's brain."

Recoiling as if she'd heard the shot herself, Jude understood how hard it must have been for Boone to put his pet out of his misery. No wonder he was so set upon calling himself a loner. Early on he'd discovered how love could hurt.

Billy flashed a broad smile. "Should have seen him. Big, strong, can't-knock-me-down Jesse Holland, letting tears drip like a girl's as we put that mangy mutt six feet under."

Jude fought the urge to reach out for Boone's hand. Proud to a fault, he wouldn't welcome the gesture, not in front of Billy. Better the man continue to misread her. He'd meant to reveal what he perceived as Boone's weakness with that story, she realized. But all Jude had seen was yet another example of the man's innate goodness.

So much for remaining emotionally uninvolved.

Nor had the ploy worked on Rooster, she noticed. The boy now stared at Boone as that poor old dog once must have, as if the sun couldn't rise without his nod of approval.

"Tell us more," Rooster prompted Billy. "I want to hear about when you two served together in the war."

"Ain't much to tell." Billy's expression went solemn. "Jesse was a regular hero, using those trailblazing skills we'd learned in the woods to make a name for himself. He was one fine scout until he deserted."

"Deserted?"

Rooster sounded like Jude felt, as if all the air had suddenly been sucked out of the carriage. Though the accusation made sense, she supposed. Why else change his identity and show such reluctance to be heading home?

"Jesse claims he has his reasons," Billy added with another sly grin, "and I'd hate to dispute them, but it sure is hard explaining my leniency to the friends he left in the lurch. Who knows how many a Johnny Reb might be alive today had Jesse been scouting before the massacre at Westport. Hate to suggest this, but maybe that's the true 'why' behind his name-changing, son. Ain't that right, Jesse?"

Jude glanced up at Boone, waiting for him to refute this,

while he looked straight at Billy. "You've had your fun," he told him coldly. "Let it go at that."

Billy nodded, turning to Jude. "Right you are, Jesse."

Staring back into his gold-flecked eyes, Jude felt manipulated. So that's what this had been about. All along, Billy had merely wanted to prove that Boone wasn't worth defending—that she'd been wrong to call him a man of honor.

And as much as she wanted to believe in Boone, Billy had set a nasty little doubt worming through her brain. A deserter? A man who left his fellow soldiers to perish in battle? She couldn't help it—the prospect left a bad taste in her mouth.

If only he'd say something, offer at least one of those reasons he'd claimed to have. But Boone just sat there, staring out the window and saying nothing, while his hard, warm thigh nudged her better senses, coaxing her to overlook his moral deficiencies and concentrate on his physical attributes instead.

Pursing her lips, she did her best to direct her thoughts away from him and onto the task ahead, but wouldn't you know the stage had to hit yet another bump in the road, causing her to slip to the left—and right into the arms of the man she'd meant to ignore.

Gazing up into his face, she could see he wasn't any happier about their collision, yet he continued to hold her long after he should have let her go. As she stared into his eyes, she could see his pain and torment, and once again, she knew a strong urge to offer solace. Boone wasn't proud of what he'd done, she sensed. Billy's taunting had indeed stirred up ghosts from his past.

Yet the very instant her gaze softened, his eyes narrowed from their vibrant sapphire to the cold gray-blue of slate. Breaking away, he pulled his hat down over his eyes, turning his shoulder to her, his message clear: *You keep to your affairs, and I'll keep to mine.*

Not liking the way her hands trembled, she gripped them in her lap. Across the way, she noticed with dismay, Billy watched with a sly, crooked grin.

Tucker was only too happy to reach Independence. Five more minutes in that stagecoach and he might have killed Billy. What the devil had he been up to, blabbering on like that about the past?

If the object had been to make Tucker look bad, he'd accomplished it deftly, the master stroke coming with the mention of his desertion. Grimacing as he remembered the confusion he'd seen in Jude's eyes, Tucker wished now that he'd said something, held her a bit longer, done anything to prevent Billy's insinuations from sinking in. At the time, though, it had seemed simpler—and certainly safer—to keep his emotional distance, a feat that grew harder the more Billy flirted with her.

It had made Tucker edgy, watching the man exert his charm, noticing how Billy appeared to be wearing down Jude's defenses. A few short days ago, she'd told Tucker that they should keep their private lives to themselves, so it was doubly unpleasant to hear her open up bit by bit to Billy. By the time they'd reached Independence, she'd gone from short, curt retorts to long, warm recitations about what it had been like growing up in Louisiana.

Listening—though he pretended to be absorbed in the scenery—Tucker realized there was a great deal about Jude he didn't know, would likely never know, and the thought left him feeling vaguely unsettled. It made him think of another old adage of his mama's: *Never know what you have till you lose it.*

Not that he'd ever had Jude, nor ever likely would. Come tomorrow, when they found Latour, she would ride out of his life forever.

No surprise there, he told himself as the stagecoach

rolled to a stop. He'd known from the start that he had no place in her life, nor she in his. As he'd told her in St. Louis, he'd long since chosen to face life wide-awake and alert and leave the dreaming to those who could afford it.

With that aim in mind, he stepped down from the stagecoach, scouting the dark streets warily, determined not to be caught off guard as he'd been in Jefferson City. Though Billy had yet to satisfactorily explain how he'd known where to find them, Tucker didn't need to be told his purpose for being there. His Cap'n didn't trust him. Nannies—that's what Billy and his two goons were—nursemaids sent to see that he did indeed deliver Latour.

Sure made things awkward, sharing close quarters with the two who had hired him for the same job. Back in St. Louis, he'd considered it his business and nobody else's, but he now conceded that Jude could feel justified in thinking he'd gone behind her back by hiring on with the Gray Ghosts. He'd asked Billy not to bring up the subject, but after the dog story, Tucker sensed his friend was just biding his time. Billy would tell Jude what best served his interests, not caring if everything exploded in Tucker's face.

Turning, he watched Billy step down and reach up to offer his hand to Jude, a gentlemanly gesture Tucker should have remembered. His regret had nothing to do with her smile of gratitude, he told himself sternly. Just didn't like to see his manners grown so rusty.

Descending from the coach, Jude looked every inch the lady. The flowered cotton wasn't as revealing as the dress it replaced, but it was no less flattering to her feminine curves. Noticing the way Billy ogled her, Tucker regretted not having time to hide her in boys' clothing before the lecher got a peek at her. Now the damage was already done. Her wearing pants would only stoke his lust hotter.

He had to get her away from Billy, he thought, as he watched his friend take her arm and lead her off down the street. It wouldn't be easy, considering Billy had taken back

Here's a special offer for *Romance Readers!*

Get 4 FREE Zebra Historical Romance Novels from the newest Historical Romance line- Splendor Romances!

A $19.96 value absolutely **Free!**

Take a trip back in time and experience the passion, adventure and excitement of a Splendor Romance...delivered right to your doorstep!

Take advantage of this offer to enjoy Zebra's newest line of historical romance novels....Splendor Romances (formerly Lovegrams Historical Romances)- Take our introductory shipment of 4 romance novels -Absolutely Free! (a $19.96 value)

Now you'll be able to savor today's best romance novels without even leaving your home with our convenient and inexpensive home subscription service. Here's what you get for joining:

- 4 BRAND NEW bestselling Splendor Romances delivered to your doorstep every month
- 20% off every title (or almost $4.00 off) with your home subscription
- FREE home delivery
- A FREE monthly newsletter, *Zebra/Pinnacle Romance News* filled with author interviews, member benefits, book previews and more!
- No risks or obligations...you're free to cancel whenever you wish...no questions asked

To get started with your own home subscription, simply complete and return the card provided. You'll receive your FREE introductory shipment of 4 Splendor Romances and then you'll begin to receive monthly shipments of new Zebra Splendor titles. Each shipment will be yours to examine for 10 days and then if you decide to keep the books, you'll pay the preferred home subscriber's price of just $4.00 per title. That's $16 for all 4 books with FREE home delivery! And if you want us to stop sending books, just say the word...it's that simple.

4 Free BOOKS are waiting for you!
Just mail in the certificate below!

If the certificate is missing below, write to: Splendor Romances, Zebra Home Subscription Service, Inc., P.O. Box 5214, Clifton, New Jersey 07015-5214

FREE BOOK CERTIFICATE

Yes! Please send me 4 Splendor Romances (formerly Zebra Lovegram Historical Romances), ABSOLUTELY FREE! After my introductory shipment, I will be able to preview 4 new Splendor Romances each month FREE for 10 days. Then if I decide to keep them, I will pay the money-saving preferred publisher's price of just $4.00 each… a total of $16.00. That's 20% off the regular publisher's price and there's never any additional charge for shipping and handling. I may return any shipment within 10 days and owe nothing, and I may cancel my subscription at any time. The 4 FREE books will be mine to keep in any case.

Name _____

Address _____ Apt. _____

City _____ State _____ Zip _____

Telephone ( ) _____

Signature _____ SP1197
(If under 18, parent or guardian must sign.)

Terms and prices subject to change. Orders subject to acceptance by Zebra Home Subscription Service, Inc. . Zebra Home Subscription Service, Inc. reserves the right to reject or cancel any subscription.

A $19.96 value.
FREE!
No obligation
to buy
anything,
ever.

Get 4 Zebra Historical Romance Novels FREE!

SPLENDOR ROMANCES
ZEBRA HOME SUBSCRIPTION SERVICE, INC.
120 BRIGHTON ROAD
P.O. BOX 5214
CLIFTON, NEW JERSEY 07015-5214

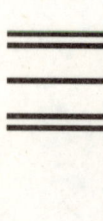

AFFIX
STAMP
HERE

a good chunk of the advance on his wages, claiming he needed it to pay their travel expenses. "Not to worry," he'd added with a casual wave of his pistol. "You'll get paid in full the instant the job is done."

Which for Tucker made finding Latour all the more imperative.

He didn't like all this hopping from place to place. He couldn't help wondering why the Federals kept shipping the man west, when most prisoners of war were sent to Rockport or Camp Chase, or another of the other camps east of the Mississippi. If Latour was not here in Independence, Tucker might have to start delving into the possibility that they'd been sent on a wild-goose chase. That someone, somewhere, didn't want Latour found.

Though he burned with a need for answers, he knew no one at the detention camp would talk to him this late at night. First thing come morning, he swore, he'd be knocking at the gate.

He had a good many things to do tomorrow, he realized uneasily. None of which included his traveling companions.

"You gonna let him get away with that?" Rooster asked in a stage whisper as they watched Billy and his bodyguards escort Jude down the street. "That buddy of yours is stealing your woman."

Tucker battled irritation. "She's not my woman. I said that only for her protection."

Rooster shook his head, sadly disappointed. "Lie to her, and maybe yourself, but don't waste words on me. I got eyes. I know what I see."

"Do you now? Tell me, old man O'Leary, what is it you see?"

"You want her bad, Boone. And that Billy, he knows it. He's looking to stir up trouble, and he don't care much who gets hurt in the process."

Boone stared into the solemn freckled face, uncomfortably aware that the boy was merely echoing his own thoughts. "That's a harsh assessment."

"It was one thing when he was talking about your dog," Rooster went on, "but that Billy crossed the line when he called you a deserter. I'm no upstanding citizen, but one thing I am is loyal—something he ain't. I don't know your story, and I ain't gonna pry, but I know the kind of person you are, Boone, and you don't leave friends in the lurch."

"Is that a fact?" Tucker refused to smile or in any way betray how the kid's observation warmed his heart.

Rooster nodded. "Jude, she's the same, just like you tried to tell me the other day. I guess what I'm trying to say is, I know she's important to you, and you can count on me to help protect her. Just wish Jude understood just how dangerous that Billy can be."

Staring at the pair ahead, Tucker was inclined to agree with him. "C'mon then," he said, starting after them. "We'd better catch up before they lose us."

Rooster beamed ear to ear as he struggled to keep up with Tucker's long stride. "Seeing I'm to be your right-hand man, think I can carry a gun?"

"You even know how to shoot?"

"Not exactly, but I can learn."

Heaven spare him from reformed delinquents. "For now I think we should stick with the basics. I'm going to need someone to help watch Billy, to figure out what's he's up to next. How about being my ears and eyes?"

"Yeah, I can do that." Rooster was unable to hide his disappointment. "But someday you think you can teach me to shoot?"

"We'll see." By this time tomorrow, Tucker thought, he'd be long gone, back on his own to pursue the life left to him. "Right now let's concentrate on watching out for Jude."

Up ahead Billy pointed to the streamers and campaign posters littering the street. "Hey, Jesse," he called back to

EVERY DREAM COME TRUE   179

them. "With the election coming up, we might just get lucky enough to catch a glimpse of your father. I hear he's on the campaign trail again this year."

"His father?" Jude asked, audibly surprised.

Annoyed, Tucker quickened his pace, leaving Rooster to trail in his wake.

"Doesn't that man tell you anything?" Billy asked Jude as Tucker strode up to join them. "Congressman Curtis Holland is his father, though I'm afraid the family will deny having anything to do with Jesse."

"Their snubbing me had nothing to do with my leaving the army," Tucker told Jude, recognizing the confusion in her eyes. "The Hollands rejected me before I was ever even born."

Billy chuckled. "Curtis wasn't a big-time politician when he first met Jesse's mama," he explained as he led Jude down the street. "A lovelier, more ladylike woman you never will meet, so it's no wonder he fell in love and married her. Too bad Sarah had nowhere near the social standing the Hollands demanded for their son. His big brother came to drag Curtis off, mere weeks before Jesse was born. Abandoned, Sarah and her boy learned to make do the best they could, but I reckon you now understand why Jesse never was all that attached to the name of Holland."

Tucker actually hated Billy in that moment, but he guessed having him relate that sordid story was the lesser of two evils. Billy could have told Jude about Curtis Holland's later visit to his mother, about the twin boys she'd been left to deliver alone nine months later. Incredibly trusting and far too loving, his mother had been an open, bleeding heart, just waiting to get trampled.

Much like Jude herself.

To his relief, Billy stopped suddenly. Looking up, he found they stood before a hotel, a far fancier establishment than Tucker would have selected. Rooster pulled up behind him, huffing like a nag heading home from a grueling day in the fields. "We staying here?" he gasped, the dollar signs dancing in his eyes.

As Billy went inside to make arrangements, Tucker made a mental note to watch the boy carefully, lest Rooster pick the pocket of some influential patron. Or worse some political crony of his father's.

But watching him might prove difficult, Tucker soon discovered, when Billy returned holding two keys. Doing the mental arithmetic, Tucker didn't need to see the patented leer to know what was coming.

"Busy night at the inn," Billy announced. "Only two rooms left in the entire establishment. Reckon the boy can sleep with us, while Jesse, lucky devil"—he leaned over to hand the second key to Tucker—"can bed down with the lady."

Fourteen

"I've been thinking that Rooster should sleep with Boone and me," Jude announced over dinner, keeping her voice low to avoid any more frowns from the other diners. Despite their baths and quick general grooming, their group must not meet the standards of the hotel's fancy restaurant. Even the waiters treated them scornfully, as if fearing such riffraff would try to skip out on the bill.

Oblivious to the negative attention, Billy shoveled his food in his face. "Don't you go worrying about the boy," he said between mouthfuls. "It's time he was with men, learning manly ways. Ain't that right, son?"

"Yeah."

"See, ma'am? It's the boy's own choice to bed down with us."

Jude felt a rising panic. Why didn't Boone object? After the way he'd run from her on the boat, he couldn't want to spend the night alone with her, yet you'd never know he had an objection now. He'd protested briefly upon being told about the lack of adequate accommodations, but once Billy countered that he'd be happy to sleep with the lady instead, Boone had behaved as if it were only natural that they share a room.

Clearly he wanted her to continue posing as his mistress, but panic gripped her at the thought of the enforced intimacy. Men were stronger than women, she knew from experience, and all too often driven by their passions. If he pressed her, surely she'd be no match for Boone's domination.

Is it his lust that worries you, a tiny voice asked, *or is it your own?*

Shying away from that thought, she reminded herself that Boone hadn't exactly been pursuing her, especially not after the night she'd unwittingly crawled into his arms. He hadn't even come to their hotel room to change, going elsewhere to remove the grime from their travels. The first she'd seen of him was when he'd shown up at the table, wearing a white shirt, black linen vest, and clean Levi's, his hair still damp from a bath. Though carefully polite, he took care not to look at her, giving Jude all the proof she needed that he didn't want to be alone with her.

That being the case, she renewed her campaign against Billy's arrangements. "You don't have to stay with these strangers, Rooster. You can—"

"It's all right, Jude," Boone said firmly. "Just let it be."

The odd note in his voice confused her, but before she could argue, he covered her hand with his own. "I think we should discuss tomorrow's plans," he announced, squeezing her hand. "I don't like the idea of a crowd visiting the detention camp. I've decided it'll be safer if I go there alone."

Across the table, Billy's frown mirrored her own. "Awfully kind of you to volunteer," he said dryly. "But you see, I have this powerful hankering to see inside that prison. I've a feeling the lady does, too."

Boone's rock-hard glare warned her to keep silent. "Let me worry about the lady," he told Billy. "You concentrate on your own carcass. Or have you forgotten you're liable to see more of that prison than you want?"

Billy made a scoffing sound. "I've slipped in and out of smaller towns than this with no one the wiser."

"That was during the war. You'll find it a good deal more dangerous now with the Federals in charge."

"Dangerous?" Jude couldn't help but blurt out.

"We're in border country," Boone said curtly, as if that explained it all.

"Heck, Jesse, she don't know what that means." Billy gulped down a healthy swig of beer. "They fought a different war in Louisiana."

"I'm afraid he's right," Jude told him with an apologetic smile. "I don't even know what border you're talking about."

Boone removed his hand from hers, his gaze studying her as if to gauge her interest. "We're real close to Kansas here," he said with a shrug. "Years back we had some trouble with local slaveholders sneaking over to vote in the Kansas elections, determined to make them a slave state, too. Fanatics on both sides started exchanging words, then blows, and things got out of hand. Both sides had been clearly established by the time war was declared, and the conflict gave the excuse to take matters further."

Across the table, Billy grinned. "You should have seen it. Kansas jayhawkers against Missouri bushwhackers. Neighbor fighting neighbor."

"Sometimes it was brother against brother," Boone interrupted grimly. "Got real ugly, with massacres piling up on either side, the violence escalating until Union troops stepped in to order Confederate sympathizers off their land. Those that weren't burned out got tossed out, leaving most of western Missouri what is now called the Wasteland. You'll find hard feelings on both sides, but the Federals, they have the power. Southerners like you and bushwhackers like Billy won't find much welcome."

"Come now, Jesse? You forget you were a bushwhacker, too?"

Boone shook his head. "Jesse Holland was a scout. He did no killing and few ever saw his face, and besides he's among the dead and missing. I'm Tucker Boone now, and of us all I stand the best chance of getting information."

"By yourself?" Billy wore his suspicion in his frown. "I don't like it."

Nor did Jude. Most likely Boone had seized this excuse to get rid of her. Maybe he wasn't trying to cut her out and find Rafe on his own, but if he thought this was the best way to protect her, he must have overlooked that it would leave her in the hands of his good pal Billy.

"If things are as tense as he says," she told Billy, "I can't see why a Federal officer would volunteer information to a man alone, an unknown quantity. A bereaving member of Latour's family, now, a poor little girl desperate to find her daddy"—she paused, blinking as if to keep the tears at bay—"why, I do believe we'd find him far more amenable."

Billy grinned ear to ear. "She could be right, Jesse."

"She could be full of . . ." Clenching his jaw, Boone tried again. "Women don't belong in prisons. There could be trouble."

"Well, then that's why me and the boys will be standing at a discreet distance."

So much for sneaking away from them once they found Rafe.

This wouldn't do, she thought, certain they'd find Rafe tomorrow. She had to find some way to talk to Boone, to convince him they had to break free of Billy.

As if sharing the intention, he tossed his napkin to the table and rose to his feet. "Fine, we'll meet in the lobby at eleven then. And now that the morning's events are settled, we should be turning in. I trust you'll take care of the tab?" At Billy's smug nod, Boone turned to her, extending his arm. "Let's go, Jude."

She fought the childish urge to slap his hand away, to refuse to go anywhere with a man who could scowl at her like that, but she was all too aware of Billy's curious gaze. If ever she'd been an actress, now was the time to play a part. Smiling up at Boone, she gave every appearance of being eager to go wherever he led.

As he stared back, she watched myriad emotions flit across his features. Irritation, certainly, and of course exasperation, but for a fleeting instant, she thought she might even see regret. Did he wish to be a million miles away—or like her, was he wishing they could have met under different circumstances, that they didn't have pasts, and probably futures, bent on coming between them?

Marching behind him to the room, facing his all too stiff back, she held little hope that the night could be anything more than an ordeal. A fact hammered home when they entered the room and he slammed the door behind them.

Unnerved by his scowl and continued silence, she waited while he strode across the dark room to light the kerosene lamp on the bedside table. As a soft golden glow blanketed the room, she couldn't help but notice how tiny it now seemed, nowhere near big enough for both her and this man. Everywhere she turned, his presence seemed to dominate—his long, hard body filling the scene. In her mind she kept seeing his muscular back as he worked to free the steamboat, his powerful arms as he'd swept Lilah up and carried her away.

Knowing she must ignore him, she strode to the mahogany bureau, only to be appalled by the image staring back at her from the gilt-framed mirror above it. How pale she looked. How frightened.

Behind her reflection she saw Boone removing his vest and tossing it onto the stuffed chair behind him. Watching him unstrap his holster, she hoped he didn't mean to disrobe in front of her.

Her gaze dropped to the richly appointed four-poster bed in front of him, and the heat flooded her cheeks. No way, no how, would she climb in there beside Boone. Thinking of how she'd cuddled up next to him on the hard, cold deck, she could only imagine what could happen under those lush covers. She might better take pillows and a blanket and make her bed on the floor.

Lord, but the butterflies were doing loop-dee-loops in her belly.

"What's gotten into you?" Boone started in, flinging the room key onto the table's surface. "I thought we'd decided you'd follow my lead tonight."

"You decided," she snapped at his reflection. "Surely you know me better by now than to think I'd ever agree to your going to the prison without me."

Image stared at image for a long, angry moment before Boone looked away, setting his gun and holster beside the key. "It's late. We should get some sleep."

For some reason his backing off annoyed her more. "I see," she said, stomping over to the bed to pluck a pillow and blanket from it. "Always the bully. You even get to decide how and when we fight."

Frowning, he watched her plop the bedding down on the floor. "What in blessed heaven are you doing now?"

"Having a tantrum. I thought it was obvious."

"Not that. That," he said, pointing to the blankets.

"Making my own sleeping arrangements." She tossed back her shoulders in a display of maidenly frost to make the primmest matron proud. "You didn't think I mean to join you in"—she blushed, nodding at the bed—"in that?"

He eyed the bed as if just now noticing it was there. "Jeez, Jude. By now you've got to know *me* better than that."

She'd have thought so, before Billy came along.

"As far as I'm concerned, this is just a job," he added emphatically. "You're paying me to find someone, and that's all there is to it."

She should feel relieved, but she merely found herself more irritated than ever. "Yeah, and part of the job was letting Billy put us in this room together?"

"I wasn't given much choice. Unless you'd rather be sleeping with Billy?"

He made it sound like an accusation, which in turn made her own reply sound defensive. "Rooster probably wanted to stick together, too. I didn't hear you arguing to get him in this room."

"Rooster wanted to stay with them. Relax, he can take care of himself—"

"And I can't? I wish you'd stop thinking of me as some frail, feebleminded dimwit, Boone."

"I have. Long ago." Sighing as if he held the weight of the world on his shoulders, he sat on the edge of the bed, reaching down for his boots. "My hands were tied, Jude. Your virtue wouldn't last five minutes with those randy louts. They're hardened, bitter men who wouldn't think twice about using you up and spitting you out. Claiming you for my own was the only way to protect you. The only thing they'd understand and respect."

He gave the words emphasis by yanking a boot off his foot and throwing it to the floor. It hit the plush green carpet with a dull thud.

As far as explanations went, it was a good one, but she resented the way it took the wind out of her sails. She wanted to be angry at him, had to be, to survive the night. "Nice friends you have," she said, letting the sarcasm drip from each word.

"Don't go holding me accountable for their actions. I never even met the others, while the Billy I knew . . . well, let's just say war changes a man."

"That's a pretty handy excuse." She was being nasty, she knew, but she couldn't seem to help herself. "Do you use it to explain away your desertion?"

He paused a moment before letting the last boot drop to the floor. "I did what I did," he said wearily. "I don't make excuses."

Watching his shoulders sag, she felt the anger drain out

of her. She no longer wanted to fight him, she ached to reach across the bed to rub his back, to ease the worry lines at his eyes. Even more, she wanted him to look at her, communicate with her, not leave her feeling awkward and angry and very much like a stranger. "Tell me about it, Boone. Please, so I can understand."

"Pray God you never have to understand," he said quietly, bitterly. "Somewhere along the line, we'd forgotten what we were fighting for. The world had gone mad, feeding on hatred and senseless killing that won nothing for no one." He turned to her then, his blue eyes dark and hollow. "Some thrived on that violence—but me, I just felt sickened. When I saw my name on the list of dead and missing, I took it as a sign. Call me a coward, but it meant I didn't need to take part in such needless suffering any longer."

His gaze narrowed, betraying that his memories went deeper, and she remembered Billy teasing about ghosts from the past. She longed to probe for more, but she knew better than anyone about the wall Boone had erected around him. Sharing confidences wasn't his way. As he'd so often maintained, he was a loner, trusting nothing and no one but himself.

As if to prove this, he stood, facing her with the bed between them. "Look, it's been a rough few nights, and I reckon we're both exhausted. I'm going to turn down the light and look out the window, so you can slip out of your, er, things and under the covers. In the bed," he amended as he reached to extinguish the lamp. *"I'll* be taking the floor."

She felt a spurt of anger at him for making the decisions again, but standing in the darkened room, she conceded that she'd sure enjoy sleeping without all her clothes for a change.

Quickly removing her dress and petticoats, she stripped down to her shift. With similar haste, she laid out her things on the bureau surface, knowing she'd need them again in the morning. Tomorrow, she thought, with a surge of excitement as she hurried back to the bed and under the covers, she would find Rafe at long last. Soon she and Rafe would be heading home to Camelot.

But on the heels of that thought, she realized with a pang that Boone wouldn't be going with them. In all likelihood, after tomorrow, she'd never see him again.

"I'm done," she called from the bed, an unexpected ache rising in her throat. "You can turn around now."

At the window Boone pulled open the drapes. A shaft of light spilled into the room from the full moon outside, framing him in its glow. Silent and solitary he stared out at the sky as if seeking answers in the great beyond. Gazing at his strong-boned features, she could see the toughness he'd honed in his body and spirit, could feel the loneliness he wore like a badge of honor. The ache swelled in her throat, made it hard to swallow.

He didn't have to do everything alone, she thought. Couldn't he see how much better things were when they worked together?

When he finally spoke, he seemed as far away as the stars he stared at. "For what it's worth, I did try to get rid of our escorts, but they had six guns between them to my one, and Billy never takes no for an answer. Watch yourself around him, Jude. He's not used to a woman turning him down."

His speech confused her. Boone being who he was, she couldn't expect him to talk about their time together, or his regret that their partnership was about to end, but with the few remaining moments left between them, she could have hoped for something more personal than a discussion about his annoying friend. "Are you saying that's why he's tagging along? Because of *me?*"

Boone shrugged. "That's the trouble with Billy. You never quite know what he's up to. All I'm saying is, don't be taken in by the lazy charm. And whatever you do, never find yourself alone with him."

He turned then to approach the bed. For a crazy, dizzying instant, she held her breath, convinced that this was it, he was coming to her—he, too, realizing this could well be their last hours together. She knew any proper young lady would fend him off—whatever he'd said about Billy's dishonorable intentions must surely go double for Boone—but she was all too conscious that this could well be the last chance she'd have to know his touch, a knowledge she'd been unconsciously craving since the first moment she set eyes on him.

Yet even as she pictured herself melting in his arms as Lilah had done, Boone reached down to the bedside table for his gun. Taking it with him, he walked over to the makeshift bed on the floor.

Jude let out her breath, hoping the ache would go with it, but it settled in her throat in a big, unwieldy knot. Though she could no longer see him, the shaft of light not extending to that part of the room, she could hear Boone settle into the bedding. She should feel gratitude, she knew, not this sadness and loss.

He truly was a gentleman, she told herself firmly, and she was lucky to have such a strong and capable man guarding her door. Impossibly stubborn and as infuriating all get out, Tucker Boone was nonetheless a good and decent man.

Still she couldn't help wishing that this once, he could have been a little bit more of a cad.

At that moment Tucker didn't feel like a good and decent man. Across the room, he could hear Jude's gentle breathing, but the fact that she'd fallen asleep did nothing to ease his own tension. The thought of her near naked body, so close and yet so far away, made him regret he'd been raised to be a gentleman. What a hypocrite he'd been, warning

EVERY DREAM COME TRUE 191

her about Billy's attentions, when all he'd needed was one word, one glance of encouragement.

Damn, he swore silently. Why couldn't she stay a boy?

He knew his cravings were stupid, that any physical contact between them could lead only to disaster, yet it didn't stop him from aching in far more than his groin. Somewhere along the line, Jude had set off a yearning he wasn't prepared for, one he could neither stop nor understand.

Yet again he gazed at her peaceful form, framed by the moonlight, sleeping like an angel on the four-poster bed. Too well, he could remember how it felt to hold her while she slept, sensing her trust, knowing her warmth. Being around Jude left him hankering for the things she took for granted: a loving home, a happy family, the kind of life he'd given up on long ago. What was it about this woman that had him thinking that if he could just touch her—could hold and possess her—he, too, could have it all?

He rolled over, angry with himself. Weakness and rank stupidity, that's what it was. Life had hammered the lesson too often into his brain for him to be so careless in disregarding it now. Some folks were meant to wander the world, restless and alone, and any attempt to do otherwise ended badly. That's how it had been with his mama, and that's how it was with him. Hard experience had proven that Billy was right, that changing one's fate was nigh unto impossible.

Useless thoughts, going nowhere. How could one woman, in so short a time, burrow so deeply under his skin? He was itching to have her, aching in every inch of his body. And there she lay, all sweetness and light, trusting him not to harm her.

As if to refute this, she began to whimper softly. He cocked an ear, thinking at first that he'd imagined it, that the sound came from outside the room. But then it was repeated, louder this time, and with considerably more force. *"Papa, no!"* she cried out suddenly.

Without thinking, he jumped up to go to her side.

Fifteen

At first Jude thought she was still dreaming. Coming off the nightmare of facing her father again, it seemed too much a miracle to be safe and secure in Boone's arms. "It's all right," he crooned in her ear. "Nothing's gonna hurt you now."

And just like that, she knew she was safe.

"It was my papa," she tried to explain. "He was after me, but he caught sight of Christopher, coming to my rescue, his little hands flailing. Papa smiled, like it was his greatest joy in life to beat that little boy senseless, and when I saw his rifle, all I could think was that I couldn't let him hurt Christopher—not again."

"You killed your father?"

She could feel Boone stiffen. Next he'd withdraw and call her an unnatural daughter like her father and Uncle Henri. She began to shiver as she always did in the aftermath of these dreams, a bone-deep shuddering she couldn't control. "I just shot him in the leg," she explained, "but I made a mistake, only wounding him. It didn't stop him. It only made him more vicious."

To her relief, Boone didn't pull away. Tightening his grasp, he ran a soothing hand down her back.

Uncle Henri would tell her she didn't deserve comfort. She deserved to relive her guilt in her dreams, he'd claim. "My mind might know it's in the past," she told Tucker, trying to explain away her own confusion. "But here in my heart, I fear I'll never get over it. That I'll never stop hating my father for the evil he did to us."

Boone took her face in his hands, forcing her to look at him. "Knowing you, I'm sure you have every right to your hatred, but stop and consider who you're hurting the most. You've got too much ahead in life to let bitterness consume you. That way he wins, and you end up wasting the best years of your youth."

"Like you?"

He nodded, frowning. "Hatred is a hard taskmaster, Jude. It can enslave you, if you let it. Then there's no saving you."

Staring into his eyes, she felt again that loneliness in him, and her own aching need to banish it. All at once she could no longer fight the pull between them, no longer wanted to. "Then let's save each other," she said, reaching up to pull his head down to her own.

His groan was his only protest, the deep-throated moaning of a man who knew he was about to drown, before his mouth closed over her own.

When his lips touched hers, Jude felt a shot of ice-cold heat rocket through her body. His arms closed around her, pulling her to his chest, and she lost all sense of the world around her. Some small scrap of sense screamed out that she was being dangerously foolish, that a wise and proper young lady would run for her life. But her body clamored for more, her heart kept protesting that she'd never again have this chance, and together, they considered the world well lost if it meant getting nearer to this man.

Boone did little to discourage her. His tongue slid over her lips, coaxing them open, setting off yet another inner explosion as it probed the moist inner recesses of her mouth. Drowning in the sweet, melting need, she lost all sense of anything wrong. Nature took over, urging her to act as instinct demanded. All that existed was the here and now, and Boone's capable hands caressing her body.

She grew intensely aware of her flimsy shift. The cotton seemed suddenly too tight and chafing, too constricting across her swelling breasts. Finding that Boone wore nothing on his own chest, she ran her hands across the coarse hair and tight muscle. Another wave of desire, a force dark and demanding, swept through her as she realized that she was here in bed with this man, doing things she'd heretofore dreaded. To her amazement, she wanted him—wanted this—more than anything else in her life.

Arching her back, giving him silent invitation, she thrilled as his warm hand slid up to cup her breast. Pulling his lips from her mouth, he leaned down to kiss the captured breast through the thin cotton. It felt so strange, so exciting. She craved more, and he obliged her, sliding his tongue over the nipple until her shift was wet, then repeating the magic on her other breast.

Leaving her dizzy with pleasure, he pulled back. Staring at her, smiling, he returned to her mouth. Kissing her deeply, he ripped away the covers separating them, then stretched out beside her, his hot, bare chest meeting her own, sparking yet another white-hot wave of passion. More, her mind cried as he continued to drink from her mouth.

Groaning, whimpering, she sidled closer, wanting every bit of them touching. Her hands traveled over him, exploring each long, lean inch she'd watched so long from afar. She touched and savored all of him—his lush golden hair, the strong planes of his chest and muscled arms, the rough denim clasping his thighs.

He responded by sliding his hands up under her shift, finding all the intimate places, before slipping it over her head. Tossing it to the floor, he paused a moment to gaze down at her naked body. Oddly she didn't feel the least embarrassed to be lying there before him. Bold, even brazen, but the fire in his gaze as he smiled at her, the reverent way he touched her flesh, made her feel she was the most desirable thing in the world. He never actually mouthed the words *you're beautiful,* but it was there in his gaze and she felt them all the same.

Still smiling, he moved down to pay homage to her breasts. If she'd been excited before with the cotton between them, the sensation of hot tongue on bare nipple drove her clear out of her mind. Hands digging into his hair, she gripped his head like a woman possessed, arching her back higher and higher to meet him.

Nor did he stop there. His hands caressed all of her, twining through her hair, delving between her thighs into her most intimate place, coaxing her there, making her forget why she should ever ask him to stop. Everything he did, everywhere he touched, made her burn so, made her yearn so, she couldn't imagine ever denying him. Moaning into his mouth, kissing his sweet, salty skin, she felt herself straining, edging ever closer to something, though her desire-dazed brain couldn't figure out what that something could be.

And then he was kneeling before her, his denim trousers somehow shed. Naked and glorious, he parted her legs as he again gazed down at her face. "You're sure?" he asked, his voice hoarse and strained as if from exertion. "God, Jude, I don't want either of us ever regretting this."

He asked too much. She didn't want to think, didn't want to stop to consider what was wise or not—she just wanted him inside her. "Quit talking," she told him, pulling his head back down to hers. "You're much better at kissing."

Which he proved by twirling his tongue around hers, sweeping away all hesitation in the rising tide of passion. Kissing her as if *he* now could not get enough, he gripped her to him, pulling her hips against his as he slowly eased into her, not pushing, always watching her face before probing deeper yet. Smiling up at him, reveling with each new thrust, she couldn't believe how good it felt, how right, as if he'd always belonged there inside her.

She clung to him as if her life depended on it, joining

the rhythm of his movements, easing apart, then coming together with more and more force. Her fingers dug into his skin as the tempo increased, each thrust touching a chord deeper and deeper within her, setting off sensations she had little time to ponder. All she could do was feel, and what she felt was wonderful.

Higher and higher he took her, driving into her, driving out all the demons that once possessed her, and with each new wave of passion, she felt more cleansed, purified, until with a furious, shuddering explosion in her inner core, Jude came tumbling back to earth—and for the first time she could remember, feeling whole.

She held tight to Boone as she felt him spasm with his own tide of pleasure, thrilled that she could give him this, wishing she could give far more. After all these years, it had taken this man to prove she could be like any woman, that she could find such intense pleasure. His touch, the way he'd looked at her, showed that it was time to let go of her hatred, to forgive herself for the past. In more ways than he would probably ever know, Tucker Boone was her salvation.

And because of it, she did not whisper the words in her heart, did not speak at all for fear of what might come pouring out of her mouth. Even when he said, "Wow, that was incredible," and slid off to lie beside her, she merely smiled and softly uttered, "Yes, yes indeed."

Lying beside him in silence, she fought the urge to reach for him, to demand he love her again and again until the morning came to pull him away. Boone wasn't one to tolerate clinging females, she'd already learned, and she had no illusions that this had changed anything. If she wanted to repay this man for all he'd helped her feel, she must let him go tomorrow, as he'd requested. With no regrets and no recriminations.

He sighed suddenly, and she tensed, expecting him to

bring this up himself. "Your father," he asked instead, "did he rape you?"

His perception stunned her. No one else had ever thought to ask, not even her brothers. "It was the man he gave me to," she explained, surprised by how matter-of-fact she could sound. "Lost me to, actually, in a game of cards." Boone was the only person she'd ever told this to, but it seemed fitting to confide in him, to complete the cleansing process.

He rolled over on his side to stare at her, plainly appalled. "He used his own kid to pay off a debt?"

She nodded. "That day I told you about, from my dream, he was beating me for running away after that awful man—" She broke off, finding there were some things she still couldn't be casual about. "Papa never did have to pay his debt, it turned out. The sadistic beast who hurt me got caught cheating, and some other drunken sot put a bullet through his black heart."

"Where was your father? Your brothers? I'd have gone after the bastard and beaten him senseless for what he did to you."

It warmed her heart, how angry he sounded, but again she felt compelled to explain. "No one knew. The man died that night without telling anyone, and I was too ashamed to speak about it. Besides, Papa thought me a boy like my brothers."

Boone's handsome face clouded. "Your own father didn't know you were a girl?"

"I was young then, and he didn't care enough to look closer." How cold and stark the words sounded, but then that was life with Jacques Morteau. "Lying about my gender was something Mama started. She didn't want him beating her for having a girl, and later she hoped it would protect me. Papa despised females. Thought them weak and useless. Had I told him what that man did to me, he'd only say it was my fault anyway—that I'd asked for it. No, the shame of that night was something I kept buried inside me. I didn't want him casting it in my face for the rest of my life."

He took her face in his hands. "All this time you've never told anyone?"

"Not until tonight." Smiling, she touched his lips with a gentle finger. "The funny thing is, I don't feel ashamed anymore. Tonight . . . you, well, it was nice, Boone. Real nice."

Tenderly he gathered her into his arms. "The world can be such an ugly place, Jude," he said softly, kissing her hair. "How have you managed to stay so beautiful?"

The words brought tears to her eyes, but she was afraid to read too much into them. The last thing he'd expect now was any gushing on her part.

"Come on, settle here up against me," he said, turning her so that her back faced him and he could tuck his arms around her waist. "If you have any more bad dreams, don't worry. I'll be right here beside you."

And indeed she couldn't have felt any warmer or safer, cocooned in his embrace, the two of them cuddled up like spoons in a drawer. She listened to the slowing cadence of his breath, grateful for this chance to fall asleep with him. For now it hurt no one to pretend that they were true lovers, that he would be there protecting her for the rest of her life. The morning would be soon enough for facing the cold hard facts. Boone would have to leave, and she had to let him, and she had to be content with what she had at this moment.

Grasping the arm he wrapped around her, she felt the ache in her throat go tighter than ever.

"Fools!" Wadding up the wire, Lance Buford flung it across the Western Union office. Why was it he could never trust anyone else to do the job right?

When he'd told his lieutenant to keep an eye on their new scout and the girl, Lance hadn't meant to be taken so literally. Cochoran took too great a risk, staying so close to them. Lance had yet to learn much about this mysterious Boone he'd hired, but he did know better than to underestimate Jude Latour. Not recognizing his daughter's caginess had cost his partner, Jacques Morteau, his life.

Maybe it was time to pull the hook on young Cochoran, Lance thought as he marched out of the office. He could put someone else on the trail. Horner maybe or LaSalle—they knew the value of discretion.

Trouble was, they rarely got such spectacular results. Billy Cochoran had a flair for the dramatic that sometimes bordered on lunacy, but no one in the gang could do the job—any job—better.

Ah, he could be worrying overmuch, Lance thought, as he started down the dusty street of Salvation. After all Cochoran wasn't the only one he had working on this. Any day now he expected to hear from Henri Morteau.

He scratched his collar, feeling uneasy about the man's lack of response. Lance would have thought cagey old Henri would jump at the chance at revenge, but after financing the train heist, the man seemed to have dropped out of sight.

Shrugging off his anxiety, Lance refused to stew over it. Morteau would come around in time, and if not, Lance could explore other options. One way or the other—and he didn't much care how—he meant to find Rafe Latour, and make that pretty little wife of his a widow.

Too bad the search had to take so long and cost so much money.

Lance didn't like being frustrated or denied what he rightly deserved. God had put him on the earth to be a wealthy landowner. Folks interfering with that made him ornery, and that made him need an outlet for his rage.

Staring at the wood-framed building at the far end of the

street, he smiled. Remembering the evening before, he decided Lilah's place was just what he needed to soothe ruffled feathers. Whiskey, gambling, and women were all part and parcel of his birthright, and nowhere could he find all three in greater abundance than in the Lucky Lady Saloon.

Determined to drown his woes in every vice the place had to offer, he strode through the batwing doors as if he owned it. Not three steps into the barroom, the proprietress herself came to greet him, all but busting out of her purple satin gown. Lord, but Lance loved big-breasted women.

"What has you looking so glum, sugar?" Lilah crooned, taking his arm to lead him to the best seat in the house. "You just sit right down, and let Lilah show you just how much you have to smile about."

He had no doubt of her ability, having spent the entire night before in her bed. Lusty and uninhibited, she'd actually liked it the rougher he played. Some women tried to fake their enjoyment, hoping to please him, but no matter what he did, Lilah couldn't seem to get enough. All things considered, he was looking forward to seeing what he could make this little tiger do for him tonight.

Reaching up, he pulled her down onto his lap. "You do that, sweet thing," he growled in her ear, biting the lobe as he reached inside her gown to pinch a nipple. "You give this old soldier what he needs."

She squirmed in his lap, making him hard with desire, acting as if she were the seducer. Lilah might be used to calling the shots, but Lance had bedded enough women to know she was hot for him, desperate for what he alone could give her, and that in itself gave him power. If he played her right, giving so much but never quite enough, he'd have her doing most anything to please him.

It hadn't escaped his notice that she, too, could be a useful alternative to fall back on. He'd been told Lilah was a powerful woman—and an undeniably wealthy one. Her money would go a long way toward making him invincible.

Not that he'd return the favor. He'd let Lilah think they were partners, but sharing anything with a woman went contrary to his plans. Despite what he'd told Cochoran and his minions, his quest had never been to save the Confederacy. Lance used such ideals, and the people who believed in them, to further his own "Cause." What he'd always sought was the position of privilege and ease that he'd been born to, a special world that included Guin McCloud and her husband's plantation. In Lance's opinion, it was the least life owed him.

And he would not rest until he had it all.

Sixteen

Tucker woke slowly, aware that something was different, but too dazed yet with sleep to identify what had changed. As he felt the warmth beside him, a smile crept over his lips. Glancing down, he found Jude nestled up against him, as naked and trusting as the day she'd been born.

The smile faded as he thought about her quiet confession last night, delving into its implications as he should have done then had he not been so exhausted. How like Jude to carry around that burden all these years. Rape. What sort of father could be so blind to her suffering, to the fact that he'd caused it?

Stupid question. He knew. It was the cruel bastard who had disregarded his own pleas. Rafe Latour was that blind, uncaring father.

A burning rage seeped into him as the pieces sifted into place. Years of hurt, anger, and hatred had fueled her thirst for vengeance. No wonder she'd insisted on tagging along, on being there when Tucker found Latour. To get back her youth, to save her belief in the future, Jude had to confront the monster who had birthed her.

Gazing down at her delicate, vulnerable features, Tucker's rage against the man took on another dimension. So much for paying any heed to talk about Latour's goodness and sense of fair play. Most monsters wore pretty faces in public, he'd learned, and here, sleeping next to him, was the proof of how vile a man could secretly be. Were Latour to walk into the room this moment, Tucker would happily kill him with his bare hands.

Looking down, he noticed he had actually clenched his fists.

Daunted by the sudden intensity of his emotions, Tucker took a mental step backward. What had gotten into him? He had other priorities—he had no business feeling so fiercely protective. Hadn't he troubles enough of his own without getting sucked into Jude's, too?

Disgusted with himself, he eased away from her and left the bed. He'd known it would be a mistake to sleep with this woman. Last night, with her hot body pressed against him, he'd deluded himself into thinking it could be just that once. In the clear light of morning, however, he could see that they'd shared far more than their bodies. By confiding in him, Jude had formed a bond between them, an involvement he'd find damned hard to walk away from.

Yet he must walk way, he insisted, as he gathered his clothes and began to dress. He had his own goals to consider. All he wanted from this woman was his wages. He didn't need guilt and recriminations, and he sure didn't need complications. His was a long, hard road that was best traveled alone.

So why then did his gaze keep straying back to that bed?

Against his will, he stared at Jude's sweet little body, curled up with her hands tucked beneath her cheek. She seemed so young, defenseless, he had to harden his heart to keep from striding over to her. Last night was a mistake, he chided himself again. Only a fool would repeat it.

Forcing his gaze away, he finished dressing. He decided not to wake her, to go to the detention camp by himself. Better to get this all over and done with, without Billy or even Jude examining his motives.

Reaching for his gun, he caught his reflection in the mirror and didn't much like the sight. Taking what Jude generously offered, then stealing away like a thief—he'd become every bit the cad she'd called him.

He imagined her waking alone, confused and undoubtedly hurt. The honorable thing to do would be to stay and explain why he was working for Billy, but that would mean more sharing and deeper involvement, and where would that get either of them in the end? Sooner or later he'd still have to leave her.

All things considered, it would be simpler and kinder if he walked off now without glancing back.

He couldn't do it though. Looking down at her—remembering how it felt to touch her, hold her, hear her laugh—he could not make his feet take a step.

As if wakened by the heat of his gaze, she stirred, a lazy, languid stretch of her naked body that proved all too dramatically what he'd be giving up if he left her now. Then she blinked up at him, looking so adorable, so desirable, he felt that now too familiar lurch in his chest.

Before he could speak, she popped up with the sheet wrapped tight to her body to stand facing him on the far side of the bed. "I forgot. We're going to the prison this morning. Look at you, already dressed and here I am—" Glancing down at the sheet, clasping it tighter, she turned red from her head to her toes. "Give me five minutes," she added, talking much too rapidly. "I swear, I won't take longer than that."

With a bright smile, she began darting about the room, gathering up articles of clothing, chattering like a bird. "I hadn't meant to sleep late. It's been years since I slept so soundly. No nightmares, not even a dream. Except that one of course," she corrected, her voice trailing off.

"Jude," he began, feeling at a loss. To listen to her now, he'd never know how completely she'd melted in his arms mere hours ago. He waited for a sign—a word, a gesture—anything to prove last night meant more than mere physical gratification.

"Don't worry," she said, refusing to look in his direction. "There's no need to explain. Last night was wonderful, and it restored my faith in men, but I never expected more to come of it. I know that you and I have separate roads to travel—and with any luck, both our journeys should start today. I, for one, would like to say our goodbyes with a smile. Let's not clutter them up with remorse."

It struck him that he should have been the one to say those words. At the least he should be welcoming her speech and the ease with which he could now stroll away, but instead he felt as if he'd been poleaxed. He *did* want something to come of it, he realized, something more than a "gee, that was swell, but I'll be moving on to someone else."

Still she wouldn't turn to face him. Clutching the damned sheet like a shield, a bright, beaming smile pasted on her face, she spoke to the mirror. "I shall always value your friendship, Boone. Let's leave it at that."

Friendship? "Whatever the lady wants," he said calmly enough, reining in all emotion. "After all, you're the boss."

"For just a few more hours."

He thought he heard a hint of regret, but saw no sense in pursuing it. He'd only be talking to her back. Her ramrod-stiff back. "I'll meet you downstairs," he told her in the same level tone. "Take your time in getting dressed."

He strode through the door, not looking back. In truth wasn't that the way to leave it? Just the way he'd lived his entire life. Boone, ever the gentleman. Ever the friend.

And once more left on his own.

"Your father is not here, Miss Latour," the officer of the day told her in a regretful tone. "We had orders for his transfer, two weeks before the surrender."

Fighting the tears she'd been holding back all morning, Jude wondered how much more she could take. She and

Boone had learned back at the hotel that the detention camp had been closed, but they could try Union headquarters for information. They'd been directed to this harried captain, but the man's tight smile warned that this might be something she did not want to know at all. "I don't understand, Captain Moore. We were told this would be his last stop—that from here, he'd be processed out and sent home."

Young and handsome, and clearly unhappy with the role assigned him, Moore audibly cleared his throat. "And so he should have been, but your father was part of a prisoner exchange, sent to an army post in the South, two weeks before the surrender."

"Then why wasn't he released and sent home from there?" The question came from Boone. It surprised Jude, since he'd been remarkably close-lipped, acting as if all that mattered was finishing the job, getting paid, and taking the first stage out of town.

Facing him, Captain Moore looked decidedly uncomfortable. "It was no ordinary transfer. The reason I remember Latour is because we were served with extradition papers. The Confederacy wanted him on charges of desertion, and as I recall, there was some mention of treason."

"No!" Jude could hardly believe that was her voice, so shrill and harsh. But it seemed too much, suddenly. After all she'd been through, she couldn't bear to hear such an unjust accusation leveled against Rafe now.

"Treason's a hanging offense, isn't it?" Boone asked calmly.

Captain Moore dropped all pretense of a smile. "I wouldn't know the laws and punishment of the Confederate government. You'd have to check the records at the post where he was sent."

"But this has to be wrong!" Jude blurted out, knowing Rafe would never betray his fellow soldiers. A more dependable man had yet to be born.

"This post," Boone asked quickly, eyeing Jude as if

afraid she might explode any moment. "Can you tell us where it is?"

Moore paused to think a moment before slowly shaking his head. "Offhand, I can't remember details, but we have the paperwork somewhere. My aide will be in the office later in the day, so if you return this afternoon, we should be able to locate the information. The Union army wants to help you find your loved ones," he assured Jude. "We have no wish to keep you from your father, Miss Latour."

Boone frowned, but Jude was too upset to pay heed. In her heart she'd truly expected to see Rafe. To learn he was still missing, to think he might even have been hanged as a traitor with no one knowing, made the setback harder to bear. She wanted to set off after him now, this instant—but it was clear that they'd stretched this busy officer's patience enough, and she had no choice but to wait out the hours for yet another frustrating lead.

Hurrying her out of the office, Boone seemed to share her frustration, and once out on the street he gave vent to it. "Wasn't that a bit too convenient?"

Bewildered, she looked up at his angry profile. "What do you mean?"

"Call me paranoid, but how many places can one prisoner be transferred to? I'm beginning to feel like a puppet, and someone is pulling my strings."

"You think he's being moved about for a reason?" she asked. Thinking back to how Rafe always seemed one step away from them, she could see a crazy logic to what he'd implied. "Who'd have the power to do this? And why?"

Boone shrugged. "If I knew that, I might be able to do something about it. A good deal more than waiting for some lazy aide to report in to work."

"And now we haven't a prayer of Billy not accompanying us." Leaving so early, they'd managed to skip out of the hotel without him this morning, but she couldn't hope he'd sleep straight through to the afternoon.

"The fun never stops," Boone said dryly.

Jude thought about Boone's theory about this puppeteer, wondering who it could be. "Why are Billy and those men following us?" she asked distractedly. "Are they being manipulated, too, or are they pulling the strings?"

Boone looked suddenly uncomfortable as he hurried them down the street. "Hard telling why Billy does half the things he does, but we can rule out his being responsible. His being here has to do with me and a debt he claims I owe him."

"Can't we lose him? You can settle up with him later, when your job for me is done."

"Yeah, well, it's not as simple as that," he said curtly. "We'll have to put up with Billy for a little while longer."

He left it at that, and Jude let him, knowing she had no intention of letting Billy know anything more about Rafe. She didn't trust that man, and if Boone insisted upon letting him tag along, maybe she shouldn't trust Boone, either.

The thought caused a pang, and she wished he'd say something to dispel her doubts, but an awkward silence had fallen between them as they walked into the hotel and up to their room. So much for easing the tension by making no demands on him. He acted as if he couldn't wait to get away from her.

Once in their hotel room, he proved this by announcing that he was going out, that he had some errands to run, and he wanted her staying put.

"Errands?" she sputtered, hurt that he could still act like the autocratic bully, that he could so effectively shut her out after the night they had shared.

"It's, er, personal business," he added, pausing at the door. "Should be back by three to go to see Captain Moore," he told her, closing the door—both figuratively and literally in her face.

She wouldn't be here at three, she told the door. She'd collect Rooster, and they'd get to Moore's office by noon,

EVERY DREAM COME TRUE

and too bad for Mr. Love-Them-and-Leave-Them Boone if he missed out on the information.

Working herself into a fine state, she stomped over to the window to watch him leave the hotel. No visit to the dry goods store for Boone, no trip to the Western Union or even the bank. With quick sure strides, he marched to the stables and rode out not ten minutes later on a big brown gelding, racing to the west.

Damn him, she thought angrily, even while knowing she should be damning her own stupidity. Obviously her little act hadn't been convincing this morning. A man like Boone, so averse to commitment, could no doubt sniff out pent-up tears a million miles away.

She could feel them stinging her eyes now, but she refused to cry, to be that pathetic. She'd made her gesture, had tried to be noble, and she couldn't resent Boone merely because he'd taken her up on it. Hadn't she known he would?

No, she hadn't, and that was why she now felt like her world was crumbling.

Startled by the sudden knock on her door, she didn't think twice before racing to open it. Logically she knew Boone was long gone, but it didn't stop the pang of disappointment at facing Rooster instead.

"Here, I rustled these up for you," he muttered, thrusting a small bundle into her arms. "Hurry and change while I hire horses. Sneak down the back stairs, so that Billy can't see you, and meet me at the stables. Way I figure it, Boone has a half hour start on us, but that should be okay. I overheard him tell the desk clerk where he's headed."

Taken aback, Jude tried to absorb the implications behind all he'd uttered, but Rooster was already off and running. "Wait," she called out. "What's going on? Where did you get these clothes? And how will you pay for horses?"

Pausing only to grin back at her, he patted his pocket. "Hurry," he called over his shoulder as he raced down the hall. "I think this could be interesting."

She called after him again, but he ignored her, disappearing down the stairs. Staring after him, Jude knew she had two choices. She could stay and make sure she got the lead she needed or risk everything by following after Boone.

Muttering to herself, she ducked back into the room to don the pants and shirt Rooster had provided, ripping up yet another petticoat to bind her breasts. Her hands were trembling when she at last crept out of the hotel, being far too aware of the risks involved and the need for haste. By the time she met Rooster at the stables, her heart was racing, too, with a mixture of anxiety and exhilaration.

If she'd hoped the boy would enlighten her as to what lay ahead, she was doomed to disappointment. Hopping into the saddle, Rooster nudged his horse down the street, leaving her to follow or be left behind.

She caught up with him at the end of town. "I must say, you never cease to surprise me, Rooster O'Leary. Since you're so grudging with your information, I suppose you're not going to tell me where you learned to ride a horse, either?"

"I spent some time on a farm," he said with a shrug, and something in his tone warned her not to press. That time couldn't have been pleasant. She wondered if the farm was where he'd learned to be so afraid of falling asleep.

Having come this far, she reasoned she might as well trust Rooster to the finish, so she rode beside him in silence, studying the countryside. The farther they rode from town, the more devastation she noticed. They'd fought a different war here, she remembered Billy saying, and with each burned field or charred building, she could see why they called this area the Wasteland.

Some attempts had been made at rebuilding. Here and there she saw barns being raised, farmers reworking the land, but such effort was rare. People must be wary, unwilling to return to the scene of so much death and suffering. No doubt it would be some time before the region fully recovered.

Passing by yet another burned-out farmhouse, she heard Rooster sigh beside her. "My folks had a place like that," he said quietly.

Surprised that he would tell her anything about himself, Jude couldn't stop the question. "What happened?"

He shrugged, as if it had happened to someone else. "Jayhawkers came one night with their rifles and torches. Next thing I knew, there was nothing left. No house, no orchard . . . no family."

It broke her heart, the matter-of-fact way he told it. He was just a boy, far too young to accept such random cruelty. She wanted to hug him, to let him know she was sorry for his loss, but being Rooster, he would reject the gesture.

"My dad," he added in the same careless tone. "He was a lot like Boone."

That explained the hero worship.

And it made her angry at Boone all over again. Cutting out on her was one thing—he had reason to avoid the scene she couldn't help but eventually make—but how could he leave this poor, adoring kid without saying goodbye? He had to know his leaving would hurt Rooster, that it would give the boy even less reason to expect much out of life.

It would serve Boone right if he felt awkward when they finally caught up with him. And if he didn't have the decency to be embarrassed, she'd make good and certain to remind him why he should.

She had her opportunity, less than an hour later, as they pulled up a short distance away from a huge rambling farmhouse, complete with a white picket fence and monstrous red barn. Unlike its neighbors, this farm was intact and fully functioning, as evidenced by the sheep in the pen and chickens pecking in the yard. A sign out front pronounced it to be the Fosterville Home for Children.

Children? Jude wondered, finding it hard to believe anyone under the age of thirty lived in the place. Where were the toys, the smudgy fingerprints, the shouts and laughter her own brothers and sisters could never contain? The unearthly quiet emanating from the house belonged more in a church. If she were a child, she would hate living in such a mausoleum.

Glancing over at Rooster's pursed lips, seeing his reluctance to take another step, the sign's significance finally dawned on her. Maybe this wasn't the actual farm he'd spent some time on, but it must have been one much like it. The sign was misleading. It wasn't a home, it was an orphanage.

Only question was, what were they doing here? More to the point, what was Boone doing here?

She could see the brown gelding, chomping at grass the orphanage kids would probably have to replant, but could find no sign of Boone himself. He must be inside, she reasoned, but as the implications sifted in and she remembered his taciturn departure, she was no longer sure she wanted to confront him.

"Quick, let's wait in that grove," she told Rooster. "We can watch from there, but it's probably best if Boone doesn't see us."

Rooster might not be one for blabbing about himself, but to his credit, he didn't waste time with unnecessary questions, either. Nodding, he followed her to the grove, both of them dismounting and concealing their horses, a feat they managed mere moments before Boone came striding out of the house. Catching a glimpse of his face, she was glad they'd decided to hide. The man didn't look much in the mood for conversation.

Any anger she'd felt toward him dissipated at the sight of his tortured expression. It had never been his intention to run from responsibility, she realized. If anything, the man had come running to face it—and emotionally speaking, it had punched him right in the gut.

EVERY DREAM COME TRUE

In three strides Boone was on the gelding and thundering off. Next to her a bewildered Rooster asked if they weren't going to follow. "Not yet," she told him, tethering her horse and motioning toward the house. "I need to find out what happened in there first."

He tried to protest, but Jude ignored him as she strode to the gate, reaching it just as a harried, middle-aged female bustled onto the porch. "Mr. Boone?" the woman cried out in a reedy, trembling voice. "Oh, dear, Mr. Boone, where are you? I have it here, the paper you needed."

Jude glanced at Rooster, who couldn't look more ready to bolt. "I'm . . . I mean, we . . . er, we're both with Mr. Boone," she told the woman. "He asked us to wait for the paper, ma'am. He wants you to give it to us."

The woman eyed her outstretched hand over her spectacles, as if sensing something not quite right. "Are you boys saying you know Mr. Boone?"

"He's, er, our uncle," Jude lied, well aware that she knew far less about him than she obviously should.

"Oh, my." The woman reminded her of a hen, the way she kept making quick, darting motions with her head, looking from one to the other of them. "Then you must be the twins' cousins."

Twins? Anxious to learn more, Jude took a step closer. "Me and Mikey, here, we're helping Uncle Tucker get the money for the farm."

It was a stab in the dark, but she struck pay dirt. Brightening, the woman held out the sheet of paper. "Well, of course you'll want this then. But do remind your uncle that the note must be paid by the end of next month. If he waits to year's end, like he'd hoped, the land already will have reverted back to the state."

Taking the paper, Jude saw that it was a notice of foreclosure for a fifty-acre plot northwest of Fosterville, land owned by a Sarah Elizabeth Holland. Boone's mother, she had to assume.

"While you're here," the woman said pleasantly, "I imagine you want to see your cousins?"

She looked so pleased with herself, and in truth she offered a lure Jude found hard to resist. She could probably learn a great deal about Boone from his brothers. What could a quick little visit hurt?

"Of course visitors are not usually permitted during work time," the woman went on, her plump face softening with concern. "I can hear Headmistress Hattie now. 'Edna Clarke' she'll say, 'you're too soft-hearted for your own good.' But what am I to do? Poor dears can't have seen kinfolk in ages, and it will mean so much to Jeremy. Jacob has learned to adjust somewhat, but Jeremy still misses his family dreadfully. He cries at night for his mother, you know. An awful thing, watching her die like that."

Those poor little boys, Jude thought, more determined than ever to meet Boone's brothers.

Rooster didn't seem nearly as eager, but he trudged along beside her as the chirping Mrs. Clarke led them through the house. "You'll have to wait in the back while I sneak them to you," the woman cautioned worriedly. "It will never do should Headmistress Hattie find out. She has strict rules about work hours."

Work hours? Jude wondered, but was afraid to speak. The silence of the house seemed even more oppressive the farther they moved into it.

Pushing them into a monklike cell with a desk, three chairs, and a single narrow window, Mrs. Clarke waddled off in search of the boys. "Don't move," she warned before she left, "or we all could be in a great deal of trouble."

"Trouble," Rooster said, the instant they were alone. "I should say so. You ever stop to think that them two boys know they ain't got any cousins? What do you think will happen if they tell anyone that?"

"We'll just say we made a mistake."

He rolled his eyes. "You can't know what it's like in

these places, Jude. That headmistress. Wanna bet she has a cane or a strap?"

Jude laughed uneasily. "Listen to you. You make the woman sound like some evil slaveholder, like the ones caricatured in Yankee cartoons."

"What makes you think she ain't? Them kids might as well be slaves. You see this place, how nice it looks? Can't get that on what the state pays them. They make up the difference by working them kids to the bone."

"The bone?" Jude asked, appalled. "How can children earn money?"

"Farming, sewing, shipped out as cheap labor. Don't feed them, don't waste much on clothes, and there's your profit. And no fear of getting caught, either. Heck, they're just kids, with no one to fight for them. Who's gonna care or even notice?"

"But that's atrocious. No, it's impossible. Boone would never let such a thing happen to his own little brothers."

"Boone wouldn't know. When he comes, they trot the boys out for a visit, all pleasant like, with the headmistress watching like a hawk in the corner."

He couldn't have made the image more vivid. "You speak as if you know this from experience."

Rooster merely shrugged, crossing to the window. "There, look at that."

Joining him, following his pointed finger, she saw children working the fields under the hot sun. Their bent postures, their lack of animation—everything about the scene seemed grim.

"Let's just say I wouldn't want to live here," Rooster added bitterly. "Even the wharves are better than this."

She faced him, aching for this boy, fearing the kind of life he must have led. "You don't have to live on the wharves," she told him. "You could always come with me to my home in Louisiana."

Far from enthused, he stared out the window. "Don't you think your folks will be wanting a say in this?"

She smiled, thinking about Guin's reaction. "At Camelot there's always a place at the table and a job to be done. Trust me, my mama will be thrilled to have you join us. She's always wanted another son."

"Yeah, but I ain't her kid."

"Nor am I. But that didn't stop her from making me and my brothers her own. It's a good place, Rooster. You'll like it. Plenty of food and love and no reason to think twice about falling asleep at night."

He gave that last a snort. The cynic in him couldn't believe there was such a place, and from what she had seen of his world, she couldn't blame him. "Can't you at least give us a try? Give yourself the chance to thrive and grow?"

"Ain't me who needs a home," he said gruffly. "It's them, his brothers." Looking about him, he shuddered. "Trapped in here, they don't stand a chance."

Impossible to hide her dismay. "Rooster, you can't expect me to take them away from this place?"

"Not alone," he said eagerly. "I'd help."

"You don't know what you're asking."

The boy shrugged, a gesture he used to mask real emotion. "You're the one who's out to save the world. Didn't know you was so selective."

"That's not fair. I already have obligations. Complications." She took a breath, determined to make him see why taking the boys with them would *not* be a good idea, but a door opened down the hallway, and both of them froze. No voices accompanied the sound, not even a whisper, just slow shuffling footsteps approaching the door.

Nor did the unnatural silence ease as two somberly garbed boys, no more than eight or nine, entered the room. Standing close enough to each other to be one body, they did much to lend credence to Rooster's allegations. The black woolen uniforms did little for their sallow expressions or their bony little frames.

"Jacob, Jeremy," she said, extending a hand in greeting as she approached them. "I'm Jude, and this is Rooster, and we've come a long way to help you."

Rooster snorted, and the boys continued to eye her suspiciously. "First things first," she went on slowly, hoping to gain their trust. "I want you to know we're with your brother."

"Jesse?" they breathed in unison, speaking with the same awe Rooster invariably showed at the mere mention of his hero's name. "I mean, Tucker," Jacob corrected, looking chagrined. "That's what he wants us calling him now."

"Yes, I know. He's working for me, helping me find someone. But boys, I need to know, do you like being here in this orphanage?"

They looked around them, then back to the door, before shaking their heads cautiously. The taller one put an arm about his sniffling brother. She assumed, from what Mrs. Clarke had said that he must be Jacob. "We stay here 'cause Jesse needs us to," he told her with a quiet pride. "It won't be much longer."

"I should say not. In fact you'll be leaving right now. With us."

Rooster's stunned expression, then slow, beaming grin was all she could ask for, and almost worth the abuse she'd inevitably take from Boone.

The boys didn't share his enthusiasm. In unison they turned fearful heads toward the door. "Headmistress Hattie won't never let us go," Jacob stated simply. "She needs to finish that order for Union uniforms."

Sickened by the woman's greed and determined to get the boys away from it, Jude hunkered down before them. "She can stop you only if she knows you are going. Which she won't, if we leave right now. This means trusting me, no questions asked. I swear to you, I mean to get you out of this awful place and back to your brother, Jesse."

The name did it. Obviously the prospect of being with their older brother was all the impetus they needed. Nodding solemnly, Jacob asked what she wanted them to do.

She held out a hand to each. "Actually I think we should run."

Before they could take a step forward, they heard a distant door slam, then determined footsteps in the hall headed their way. Jude turned to Rooster. "Any suggestions?"

He nodded at the open window.

"Help them outside," she whispered, nudging the boys in his direction. "I'll prop one of these chairs against the door."

She managed to wedge the chair in, just before the knob began to rattle. "Jacob Holland, open up this instant," a stern voice commanded, a far cry from the timid Edna Clarke. Plainly the dreaded Headmistress Hattie. "Open this door, boy, or I'll give you the caning you richly deserve."

Racing to the window, Jude gave a few forced coughs, hoping the woman would think the boys—at least Jeremy—were still in the room. The longer she kept rattling the door, the more time they'd have before an alarm could be sounded.

Jude was lifting her leg over the windowsill when she saw the chair give way. Chanting a series of prayers and promises, she raced across the yard, chickens scattering out of her way. Up ahead she noticed the quick-witted Rooster had brought the horses closer and already had both boys mounted, all three skinny behinds securely in one saddle. "Go," she shouted as she neared. "Get them out of here. I can catch up later."

It wasn't much of a jailbreak, considering their only pursuit was by two middle-aged women running as far as the gate, Mrs. Clarke twisting her hands in her apron and

Headmistress Hattie shaking a fist in the air. Still neither Jude nor Rooster saw any reason to slow until they were a good ways down the road.

Coming to a stop at last, they both broke into chuckles, while the two little boys looked more solemn than ever. "Hey, crack a smile," Jude told them. "We did it. You're free."

Jacob looked over his shoulder. "Yeah, but this isn't the way to Jesse. He took the north road to the farm."

Remembering the bill for back taxes, Jude knew they must mean their family home. She exchanged a worried glance with Rooster, who nodded at the boys clutched together on the saddle behind him. "We'll never make it there and back to town again. Maybe I should take these two back to the hotel and let them get rested up. You go after Boone."

It was a monumental thing, leaving the safety of Boone's two little brothers in the hands of the boy who had stolen her carpetbag, but she realized that earning her trust was important to Rooster. And in truth did she have another option? "Okay, but no buying sweets or running wild in the halls."

"Yeah, yeah. If you don't sound like a mother."

"I didn't hear your promise."

"Okay, I promise. Happy now?" He softened the words with a reluctant smile. "Don't worry, Jude. Me and the boys will be fine."

Jacob and Jeremy didn't look fine. Their sad little faces as they rode off, with lips atremble and eyes wide with fright, might have had her reconsidering if she wasn't so worried about Boone. She couldn't forget his fierceness as he'd thundered off, and she was afraid he was liable to do something foolish.

Racing along the north road, she knew an impatient need to see him. She didn't know what she could do to stop him from acting rashly, or even what to expect when she found him. Her fears ran the gamut from finding him holding a gun to a prospective buyer's head, to wrecking the place before letting anyone else have it—but nothing in her imagination prepared her for the sight that greeted her eyes when she at last pulled up to the Holland farm.

Tucker Boone stood alone on the grassy knoll, staring blankly at a sunken hole in the earth. He didn't move, didn't even turn his head as she rode up, as if unaware that anything but his own private hell existed.

And it must have been far too like a hell that night, she thought, as she dismounted. Everywhere she looked, she could see traces of the fire—the house, the barn, the woods—nothing had been spared the torch. Here and there patches of grass and wildflowers had sprouted up from the ashes, silent testimonials to the persistence of life—but nothing else remained to prove anyone had lived here, save perhaps the charred foundation at which Boone now stared.

She dismounted slowly, searching for the right thing to say, for anything that would not sound inane, for she had never seen anyone in more need of comfort. Aching for him, she longed to hold him tight, to cradle his head against her heart.

"Go away, Jude," he said lifelessly. "There's nothing for you here."

All things considered, it was far from an auspicious start.

Seventeen

Boone didn't know if he was glad or sorry to see Jude standing there, viewing this testament to his past. Leaving their hotel room this morning, he'd tried to make peace with the fact that they'd follow separate paths, so to see her here now, where his hopes had begun and so painfully ended, was just one more twist of the knife in his soul.

Staring at her, it struck him suddenly, and far deeper than he'd like, how perfectly Jude blended in with his dreams for this place. He wasn't fooling anyone, certainly not himself, by barking at her to go. He didn't want her to leave—he wished for some small miracle to entice her to stay.

But there were no miracles—not here, not for him. What was it with fate, that it seemed so bound and determined to deny him, yet at the same time tempt him with visions of what might have been. . . .

All too soon they'd be taking even this land away, and there wasn't much he could do to stop them.

"What happened here?" Jude asked in a hushed voice, looking about her with a pained expression. "Was it the Federals who burned down your house?"

How like her not to stay in the hotel like he'd asked her, to spend the time tracking him here. *Your house,* she'd said, yet how could she have known? No one in Independence could connect him with this place. Except maybe Billy and Lord only knew what he might have told her.

"It might have been easier to take if it were Federals," Tucker answered, wanting her to know his version of the story. "Even jayhawkers would have been understandable. Hell, war is war, and you have to expect casualties, but nobody ever warned me to expect such brutality from my own side."

"Confederates did this?" Her dark eyes went round with horror. Obviously this was something no one had told her. "Are you sure?"

He couldn't stop the bitter laugh. "That's exactly what Colonel Shelby asked. He wondered if maybe bushwhackers had burned us out, members of my old troop getting revenge on me for mustering out of the unit to join the regular army. Some of them could be a vicious bunch, and I'd have wondered, too, had I not then been tracking for Confederate troops in the area. As scouts we often caught wind of upcoming maneuvers, and I'd heard that one local unit had an eye on Curtis Holland. He was running for Congress as a staunch Unionist, and they seemed to think they could force him to withdraw from the race by threatening his mistress and her family."

"Your mother," she said quietly.

"She was his wife, not his mistress!" At her startled expression, he tried to ease his tone. "The Hollands had the marriage annulled, but my mother never signed the papers. In her heart she was wed until the day she died."

Despite gentling his voice, Tucker could hear his rage and bitterness in every syllable and he imagined Jude could, too. "Holland had abandoned my mother years ago," he went on, reasoning Jude might as well know the whole of it. "So it made no sense to think he would care what happened to her. The last time he visited was in '57, a three-day stop at the whorehouse that left my mother crying, and with yet two more babies to care for. I was fifteen then, and feeling my oats, so I went storming to that fancy house of his. Never did get to talk to Curtis, but his brother, who was his campaign manager, seemed interested in my threats. Soon after, lawyers drew up the deed for this farm. Mama called it proof that Curtis truly cared about us, but I knew it was just a matter of greasing wheels and easing a guilty conscience. He certainly never bothered to come see his sons."

"It was his loss then."

Jude, ever the defender of lost causes.

"Yeah, well, what Curtis Holland did or didn't feel had no real bearing on that raid. I tried explaining this to the captain in charge, hoping to disabuse him of the notion that our farm held any military value. I talked for over an hour to that man, explaining that he'd be doing Curtis a favor. He'd just be relieving the man of an unwanted responsibility, '62 being an election year and the Hollands not anxious to have their dirty laundry aired. The captain listened politely, looking me in the eye, and I left for another mission, believing he'd spare my mother's home. It wasn't until later in the week that I learned the man had been pacifying me and laughing behind my back."

A slow rage built inside him as he thought of Latour that day, so calm and reassuring to him, then so brutally cold to his mother the same night. "Needless to say, he attacked anyway, and so viciously, no one could doubt his intent. If I've learned nothing from war, it's the fact that some men just plain enjoy killing. A woman with two small boys and no man to protect them must have been a ripe plum too hard to resist. And stupid, trusting me landed the prize in his lap."

"Boone, no." Gripping the reins to her horse, Jude shook her head. "You can't be blaming yourself for what those men did."

How could he not? "I should have been here. My mother begged me not to go off to war, said she couldn't keep the farm going without me, but I didn't want to be a farmer. I wanted to raise horses, and when the bushwhackers came by, tempting me with tales of the loot they'd won in their raids, I saw my chance to earn money. I was as bad as the rest of them. It didn't dawn on me, until too late, that for me to prosper, others had to suffer."

"But you were young—"

"I was old enough to know better," he growled, his anger directed at himself. "I tried making amends by joining the regular army, which was by then planning its invasion of Missouri, but I might better have come home. I left my mother alone to face those soldiers, to protect this farm and my four-year-old brothers. They say she must have known what was coming the instant she heard horses riding up because she made the twins hide in the root cellar. Neighbors found the boys days later, still huddled in the corner, too frightened to move or speak."

"Oh, Boone."

He looked away, guilt and regret tightening his throat. "I was fifty miles south of here, serving my own interests, while my fellow soldiers beat my mother senseless and left her to burn in this house." He turned back to Jude, fixing her with his gaze. "You still wonder why I left the army without looking back?"

"No." She stared back, her gaze and resolve never wavering. "In your place I'd have done the same."

He nodded, silently thanking her for that concession. "Even after it was over and done, no one had the decency to inform me. My little brothers were carted off to an orphanage. When I finally learned the truth, it was too late to help them. By then the state had custody."

"But surely you were old enough to assume responsibility?"

"Do you think a Union state would hand over two young boys to Jesse Holland, known bushwhacker? Present myself as their brother, and I'd have been condemned as an outlaw and clapped in prison. No, I had to pretend to be their uncle Tucker. It gets me visiting privileges, but without a

EVERY DREAM COME TRUE 225

home or visible means of support, I'm told, no judge will grant me custody."

"But your brothers have this farm," she protested. "The land, at least, they should have inherited."

"Yeah, and with it seven years in back taxes." He kicked out at a stone at his feet, venting his frustration. The lawyer now said he had to pay up by the end of the month, not at year's end like he'd hoped, but where would he get that kind of money in the next few weeks? "This is it," he told Jude wearily, gesturing around him. "This is me, my future, the sum and total of what I am worth. A whole lot of hopes and dreams gone up in smoke."

"You can't really feel that way." Tying her horse to the stump beside the gelding, she strode over to the foundation. "Just look around at all the potential," she said fiercely, gesturing with her hands. "All it needs is a little rebuilding. Look at those fields, the pastureland—and this is such an incredible location for a house. Put a window right here, and I bet you can see clear down to the river."

"You sound like my mother." With a reluctant smile, Tucker realized Jude even acted like her: the dreamy expression, the ability to see good in a stone. "I remember the first day we came here. She ran about, excited by what could be done with a little hard work. I don't think I'd ever seen her so happy. Now that we had a place to call our own, she said, life would be so much better."

Jude smiled back at him. "Wasn't it?"

"For a time." It hurt to think of that interval, so pleasant, so brief. "Just long enough to get my hopes up. That pastureland you mentioned"—he nodded out over the fields—"I dreamed of putting it to use raising horses. Before the war of course. Before all this."

She didn't look at the pasture—she stared at him, into him. "They took away your home and family. You can't let them rob you of your dream, too."

He snorted. "Dreams cost money. And they rarely come true."

"So just like that, you're giving up?"

"Just like that?" Seeing her flinch, he realized he should temper his tone. "I've worked my tail off, taking jobs I didn't particularly enjoy and wasn't much proud of, only to find myself still a good deal short. And now I'm told I have less than three weeks to get the rest, or the land will fall under state custody, too."

"But that's so unfair." Her lovely face clouding, she moved closer. "Can't you talk to someone? Explain the circumstances and offer to pay some now and the balance within a reasonable time?"

"I've tried. I get the impression that somebody else has his eye on the property, someone with better political connections than mine."

"But your father's a congressman."

Hard to miss the harsh ring to his laughter. "Curtis Holland hasn't lifted a finger to help in the twenty-four years of my existence. Hell, he's never even acknowledged my existence. No, I'm alone in this, a bald fact I accepted a long time ago."

"Tucker Boone, the loner." She shook her head. "You know what I think? You're a fraud. All your talk about dreams being too expensive is just that, mere talk."

"Well, thanks for being so understanding."

She moved closer yet, coming over to stand right in front of him. "There you go again, trying to put up that wall between us, but it's not going to work this time. I know you better than you think, because I used to be the same. So determined to fight life my way, convinced the whole lousy world meant to conspire against me." Sighing, she reached down and held up the locket she always wore around her neck. "I got lucky. Fate brought me a wonderful woman who later adopted me and taught me that life doesn't have to be so grim. When she gave me this locket, she called it a symbol of trust. My proof that there was at least one person in the world standing behind me, willing to help. Heck, I've since learned that the world abounds with people like Guin. You don't need to take on all of life's problems alone, Boone. You could let others help."

"Really?" he said dryly. "I haven't noticed a line forming at the door."

She frowned up at him. "Maybe that's because you keep slamming the door in our faces. I happen to know that Rooster would walk across fire for you and so would your brothers. Let us in, Boone. Dreams are more fun and far more productive when you dream them together."

Together. Staring down at her face, struck anew by how achingly beautiful this woman was, Tucker fought the urge to gather her up and hold her close. "When you say *us,*" he found himself asking, "are you speaking in general terms, or are you including yourself?"

She looked at her feet, and for an instant he feared that he'd pushed too hard too soon, that maybe he'd pushed her away.

"I want you to know," she said in a voice so small he had to strain to hear her. "Back in the hotel room, I lied to you."

Here it comes, he thought, angry with himself for hoping for more.

"I know you said you didn't want regrets," she said in a rush, "but I'm sorry. What happened is too important for me to pretend I can so easily forget it."

"Jude—"

"No, let me finish before I lose my nerve. I blathered all that nonsense about separate paths and uncluttered goodbyes only because I thought it was what you wanted to hear. Maybe it was, but I see now that what you want and what you need are two different things."

"Oh, really?"

"Really!" She stared up at him, so serious, so intense.

"I've been watching you, Boone. You need . . . no, you deserve . . . to have someone standing in your corner. Someone not afraid to fight for you, ache for you, push you when you start getting that urge to give in. Someone who believes in your dream with you and won't let you give up until every one of them comes true."

He didn't know how she did it. He, who by now ought to know better, found himself tempted to throw caution to the wind and just take her at her word.

Lifting her locket over her head, she gave him a shy smile. "After what you've told me, I know you have every reason to be wary, so I want you to take this as collateral, until you have this place bought and paid for. If I ever let you down, you get to keep it, or toss it, whatever you decide."

Humbled by the offer, he tried to push the locket back. "No, Jude, I know what that locket means to you—"

"All the more reason why I want you to have it." Setting her gift in his hand, she closed his fingers over the locket. "I want you to have proof, every time you look at it, that someone cares enough to stick around."

He could barely speak, his throat felt as raw as freshly slaughtered beef. Cupping the locket, he felt empowered, capable of anything. In her gentle, ingenuous way, Jude had said that she believed in him. And her incredibly deep and welcoming eyes told him so much more.

It could never work—they still had different paths to follow—but gazing at her, Tucker felt an incredible rush of hope, which fueled an even stronger rush of desire. It took all his willpower not to lower her down to the grass and pound himself into her. "Thanks," he told her quietly, slipping the locket over his head. "I promise, I won't let anything happen to it."

The woman had a smile that could melt his bones. "I know. I trust you, Boone."

She shouldn't. He could list all the reasons why not in

his head, primary of which were his rampaging carnal urges, but sharing that list with her would merely scare her off—and that was the last thing he wanted at the moment. God, but he burned to kiss her.

He knew he shouldn't—he could list all the reasons for that, too—but she was right there, moving closer until they were touching, and the temptation became impossible to resist. Reaching down, he dug his hands into her hair and pulled her head to his.

Given what she'd confided last night, he knew he should be gentle, but how could he hold back when here she was in his arms after he'd thought never to hold her again? Parting her lips with his tongue, he delved inside her mouth, starved for the taste of her. Just a kiss, he tried to tell himself, but already his hands were stroking her soft arms, her back, her beautiful face.

"Damnit Jude," he groaned against her mouth. "How can I be a gentleman with you in that damned dress?"

"But I'm not." She pulled away, looking up with a confused expression. "Rooster found me pants and a shirt."

So he had. Funny, Tucker hadn't noticed. He supposed she could be wearing a grain sack, and all he'd see was the woman he'd made love to. Just the mere thought of the passion they'd shared had his groin tightening.

"I want you," he told her, his voice low and hoarse. "Here. Now."

With a shy smile, she reached down to undo the buttons of her shirt. He couldn't help but notice how her hands shook as she did so. "I want you, too. So very much. But I'm so new at this. I've never been with another man. At least not . . . not like this."

Gazing into her wide-open eyes, he saw the enormity of what she was offering. This time he couldn't delude himself into thinking this would be a mere exercise in mutual pleasure like it had been with Lilah and the other females in his life. A woman like Jude deserved so much more than a quick roll in the grass.

So be it, he thought, staring down at her lovely face. Over time she would figure out that he wasn't much of a bargain, but until she left, for as long as she entrusted herself in his care, he'd do his utmost to cherish and protect her.

And what better place to make his silent vow, than here on the land that meant so much to him. They kept getting tangled up anyway, Jude and his dreams for the future. Might as well accept that they were one and the same.

"Here, let me help." Gently he moved her hands to the side. Inside him the carnal urges still raged, but he could control them, if that was what Jude needed to keep from getting spooked. He could forget his own physical need. He would stroke her and coax her and watch her face go wild with passion.

But being Jude, she had other ideas. Even as he was undoing her last button and sliding the shirt off her shoulders, she was reaching for the buttons of his shirt. No demure miss, not his Jude. Her fingers sliding over the bare skin of his chest wreaked havoc with his resolve.

By the time he'd unwrapped the cotton strips with which she had bound her chest, his own hands were shaking— with the effort of keeping himself from devouring her whole. She could have no idea how damned near perfect she seemed, with her head back and those luscious breasts offered up to him. *Be gentle* he kept repeating like a mantra in his brain as he lowered his head to lave one dusky nipple and then the other. She answered such stiff self-control with low, soft moans deep in her throat.

Which in turn fueled his hunger. He wanted to take it slow, but she felt so good, tasted so good, and he wanted her entire breast in his mouth. Cupping both, he took the left one, twirling his tongue over the nipple in ever-widening circles, until his mouth all but engulfed her breast. At her moan, he began a long, slow withdrawal, sucking the nipple up and out to complete erection. Giving it one last flick of the tongue, he moved over to repeat the ritual on the right.

He could have stayed there all day, worshiping her breasts, but he had more, so much more, to teach her. "Let's get undressed," he said, his voice hoarse. "I want to see all of you."

She seemed startled and again a bit shy, but untying the rope holding up her pants, she let the rest of her clothing fall to the ground. Standing there, staring at her, it was all Boone could do not to throw her down and ram himself into her. Her dress, for all its suggestiveness, hadn't begun to do her justice. From the creamy skin of her high full breasts to the tiny waist, flared hips, and long shapely legs, Jude was a vision, his every fantasy come true. The perfect woman, every last inch of her, yet she stared up with a worried expression, as if waiting for his assessment and unsure of what he might say.

Boone said the only words that came to mind: "God, woman, has no one ever told you how incredibly beautiful you are?"

Blushing, she shook her head, but he could see the words pleased her. "I want to see you now," she said shyly, reaching to undo the button at his waist.

Again he moved her hand away, knowing that if she continued, he'd lose all control. "First things first," he told her gently, and with her help, shoved the shirt from his shoulders and laid it out on a soft patch of grass. "It's not much of a bed," he told her, "but the best we can do under the circumstances. Shall we?"

She grinned. "As you said, first things first," she said, her fingers tracing the vee of his partially opened fly. "C'mon, Boone, fair is fair."

"God, woman, do you know what you're doing?"

She shook her head. "No. All I truly know is that I want this, you and me, with nothing between us." Undoing the last button, she slid her hands inside the waistband and down his buttocks, slipping the denim down over his hips. The combination of the cool breeze, and her warm, nimble fingers on his flesh, forced the tightening of his groin into a full erection. Now if that doesn't scare her away, he thought, angry at his lack of self-control.

It wasn't fright he saw in her gaze, only wonder. "Oh, Boone," she breathed, moving up to press her hot body against him. "Has no one told you how beautiful *you* are?"

That did it. Losing the last shreds of sanity, he swept her into his arms, kissing her as if he might never hold her again. Digging her hands into his scalp, she held on for dear life, giving as well as she got, her body pressed so close he had to be aware of every delicious inch of her.

Lowering them both to the ground, he tried to remember to take it slow, but her hands were exploring him, stroking, kneading, digging into his flesh. When he kissed her breasts, she arched her back in offering—when he moved lower, she opened her thighs to his touch and taste. Welcoming him, giving herself up to him, she made Tucker ache to please her, to draw those deep, guttural groans from her throat. It all seemed so perfect—the two of them alone, with the warm sun looking over them, the breeze soughing through the meadow—surely it couldn't get any better than this.

He was wrong. She was sheer delight, always surprising, never doing the expected. Just when he thought it was time, that she was ready for him to take her, she reached down to his groin and took him into her hands with warm, sure strokes. Hers wasn't the practiced touch of Lilah, but rather the caress of a lover, fascinated by the feel and taste and smell of his arousal. Gazing at her smiling face, he could see she took pleasure in pleasuring him, a fact that drove him half mad with desire. How easily he could drown in her deep brown eyes. He felt so strong when she gazed at him like that, as invincible as a god come to earth.

EVERY DREAM COME TRUE

But in truth she was the goddess, a sweet, impossible miracle, alive and breathing beneath him, bringing all the wonder and magic he'd been missing in his life. Wanting to adore her, worship her, he rolled them over so that she was atop him, and he could watch every last expressive movement of her face as they came together.

And, oh, how he relished her first startled blink as he lifted her hips and slid her down his erect shaft. How he savored her glazed look of pleasure, her eyes slowly closing as the rhythm of his thrusts took over, and she began riding him in earnest. And, oh, how he treasured her ever-deepening groans, her wild abandon as their tempo quickened, and he drove deeper into her hot welcoming body.

Reveling in the sounds of her pleasure, the sight of her lovely face lost to passion, he lost all control. He squeezed her buttocks, ran his hands over her breasts, but he could not get enough of this woman. Clasping his hands at her waist, directing her movements, he pounded her against him, driving himself ever deeper inside her, as if by so doing he could make them one. In that untainted, still trusting part of his brain, he truly believed if he could but reach the core of her, touch the very essence that was Jude, he would bind them together in a way that could never be undone.

And so he kept thrusting, holding on to her for all he was worth, until he heard her cry out, a fierce, piercing yell of triumph. Feeling her spasm around him, he lost it. Every particle drained out of him and into her body, a sacrificial outpouring to his goddess that left him dizzy with joy and aching with sorrow.

He had done it, had felt her soul in that shattering, blinding moment of passion, but each subsequent thrust merely drew him farther away. More than life itself, he wanted to keep throbbing, to stay forever within the warm cocoon she offered. It was heaven here inside this woman. It was home.

But nature had designed him otherwise, and all he could

do was hold tight to her waist, watching her face as the last, dying spasms rocked both their bodies. Gazing up at her, he felt a million emotions rush over him, but mostly he felt gratitude. Even if she left this moment and he never saw her again, he'd be richer for the time he had known her. In her own unique way, Jude had managed to open a window to his soul, bringing light and warmth and goodness to shine in the dark, shadowed corners. She'd shown him what a joyful thing it could be, making love.

And he knew it would never be the same with any other woman.

Reaching up for her, he pulled her down against him. Awash with tenderness, he kissed her hair, letting the magic thrive for a few moments more. All too soon, reality would find them, but for now, for as long as he could make it last, he wanted to believe that their idyll could go on forever.

As if in agreement, Jude sighed happily. "Ah, Boone," she said softly. "You truly are a gifted man."

How like her to take such a serious moment and make him chuckle. "I assume I'm to take that as a compliment?"

"You are." She sighed again. "I'm not trying to boast when I say that I've been wooed and courted by more beaus than I care to count, but never once before was I tempted to do something like this."

"Are you telling me a beautiful girl like you got to the ripe old age of twenty-one without even once contemplating marriage?"

She shook her head. "I couldn't find a man I wanted to spend the day with, much less the rest of my life. I don't know what it is about you, Boone, but you just have to look at me and I swear, my knees turn to mush." She popped up, resting her elbows on his chest as she grinned sheepishly down at him. "Not very smart of me to admit that, was it?"

No, it probably wasn't, but it was so typically Jude.

Reaching up, he traced his fingers across her lovely face. "You've got me feeling pretty mushy myself."

"Truly?" She seemed genuinely surprised and no little delighted.

"Let's just say I've gotten to my own ripe old age without ever before contemplating the state of wedded bliss."

She froze, her gaze boring into him.

Too late he realized what his admission implied. She'd started him thinking about terms like love and commitment, without seeing it through to the end. Sure he wanted to be with her, but what sort of lout would saddle this sweet, giving woman with a borrowed name and the life he'd have to lead? Fear and drudgery, that was all Tucker Boone had to offer, a life lived with one eye glancing back over a shoulder and the other to the long, grueling day ahead.

"Contemplating and offering are two different things," he said brusquely, rolling her over to her side. "Sorry, but I'm not the marrying kind, Jude."

He sat up, turning away to reach for his clothes. He hated to end the magic between them, but it wouldn't be fair to leave her with any illusions. "My road's a hard one, and I've got to go it alone."

He felt her hand on his shoulder. "It's all right, Boone. I wasn't pressing for a proposal. I know better than that."

It ate at him, the apology in her voice. He was the one who'd done things to be sorry for, not Jude. Was still doing them, if her wounded expression was anything to go by.

More than he thought possible, he yearned to hold her tight to him, to beg her to give him the chance to turn this place around so he could make a hard, honest living, but he was far too conscious of the past and the lies he'd put between them. Now with the note due on the farm, he *had* to take the Gray Ghosts' money. Jude wouldn't look at him so kindly, he knew, once she learned that all along he'd been humoring her, that she had never had any hope of being there when Latour met his end. Tucker Boone, the lover she trusted, would cheat her of her vengeance by giving the man to the Gray Ghosts instead.

He almost did it. He came this close to confessing everything, when he heard the horse riding hard in their direction. He felt Jude's fingers tighten on his shoulder before, with a little shriek, she pulled away to scramble for her clothes.

They dressed much faster than they'd shed their clothing, though Jude's fingers shook no less as she madly did up the buttons. Facing him from a ten-foot distance, she began to laugh. "Will you look at us?" she said with a contagious grin. "Running about like naughty children caught in the act. When you stop to think about it, what are the chances it's someone we know, or that he'll even glance in our direction?"

Pretty good, apparently. Slowing as he rounded the bend, the rider was only too familiar.

"Christopher!" Jude said, clearly as surprised as Tucker himself. "What on earth are you doing here?"

Eighteen

Jude was glad to see her little brother, truly she was—but she couldn't help wishing she'd had just a while longer alone with Boone. Her heart hurt, thinking about his tortured confession, and she wanted to help heal some of the wounds that the war—and his father's neglect—had caused, just as he'd done for her. But she imagined Boone would resent his private life being openly discussed, and even if not, her brother's scowl as he dismounted discouraged conversation.

Holding the reins tightly, Christopher looked very much like the scolding parent, his cool, assessing gaze resting first on her, then growing more displeased as he studied Boone. He must guess something of what they'd been up to—Lord, he'd have to be deaf, dumb, and blind to miss the tension in the air between them—but at least he had the good sense and discretion not to remark on it. He knew she'd clock him if he did.

It didn't stop her brother from casting another suspicious glance at Boone, however, as he announced to Jude that she had to come with him. "We've got a complication," he added sternly.

"What complication? It's not Guin, is it? She isn't sick?"

Christopher shook his head, keeping his glare on Boone. "If you'll excuse us, these are matters my sister and me need to discuss in private."

"And where is he supposed to go?" Jude found herself

resenting her brother's attitude. "What can you say that he can't hear?"

"It's a family matter, Jude." Christopher seemed no less adamant. "Personal business."

Boone held up his hands. "Say no more. I'll ride on ahead while you two talk. We need to be heading back anyway to see Captain Moore."

"It's not necessary," she insisted, panicked at the thought of Boone riding away without her. "Tell him we can all ride together, Christopher."

Meeting her brother's frown with a level gaze, Boone shook his head. "It's all right. I can use the time to do some thinking." He turned to her then, causing her heart to dip. "I'm sure you'll agree that you gave me a lot to consider."

Smiling, donning his hat, he strode over to his waiting horse. Watching him mount in a quick, fluid motion, Jude fought the urge to ask what he meant by that. Would he be thinking about their working together, about whether or not to trust her, or possibly . . .

Stop fantasizing, she warned herself, or the man would break her heart. Hadn't she heard him say he wasn't the marrying kind?

She hated to let him go with so much left unresolved between them, but he kept shifting in the saddle, and she could see he was anxious to leave. And no wonder with the dark looks Christopher kept shooting at him.

"I'll slow down near town so you can catch up," Boone said, turning the gelding toward the road. "It might be best if we rode in together." With a nod to each of them, he flicked the reins and trotted off.

"What was that all about?" Jude demanded, rounding on her brother the instant Boone rounded the bend. "Could you have been any ruder?"

"Yeah, well, could *you* have been any friendlier?" Christopher snapped, sliding up onto his saddle. "I thought you agreed to be cautious around him."

She blushed. Lord, what got into her when she was alone with Boone? She couldn't seem to keep her hands off him. Any more than he could keep his off her.

"Look at you," Christopher went on. "Grinning like the village idiot. It would seem Patrick was right in sending me to keep an eye on you."

Daunted to have him staring down at her, she marched to her own horse. "So now you're the family spy?" Angry at both brothers, she climbed up into the saddle with a huff and urged the animal onto the road, talking back over her shoulder. "At twenty-one years of age, I certainly don't need my little brother watching over me. As for Boone, I suggest you find some way to like him, for if I have my say, you and the entire family will be seeing a whole lot more of him."

Urging his own mount to catch up to her, Christopher couldn't have looked more alarmed. "You can't mean what I think you mean. You can't bring him home. Are you forgetting he's a hired gun?"

Letting him pull up beside her, she faced her brother down. "I know exactly what he is."

"Yeah, well, it's not his real name. Uncle Ham says he uses an alias."

"I know."

Christopher got that stubborn look he always got when arguing with his older siblings. "Did you know he's a criminal, wanted by the federal government? That he once rode with the Gray Ghosts?"

"I even know his reasons." She stared at the road ahead, letting him know she could be stubborn, too.

"All right, he's obviously been confiding in you, but just how much did you tell him?"

Thinking back, she decided she might better keep those

conversations to herself. "Boone's a good man," she said stubbornly.

"Jude, you're scaring me. What's going on here?"

"Nothing." That much at least was true. "We're friends, that's all. He's told me . . . things. That place back there was his home, burned out by his fellow soldiers during the war. Because of it, he's got a lot of bitterness and guilt. It's led him to desperate acts, but he's bone-deep decent, Christopher. Give yourself the chance to know him, and you'll see what I mean."

Giving her a hard, long look, her brother shook his head. "Looks like I'll have plenty of opportunity. I'll be tagging along with you two from now on."

"On Patrick's orders," Jude said with a sneer. "I'm only surprised that our worrywart brother didn't come himself."

"He wanted to." Christopher tightened his grip on the reins. "But back home the stakes have changed. George, Mrs. Tibbs's nephew from Boston, has come to New Orleans to stir up trouble. You know he's always felt that her estate should go to him."

Jude nodded. "Yes, but Mrs. Tibbs never trusted him or even liked him much. That's why she said she was leaving her money to Rafe."

"You and I and half of Louisiana might know she swore she'd never let that weasel touch a dime, but that hasn't stopped George from filing a petition contesting the will. He claims his aunt became senile in her declining years and was therefore easy prey to a conniving criminal the likes of Latour."

"Criminal? Rafe?"

"I'm just quoting George's own words. He claims he has proof that Rafe was brought to trial in Baton Rouge and convicted of treason."

"Baton Rouge?" Jude asked, appalled that all along Rafe had been so close to home. "Are you sure that's where he said?"

"George repeated it a good dozen times, adding that he has reason to believe Rafe was hanged for the crime, and buried in an unmarked grave. As yet he hasn't presented concrete proof of this, so that's our job—to go to Baton Rouge and find out what really happened there."

"I don't understand. Why didn't you go straight to the capitol, instead of coming all this way after me?"

He looked suddenly sheepish. "Don't get mad, but I've been following you. I got the message from home at the Independence Western Union office."

"You've been behind us all the way?"

"Well, I lost you for a while between St. Louis and Jefferson City, but then I happened to see you getting on the stagecoach. I asked at the livery stables this morning, and they told me you were heading out this way. I was sure glad to see you. I was starting to think I'd have to ride clear into Kansas. I would have though," he added solemnly. "I knew you'd want to hear what I had to say."

Jude wasn't sure that she'd *wanted* to hear such dire news, but Christopher was right. She had to know what was happening, else how could she find and save Rafe? "You don't really think he's dead, do you?" she asked, feeling chills of fear and dread.

He shrugged, a clear sign that Christopher was disturbed by the prospect but unwilling to express an unmanly emotion. "I don't want to think it, but we can't hide from the truth. We have to get to the bottom of this."

"You're right. We'd better make arrangements to go to Louisiana. Boone and I were waiting for the Federals to tell us where Rafe was sent. I guess I should ride on ahead and tell him there's no need to go back to that office."

Christopher reached over to grip her arm. "Let him go, Jude. You and me can start riding for home from right here."

"Just like that, you want me to vanish? No goodbyes, no explanations . . ."

Frowning, Christopher released her arm. "We don't need him anymore. He'll just get in the way."

If he thought Boone was a problem, just wait until he saw Rooster and the twins, not to mention Billy. She'd have laughed had it been a laughing matter.

Christopher was asking her to choose, a choice she was not prepared to make. She'd do anything for her family, but she'd just sworn to Boone that he could trust her, and if she left now, she'd be going back on that promise. "I offered him a job, and I'm not going to renege on it," she insisted stubbornly. He needed those wages, she realized, to help buy back the farm.

"But I got a bad feeling about all this. I don't trust him, Jude."

"You don't know him."

"Maybe not, but I know you, and for all your blustering, you're too softhearted for your own good. What if he's just been handing you some hard-luck story, and the next thing you know, he rides off with all our money?"

Remembering the stolen carpetbag, she grimaced. "That won't be a problem."

He gave her a funny look. "You sound pretty sure of him."

"I am."

His expression turned sly. "I couldn't help but notice he was wearing your locket. You never take it off. Mind explaining what it's doing around his neck?"

She did mind. The moment she'd presented it—and the lovemaking that had followed—had been so private, so special, she didn't want Christopher spoiling it with his cynical sneer. Yet she had to tell him something to make him understand the depth of her commitment. "Guin gave me the locket as a symbol of trust," she told him slowly, choosing her words with care. "And I've passed it on with the same intent. She taught me that sometimes you've just got to have faith in people. I'm trusting my instincts, Christopher. They haven't let me down yet."

"Well, I'm going by instinct, too. And it's telling me he's lying to you, Jude. He's hiding something he doesn't want you to know."

"If so, he has his reasons," she repeated stubbornly. In her mind she could see Boone's tortured expression as he spoke of his mother's death, his dream to build a life for his brothers. "He's coming with us, Christopher. And that's the end of the discussion."

"Damned stubborn female," her brother grumbled. "Fine, I'll put up with him, since you're forcing him down my throat, but I have some conditions of my own. I don't want that man knowing our private family matters."

Remembering what she'd told Boone about their father, she couldn't control the color flooding her cheeks.

"Damnit, Jude, you didn't tell him about the inheritance, did you?"

"No." She hadn't, and she felt bad about it, too. She'd asked Boone to trust her, yet it wasn't trustworthy to keep secrets from him. "I left it hazy, the reason we're tracking Rafe down. Boone thinks I'm after some sort of revenge."

"Good. Let's keep it that way." He must have seen her frown, for he worked extra hard at convincing her. "There's more at stake here than your personal feelings. You need to think about Rafe's life and our family's future. Once all is said and done, you can tell Boone the truth, and you can even blame me for forcing you to lie to him. But if I'm right, and he *has* been lying, then won't you feel better knowing you haven't jeopardized anyone else in the family?"

She thought of Boone, riding alone up ahead, his exile self-imposed to give her time with her brother. She wanted to rush to his side, to stay there and unburden her heart, but she knew Christopher wouldn't belabor his point without cause. When he had a feeling, she'd learned, it was generally wise to listen. "You're asking me to make a hard choice."

"No, all I'm asking is that you wait and see. You don't have to lie to him. Just don't volunteer information."

Maybe he was right, she tried to tell herself. All things considered, it was probably best to err on the side of caution. She wouldn't be hurting Boone, at least not directly. She'd be tending to the good of the greatest amount of people. She had to protect her family, for heaven's sake.

"All right, we'll try it your way for now," she told Christopher curtly. "But I hope to God I have the chance to prove you are wrong about him."

"That makes two of us," her brother muttered under his breath.

Tucker rode into town beside Jude and her brother, in a silence so thick a bayonet couldn't slice through it. He didn't know what they'd discussed, but whatever Christopher said to Jude had made a marked difference. She continued to speak politely enough, but instead of gentle smiles and heartfelt confidences, all she gave him now was the courtesy due a stranger. The last few hours might never have been.

With each awkward step they traveled, the urge intensified inside him to say the hell with finding Latour, to turn their horses and return to the farm. They had been able to talk there. Given time, surely they have could come to an understanding.

Anything would be better than this painful, frozen silence.

Or so he thought until he heard the sharp *"Psst,* Boone!" from a break in the buildings to his right. Rooster stood in the shadows of the alley, his gaze taking in everything, his body poised for flight. *Trouble,* Tucker thought instantly.

Dismounting, he motioned Jude and Christopher to follow as he cautiously led his horse to the alley. "What's wrong?" he asked Rooster as he reached him.

"Nothing yet." The boy frowned, glancing back over his

shoulder. "But that buddy of yours brought in reinforcements. They're waiting outside the hotel. Billy's none too pleased about you two cutting out on your own."

Tucker wasn't surprised, except maybe by the added manpower. "When you say reinforcements," he asked the boy, "how many are you talking about?"

Rooster shrugged. "I dunno, maybe a half dozen or so. I recognized at least two of them as the ones who jumped me in St. Louis."

Now that Tucker hadn't expected, though thinking about it, he didn't see why not. Billy would want to keep an eye on Jude . . . and her carpetbag. That meant the Gray Ghosts must have both her money and the Confederate uniform. He had to find out what else she had in that bag, to know ahead of time what else Billy might use against them.

"Where does this alley lead?" he asked Rooster.

"A barn. I think someone once kept horses in it, but it's empty now."

"Good, we can go there then." Looking behind him, he made sure Jude and Christopher followed. "We need to reconsider our strategy, which might best be done in private."

"You couldn't find anyplace better." Rooster puffed out his skinny chest. "Me and the boys have been hiding there for hours, waiting for you to come back."

Tucker began to feel uneasy. "What boys? You're not alone?"

"I guess that depends on what you mean by alone. Sorry, but them twins ain't much help making decisions. Especially Germy."

"Germy?"

Rooster grinned sheepishly. "No disrespect meant to your family. It just seems to fit him. You know, the way he's always sniffling and all."

Tucker halted and the others, horses and all, stopped behind him near the end of the alley. "It's not the nickname

I'm objecting to, Rooster. I'm assuming—and I hope you'll correct me if I'm wrong—that we're talking about my brothers, who I could have sworn I left safe and snug in a state-supervised institution."

Rooster snorted. "A prison, more like."

"Jude?" Christopher asked, his gaze darting from her to Tucker and Rooster. "What's going on here?"

"Yes, Jude," Tucker seconded. "Mind telling me what my brothers are doing, hiding in some abandoned barn?"

She faced him with her hands planted stubbornly on her hips. "For heaven's sake, you couldn't expect us to leave them in that awful place."

His hands tightened on the reins. "They were safe in the orphanage."

"Were they?" Burning with indignation, she faced him down. "Did you ever see where they sleep, what they eat, the hard work they must do?"

He felt uneasy again, knowing he hadn't exactly had time to keep a proper eye on his brothers. He'd wanted to believe the place was all right, because what was his option—kidnaping them and dragging them around with him? Considering his line of work, they were still better off where they were.

"You should have seen Jude," Rooster was saying beside him. "There was Headmistress Hattie, marching down the hall in pursuit while Jude barred the door with a chair. She was great, Boone. Jay Cob and Germy can't stop talking about how brave she was to rush in and rescue them like that."

"Brave?" Tucker exploded. "Or downright irresponsible? Is this getting to be a habit with you?" he asked angrily, turning to face her. "Just how many strays are you planning to collect along the way?"

If he'd expected to see contrition, he'd forgotten who he was dealing with. "They're not strays," she said, her cool voice drawing a line between them as effectively as her stiff posture. "They're your brothers."

Strays might have been a poor choice of words, but he wasn't backing down from his anger. "That's my point, Jude. The twins are *my* brothers, *my* responsibility, not another lost cause for you to adopt. They've been through hell and back, and what they need most now is a stable environment. Whatever you claim is wrong with that home, at least there I could be sure they had a roof over their heads, clothes on their backs, and food in their bellies."

"Gruel," Rooster sneered.

"What they want is family." Jude punctuated her stance by folding her arms across her chest. "Your brothers aren't hankering after food and shelter. All they really need is you."

It didn't matter that she was right—what she wanted was impractical. "What about your search for Latour? Isn't it complicated enough, jumping from one city to another, without dragging a bunch of kids around behind us?"

"Don't you worry none about the twins," Rooster reassured. "I'll make sure they toe the line."

And wouldn't that be a case of the blind leading the blind? Tucker thought, but seeing Rooster's pride in his offer, he kept his misgivings to himself. "Their behavior is the last of my worries at the moment. I can barely fund my own trip. Where in blazes will I get travel and food money for the rest of you?"

Grinning, Rooster reached into his shirt and whipped out a wad of bills. "This one's on me, Boone. Didn't I say I'd pay you back?"

"Oh Rooster," Jude said, her voice heavy with disappointment. "I thought you'd promised there would no stealing."

"But I didn't steal it. Not exactly."

"Theft is theft," Boone said sternly. "How can it be *not exactly?*"

Rooster shrugged, but his expression was considerably less hangdog than the situation would warrant. "Let's just say I liberated it from Billy. Like you said, stealing is stealing, and in this case, one good theft deserves another."

"Maybe," Boone said, realizing the cash must originally have come from the carpetbag. "But then, by rights, the money should go to Jude."

"Me?"

Boone fought the exasperation. "What Rooster is trying to say, if I'm following his logic correctly, is that Billy's thugs were the men who took the money from him."

"Darned near killed me doing it, too."

"Be that as it may," Tucker added, frowning at the boy, "you also neglected to mention where you got the cash in the first place. You seem to have forgotten a certain carpetbag you misplaced."

"Jeez, Jude, who is this kid?" Christopher asked his sister. "What are you doing with him, and what is this about stolen money?"

Noticing Jude's hesitation, Tucker made the introductions. "Christopher, meet Rooster O'Leary, one of Jude's"—no, better not call *him* a stray—"er, protectors. Rooster, this is Jude's brother, who I'm willing to guess means to be sticking around, too."

Jude shot a look at her brother. "He brought me information."

From the way Christopher watched his sister, Tucker figured he had come primarily to protect her—probably from himself. "Great," he muttered. "Another mouth to feed." He turned to Rooster. "Go on, give Jude her money so she can start managing this little menagerie."

"But Boone—"

"Hand it over."

No doubt recognizing Tucker as an unmovable force, Rooster laid the wad of bills in Jude's hands, albeit begrudgingly.

"All of it, Rooster. And I do mean the bills you've got stashed in the bottom of your shoe."

It was a guess, but the boy's chagrin proved it was a good one. "That ain't fair, Boone. I risked my neck getting that money. I deserve a commission."

"Personally I'd think the cash you've stuffed in your waistband will more than cover it, but you'll have to work that out with Jude. I do know, however, especially after our talk, that you'd never do anything to willfully cheat her."

Grumbling under his breath, the boy dug into his shoe, then waistband, before handing over a few more bills. Most likely Rooster had an emergency fund hidden somewhere else on his body, but Tucker figured he might as well keep it. The boy needed some sense of security, and besides, the point had been made bluntly enough. Rooster had to learn to be more trustworthy and Jude to be more wary.

Though she didn't seem to be heeding his message that well. The way she beamed at Rooster, you'd think the boy was her savior. "This is wonderful. I was wondering how we'd finance our trip. Now we can go straight to the stage line and make arrangements."

"Aren't you forgetting Billy?" Tucker said dryly. He certainly hadn't.

Jude's expression as she turned to Tucker sobered drastically. "We're not going back to him, Boone. You can, if you have to, but I'm not and neither are Rooster and my brother."

"Who the heck is this Billy?" Christopher asked. "And why are you all so afraid of him?"

"I ain't afraid of nobody," Rooster said stubbornly.

He should be. Thinking of how Billy would react when he discovered the money gone, Tucker realized Jude was right. None of them could return to the hotel now. "I'm not sure we should be discussing this here in the open. Let's get to that barn."

He started leading his horse, leaving the others to follow.

Rooster raced to keep up with his long strides. "You ain't mad at me, are you? I was only doing what you asked, looking out for Jude. That Billy had no business with her money."

"I'm not mad."

"Just worried, huh? These new men, they're them Gray Ghosts Jude's so afraid of, ain't they?"

Rooster and his sharp perception would be the death of him yet. "Maybe, but I think the less said about it to the others, the better."

The boy nodded. "You ain't going with them, are you?"

He should. Every instinct of self-preservation—for himself and the ragtag group around him—screamed out that the Gray Ghosts would now track them down with a vengeance. Yet he wasn't willing to risk what Billy might do to Rooster for taking the money. He'd get them all to safety and then send a wire to Salvation, letting the Gray Ghosts know he was still on Latour's trail. With any luck he could still come out of this with his wages and everyone's life still intact.

Leading them all into the dark, hushed barn, he tethered his horse and turned to Jude. "Watch over them. I'll be right back."

"Where are you going?" she asked, grabbing his sleeve.

She shouldn't touch him, he thought, not if she wanted to maintain the distance between them. Staring down at her, he wanted nothing more than to take her in his arms and forget the rest of the world existed. "Someone's got to talk to Captain Moore," he told her, pulling away.

"But Boone—"

"For once, don't argue. We need that information, and it'll be safer if I venture out alone."

"But you don't have to. That's what I'm trying to tell you. Christopher already told me that R-"—she hesitated, glancing back at her brother—"uh, Latour was sent to Baton Rouge."

"How do you know?"

Tucker asked the question of Christopher, who faced him with a stony glare. "I've been asking my own questions, Mr. Boone. I'm not nearly as trusting as my sister."

Hard to miss the implication. Clearly the boy had learned more than was comfortable about Tucker's past. At least he was honest. Tucker had to respect that. "I guess we'll be heading to Louisiana then. But not until dark—"

"But my things," Jude interrupted. "My clothes are still at the hotel."

"I could sneak back," Rooster suggested. "Nobody will be looking for me."

"We're not going to risk Billy finding us for a damned dress. It's going to be hard enough spiriting this group out of town as it is."

Jude smiled up at him. "By group, do you mean all of us? Even your brothers?"

It was insane, he thought with a shudder. He'd never be able to keep them in line—the frightened twins, the conniving Rooster, the ever-scowling Christopher. If he had any sense, he would put down his foot and demand that they all return to Salvation, leaving him to go it alone.

But gazing down at Jude's beaming grin, seeing her hopeful expression and obvious pleasure, he just couldn't tell her no.

"Yeah," he told her. "No doubt I'll live to regret it, but we all go together. From now on, if anyone asks, we're just one big, happy family."

Nineteen

Jude stood on deck, watching their approach to Baton Rouge. She saw little activity on the docks this close to dawn, but she'd rather watch empty streets than listen to the argument behind her. The past three days, Rooster and Christopher had yet to reach an agreement—on anything. On the stagecoach, and now on the journey downriver, the pair seized every opportunity to prove one another wrong. Jude didn't know why they'd taken an instant dislike to each other, or how to stop the friction between them, but their constant battling did not bode well for Rooster settling into life at the Latour family plantation.

She'd tried pointing out to Christopher how he and Rooster intimidated the twins with their yelling, but he'd merely countered that everything intimidated those two, a sad fact she couldn't dispute. Though Jacob and Jeremy had been sharing quarters with her—while Boone and the older boys slept on the more economical main deck—the twins continued to keep to their side of the tiny cabin, cowering on their cot, answering her polite inquiries with a yes, no, or shrug of the shoulders. So much for Boone's idea of being one big, happy family.

And in her opinion, Boone was to blame for that.

She tightened her grip on the rail. No promises had been made, so she had no real right to resentment—only why was she alone with her menagerie, while he spent every day and half the night in the gaming room? It hadn't been easy, watching out for two boys who wouldn't speak to her, bullying them to finish a supper they didn't want to eat, hustling them into bed early so they could sleep between nightmares. She longed for Boone's help with them, or even his advice, but she never saw the man. When he wasn't playing cards, he was stretched out on the main deck, stealing a few hours' sleep. Obviously he meant to avoid her, and the reason was as plain as the nose on her face.

Everything had been fine between them, wonderful in fact until the conversation shifted to marriage.

Despite her attempts to reassure him, but he must have seen her words for the half-truths they'd been. Maybe she didn't *expect* marriage, but that didn't stop her from *wanting* to spend time together. She'd gotten used to having Boone around. Not that she missed his bullying, but she'd had a taste of what it could be like to talk with him, laugh with him, lie in his warm, comforting arms at night—and she wanted more of it. She wanted to discuss what had happened between them and perhaps even devise some way to deal with the future, but instead he was off having a gay old time, while she kept guard over his brothers and played referee for the older boys' verbal sparring.

Hearing Christopher and Rooster shout "Did not," "Did to," for the rest of the world to hear, her already frayed temper snapped. "Stop it, both of you!" she called out as she marched over to them. "I'm sick to death of hearing you two fight, and I'm sure the rest of the boat is, too. We're moments away from docking, so I suggest you save your energy for whatever the day might bring."

"He was in the gaming rooms again last night," Christopher said, stabbing a finger in Rooster's direction. "Wanna bet he was trying to pick another pocket?"

"A lot you know." Rooster stood firm, the picture of righteous indignation. "I promised Jude not to steal, and I ain't even tried. I was looking for information."

"Yeah, and I'm the king of Prussia. All you were looking for was trouble."

"For heaven's sake," Jude intervened. "You're driving me insane with your scrapping. You've got to learn to get along."

"Why bother?" Christopher glared at the younger boy. "You're out of your mind, Jude, if you think you can bring this . . . this wharf rat home to the family."

Rooster flinched at the "wharf rat," but he faced Christopher squarely. "Yeah, as if I'd ever live anywhere such a . . . a bag-o-wind calls home. I'm only here to help Jude find this guy she's after. Then I'm off to St. Louey."

"Hallelujah! Why not leave right now? I bet the other thieves can't wait to have you back."

"Christopher!" Jude grabbed his wrist, appalled. "I can't blame Rooster for being afraid of our family, the way you're treating him."

"I ain't scared," Rooster insisted.

Jude ignored him, too busy with her brother. "Did you bother to ask why he was in the gaming room? Or just jump at the chance to assume the worst?"

"Doesn't take much assuming. He did steal your carpetbag, remember."

"That was before I knew her," Rooster said quietly. "And I needed to eat."

Dropping Christopher's wrist, Jude turned to Rooster. "I believe you, but maybe it would help if you explain what you were doing there."

"Helping Boone. Doing him a favor."

"Saint Boone." Her brother's sneer matched his tone. "Tell me, was he walking on water when he asked for this favor?"

"Christopher!"

"Ah, forget it, Jude." His voice changed pitch, almost wavered. He looked as if he'd lost his best friend. "I don't know why I bother talking to you anymore. Obviously you think the man walks on water, too."

Watching her brother stomp off, Jude wondered what had gotten into him. "It's not like Christopher to be so unreasonable," she tried to explain to Rooster. "I don't know why he lashed out at you like that. He's far from a saint himself."

"He's a guy, likes to be in control of things," the boy said with a shrug of his thin shoulders. "He came after his sister to protect her, only you ain't saying what's going on. I reckon it scares him."

Now that Rooster mentioned it, she could see her brother must be feeling as shut out as she felt by Boone. Caught up in her own concerns, walking the fine line between what could or could not be revealed, she'd never discussed anything with Christopher. That was the trouble with keeping secrets, she knew. People you loved were bound to get lost. "It's still no excuse for his rude behavior," she told Rooster. "All of us are scared."

"Not me." Rooster stuck out his chin. "That ain't my objection to meeting your family."

Jude recognized the pose. Reject before you can be rejected. "Indeed. Then what is the problem?"

He wouldn't look at her. "Your folks don't need the likes of me."

"Ah, Rooster, I wish you'd let them be the judge of that. Christopher notwithstanding, I promise my family will be glad to have you. Your circumstance or background doesn't matter to them. It's the person you are inside. Believe me, the fact that I call you my friend will be enough for any Latour to accept you."

Rooster snapped his head around to stare at her. *"Latour?"*

Too late she remembered Christopher's request not to reveal their relationship to Rafe, but Rooster, ever adept, had already figured it out. "That's the man we're tracking, huh?" he went on, thinking aloud. "He some kin to you?"

Senseless to deny it now. "Technically he's our uncle, but years back, he and his wife adopted my four brothers and me."

Rooster nodded as if he'd expected this, then tilted his head to study her. "This home of yours, it's called Cattle Lot?"

"Camelot," she answered automatically, confusion and curiosity making her forget Christopher's warning. "Why do you ask?"

"This guy in the gaming room mentioned it to the man I was watching. The guy says his boss, a Henry More Toes, has an eye on the place. It's supposed to be on the auction block come next month."

There was so much in that statement to upset her, from the threat against Camelot to the identity of the men discussing it. "This boss," she asked, tackling the most serious issue first, "are you sure his name wasn't Henri Morteau?"

"Yeah, that's it. You know him?"

She stifled a shudder. "He's my father's brother. My birth father. Uncle Henri has more money than Midas, but you'll never meet a more selfish, vindictive man. He doesn't want Camelot, not really. He just wants to destroy Rafe."

"But why?"

Chilled inside, Jude remembered the nightmare of her father's death. "It's a big misunderstanding. Uncle Henri thinks Rafe killed his brother, and because of it, he's caused us a lot of trouble over the years. I don't like that one of his employees is here on this boat."

Rooster frowned. "I wasn't thinking he could be trouble, too."

"Too?" she asked, alarmed.

"The guy he was talking to—the one I was watching—has been tailing us, at least since St. Louey."

The chill inside her deepened. "Not the Gray Ghosts again?"

Rooster nodded as if pleased with her deduction. "Boone thinks so."

Clearly they hadn't left the gang behind in Independence. How in blazes did Billy and his goons keep learning their location? "You say Boone knows about this man?" she asked aloud, not comfortable with the fact.

"He said he would bear watching."

Bear watching? she thought, wondering why he'd never mentioned the man to her. But then when would he have opportunity, avoiding her as he'd been.

"That's what you were doing in the gaming room?" she asked Rooster. "Watching this man for Boone?"

"Partly." Rooster looked away, suddenly evasive. "The guy wasn't gonna let anything slip around Boone, but nobody pays heed to a kid. I figured I could just sneak past, and if I overheard anything good, I could pass it on."

"Back up a minute." Jude reached out to turn his head so he faced her. "What do you mean by partly? What else were you doing there?"

"Watching out for Boone. Helping him win."

"He's cheating?" Stunned, Jude released his chin. Bad enough to hear Boone could be so dishonest, but to use this impressionable boy?

Rooster shook his head vehemently. "He don't have to cheat. Not the way he plays. But I figure it don't hurt to be on the lookout for who is. Back in the shadows, I can see who's packing an extra ace or dealing from the bottom. I find the cheats, and then Boone can avoid them."

"You say he's winning?" Jude asked, focusing on that thought.

Rooster beamed. "You should see him. One night, I watched him bluff a pair of deuces against a full house and come out a winner."

For the life of her, Jude couldn't figure the man out.

How could he indulge in drinking and card playing with a Gray Ghost on the prowl? Or let a kid like Rooster do his spying for him?

Noticing how the roustabouts began to scurry across the deck with their ropes, she decided it might be wise to get to the bottom of this before they took to the streets of Baton Rouge. She'd stand in wait at the gangplank, pouncing on Boone the instant he came down the stairs. Thanking Rooster for his information, she told him to gather the others so they'd all be ready to go ashore.

"Boone, too?" he asked.

"Boone especially." No doubt about it—she and that man had to talk.

"Cap'n, you in there?"

Recognizing Billy Cochoran's voice outside the door of Lilah's bedroom, Lance left the bed to retrieve her clothing. As much as he enjoyed watching her dance naked for him, he didn't want her around when he talked to his lieutenant. Like the lady herself would say, no sense mixing business with pleasure.

"Cover yourself," he snapped, shoving her behind the dressing screen and tossing her clothes in after her. "And find something else to do for a half hour."

Green eyes flashing, she eyed him over the screen. "This is my place, lover. Who are you to order me from my own bedroom?"

"The man who's going to make us both a lot of money." Crossing the room to the door, Lance found it hard to disguise his annoyance. Lord spare the world from grasping, managing women. "It's man talk," he said soothingly. "Business."

"I thought we were partners." She still pouted, but at least she began dressing. "With all the cash you've sucked out of me, I think I deserve to know what you're up to now."

Lilah might be a prize in bed, but out of it, she was far too demanding. "It has nothing to do with you," he told her, resenting the need to unruffle her feathers. "Don't worry your pretty little head about it, sugar. It's just a little mess from my past I need to clean up."

"Cap'n?" Billy repeated from the other side of the door.

"C'mon in, Lieutenant." Yanking it open, happy to be interrupted, Lance ushered his lieutenant to the table by the window. "And to what do I owe the pleasure of this visit?" he asked as he poured a whiskey from the bottle there.

Taking the glass, Billy stared at Lilah, who was still making noises behind the screen.

"Don't worry," Lance assured him, pouring a drink for himself. "The lady's just leaving. Aren't you, darling?"

Barefoot, her gown half buttoned, Lilah stomped over to them. Lance frowned, not liking the way her gaze assessed Billy. The last thing he needed was these two comparing notes. Hoping to distract Lilah, he took her in his arms, devouring her mouth, squeezing her breasts for good measure. "Come back in a half hour," he whispered in her ear, "and I promise, I'll make it worth your while."

She pulled back, a reluctant grin playing at the corner of her lips. "You're the devil incarnate, Lance Buford. Lord alone knows why I put up with you."

"We both know why." Conscious of Billy, studiously looking elsewhere, Lance grabbed for her again, cupping her buttocks hard and rough. He'd show his lieutenant how well he handled women, how he showed them who was boss. "A half hour," he told Lilah with a slap to her backside.

"Maybe. If I'm in the mood." Tossing back her head, she marched away in a huff, but the act didn't fool Lance. She'd be back, and crawling on her knees if he told her to, more than eager to please him. That woman was a master at the art of seduction, he thought with a sigh. Too bad she'd begun to bore him.

No matter. He'd soon be going home to Guin.

Turning his attention back to the business at hand, Lance found Billy eyeing the retreating Lilah, grinning as she so predictably slammed the door. Again Lance saw how those two together could make for a dangerous alliance. "Why are you here?" he asked brusquely. "I hope you have good news, after so rudely interrupting my rest."

Billy's smirk betrayed a knowledge of how *un*restful his captain's activity had been, but he had the good sense not to remark on it. "We lost Boone," he stated baldly instead. "He gave us the slip in Independence."

This Lance already knew, having intercepted the wire from Boone, which was why he'd sent Ed Harkley in pursuit. Good to know his lieutenant remained honest, though. Inexcusably inefficient, but Cochoran didn't have to die as long as he continued to tell Lance the truth.

"What about the girl?" he pressed, since Harkley had wired that Boone was traveling alone. Lance didn't like loose ends, especially when that end was the troublemaking Jude Latour.

Billy merely shrugged. "I had men posted at the hotel and at the Union offices, and neither Boone nor the girl ever showed up."

"In short they outsmarted you."

Lance expected to see anger, even remorse, but Billy just wore a smirk, as if it suited his needs just fine that the pair had eluded him. Lance didn't like thinking his subordinates might have intrigues of their own. "This late in the game, we can ill afford to have the girl running loose," he growled.

"Point noted. Mind telling me why this female is so important, Cap'n?"

He did indeed mind. Knowledge was power, and as such, Lance meant to keep Jude Latour's background to himself.

He needed her where he could find her though. To use as bait, obviously, to draw Latour in his trap and keep him there, but it hadn't escaped his notice that Jude could also serve as a bargaining tool. Henri Morteau would be more anxious to help him, after all, if Lance could offer two Latours for the price of one.

Henri hated the girl, certain she'd played a part in his brother's demise. And since her interference and testimony had led to Lance's own prison term, he had no qualms about offering Jude up to her uncle's thirst for vengeance. To do that, however, he had to know where she was at any given moment.

"Forget Boone for now," Lance told Billy, downing his whiskey in one gulp, "but I suggest strongly that you find the girl and bring her to me." He slammed his glass to the table. "Have I made myself clear, Lieutenant?"

"That you have, Cap'n." Billy's tone was properly submissive, but Lance detected an evasiveness in the gold-tinted eyes as he, too, set his empty glass firmly on the table. "To track her down, though, I'm gonna need more funds. These days, traipsing about Missouri ain't cheap."

Lance longed to backhand the man for his attitude, but he resisted the urge. Having no one else he could spare at the moment, he had to rely on Billy until Jude was in his hands.

Reaching into his pocket and peeling off bills from the wad Lilah had just given him, Lance made it clear that this would be the last of it until the job was completed. "And if it isn't done to my satisfaction," he added, "I'll take the repayment out of your hide."

"Sure thing, Cap'n." Saluting him, Billy went to the door. "But really, when it counts, have I ever let you down? Don't I always get my man?"

"Yeah, but in this case, you're after a woman."

"That she is, Cap'n," Billy said as he left the room. "Ah, yes, that she is."

Although Billy's parting shot added to the uneasy suspicion that he had his own hidden motives, Lance let him go. If it became necessary, he had the resources and power to rein in his lieutenant, but for the time being, what mattered most was finding Jude Latour. In truth what did Lance care what Billy did to the girl, as long as he left her alive for his own fun?

Revenge, Lance thought with a chuckle. As the poets would say, it was sweet indeed.

Intent upon disembarking, Tucker nearly stopped in his tracks at the sight of Jude, standing alone by the gangplank. From behind, with her slim hips encased in trousers, he supposed she could be mistaken for a boy, but no one could possibly make that mistake when gazing at her profile. Watching her stare out over the rail, he could feel his entire body react to the sight of her, remembering all too vividly what lay beneath the denim and flannel, a memory that had tortured him day and night since they'd left Independence. What he wouldn't give to march up and pull her into his arms, to kiss her soft red lips as if he owned them.

But he didn't own them, nor had he a prayer of staking a legitimate claim, which was part of why he'd been avoiding her. A wasted effort, it would seem. One glance and here he was, yearning for the impossible all over again.

Leave her be, his conscience insisted. *Walk away before she sees you.*

Too bad the rest of him had different ideas.

His legs kept him marching forward, his eyes remained on her profile. His conscience screamed at him to walk in the other direction, but for the life of him, Tucker could remember nothing but the feel of her warm soft body next to his.

She turned to him as he approached, her dark eyes watching his every moment, as alert and wary as a deer in the forest. Everything about her seemed tense, a far cry from the soft, yielding woman he'd made love to at the farm. "I see Rooster dragged you from the gaming tables," she said, her words clipped and abrupt.

Inwardly he flinched, but outwardly he stayed as cool and calm as she. "I have business ashore," he said, nodding at the docks. "Or had you forgotten?"

"I've forgotten nothing." She pinned him with her gaze. "Why have you been avoiding me, Boone? Do I scare you that much?"

Ever direct, she'd gotten to the heart of the matter. That soul-draining gaze of hers frightened the hell out of him.

But that wasn't why he'd been keeping his distance. "I'm not scared of you, Jude," he told her quietly. "I'm scared *for* you. You and the boys. I don't want to put your lives in any more danger."

"Is this danger from the man Rooster overheard in the gaming room?"

He smothered an oath. "He wasn't supposed to tell you about that. I didn't want you worrying."

"That's just great, Boone. You can't trust me with the information, but you can send a twelve-year-old boy into that den of iniquity to play your spy."

It stung, that she could think that of him. "I never sent Rooster anywhere. In fact I kept chasing him away. You think I'd want him taking risks like that?"

"But he said that you . . ." She closed her mouth, shaking her head. "Never mind, I forgot for a moment it was Rooster we were talking about. This man, you really think he's one of the Gray Ghosts? That he means us harm?"

He shrugged, wishing he could reassure her, but she had asked for honesty. "I never met the man myself, but I've seen Ed Harkley's face on many a post office wall. I can't imagine why Billy would send a ruthless killer after us, but if he did, Harkley is expecting to find me with a woman. I figured with you dressed as a boy, you'd be all right, but the less we're seen together, the better. You're safer hiding out with the twins. No one's looking for a bunch of boys."

"I wish you'd explain that to your brothers. They can't understand why you don't come visit. I think they believe I'm somehow to blame."

Hearing the weariness in her tone, he realized how hard it must have been for her these past few days. "It's almost over." In more ways than one, he thought unhappily. "With any luck I'll find Latour today."

"You'll find him?" she pounced. "Don't you mean we?"

"Ed Harkley will be tailing me. Do you want him figuring out who you are, who the boys are? Be reasonable, Jude. This is no time for theatrics."

"My theatrics saved your butt on many an occasion, Boone."

Bad enough he couldn't touch her—he couldn't stand to have her angry at him, too. "I know," he said gently. "And there's no one I'd rather have beside me. But if something should happen, who will take care of the twins . . . or Rooster?"

"You expecting something to happen?"

She was too sharp for her own good. All Boone knew for certain was that he couldn't have her meeting up with Harkley. "I don't know what to expect," he told her honestly enough. "But I can't leave my brothers alone and unprotected. Not after what they've been through already."

"No, you can't." She pulled herself up to her full height. "You stay with the twins. I'll go to Union headquarters."

"You?"

She stiffened. "Well, thanks for the vote of confidence. Think with your head and not your pride, Boone. I'm still better able to get the information—and more to the point, this Harkley won't know to follow me."

"He will, if he sees us talking."

"Then I guess I'd best be going, hadn't I?"

He reached for her. "Damnit Jude, you don't know what you're asking—"

"I'm asking you to trust me," she said, facing him stubbornly. "If you can't, you might as well just give me back my locket right now."

Give her the locket and get it over with, his conscience warned. She'd be demanding it eventually. He'd left Billy behind for convenience and safety's sake, but basically little had changed. Though he'd earned a bit gambling, it wasn't enough to pay Lilah off or cover the taxes for the farm. To have hope for the future, or any chance with Jude, he still had to deliver Latour to the Gray Ghosts.

But tell her the truth now, and she was liable to go off half-cocked, causing Lord alone knew what danger to herself and the others. "Go on, then," he told her, "but come back for me once you find him." He released her arm. "And hurry. Remember this boat will leave port in two hours."

"I know."

The catch in her voice nearly had him reconsidering. For two bits he'd love to grab her hand and run far away from the past that threatened to come between them, but persistent ghosts haunted them both. Driven by private demons, Jude wouldn't give up until she'd laid those ghosts to rest. *Trust me,* she'd asked, and how could he refuse her?

But he wouldn't let her go unprotected. "Take this," he told her, reaching for his Colt. "Use it if you need to."

Her eyes searched his, as if understanding his reluctance to part with his weapon, her slow smile appreciating the sacrifice. "Thanks," she told him quietly. "You won't regret it."

Let's hope not, he thought, watching her hurry down the gangplank, but he couldn't shake the feeling that he should have gone in her place.

A sensation that merely worsened when he glanced up to see Ed Harkley scowling down at him.

Twenty

"Rafe Latour is dead," the Union colonel stated baldly, handing Jude a stack of papers. "As you can see, he was executed for the crime of treason."

Hands trembling, Jude stared at the official documents, battling disbelief, holding back tears. Posing as a boy, she couldn't be crying in public. Besides, she'd taken an instant dislike to the fat, smug Colonel Porter, and she refused to show even a trace of weakness in front of him.

Inside though she grieved for the man who had been more a father to her than the one who had birthed her. Rafe couldn't be dead. It couldn't be possible that she'd come all this way just to find she was too late to save him. What would she say to the rest of the family? Dear God, how could she ever tell Guin?

Somehow she got through the rest of the interview, though she'd never afterward remember one word she'd uttered to the self-righteous colonel. All she'd recall was the need to hurt him as much as his careless speech devastated her. How dare he smile when he talked of Rafe's death. How dare he smirk.

Leaving the Federal offices, she headed in the direction of the docks, feeling lost and adrift. After all this time, all this hoping, what did she do now?

Boone, she thought, quickening her pace. More than anything she needed his strong arms around her.

Only it wasn't Boone who grasped then steadied her so she wouldn't go tumbling into the street. "Miss Latour?"

Looking up, she recognized the handsome young private who had ushered her into the colonel's office. "Forgive me, miss. I don't mean to startle you, but I just couldn't let you go without hearing the truth."

She blinked, dazed and instantly wary. How could he know she was a girl?

"Maybe you don't remember me," he explained, "but I used to go hunting and fishing in the bayou with your brother, Peter. I'm Bartley Remmers. Me and Peter lost touch, I'm afraid, having served on different sides in the war."

"Oh, Bart, of course I remember you." He'd had a bit of a crush on her, as she recalled, the young-boy kind that pulled braids and left frogs in your bed. "Forgive me, my wits are a bit addled by all I heard in there."

Face grim, he took her arm, drawing her out of sight of the Union office. "I must make this quick. I could be court-martialed for what I'm about to tell you, but your family was always kind to me, and I can't let you suffer because I didn't speak up. There wasn't a hanging, miss. Wasn't even a trial. Your uncle was handed over to a civilian after money changed palms."

"Rafe's alive?" she asked, gripping his hands, so overwhelmingly relieved her knees nearly gave way.

At Bart's nod, her questions began to multiply. "I don't understand," she told him, remembering Boone's suspicion that there might be some unseen force working against them. "Who was this civilian?"

Bart glanced over his shoulder. "Swear you won't tell where you heard it, but a New Orleans lawyer came swaggering in two days ago with a sackful of cash, which I was told to put into the colonel's private safe. Next thing I know, this Lloyd Mathews has a small army of guards marching your uncle to the dock."

"Did you say Lloyd Mathews?" Jude asked sharply, recognizing the name. Mathews was her uncle Henri's factor and general man of business.

Bart nodded. "He drew up the list of formal charges as well as the death certificate the colonel showed you. If you have your own lawyer look at those papers, I'm sure you can prove that they're forged."

Bribery, forgery, kidnaping. Colonel Porter had been so pleased with himself, but they'd see if he smirked when faced with his own court-martial.

In the meantime, though, Jude had no wish to cause trouble for Bart. Thanking him and urging him to come visit at Camelot, she took her leave before he was caught talking to her.

She headed straight for the dock, knowing she had to be on that steamboat when it sailed downriver. Somehow they had to find out where Uncle Henri lived these days, and quick, before anything worse happened to Rafe.

Lord, she felt as if her head had spun around twice. Just when she thought she was headed in the right direction, something started her off in a new one.

Like now—finding Boone in front of the Western Union across the street.

Stunned she stopped where she stood to gape at him, wondering what on earth he was doing there when he should be back on the boat. *Someone has to stay with the twins,* he'd insisted, but where were they? They had maybe fifteen minutes before the boat sailed. Was he planning on missing it?

As if hearing her doubts, he glanced over at her, a sharp frown creasing his handsome face. *He* was angry to see *her?*

When she took a step forward, he gave a dismissive shake of his head. Bewildered, growing more suspicious by the moment, she would have gone rushing at him if not

EVERY DREAM COME TRUE   269

for the tug on her elbow. Spinning around, she faced the somber features of Rooster O'Leary.

"What in blazes is going on?" she asked as he dragged her away. "What are you and Boone doing here? Who's with the twins?"

"Your brother." Rooster's sneer told her what he thought of Christopher's abilities. "Boone's here to make a conversion, he said, to help you get to them offices and back."

"Conver- . . . oh, you mean a diversion?"

"Yeah, that's it. That man, the Gray Ghost, saw him talking with you on the boat. Boone figured it'd be better if he was the one followed, not you."

"But I don't get it. Why would Ed Harkley bother following me? I thought Boone's the one the Gray Ghosts are after."

Rooster shrugged. "I'm just a kid. No one tells me nothing. Ask Boone."

"And how can I do that? In case you didn't notice, the man isn't exactly anxious to talk to me."

"He'll be around," Rooster reassured her. "Just give him time to shake lose of that Harkley guy."

"Time is something I don't have. I have to get on that boat." Nervously she looked toward the dock. If Uncle Henri had Rafe, he was in serious danger. "If we're lucky, we have ten minutes before it sails." As if on cue, the vessel gave a long, mournful blast of its horn.

"Yeah," Rooster conceded reluctantly. "I reckon you'd best get going. Boone will want you, not your brother, watching out for his kin."

Overwhelmed by all that was happening, it took her a moment to realize what Rooster had said. "You aren't coming with me?"

"Boone ain't leaving without getting that Gray Ghost off your trail. And me, well, I aim to talk him into letting me help."

"What do you mean, talk him into it?"

His grin went sheepish. "He tried to send me back to the boat—but, hey, you think I can let him go it alone? Somebody's gotta watch out for that man."

"Don't be foolish. You can't take on a hired killer." Scared for him, she reached for his arm. "I'd never forgive myself if anything happened to you."

"Jeez, Jude," he said gruffly, pulling away. "I ain't that dumb. I'll be with Boone. We'll be watching out for each other."

How proud he sounded, how sure of Boone. "But I thought you'd be coming home with me. What about meeting my family?"

He wouldn't meet her gaze. "He needs me. Can't turn my back on that."

No, he couldn't. Rooster was undeniably loyal, and somewhere along the way, Boone had become family to him. As the adult Jude knew she should keep at him, coaxing him to take the safe and sane route to Camelot, but the child in her recognized the stubborn set to his shoulders. Having adopted the pose often herself, she knew Rooster wouldn't be swayed, no matter what she said or did.

Hearing a second blast from the steamboat, she made her decision. "Take this, then," she said, reaching into her waistband for Boone's pistol.

His eyes went as wide as the Mississippi. She could have handed him a king's ransom, considering the reverence with which he clasped that weapon. "This is Boone's gun, ain't it?" he asked.

"Do you even know how to shoot it?"

He didn't need to answer—the sudden color in his cheeks gave him away. She raised her eyes heavenward. "Let's just pray that God does indeed watch out for children." And fools, she added, hoping she wouldn't regret giving him that gun. "And let's also pray that you never need to use it."

"We'll be fine," he reassured her, reaching out to pat

her arm. "Why, before you know it, I'll be showing up at that Cow Lot of yours."

"It's Camelot. And I expect to see you both coming down that drive." She took his hand, past caring if the display made him uneasy. "Tell Boone . . . I need to see him. There's so much to explain." She started as the steamboat gave a double blast, its last warning before the gangplank was raised. "Tell him . . ."

Now, faced with the fear of never seeing Boone again, she thought of a million things she could have said. She should have given him the chance to explain away her doubts and fears, should have trusted him with the truth about Rafe. "Tell him I want the chance to bring everything out in the open, to make it good and honest between us. And tell him to hold tight to that locket."

"Hey, you ain't gonna cry, are you?"

"I never cry," she answered sharply, realizing how much it sounded like his own claim of never being afraid. "Oh, Rooster, I'm gonna miss you," she said, giving him a quick, fierce hug.

Telling him to take care of himself and Boone, she ran for the docks before she could shame herself with tears. She never had been much good at goodbyes.

Still feeling shaky, she ran up the gangplank, only to find a glaring Christopher waiting with a frightened twin on each side.

"Where's Boone?" he barked at her. "Did you know that wharf rat's taken off, too?"

"I saw them." She brushed past him, intent upon making the arrangements for continuing their journey. "They'll be staying in Baton Rouge."

"And why am I not surprised?" Her brother followed behind her, clearly determined to dog her heels. "What about his brothers?"

"Don't start," she snapped, quickening her pace. "I've had about all I can take already."

"What's going on, Jude?" Christopher called after her, dragging the twins with him. "Where the devil are you going?"

Hearing the panic in his voice, she remembered Rooster saying her brother was scared. Turning back to him, seeing the twins' frightened faces, she realized they'd all needed reassuring. "We're going home," she told Christopher wearily. "Back to where we can put an end to this, once and for all."

Not blessed with the same sense of imminent closure, Tucker left the Union offices more confused than ever. The colonel had refused to tell him anything, him being the third to ask about Latour today. The first, a boy, had to be Jude, Tucker reasoned. The man had to be Ed Harkley.

One would think he'd want to avoid being recognized. Then again Harkley had committed his crimes in Missouri, so maybe there were no wanted posters here in Louisiana. Of course, if he were like Billy, he'd take bearding the lion in his den rather than risk angering his Cap'n. No doubt Harkley had already made his report, making it clear that Boone was shirking his own duties.

Tucker cursed, wishing he'd thought to contact the Gray Ghosts earlier, when he'd wired his poker winnings to Lilah. Being fifty dollars short, he'd asked the blasted female for an extension, promising to get the last to her by the end of the week. Which, in essence, gave him five short days to find Latour.

He had to find Jude, but he hadn't the least idea where she'd gone. Odd how unsettling it was, finding himself alone.

No, not all alone he soon discovered, feeling cold steel press into his spine. "Question and answer time, Boone," Harkley muttered behind him. "But first, nice and easy like, I want you handing over your revolver."

"I'm not carrying one."

"Well, now reckon I'd best check for myself." Patting his sides, Harkley kept his gun against Tucker's spine as he searched for concealed weapons. "The Cap'n will be interested in hearing what lengths you'll go to, protecting that young filly. Pretty clever, hiding her looks in boys' clothing. Never would give her a second glance myself, had I not seen your tender parting. You got it bad, Boone. Hell, I'd feel sorry for you, save I know who's paying my wages. And the Cap'n, you'll find he don't take kindly to being betrayed."

"Nobody's betraying anyone," Tucker said with faked scorn. "Put the gun down, Ed. We both know you'll never find Latour without me."

"On the contrary. The colonel gave the information to the girl." Harkley bent down to frisk his legs. "Face it, Boone, you're expendable."

No surprise there. He knew the man meant to kill him, but Tucker had no intention of letting this coldhearted bastard go after Jude next. Somehow he had to reach the knife strapped to his ankle before Harkley could shoot him. Tensing as the man's hand reached his boot top, Boone was ready to move, and damn the consequences, when he heard the grunt behind him. He glanced over his shoulder to find Harkley slumped in the dirt and Rooster standing over him, holding a far too familiar revolver.

"Jude said she hoped I wouldn't have to shoot it," the boy said with a grin. "Don't reckon she expected the other end would work as well."

Boone reached out for the weapon, taking it before Rooster could hurt himself. "That was some quick thinking. Thanks, I owe you."

Rooster beamed. "Yeah? Then how about them shooting lessons? That way I won't have to wait for the guy to bend over next time."

"If I have my say, there won't be a next time. What are

you doing here anyway? I thought you sailed off with Jude and the others."

"Somebody had to watch your back."

The boy's stiff tone and stance told Tucker that it hadn't been an easy decision to remain behind, that Rooster had wanted to go with Jude. "You're right," he conceded, not wanting to make light of the boy's sacrifice. "The least I owe you is lessons. But for the time being, mind if I carry the gun?"

Rooster grinned. "I could always take his," he said, toeing Harkley with a surprisingly expensive shoe.

Given the boy's larcenous nature, Tucker didn't want to know where the shoe or his other new clothes had come from. "Maybe we should take it. The man'll be mighty angry when he comes to."

"Well, I was thinking. You said he's got this price on his head. Well, how about if we go tell the sheriff he's here? He can't hurt nobody in jail."

Tucker thought about the necessary explanations, how it could well reveal his own past as a bushwhacker. "It's a good plan," he told Rooster, "except I can't really afford to be talking to the law at the moment."

"You watch him then and keep him here till I get back." Rooster flashed an impish grin. "I won't mind having the reward money all to myself."

Tucker thought of the extra fifty dollars he needed, but fair was fair. "Go on, get the sheriff," he told the boy. He could watch Harkley from a safe distance, and when the law arrived, Tucker could slip off with no questions asked. He'd head straight for the Western Union office and send a wire to Salvation.

"Wait." He realized that Jude probably had a good idea of where to look for Latour next. "I don't suppose Jude told you where she was going?"

"Home," Rooster said with a grin as he darted off. "To someplace called Camel's Lot."

* * *

Sitting at the bar in the empty Lucky Lady saloon, nursing his tenth whiskey of the morning, Lance Buford wondered what was taking Renny Claiborne so long at the Western Union office. What was he doing, sending wires to himself? At this rate Lilah would be back from her predawn meeting with her bank manager. If the truth be told, he was getting sick and tired of Lilah Matlock with her ten thousand questions, and he was double-damned tired of waiting.

Draining his pewter mug, he tossed it into the long mirror behind the bar. He sighed at the satisfying sound of shattering glass.

Hell, who needed a mug anyway—he could drink straight from the bottle.

Smiling at his reflection in the sole remaining shard, a wide jagged piece in the corner, he was reaching for the bottle as Renny strode in through the door. Lance watched his image stop dead at the sight of the broken mirror. "What happened here?" Renny asked, his right hand sliding closer to his gun.

"I got impatient," Lance snarled as he raised the bottle to his lips. "Be grateful you weren't here to take it in the eyeballs. Where in hell have you been?"

Renny actually looked hurt. "I had to wait for the place to open. I'd have tried breaking in, but you told me not to take any chances."

So Lance had. This damned witch-hunt had him edgy, all those Federals itching to burn bushwhackers at the stake. "Well, don't stand there gaping." He waved the bottle, gesturing Renny closer. "Tell me what Harkley reported."

Renny, who'd been heading for the whiskey bottle like a homing pigeon to its coop, came to an abrupt stop.

"Weren't no message from Ed," he began hesitantly. "But you did get one from Boone," he added quickly.

Boone? Taking another swig from the bottle, eyeing Renny in the shard of glass, Lance struggled to remember why the name seemed familiar. Lord, but his brain had gone fuzzy.

"He tracked Latour to Baton Rouge, Boone said, but now he's heading down to New Orleans."

Boone was Billy Cochoran's friend, Lance remembered. Good old Jesse Holland—Congressman Holland's by-blow. "Hmm, New Orleans. But there's no word from Harkley, you say." Strange, Harkley should have been there, watching Boone send his wire, sending his own report minutes after. "Nothing at all?"

"Well, sir, that ain't entirely accurate." Looking away, Renny appeared suddenly uncomfortable. "You had another message. From a Henry Morteau."

Bottle halfway to his lips, Lance spun on the stool to face him. "It's Henri, you jackass. *On-ree*. What did he say?"

At each enunciated syllable, Renny flinched like a dog expecting a whipping. "Weren't much. Just that he no longer requires your services."

"Son of a bitch!" Lance was so angry, he could barely breathe. So that was why Boone was going to New Orleans. Morteau had Latour. That cagey Cajun bastard had gotten the jump on them all.

No longer needed his services? Well, they'd just see about that.

Lance slid off the bar stool, standing none too steadily, just as Lilah loomed in the doorway. Awesome in her outrage, she seemed—at least for a moment—unable to speak.

The moment didn't last long. At her shriek, Renny melted into the shadows.

"What in hell happened here?" Lilah sputtered. "Do you have any idea how much that mirror cost me?"

Lance could care less, his attention riveted on the carpetbag in her hands. "Did you get it?"

She clutched the bag to her chest. "I cleared out his account, along with several others, but don't for a second presume that you're gonna touch it. This money is going to buy me a new mirror."

Logic told Lance that Lilah needed to be soothed, that she'd come around if he took time to stroke and pet her, but frustration—and the whiskey—was burning a hole in his brain. Here he was, on the brink of his moment of triumph, and first Henri Morteau, and now this bitch, meant to stand in his way?

"Give me the bag, Lilah," he said, as he edged toward her, almost laughing at the gun she drew, one of those dainty little single shooters women favored. "Hope you're a crack shot," he warned as he neared. "You've got to hit me square on, sugar, or I'm just gonna keep right on coming."

One hand clasping the bag, the other wavering as she aimed her pistol, Lilah looked remarkably unsure of herself. Easing closer, Lance pressed his advantage. "You don't want to shoot me, now do you? Think of the fun we've had in that bed of yours, how my tongue feels in your mouth, on your breasts, in your—"

"Stop it! Damn you, Lance Buford. Damn you."

He stepped up to take the pistol away. "Thank you, sugar." He yanked the bag from her hands. "You sure have been sweet, but I've got to be moving on."

"You can't leave me." She reached for him, her fingernails like talons digging into his skin. "We're partners. You said I'd be your woman."

"And so you were, for a time, but the time is now over." He laughed nastily. "I do hope you weren't expecting marriage. Look at yourself. You're a whore. I told you I need a lady."

"You bastard," she hissed, removing her hand to swing at his face.

Lance grabbed and held her wrist in a death grip. "Actually a bastard is one thing I'm not. My mama was the only female my daddy did marry, a single act of honor that made me a gentleman with all the rights and privileges of that class. That's what this is about, sweetness. Me taking my rightful privileges. You see, I'll be using the money you so generously appropriated to establish myself a dynasty. And I already have the lady picked out. Her name is Guinevere, a queen whose boots you're not fit to lick."

She wrenched free of his grasp, her green eyes flashing fire. "Take the money, but when those depositors come screaming for blood, I'm not assuming the blame for this. Any dynasty you establish will be from behind bars."

Staring into her eyes, he saw that she meant it, that he'd gone too far to charm his way out of this. In his mind he had but one option—backhanding her—and so hard she went flying, falling and cracking her head on the corner of a table.

Savoring the sound of bone hitting wood, Lance watched her slump to the floor. "That's what happens to women who cross me," he told the slack-jawed Renny Claiborne, stepping tentatively closer.

"Is she dead?"

Lance shrugged. "Don't know and don't much care." He gestured at the bar. "Quick, knock down those bottles and spill whiskey on the floor. This is my going-away present to the citizens of Salvation. After all these years of her bleeding them dry, I'm taking the initiative and putting a torch to her place."

"With her in it?"

"You got a problem with that?"

Renny shook his head vehemently. "You're the boss, Cap'n."

That he was, a fact Lilah would have been wiser to remember. Stepping over her unconscious body, he went behind the bar for a bottle to fashion himself a torch. Yes,

EVERY DREAM COME TRUE 279

let this be an example of what happened to those who crossed him, he thought with great satisfaction.

Soon he'd be getting to the others on his list.

When Renny finished sweeping the bottles to the floor, Lance grabbed the bag of money and led the way out of the saloon. They stood at the door a moment viewing his handiwork, before Lance lit his makeshift torch. Readying his aim, he thought he saw Lilah stir, but he flung the bottle anyway. "Sweet dreams, sugar," he said softly as he turned his back to the rapidly creeping flames.

Out in the street, seeing the sun rise in the sky, Lance was blessed with a sudden clarity, as if all the alcohol had cleared from his brain. "Hurry and fetch our horses," he told Renny, "and meet me in the southwest corner of town."

"Where to, Cap'n?"

Lance patted the sack of money. "Back home to Louisiana, Renny. Got me a hankering to pay a call on old friends."

Pacing across the entrance hall at Camelot, Jude wondered what kept her brothers. A full day and a half had passed since the four of them had gone to New Orleans. They should be back by now with word of their uncle Henri's whereabouts, and with it knowledge of Rafe's current location.

And why hadn't she heard from Boone? It drove her crazy, not knowing if he were all right, if Rooster were with him, if she'd ever see them again.

Sick with worry, she quickened her stride, cursing the petticoats swishing around her ankles. She'd tried pointing out the inconvenience of a skirt, but Guin had insisted that as long as her daughter stayed in this house, she would dress and act like a lady. Out of love and respect, Jude acquiesced, but the instant she learned Henri's whereabouts, she vowed, not even her mother could stop her from changing back into pants and riding out with her brothers.

Engrossed in her thoughts, she didn't realize she had company. It wasn't until she turned back toward the stairs that she noticed Boone's brothers standing on the third one up. "Jacob, Jeremy, I didn't hear you."

"No, don't reckon you did, ma'am."

Staring at their grim little faces, she winced. She'd virtually forgotten the twins. "Boys, what's wrong?"

"We need to speak to you." As ever Jacob did the talking. Jeremy clung to his jacket, looking equally solemn and twice as scared. "We have to know if Jesse . . . I mean, Tucker . . . will he be coming back for us?"

Jude took a step forward, intending to comfort them, but she stopped at Jacob's next words. "Because if not, we should be getting back to the home."

"The orphanage? Why on earth would you want to go there?"

"We don't want you thinking we're not properly grateful," Jacob said awkwardly. "It's just, well, Jesse will know to look for us there."

"Nonsense. He'll be coming here to Camelot."

Jacob eyed her like a disappointed parent. "How's he gonna find it?"

Unfortunately it was a question she'd been asking herself. Now, too late, she saw the consequences of not telling Boone about herself. Her only hope that he'd find her was in the little information she'd given Rooster. And given the boy's talent for confusing the name with various livestock, he and Boone were just as likely to be on their way to some cattle ranch out west.

Mistaking her pained expression for an answer, Jacob cleared his throat. "It's clear, ma'am, you have troubles enough without us being a burden, too."

Burden? Was that how she'd made them feel? Horrified, she approached them, coming to a stop at the bottom of the stairs. "Oh, boys, you can't really *want* to go back to that orphanage?"

Jeremy answered with a sharp shake of his head, but Jacob tempered his response with mature logic. "Wanting and needing are different," he said firmly. "You folks don't need us here. We're just in the way."

His words shamed her. Lost in her preoccupation, she'd neglected these poor boys, left them to think they were not wanted here. Why, she was no better than Headmistress Hattie.

And no wonder they preferred the orphanage. Since her return, Camelot had been twice as somber as that awful place. Where were the shouts and laughter that usually rang through these halls? What had happened to the games and good-natured teasing her brothers and sisters usually shared?

Silly question. *She* was what happened. Obsessed with her worrying, she'd infected the entire house. And it was time she did something about it.

"I can understand your needing to get back home," she told Jacob. "But the thing is, I really need your help here."

"Us?" Jacob looked down at Jeremy, who was still clinging to the jacket as if his life would end should he let go. "What can we do?"

She eyed them solemnly. "Maybe you haven't noticed, not knowing my family, but my little sister Amanda hasn't laughed once since we got here, my brother John hasn't tried to tease me, and I can't remember ever seeing little Jeanie so somber. It's probably because they're missing their papa, but the gloominess has got to stop. They need some exercise to chase off the doldrums."

"Exercise?" Jacob asked, both boys clearly suspicious. "Like in work?"

Imagining what they must have had since their mother's death, Jude ached to hug them. "No, like in play. Have you ever played blindman's bluff?"

They shook their heads warily.

Reaching for their hands, she tugged them down the stairs. "It's not hard to learn. I'll explain the rules while we go find the others."

She couldn't precisely call them eager as she dragged them outside, but they did seem curious. All in all, she found it a step in the right direction.

And hours later, watching them scamper on the lawn with her sisters and brother, she decided they'd all taken a giant leap forward. Something magical happened when children played together: bonds were formed, a communication that needed no words or language. For a while problems could be forgotten. Jacob might never actually laugh, but he relaxed enough to occasionally smile, and he'd even shed his heavy black jacket. Jeremy had let go of it long since, his attention caught by eight-year-old Amanda. Jude had asked her sister to take him under her wing, but the two appeared to have a good deal in common. It did her heart good, seeing Amanda whispering in his ear, and Jeremy grinning broadly.

If only there were a game to help her get her mind off her troubles. Where the devil were her brothers?

Hearing an engine in the distance, she felt her heart leap into her throat. She nearly ran back to the house to change into boys' clothing, but listening more closely, she realized the boat must be close, maybe just around the bend. She'd better get down to the pier if she wanted to be there to greet them.

She started down the drive, cursing her skirts for impeding her progress. Lifting them up, she began to run, watching the river for the first sign of the steamboat. Unfortunately she was looking in the wrong direction.

It took the blast of a horn to alert her to her mistake, but by then the southbound vessel was pulling up to the pier. Staring at it, she wanted to shout at its captain to shove off, that they weren't expecting company, when she noticed who was waiting at the gangplank to disembark.

"Boone," she cried out, running the remaining distance to the dock.

Twenty-one

Catching Jude as she ran to him, Tucker swung her up into his arms. He savored those first few moments of holding her, treasuring her warmth, breathing in the sweet floral scent of her hair, marveling at how much he had missed her in their three-day separation. So much for his hope that he could one day forget her.

"Ah, Boone," she said, as he set her back down on her feet. "I'd begun to doubt I'd ever see either of you again. I should have known Rooster would get you both here in one piece." She beamed at the boy coming up behind them.

"He was a big help," Tucker said dryly. "Helped me waste the better part of a day, combing the streets of Baton Rouge for him. I wasn't expecting to find him at the Tally-Ho Tavern, knocking back sarsaparillas."

"Hey, I had to wait for my reward," Rooster protested. "It paid for our passage, if you recall."

"The second passage, which we needed only because you didn't get the name right in the first place. Caramel Lot. It's a lucky thing that riverboat captain knew the neighborhood." The man had given Tucker an earful about the Latour family, too, enough to warn that he wouldn't find Jude doing chores in some modest farmhouse, as he'd let himself believe. From the river he'd seen the sprawling plantation house with its bold columns and many railed porches, a mansion that put her in a class so far above him, he might as well reach for the stars. Now, gazing at her expensive brushed cotton gown, all the yards of Belgian lace, he knew for certain he'd never find a place in the life of this elegant stranger. He couldn't even afford the repairs on such a dress.

"Reward?" she was saying to Rooster, eyeing his new clothing suspiciously. "Let's go up to the house and have a lemonade while you explain to me just what you've been up to."

The kid grinned as he stared up the winding, tree-lined drive. "I saw some kids playing on the lawn. One even looked like Germy."

"Jacob's there, too." Jude gestured toward the house. "Go on and join them. I'm sure they'll be thrilled to see you."

"I reckon it's Boone they'll be wanting to see."

He was undoubtedly right. Tucker was anxious to see them as well, but he needed a few moments alone with Jude. Time to look at her, talk to her, thank her for taking care of his brothers, but more importantly, to tell her the truth about his involvement with the Gray Ghosts. After Rooster had told him about her parting words about wanting honesty between them, he'd realized that it was the least he could give her, the least she deserved.

"Tell the boys I'll be along in a moment," he told Rooster, "but right now I need to talk to Jude."

"Yeah, maybe I will go find those two," Rooster said slowly, looking from Jude to Tucker. "If you're sure you don't need me."

Tucker shooed him off, knowing all he'd need the boy for was an excuse to avoid the inevitable.

"I'm glad we have this brief time alone," Jude said as they watched Rooster vanish up the tree-lined drive. "I've something I need to say to you, too."

Tucker turned to her, intending to spill his guts, but one look at her lovely face, and all he could think of was kissing her. A sentiment she obviously shared, for in the next instant, she was in his arms, reawakening every fantasy he'd ever known. Tasting her lips, drowning in the sensual heaven of her mouth, he grew achingly aware of all he'd missed, all he could lose forever.

"No, I can't do this, not until I've said what I have to say." Jude pulled free, speaking quickly, as if desperate to get it all out without interruption. "You're going to think me a hypocrite, spouting off about trust and honor when I've been so dishonest myself. I can't blame you for being angry. I know I can never forgive anyone who lies to me."

I can never forgive anyone who lies to me. Hearing those words, Tucker knew a sinking sensation. That's what he'd been hoping for, forgiveness, but his chances looked worse and worse. "It's all right," he told her, pulling her against his chest, wanting to stall a little while longer. "I'm sure you had your reasons."

She shrugged. "Christopher made me think so, but I know now that I was wrong to keep the facts from you. You deserve to know that Rafe is our father."

This was her big secret? Hugging her tight, he spoke into her sweet-scented hair. "Don't worry about it. I already figured it out, that night you told me about him in Independence." Feeling her stiffen, he hastened to explain. "Ah, Jude, nobody could blame you for wanting revenge."

"Revenge?" She pulled back, clearly confused.

No less than himself. "Isn't that what this has all been about," he asked, feeling himself floundering. "Your getting back at him for what he did to you?"

"But that wasn't Rafe. That was my real papa, Jacques Morteau."

Morteau? Tucker frowned, finding something tauntingly familiar about the name.

"I could never hurt Rafe," she went on earnestly. "I owe him my childhood, my life. That time I told you about, when I shot Papa in the leg? Well, he came after us, swearing to beat us all. Uncle Rafe was a bachelor then, so it was easy for him, but he took my brothers and me in and hid us at his shack in the swamp. He was working hard to build Camelot. It was his dream to make a real home for all of us, but Papa and his friends tried their best to destroy him."

Jude grimaced. "They came to the swamp one day when Rafe was away. Papa was going to hurt my brothers, so I had to trick him, and he . . . he fell to his death. It was all my fault, but Rafe insisted on taking official blame. He and Guin felt that we kids had been through enough already."

Listening to her, Tucker found it hard to reconcile her tale with his own experience. The Rafe Latour she described was a far cry from the monster who had killed his mother.

Jude sighed heavily. "The trouble is, by protecting me, Rafe made Papa's brother angry at him. Uncle Henri is the one who wants revenge. I think he's been behind all Rafe's transfers. He's the puppeteer, pulling strings."

Tucker shook his head. "Isn't it an awfully elaborate scheme? Surely he could find more direct means of revenge."

"You don't know Uncle Henri. It's just the kind of game he loves to play. He fancies himself the great manipulator, as patient as Job. For years he'd been toying with Rafe—flooding the fields, burning buildings, destroying Camelot's credit—but a friend or neighbor always baled us out. When the war began, and the harassment stopped, we thought he'd given up—but down in Baton Rouge, when I heard his lawyer had taken Rafe away . . ."

"Wait, what is this?"

She frowned. "I forgot, I didn't have the chance to tell you. I was told Rafe was hanged for treason, but luckily a friend saw the colonel taking money to falsify records. That's when I realized I'd been led there, just so that awful man could tell me Rafe was dead. Knowing I'd bring the news home, Uncle Henri wanted the whole family suffering. In a few days' time, he'll probably send some sign that Rafe's still alive. Not much of a sign, just enough to raise our hopes, so he can dash them again. He's just biding his time, enjoying our misery, waiting to watch us lose Camelot to the auction block."

Tucker couldn't help but notice the similarity to his own position with the farm. "You owe back taxes, too?"

"With us it's the creditors. It's been nigh on impossible, keeping the place going with the war and the embargo. A family friend bequeathed her estate to Rafe, but he has to be found, alive or dead, before anyone can claim the money. That's why Henri is hiding him, to make sure we can't save our home. He wants Rafe's dream to die with him."

Again Tucker found it hard to connect the Latour she described to the man he'd hated so long.

She sighed. "The minute we lose Camelot—and you can bet that when the dust clears, Henri will be holding the deed—Rafe will be executed."

Watching her face, seeing her worry, Tucker's uneasiness deepened. What was it about the name *Morteau?*

"We have to find Rafe and soon," Jude told him, her gaze pleading. "My brothers went to New Orleans looking for Uncle Henri, but they've yet to return—and I'm getting worried. What if something happened to them, too?"

Staring into her eyes, Tucker was hard put to remember his hatred. Jude, with her warmth and caring and undemanding trust, had him rethinking his own need for revenge. How petty it seemed in the face of this threat to her family. He still had no love for the man, but destroying Latour now would break her heart, and how could he live with that on his conscience?

Maybe he should find some other way to earn his money. Let Billy . . .

With a flash of cold dread, he remembered the wire he'd

sent in Baton Rouge, telling the Gray Ghosts he was on his way to New Orleans.

"I need a horse," he told her abruptly, thinking that while he was in town, he'd send another wire detouring the gang to Mississippi or maybe Alabama. "I'll also need the fastest route to the city. I'm going after your uncle," he added as she blinked at him in confusion. "And hopefully your brothers."

With a determined smile, she turned toward the house, tugging him behind her. "Very well, then come with me. You can chat with Guin while I change."

"Whoa, Jude, forget it. I'm going alone."

"Sure you are," she said conversationally, bulldogging ahead. "And I'm going to sit here chewing my fingernails to the bone waiting for word from you."

"I mean it, Jude. This could be dangerous."

"All the more reason you need my help. I can't believe we're still having this argument, Boone." She stopped, turning to face him. "What does it take to get through that hardheaded skull of yours?"

"Is this the pot calling the kettle black?" He stared her down, fighting worry and exasperation. "Think this through, Jude. Past the this-is-what-I-want phase."

"Obviously I've given it more thought than you. Face it, you'll need me to identify the people you're going after. Or were you planning on running around shouting their names, hoping they'll come to you?"

He almost told her he knew damned well what Rafe Latour looked like, but in the very same instant he remembered where he'd heard the name Morteau. Billy had mentioned it, that night in St. Louis, as the man his Cap'n worked for. The Gray Ghosts had been helping her vicious uncle Henri build his trap around her family.

And Tucker Boone had played too large a part in it.

Hands on hips, she gave her ultimatum. "I'm going with you, Boone, and you can't talk me out of it."

Oh, he could stop her, he thought ruefully. He just had to tell her the truth.

It wasn't so much the prospect of her anger that held his tongue, but the look of dismay—no, disgust—that he'd see on her face. Both of them knew he'd had his chances to confess, but he hadn't taken them and now was too late. He had to fix things, make them right again, before he could confess what he'd done. "Fine," he told her, recognizing it was useless to argue. "But you'll do what I say this time, you hear?"

They both also knew she had no intention of obeying him, but he wasn't giving her the choice. He'd take her with him to the authorities, but he'd leave her there, where she'd be safe, while he did his own investigating.

Looking up the drive, hearing the children's chatter, he realized the rest of her menagerie might need protecting, too. It might be too late to stop the Gray Ghosts—they could have acted on the message he'd sent them already.

"Before we leave," he asked Jude, "is there somewhere the twins and the rest of your family can go until we get back?"

"They can go to Roseland, my uncle Ham and aunt Edith Ann's place," she told him, her face puzzled. "Why? Are you anticipating trouble?"

He shrugged, not knowing what he expected, only that his anxiety increased by the moment. "I figure it's better to be safe than sorry."

"I suppose." She tilted her head, clearly bewildered. "But I must warn, it would be just like Guin to refuse to leave the house unprotected. And knowing Rooster, he'll put up a fight if we don't take him with us."

This was why he liked working alone, Tucker thought impatiently. Who had time for all these little rebellions? "Then convince them," he threw over his shoulder as he headed up to the house. "Just bully them like you bully me."

* * *

Feeling very much bullied, Guin Latour drove the wagon loaded down with children, gazing back over her shoulder at the pair bidding them farewell in the drive. As worried as she was, Guin couldn't stop the smile as she thought of how Jude had argued with the handsome Mr. Boone. Their little girl had chosen one heck of a time to fall in love.

Guin only prayed the man didn't break her heart.

Though she feared it might be inevitable, the way those two refused to give ground to each other. Then again she and Rafe had fought at the beginning, before realizing they shared the same dream for the future. Maybe, like herself, Jude had to learn not to be so mule-headed.

Indeed it was the girl's stubbornness that had her riding now for Roseland. Guin hadn't wanted to leave her home unprotected, but she knew Jude wouldn't leave until she agreed, and Guin would do nothing to stand in the way of anyone finding her husband.

Last night she'd had a dream—a nightmare, really—in which she'd stood facing Lance Buford again, assuring him that she could never marry him. At first she hadn't been sure why, only that it was imperative that she hold on and wait, but when Rafe had walked into the dream, so tall and proud and heartbreakingly handsome, the tears had sprung to her eyes. Tears that stayed on her cheeks when she woke in the morning.

In her heart Guin considered it a sign. Rafe had seemed so real, so solid to her, she was convinced that he was alive. So desperate was she to find him before it was too late, she'd have gone herself to New Orleans, if not for her younger children. She had to see them—and the twins—safely settled at Roseland.

But that didn't mean she would stay there herself.

Grinning at Rooster, seated beside her on the bench,

Guin had every intention of being at Camelot, guarding the fortress, until her husband came home.

Hurrying behind Boone to Union headquarters in New Orleans, Jude tried to shake off her uneasiness. As she'd feared, Guin hadn't wanted to leave Camelot, and their refusal to take him along had left Rooster feeling thoroughly affronted. After much deliberation, Guin had taken the boy aside, after which they'd both agreed to Boone's request. It made Jude uneasy though, watching Rooster's wide grin as the family rode off to Roseland.

But she had no time to worry about it. She and Boone had enough on their minds, trying to locate her uncle. On the trip downriver, they'd decided to start with the authorities. Or rather Boone had decided, and she had thought it political to agree with him after he'd allowed her to tag along. If nothing came of their visit—and she didn't think it would—she had friends in the French Quarter, Creoles she'd met during visits to her great-grandparents, who might know better where a man like Henri Morteau might be hiding.

Struggling to keep up with Boone in her skirts—Guin had refused to allow her daughter to go parading around New Orleans dressed as a male—Jude entered the building a good ten strides behind him. He made no attempt to wait for her, but marched across the huge, crowded room to a central desk, determined to get the attention of the harried sergeant standing behind it.

Unfortunately Boone was not alone in his efforts. A small horde of civilians and military personnel swarmed the desk, shouting for the sergeant's attention. In obvious disgust Boone strode back to Jude, waiting in an oasis of relative quiet in the corner. "This could take longer than I'd hoped," he told her gruffly. "From what I can hear, there's been a murder. The newsmen want information, the military isn't giving it, and no one can be heard over the battle."

"What can we do?"

"You stay here and watch for an opening. I'll go scout out the place, see if we can slip by into the offices unnoticed."

She grabbed his sleeve. "What if we get separated?"

"I'll be right back, all right?"

He seemed distracted, and she didn't like the way he wouldn't look at her. She had the sudden ugly sensation that if she let go now, she might never see him again. "You never told me. Back home by the river," she went on, noticing his blank expression. "You never did say what it was you wanted to talk about."

His face tightened. Staring at his profile, she could see the strain in every line. As he turned to her, she tensed, afraid of what he might tell her, but his features smoothed into a smile. "I wanted to thank you for taking my brothers under your wing. Being with your family has done wonders for them. I haven't seen them that happy in a long, long time."

She smiled back, remembering how the twins had flown into his arms, all dirty and disheveled and looking like normal, active little boys. "There will always be a home for them at Camelot. They can stay with my family while you do what you must to get back your farm."

The strain was back in his features, in every muscle of his body. "You should watch that generosity, Jude. Folks are bound to take advantage of it."

Alarmed by his cold, almost cruel tone, she took his hand. "I hope you know there's a place for you, too. Wherever I am, you can always find a home."

Clenching his jaw, he pulled his hand away to gesture to the desk. "See what you can do about getting us in to talk to someone. I'll do some scouting."

She couldn't believe that he meant to leave her here.

"Please don't go," she blurted out as he took a step forward. "Why can't we do this together?"

"Damnit, Jude!" he exploded. "For once, can't you do as I ask without an argument? This can take hours, and we don't have hours."

No doubt seeing her shocked expression, he took a deep breath and spoke in a more controlled tone. "I'll be back for you, Jude. You have my word on it."

She stared into his eyes, needing to believe him, yet sensing he was hiding something from her. "What is it, Boone? What are you *not* telling me?"

"Let it be," he growled at her, mouth tightening as he strode off. "Let's just do what we have to do."

She stood there frozen, watching him walk away from her. Her heart screamed out to him to come back, but her mind felt battered. Had that been her Tucker Boone, talking so harshly, ignoring her pleas? He could have been a stranger, the way he couldn't wait to be quit of her.

Biting her lip, she refused to feel hurt, to play the victim. Who did Boone think he was, ordering her around? If he wanted to pretend the last few weeks had never been, then maybe she should remind him that he was in her employ, and bound to follow her orders. Primary of which was to stay close to her side.

She started forward, meaning to go after him, when she heard her name from across the room. Spinning, she spotted Christopher, waving his arms and motioning for her to join him.

He wasn't alone, she saw as she hurried over. Patrick, Peter, and Paul sat slumped in chairs behind him, scowling at the three burly guards standing at attention to their right. All three brothers rose when they noticed her approach.

"We're being held for questioning," Christopher explained before she could ask. "But I don't think they believe we had anything to do with the murder."

Remembering how Boone had mentioned a murder, Jude

looked from one brother to the next, the implications slowly sifting in. "Uncle Henri?"

"He, his lawyer, and a half dozen men were gunned down at his shipyard," Patrick explained with a grimace. "Can't say we much enjoyed finding them."

No, he wouldn't have, not with his sensitive nature, but Patrick's grim expression brought home a frightening prospect. "Did you find Rafe?"

"Don't worry, he wasn't one of the victims," her brother Paul said, shaking his head. "Though we did find some ropes and signs of a struggle."

"We're guessing somebody went to Uncle Henri's after him," Peter added. Being twins, they often finished each other's thoughts. "And they killed whoever got in their way."

"A whole slew of somebodies," Paul continued, "judging by the muddy footprints. Which, incidentally, gets us off the hook. They say the boots that made those prints were army issue. Confederate army."

She glanced at her brothers' simple shoes, glad that they'd shed all visible reminders of the war. "It had to be the Gray Ghosts."

Christopher nodded. "They're not saying, but that's what I'm thinking."

She stared at him, thinking aloud. "But they operate out of Missouri. What would they be doing down here, and what on earth would they want with Rafe?"

Christopher looked her straight in the eye. "Maybe you should be asking Boone these questions."

"Boone?"

"C'mon, Jude, it's not like you to be so blind. Rafe fought in Missouri, maybe even served with a Gray Ghost or two before he was captured. Remember how your good friend Boone knew about the train derailment? What if he's just been using us so he and his friends could get to Rafe?"

"No!" The first was automatic, the rest a product of

slow reasoning. "He had nothing to do with the attack on Uncle Henri. He was with me. Still is."

"Yeah? Where?"

She glanced helplessly over her shoulder. "You can't see anything in this mob, but he's here somewhere, trying to find us a way in to talk to an official." Even as she uttered the words, she realized how lame it sounded, especially when she remembered how tense he'd been when she tried to detain him. "I'll go find him," she offered, needing to see Boone's face. "He'll explain everything."

"Jude, wait." Patrick grabbed her arm, his face clouded with worry. "There's something else you should know. They say there's a witness who saw a good-looking, fair-haired gentleman walk into the shipyard. Christopher insists it's this Boone of yours, but because of what you just said and something else that was mentioned, now I'm not so sure."

"Something else?"

"The witness claims another man called him Cap'n. Cap'n Buford."

A frisson of fear shot through her. Lance Buford? Long ago the man had tried to burn them in their beds, hoping to kill Rafe and thus gain Guin and her daddy's plantation. "But it's impossible," she protested. "Buford's in prison."

Patrick looked more solemn than ever. "So I told the lieutenant, but he said many prisoners were furloughed off to the battlefield. When you think of it, it's only natural that he and Henri Morteau would join forces. Just as predictable as it ending badly for our uncle."

Her mind reeling, Jude barely heard her brother. If *Lance* had Rafe, things were drastically worse. He hated Rafe and had no reason for keeping him alive.

So why hadn't Lance killed him with Uncle Henri? Why untie and drag him off? "Oh, God," she cried as the awful truth dawned on her. "He's taking Rafe to Camelot. To Guin."

Patrick, who'd fought through that awful time with her, understood in a flash. "Buford still needs to prove that he's the better man."

She nodded fearfully. "We've got to stop him."

"We can't go anywhere," Christopher said, again nodding at the guards. "They're keeping us here until this mess is cleared up."

Patrick took her by the hands. "I'll try to get the lieutenant's ear so he'll send some soldiers, but in the meantime, you gather up friends here in town and hustle them upriver to Camelot. We should never have left Guin alone there."

"We didn't. Boone insisted everyone pack up and go to Roseland until we got back."

"And you don't think that was odd?" Christopher muttered behind her.

Unsure of what he meant, Jude turned to question him, but Patrick distracted her with a more dire concern. "I'm glad Guin is safe, but it won't stop Buford from taking his revenge. It won't be the first time he's torched a house."

"And just like the first time, he'll want Rafe in it," Jude said, appalled. "I'll go find Boone. He'll know what to do."

"Forget Boone," Christopher snarled. "Go find Charlie Lawton and the Bakers. They'll stop that sick bastard from doing any more harm to this family."

"He might be right." Reluctantly releasing his grasp on her hand, Patrick shooed her off. "Speed is vital, and you'll find safety in numbers."

"I'll do what I can," she answered evasively. "You boys do your best to get home as soon as possible."

She left them, making her way across the crowded room. Doubt and worry haunted her, but she refused to leave without Boone. Only imagine how he'd feel to come back for her and find she'd gone off without him?

After a while she could imagine only too well, finding

no sign of Boone anywhere. Thinking—hoping—he might have stepped outside for a moment, she marched through the door to glance up and down the street. Frustrated, she was about to go back inside when she felt a hand grip her shoulder. She whirled, ready to lay into him, but it wasn't Boone she faced. Holding his gun to her side, Billy Cochoran flashed his patented grin. "You can't know how long I've been looking for you, sweet lady. Come along, there's someone I want you to meet."

She wanted to run, to scream bloody murder, but she had to go with him, his gun being quite persuasive, as were the four heavily armed men at his side. She did protest when they neared the docks, having a healthy fear of what happened in shipyards, but Billy ordered her bound, gagged, and blindfolded. "Got no time for female hysterics," he told her nastily when the order had been carried out. He then barked at a man he called Preacher to hoist her up over his shoulder.

In this ignominious position, she was carried aboard what she assumed was a boat and dumped onto a cold, hard deck. Left alone and unable to see, she had more than ample time for the fears to fester. Where were they taking her? What would they do to her? And most importantly, what was happening to Rafe?

Fighting panic and frustration, she prayed Patrick had gotten free of the Union offices, that her brothers were racing to save their home. Feeling the boat engines rumble to life beneath her, she knew she'd be powerless to stop anyone.

"Be a good girl, and I'll take off the blindfold," Billy said into her ear. "I might even take off the gag if you swear to keep quiet."

"Why are you doing this?" she asked the minute both cloths were removed.

Hunkered down in front of her, Billy wasn't grinning now. "I want you to know, I'm sorry about this," he told her, reaching down to slice the rope at her wrists. "Got no wish to be hurting a sweet thing like you, but I got my orders. Got to be looking out for myself, same as everyone else."

"And your orders are?"

"Mainly to see that you cause no trouble. Be a good girl, now, and nurse the prisoner." He nodded to a dark form on the other side of the barge's open deck. "Had to hit him a mite hard to subdue him."

"Prisoner?" She moved closer to the still form, sensing who she'd find.

Rafe! Dropping to her knees, she nearly sobbed with relief. All these years of waiting and worrying, and here he was in the flesh.

Though with the blood caked on his face, she could scarce make out his features. Touching him gently, she felt an ugly tug at her heart to discover that he hadn't reacted. She felt for his pulse, overjoyed to find it stronger than he appeared himself. Poor Rafe looked so pale and emaciated. And obviously he'd been beaten to within an inch of his life.

"What have you done to him?" she lashed out, appalled to hear her voice tremble.

"Worry less about what we *have* done to him," someone drawled behind her, "and more about what we *will* be doing in the near future."

Looking up, she found herself facing the evil Lance Buford.

Twenty-two

Christopher paced across the small area they'd been ordered to wait in, unable to think in all the noise, a din that increased as more and more people poured into the room. Uncle Henri's death sure seemed to have caused a commotion, or else this town just needed something else to think about after losing the war.

What was keeping Patrick? he wondered, glad that at least Jude had gone for help. He'd watched her slip out the door alone nearly an hour ago, and it gave him great satisfaction to be right about Boone. From the look on her face as she left, the man had been nowhere around when she needed him.

A satisfaction short-lived, though. Looking up, Christopher saw Boone striding toward him through the mob, his scowl as dark and threatening as a November sky. "Where's your sister?" he barked. "Where is Jude?"

Christopher had no intention of telling this man anything. Setting his shoulders squarely, he faced Boone down. "Where were *you?*"

"I don't have time for games." Boone glared from him to Peter and Paul, who were now wandering over to see what was going on. "I just learned Billy and his Gray Ghosts are in town, and I want to make certain your sister is safe."

"Gray Ghosts?" Peter asked. "Isn't that the group that killed Uncle Henri?"

"Morteau is dead?" Boone's gaze narrowed as he glanced at the desk. "Of course the murder," he said slowly. "What about Latour?"

"We think Buford took him back to Camelot," Paul volunteered, to which Peter added, "To punish Guin."

"Why are you telling him all this?" Christopher snapped at his brothers. "He's just Boone, the man Jude hired. He doesn't need to know family business."

"You'll have to forgive our little brother." Paul frowned at him. "He tends to be overprotective when it comes to Jude."

"I noticed." Boone gave Christopher another scowl. "I'm trying to protect your sister, too, damnit. You don't know what these men are capable of."

"We know what they did to Uncle Henri," Christopher sneered before stomping off, having no stomach to listen while Peter explained what their uncle, father, and Lance Buford had done in the past.

He didn't like the way things were working out. This should have been his adventure with his big sister, him and Jude finding Rafe together, only everyone else kept getting in the way. Braggarts and show-offs, all of them, from that aggravating Rooster to Saint Boone himself.

Bad enough Jude had to hang on every word the man had to say, but now his brothers did, too? *I'm trying to protect your sister*, Boone boasted, as if Christopher wasn't capable of looking out for Jude himself. It had him wishing he hadn't nicked the man in the shoulder, that he'd hit Boone square in the chest.

Working himself into a state, he was taken aback to see Boone marching to the door. Unnerved, Christopher went to his brothers. "What was that all about?" he asked, trying to sound casual. "Where's he going in such a hurry?"

"Home," Peter offered at the same time Paul said, "After Jude."

At Christopher's colorful oath, their brows raised. "I'm

telling you, Boone can't be trusted," he insisted. "That's it, I'm going after him myself."

Paul reached out to stop him. "Are you crazy?" He nodded at the guards. "Did you forget our friends with the guns?"

Christopher had, but he'd never admit it to his brothers. "I'm not that dumb," he told them. "You two make a diversion so I can slip away unnoticed."

"They're going to realize you're gone eventually," Peter pointed out. "They're bound to come after you."

"Good. I'll need some extra muscle to take on Buford."

Peter and Paul exchanged glances, a slow grin appearing on both faces as they realized how the added reinforcements could save the day. With dual nods, they headed back to their seats, shouting and shoving, then wrestling each other to the ground. When the guards rushed at them, Christopher dashed for the door. Five minutes later he was running down the road, hot on Boone's heels.

He caught up with the man by Jackson Square. "If you're looking for passage upriver," he told Boone breathlessly, "you're heading the wrong way. Stumpie Whitaker has the fastest boat on the bayous."

Boone merely nodded, falling into step beside him, treating his advice with the respect it deserved. For a fleeting moment, Christopher almost liked him. "This is just to save Jude," he added in warning. "After this . . ."

"Don't worry," Boone said darkly. "After *this* I doubt you'll have to deal with me again."

Jude sat in the front parlor at Camelot, shivering though it wasn't really cold, cradling the still unconscious Rafe in her lap. On the other side of the door, she could hear Lance Buford giving Billy an earful. It wasn't enough to have found her, apparently—Billy shouldn't have left Boone on the loose. "Get out there and watch for him," Lance shouted. "He'll be showing up here soon enough."

Jude winced as the door slammed shut, knowing she'd be his next target. The self-absorbed greed in Lance's cold eyes set her skin crawling. As a boy he must have been the kind to pick the wings off butterflies, then sit smiling while they suffered and died. Much like he'd studied her and Rafe on the trip upriver.

Any illusions of appealing to this man's mercy had died when they'd arrived here at Camelot, and she'd listened to Lance's mindless rage at discovering Guin wasn't here. Right now whatever men weren't guarding the house were scouring the grounds for her, and Jude knew it was a mere matter of time before Lance turned on her to learn Guin's whereabouts. She'd made the mistake of being too smug about finding the house empty, and Lance's sneer warned that he'd noticed.

He stormed into the room a moment later, one hand clutching a stuffed carpetbag, the other aiming a pistol at her heart. Instinctively she shielded Rafe's head with her hands, prepared to protect him, but wishing he'd wake, well and whole, to help her fight for their lives.

"Where is Guin?" Lance growled, his tight features betraying his frustration.

Jude shrugged. She knew her indifference would anger him further, but she refused to let this man hold more than her body hostage. "You seem to be having trouble keeping track of your victims."

As she'd expected, his face contorted with rage, the lines of cruelty and dissipation etching deeper. Gazing at him, Jude watched the charming facade vanish, revealing the monster underneath.

"I do hope you're not expecting Boone to come after me," she told him. "Last I saw, he couldn't wait to leave me behind."

In the blink of an eye, the mask slipped back into place,

and Lance Buford was once more the gallant Southern gentleman—in looks if not speech. "Dear girl," he said, shaking his head sadly, "did you truly think it was you Boone wanted?" He gave an amused laugh. "How vain. This is what he was after," he said, tossing the bag onto the sofa. "This is what he'll come back for."

She couldn't help but notice the bills poking out the sides. "Money?" she couldn't stop herself from blurting out, her stomach knotting.

"Don't get me wrong," Lance went on, striding behind the sofa. "You're a fine-looking woman, Jude Latour," he said, leaning over to stroke the pistol along her cheek. "If I weren't preoccupied with Guin at the moment, I'd enjoy having a go at you myself—but take it from one who knows, no man's lust is ever as powerful as his greed. Take Boone, for example. He likes the skirts as much as any red-blooded male, but faced with the choice, he'll invariably take the cash."

She wanted to protest that Boone wasn't like other men, that Lance didn't know him at all, but she couldn't forget how Boone had let Billy ride with them, how the Gray Ghosts had dogged their trail. What had he been doing at the Western Union office in Baton Rouge? she wondered. For that matter, what was he doing now?

"Did you hear that?" Lance walked slowly to the door, pistol at the ready.

Jude's heart leapt, hoping Boone had come to save her, but then she realized his being here would only prove Lance's point. When she heard the voice raised in protest, her spirits plummeted farther. What in the name of all good sense was Guin doing home?

She didn't wait long to find out. Grinning smugly, Lance took a furious, wriggling Guin from the man holding her and dragged her into the room. "Come on in, Guin, honey. We've all been waiting on you for the party to begin."

In the tailored riding habit, with her blond hair piled

atop her head and her classic features tight with disdain, Guin seemed as regal as ever as she strode into the room. "You've sunk to a new low, Lance Buford," she told him imperiously, acting as if the pistol trained at her chest were beneath her notice. "Just what is the meaning of this? How dare you invade my home!"

"Still the queen of the castle." His appreciative smile belied the threat he posed. "After all this time, how reassuring to find that some things never change. I'm sure gonna enjoy this, but you two ladies will have to excuse me a minute, while I get old Preacher to find us a pail of water to wake up the guest of honor. Wouldn't want your precious dirt farmer to miss a minute of the fun."

"Rafe Latour is twice the gentleman you'll ever be, Lance Buford," Guin told him proudly. "Which is precisely why I married him and not you."

Heartfelt words and all too true, but Lance's murderous expression showed Guin's mistake in uttering them. "We'll see about that," he said darkly as he strode from the room.

Turning, Guin seemed to notice for the first time that she wasn't alone. "Jude, oh, my God . . . is that—" She ran to the sofa, kneeling before them, her face white with fear. "Is he . . ."

"He's just unconscious," Jude said softly. "They beat him pretty bad."

"My poor darling," Guin crooned, running her hands over Rafe's face. "Oh, God, Jude, he is alive. You've brought him home to us, at long last."

Jude didn't have the heart to point out that she hadn't brought him here, that Guin might be celebrating prematurely. Easing Rafe's head off her lap, she stood up and let Guin take her place on the sofa. She'd waited too long to see her husband to have even this brief reunion taken from her.

"We have to get Rafe out of here," Guin said solemnly,

cradling her husband as if to shield him from harm. "Lance is insane. He'll kill him."

"I'm afraid you're right. Oh, Guin, I thought you were going to stay at Roseland. Why did you come back?"

"I only said I'd *go* to Roseland, not stay there." Guin gazed up at Jude. "How else did you think I could convince Rooster to stay behind with me, except by asking him to come back with me as my protector?"

Jude had known they'd both given in too easily. "He's not much of a protector. He's just a boy."

"Quite a resourceful one, though. He created a diversion, running through the bushes so I could sneak up here and see who was in my house." Her face clouded. "Lance must have the place surrounded. His men grabbed me before I even hit the porch."

"I don't suppose you brought a gun?"

"I did, but I left it with Rooster." Seeing Jude's crestfallen expression, she added, "Oh, honey, you know I can't shoot."

Neither could Rooster, Jude thought unhappily, watching another hope be yanked away. She just prayed the boy had the good sense to take off running. No sense in them all getting killed.

Killed. Looking down at Rafe and Guin, thinking of all that they'd done for her, Jude understood the true enormity of their situation. She had to find some way to stop Buford.

She moved about the room, looking for something she could use in defense, but they kept no weapons in the parlor. By the door she noticed a two-gallon container of kerosene—no doubt Guin had been filling the lamps—but she had no way to light it, and besides she couldn't risk setting fire to the house. Reaching for a pair of sewing shears, she heard another commotion in the front hall. Guin looked up at Jude, mirroring her alarm, neither prepared for Lance's return.

Nor was Jude any more ready to see Boone.

He burst into the room with his hands raised, Billy holding

a pistol to his head. Hiding the shears in the folds of her skirts, Jude watched Lance march in five paces behind them.

"Isn't this splendid?" Lance beamed at Guin. "Everyone's shown up for our little party."

Jude watched Boone. Had he, like Lance suggested, merely returned for the money? She had to know what he was doing here, needed to find some excuse to explain away the obvious, but he refused to look her way.

Lance, however, couldn't wait to catch her attention. "See, I was right and you were wrong. Here's Boone, right on schedule, come to collect his money."

Look at me, she pleaded silently. *Give me some sign that I wasn't a fool to trust you.*

Instead his gaze went to the bag on the sofa. "So there really is money?" he asked casually. "After the cold reception, I wasn't sure I'd be getting paid."

Jude felt a part of her heart wither.

Lance gave a nasty laugh. "You've got nerve, Boone. Gotta give you that. But really, why should I pay you a cent? We got to Latour before you did."

"Who told you where to find him?"

Jude stared at him in shock. She needed him to protest his innocence, not add to his conviction.

"Yes, you were quite helpful," Lance agreed amiably. "But let's face it, Boone, you failed to stop the girl from getting in our way."

"I didn't hire on to play baby-sitter."

Amazing how much that toneless retort could hurt. In one short sentence, Boone had reduced their time together to a tedious task he'd been paid to do.

Typically Lance laughed. "No, you had your own agenda, right from the start. You wanted to repay Latour for killing your mother."

"No," Jude said softly, her mind reeling from one painful revelation after another. So vividly she could see the hatred on Boone's face as he spoke of the rebel captain who raided his farm. "It wasn't Rafe. He'd never do such a thing."

"Such touching faith," Lance sneered. "I should warn, Boone, they all think the sun rises just to shine on that man's head."

"Faith is a thing earned, Lance Buford," Guin told him coldly. "A concept you never quite grasped."

"As long as we're tossing out clichés, never forget that might makes right." Lance smiled, stroking the barrel of his pistol. "Men like me and Billy and Boone here, we don't have much use for lofty concepts. Faith never pays the bills, dear heart. To have real respect, real power, you've got to have cold, hard cash."

Jude silently willed Boone to argue, to insist Lance was wrong, but he stood silently, hands raised in the air, still refusing to so much as glance at her.

"Guin is right," she said angrily. "Rafe is ten times the man you'll ever be."

Boone pointedly ignored her. "You accuse me of having my own agenda, but what about you, Buford? Those lost souls outside, following you to keep the Cause alive, do they know the real reason you brought them here? Billy, do you?"

Gaze narrowing, Lance turned in his direction. "Clever, Boone. Divide and conquer. Trouble is, you can't break the bond between my men and me. Staring death in the face together keeps us looking out for each other. But I don't imagine that's something a deserter like you can ever understand."

Boone looked at Jude then, an involuntary reaction he obviously regretted, for barely had their gazes linked when he looked away. Jude thought she saw guilt, but like Christopher suggested, maybe she saw only what she wanted. All those tender moments, letting her get just so close before backing off—it would seem he'd just been charming her like he sweet-talked Lilah and all his other women.

From the start he'd been wearing a mask, much like Lance himself, using her to get Rafe so he could collect his blood money.

Gazing at Boone's profile—remembering how it felt to hold him, love him—Jude felt another part of her die.

"These Latour women understand loyalty," Lance was saying, strolling up behind Guin, leaning down close to her face. "They're regular tigresses when it comes to protecting their own." He rubbed his gun barrel along Guin's cheek. "Ain't that right, sugar?"

Gripping the shears, Jude took a step forward, wanting to plunge the blades into his cold, black heart, but Billy called out, "Cap'n, the young one. I wouldn't turn my back on her if I was you."

"How astute of you, Lieutenant." Straightening, Lance called out, "Renny? Get your carcass in here to keep an eye on this she-cat so I can deal with Latour."

"What are you going to do?" Guin asked fearfully as Renny Claiborne strode over to Jude, his pistol trained at her head.

"Yeah, Buford," Boone taunted, "why not tell us all what you really mean to do? Somehow I'm thinking it has precious little to do with the Cause."

"You think I'd waste my time on any cause but my own?" Lance gave a scornful chuckle. "I knew the Confederacy never stood a chance against them Northern millionaires. You have to beat the Yankees at their own game, by amassing as much money and political power. That's my *cause,* and the only one I believe in."

"Hear that, Billy?" Boone said over his shoulder. "Greed. That's all this has ever been about."

Jude watched Billy's grip loosen on his weapon.

"Hell, no, it's been about foresight." Lance snorted. "I saw the opportunity your Missouri border offered. Government-sanctioned robbery—that's what it was—from which I stood to make a killing. See that," he said, nodding at the bag on the sofa. "There's more in the bank, plenty enough to set up my own little empire, here in this house, with my beautiful Queen Guinevere at my side."

Guin glared up at him. "You're forgetting I already have a husband."

"Well, now, thank you for bringing that up." The smile Lance gave Guin chilled Jude's bones. "I aim to rid you of that inconvenience," he drawled, his gaze going from Guin to Rafe. "But how? I do hate to shoot a man in the back."

"This is insane," Jude couldn't stop herself from crying out. "You'll never get away with it, not with all these witnesses."

"You know, Guin, that's one smart little girl you raised. Too bad those witnesses aren't particularly reliable. I doubt the authorities will pay them much heed once a certain young lady's carpetbag is discovered at Morteau's shipyard with her and Boone's belongings inside it." He turned to frown at Boone. "Still she could be right. The less said against us the better. Billy, why don't you take your old friend out back and show him how we deal with deserters?"

Billy's grip wavered. "Cap'n, you sure—"

"That's an order, Lieutenant. Unless you're planning on becoming part of the body count when we're finished."

"What makes you think he won't kill you anyway?" Boone asked calmly. "Once you've finished his dirty work, you'll be expendable, too."

Lance turned, aiming his gun at Jude. "Best shut your mouth, Boone, or I'll shoot the girl. Bad enough selling her out, but to add her death to your crimes?"

"How did I sell anyone out?" Boone's tone held a sharper edge. "I never got paid, remember?"

"Sorry about that," Lance said with a vicious grin, "but you can't spend the money anyway, not where you're going."

"You won't spend it, either," Boone told him, looking as hard and mean as Lance himself. "I'll see you in hell first."

"Get him out of here, Lieutenant." Lance waved his gun in dismissal. "I have more important matters to deal with."

Jude told herself it had nothing to do with Boone being dragged away. This was her chance, and she had to seize it. She crept forward while everyone else watched Billy shove Boone out the door, but her skirts and Renny Claiborne got in the way. He grabbed her from behind before she could raise the shears to strike.

Sneering, Lance took them from her and tossed them to the ground. "What is it with you women and scissors?" he said angrily, rubbing the scar on his arm. "Hold on to her, Renny," he snarled. "I don't want her going anywhere until I'm through with Latour. Then I can take my time and pleasure killing the little bitch."

Jude felt too numb to know fear. As grim as life seemed a short time ago, at least she'd had hope for the future. *I'll come back for you,* Boone had promised mere hours earlier, but his sole concern had been with that bag on the sofa. Had everything between them been a lie?

How he must have laughed at the naive trusting fool who had offered her locket. The fact that he could take it—that he could let her stumble through her confession about lying to *him,* all the while knowing he would bring her to this moment—proved how cold and ruthless the man could be. She should be glad that he was getting what he deserved, but all she could feel was the pain of his betrayal.

As if to prove she had other things to worry about, Lance turned to smile at her. "Well, now, Miss Latour, what say we get this party started."

Twenty-three

A half-moon lent a strangle glow to the night as Tucker walked across the backyard, Billy's gun barrel jabbing into his spine. He wondered how many Gray Ghosts lurked out here, waiting to pounce. Lord knew, he hadn't taken two steps onto the porch before they jumped out of the shadows to grab him.

He also wondered what had become of Christopher. The boy had been far enough behind him to escape detection, and Tucker hoped that he'd gone for help. That was why he'd been playing Buford's game, hoping to stall for time.

Too bad he seemed to be running out of it.

He thought of trying to wrestle Billy for his gun, but he didn't dare ignore Buford's warning. The man had seen right through his bluff—he'd known Tucker would do anything to keep Jude from harm. If only Jude could have seen it, too—but from her horrified expression, Tucker doubted she'd ever again believe a word he uttered.

"This way," Billy said behind him, directing him to follow a path through the undergrowth, jabbing the gun into his back.

Tucker knew his sole remaining hope—a slim one at that—would be to talk Billy out of killing him. "I hope you realize," he said quietly so only his friend could hear. "Sooner or later that man will have you all dancing at the end of a rope."

Billy likewise kept his voice low, but no less intense.

"You think you know a person, but you never do, not really. His lying, his using the boys and me, it just ain't right, Jesse. Tain't right at all."

"Neither is marching me out to the woods. We go way back, Billy. Can you really kill me just because some maniac fancies himself an empire?"

"Reckon I can't. No, don't turn around," he hissed, poking with his pistol. "I don't know who's watching. I figure we need to go all the way to the swamps before we can skirt around back to the house and make our move."

Tucker couldn't trust what he heard. "You'll help me save the Latours?"

Billy laughed softly. "Seems like old times, don't it, me and you tracking through the woods? Hell, Jesse, this is liable to get me killed, but I can't condone killing innocent women for financial gain. For me this was never about the money—well, at least not entirely. I still have some scruples left."

And thank the good Lord for that. "What do you suggest we do?"

"See how the undergrowth to the right stretches clear to the house? You're the scout. Get us past the guards and over to that point, and from there, it's a short skip to the back entrance. If we're smart, and real careful, we can duck in through that door and sneak up on the cap'n unawares."

"You know an awful lot about this place."

"Yeah, well, let's just say I thought it prudent to check my surroundings, in case I had to get out quick." The gun left Tucker's back. "I think this is far enough. We can stop here. I'll just fire a few shots in the air—"

Tucker reached out to stay his arm.

"Cap'n has to think you're dead," Billy insisted. "If you're worried this will upset the little lady, never fear—she'll be seeing you alive and well soon enough."

"I don't imagine she'll care one way or the other, not after the picture I let Buford paint of me." Tucker removed his hand, realizing Billy was right, that Buford would be less inclined to pull the trigger if he thought he had all the time in the world for his plans.

"Don't reckon she will, from what I've seen of the little lady. That is one proud and stubborn female. Want me to put in a good word for you?" Billy added with a grin, firing two shots at the sky.

That would be a big help, Tucker thought wryly. "Thanks, Billy, but I can handle this one." He doubted there was much anyone could say in his behalf.

"Let's wait here just a minute or two to give me time to dispose of your body." Billy gestured to a log, where he took a seat.

Tucker understood why they should wait, but he couldn't sit, too worried about what might be going on in that house. Pacing before Billy, he found it eerie here in the semidark, the sounds and smells of the bayou unsettling him further. Knowing Jude could scout their way through these paths blindfolded, he wished she were with them—but after seeing her face as he left the parlor, he figured missing her was something he'd have to get used to. "Say we get to Buford," he asked, refusing to follow that train of thought, "what will you do afterward? You can't go back to the Gray Ghosts or to saving the Confederacy."

"No, don't reckon I can." Billy wore a pensive expression. "Listening to him in there, I could see you was right. Ain't no hope for the South. I gotta be thinking about saving my own neck now. Hell, maybe I'll head out west, like you suggested—take a new name for myself. Or I can always hire on with the Younger brothers. I hear them and the James boys are going into business together."

Getting involved with other bushwhackers didn't seem a good idea to Tucker, but he said nothing. Being Billy, he'd do as he pleased anyway.

Billy sighed. "Gotta say, something like this makes a man stop and take stock. I'm thinking I was wrong that night in St. Louis, that there ain't no such thing as destiny. If there was, I'd be taking the easy way out, yet here I am, choosing to risk my neck to help a friend. And feeling mighty good about it, too."

Tucker had to smile. "You head out west, Billy," he found himself advising anyway. "Out to California, or Colorado, where you can start fresh."

"What about you, Jesse? You looking to settle down with that little filly?"

Tucker stopped pacing to glare at him. "She's not a damned horse."

"Begging your pardon. No need to get so testy." Rising slowly to his feet, Billy once again wore his lazy grin. "C'mon. Let's go get her then."

"Do I get a weapon?"

Hard to miss that instant of hesitation before Billy reached down for Tucker's revolver. Two shots left, Tucker remembered as he took his weapon. He'd have to make each one count.

They made their way in silence, Tucker concentrating on all movement in the bushes. Hearing a twig snap a short way from the house, he pulled Billy back behind a tree, seconds before two men crept past on the intersecting trail ahead. "A patrol making their rounds," he said when they'd gone, taking heart from the possibility that it was less strength in numbers, and more mobility that enabled them to keep an eye on the place. "How many men do you figure are out here?"

Billy shrugged. "A dozen, maybe."

"Are they all as loyal as Buford thinks?"

"Divide and conquer?" Billy grinned. "Like the man said, loyalty is a prime motivating factor, but then again so is greed. I can name a good six who will go with whoever is holding the money. The others I might be able to turn to our way of thinking, given the chance."

"Let's hope you get it. We've got maybe five minutes

before the next patrol comes by. Think we can make a break for it?"

"Yeah, let's do it."

It did seem like old times, Tucker thought—it felt good having his friend fight at his side again. Gripping his Colt, he led the way through the undergrowth, his gaze on the entrance Billy described. They had a good twenty feet of open ground to cross, so they might better do so separately. "You first," Tucker told him, gesturing at the door. "Stay low, on your belly."

Watching Billy crawl away, Tucker thought he heard shouts coming from the front of the house. He froze—the air itself seemed to freeze—as he imagined all sorts of horrors. He waited for the sound to be repeated, but other than the eerie whisper of the breeze and the constant drone of mosquitoes, he heard nothing more while Billy covered the distance and slipped through the door unnoticed.

Hold it open for me, Tucker pleaded silently as he began to crawl across the yard, conscious of how near they were to the end of their five minutes. If that patrol came along now, he'd be hung out to dry.

Peering through the dark, he found the door ahead slammed shut.

The distance felt like miles. Worse, he heard the shouting again, definitely female, and definitely pleading. Gripping the Colt, cursing himself for not stocking up on ammunition and Billy for being undependable, he crept through the grass. A few feet from the door, close enough to get up and push through it, he heard the snap in the bushes behind him. *Hold on, Jude,* he willed her as he froze there on the ground, praying the shadows would hide him, that the patrol wouldn't notice.

Trouble was, he couldn't see them, and thereby couldn't know whether or not they'd passed by. He had to lie there, ticking off the minutes in his head, giving them what he hoped was time enough to go, before rising slowly to a crouch. Thanking the fates that the door wasn't rusted, he pushed through and found himself enveloped by total blackness.

"Damn you, Billy," he muttered under his breath, feeling his way through the dark to what he assumed was the front of the house.

"I'm right here behind you, Jesse."

Even with the whisper, Tucker could hear the amusement in Billy's voice. "The shouting?" he asked, stifling irritation. "Can you tell where it came from?"

"I'm judging the front hallway, but I guess they could still be in that parlor. Reckon we should take the door to your right."

"Let's go then." Easing his way through the dark, groping with his hands, Tucker at last felt a knob. He turned it slowly, blessing Latour's household maintenance as once again, the door slid open silently to reveal a hallway bathed in kerosene lighting. He could hear Buford's cold, penetrating laughter.

"Thanks for the pail of water, Preacher," the man was saying. "I'd say Latour looks awake enough now. Can't you just imagine the remorse he must be feeling for killing his old enemy, Henri Morteau? String him up, boys. Let's put the poor man out of his misery."

"No!" Jude cried out.

"Damn you, Lance." Quickening his pace, Tucker recognized Guin's quiet voice. "You swore if I signed that marriage license, you wouldn't do this."

"I told you both to shut up." From his tone Buford was losing patience.

"You won't get away with it," Jude kept on, never one for letting prudence get in the way of her emotions. "No one will believe a convicted criminal."

Tucker heard the slap of palm against flesh. The bastard had backhanded her. "One more word," he heard Buford snarl, "and it will be your last."

Feeling murderous himself, Tucker reached a partly opened door to the hallway in time to watch Preacher and Brady Watkins slip a noose around a groggy Latour's neck. They had him propped on a chair beneath the circular stairway, the rope attached to the banister above. The plan must be to knock the chair out from under him and make it look like suicide.

But Tucker's concern was with Jude. Peering through the crack in the door, he found her to the far left, struggling in Claiborne's grasp. Wasn't great odds, just him and Billy against these four, and with only two shots in his revolver. They should probably split up, Billy going to the door on the far side of the stairway. Glancing over his shoulder to convey this, Tucker noticed with a sinking sensation that Billy had once again vanished.

"You won't ever be able to live here at Camelot," Jude ground out. "I'll make sure everyone knows what you did."

"And what makes you think you'll be alive to tell them?" Unable to resist the opportunity, Buford strolled over to gloat.

Damn you, Billy, Tucker thought. With him there to make a diversion, Tucker could have tried for Buford, but with the man's gaze and gun now fixed on Jude, he didn't dare take the chance.

"I don't have to be alive," Jude tossed back. "Folks hereabouts know you. They and my brothers will be asking about the corpses you left littering the place."

"And did you think I wouldn't say anything, either?" Next to her, her wrists tied behind her, Guin stood with quiet dignity. "Are you that self-absorbed you didn't realize I'd be shouting from the rooftops that you murdered my husband?"

Buford shook his head sadly. "The object was always to marry you, sugar, not live with you. I have a signed license giving me all your assets, so why would I put up with your carping? And don't worry your pretty little head about corpses. You'll all be floating face first down the Mississippi. Pity, considering your beauty. Only imagine what muddy water and hungry fish can do to a body, if and when they ever find you." His laughter rang through the hall.

Tucker tightened his grip on his weapon.

"Gentleman, I think we've delayed enough." Buford grabbed Guin so she could do nothing to stop them. "Give that chair a good, stiff kick."

Watching Jude's face, Tucker saw her desperation. She was going to do something stupid, he realized. Being Jude, she wouldn't think about the risk to her own life in her attempt to save Latour. Eyeing the rope, then his revolver, Tucker grimaced. He hated wasting a precious bullet, especially on a man like Latour, but what was his choice? Someone had to save Jude from her own selfless folly.

Taking aim, he shot out the rope in its middle as the chair went flying. Latour fell to the floor with a thud. Brady and Preacher went ducking for cover behind the stairs.

"Fools," Buford screeched. "Get the bastard that shot that gun."

"I got him, Cap'n," Billy called out, jabbing the ever-present gun barrel once again into his spine. "Trust me," he whispered in Tucker's ear as he grabbed the Colt. Remembering those prime motivating factors he'd called loyalty and greed, Tucker had to wonder which motivated Billy's current actions.

"Sorry about that," Billy apologized to Buford as he forced Tucker into the hallway. "He got away from me in the woods. I had to track him to the house."

"Hell and damnation," Buford raged. "Preacher, get us another rope."

"I'll have to go clear out back."

"Get it," Buford shouted, "lest you want me shooting you, too. For pity's sake, Boone, why couldn't you leave well enough alone?"

"I tend to react poorly when folks try to kill me."

Tightening his hold on Guin, Buford nodded at Latour, who was struggling into a sitting position. "I'd have thought you'd rather see him swing." His gaze went to Jude, still wriggling in Claiborne's arms. "You know, before I kill you in front of these ladies, I've something I should share with you. It's really quite ironic, actually, that all this time, tracking down Latour, you never once stopped to think you could be after the wrong man."

Tucker ached to haul off and slug his smirking face. "What are you ranting on about now?"

"Rafe actually did try to call off that raid on your farm, but the papers got conveniently lost in the shuffle. Right along with the official leave he'd gotten to deal with family matters. He'd just learned about my release from prison, you see, and was anxious to get home to protect his family."

"Are you saying he didn't burn the farm? That you did?"

Lance shrugged. "I saw a chance to rise in the ranks and took it. I also thought Curtis Holland would have left his mistress with some money, but live and learn, I always say. After it was over, good old Henri was all too happy to arrange things to blame Latour. He'd been captured by Yankees by then, unable to protest or prove his innocence, so Henri found it remarkably easy to document his guilt. That's the true value of money, my friends, the ability to rewrite history to your satisfaction. Henri's now dead, of course, as will be anyone else who might reveal the truth."

"What about those who raided the farm with you?" Tucker asked, needing to know if Billy had taken part in his mother's death. If so, there was no sense hoping he could ever trust him again.

"If they're not Gray Ghosts, they're dead and buried," Buford said, telling him nothing. "Just as you soon will be."

"I don't think so, mister. I got this fine old shotgun saying otherwise."

Rooster stood in the doorway to the left, toting a weapon

too large for his skinny frame. Aware of the boy's lack of skill, Tucker stifled a groan.

"And I got this big old repeater," Christopher added from behind Tucker.

His appearance did little to lighten Tucker's spirits, his shoulder reminding him of that kid's inaccuracy with a weapon. If they started shooting, Guin and Jude could be caught in the cross fire. Hell, they were all liable to be eating bullets.

"If our friendship ever meant anything," he hissed at Billy, holding out his hand, "give me my gun."

"Friendship, nothing," Buford spat out. "You have your orders, Lieutenant."

Billy shook his head sadly. "Sorry, Cap'n, but it just ain't right, what you did to Jesse's mama."

Tucker felt a surge of faith in his fellow man, not to mention outright relief, as his Colt dropped into his grasp. He liked to think Billy had known the boys were there and had merely been waiting for them to get into position.

Gripping his revolver, Tucker kept his eye on Jude. Clearly rattled by the change in circumstances, Claiborne might be less apt to put his life on the line. "Give it up, Buford," Tucker warned, nodding at Guin. "Her sons are on the way with the law."

Buford merely laughed. "Wouldn't think you'd want to be talking to the authorities, either. Why, I just need to mention that you're the bushwhacker, Jesse Holland, to have you transported to a Missouri jail. Though with the evidence we planted at Morteau's, you'd probably hang right here in Louisiana."

Tucker had no intention of going to jail, not before he saw his brothers safely settled. "I'll take my chances," he said coldly. "How about you, Buford? Think you can make it out of here alive with four guns trained on you?"

Buford didn't bat a lash. "Four on three isn't bad, considering two of yours are kids."

"Five on two, Buford," Latour said feebly from the floor. Somewhere in the confusion, he'd gotten the gun from Brady and now held it to the man's head.

Visibly edgy now, Buford backed up closer to Claiborne. "Yeah, but we have your women," he said, motioning his accomplice back toward the parlor. "You won't be taking chances with their lives."

Tucker shared Latour's frustration. Though known as a crack shot, Latour was obviously keeping himself upright by sheer force of will and his aim was bound to suffer. Switching his attention back to Buford, Tucker saw the man's face darken.

"Where did Cochoran go?" Buford shouted. "And damnit, where's the redheaded kid with the shotgun?"

"I was watching Latour," Renny said needlessly, earning Buford's fury.

"Get the girl back into the parlor," the man snapped, looking ready to shoot the next thing to move. "Let's get the bag of money, and get the hell out of here."

With the struggling women impeding their progress, Buford and Renny didn't get far before Tucker reached the parlor door. The fact that the carpetbag was no longer on the sofa helped slow them down. "Damn you, Boone," Buford growled, the blood vessels in his forehead about to burst. "How the hell did you get my money?"

Tucker now guessed where Billy had gone, but he saw no sense in correcting Buford. "Let's make a trade," he bluffed. "The women for the bag."

"I'm not stupid." Buford backed Renny and their hostages to the veranda doors. "These females are my sole hope of getting out alive. I have more cash in Missouri, and I might better build my empire there. I know a certain farm being sold for back taxes that ought to suit my needs just fine."

Over my dead body, Tucker thought, weighing his chances of rushing the man as he tried to slip out the door.

"Give us to the count of one hundred to get away," Buford said, anticipating the move. "I see or hear you anywhere near, and the girl gets it in the head."

With only Christopher at his side and one shot left in his revolver, Tucker couldn't chance it.

"Quick, grab the lamp on the table, Renny," Buford directed, snatching up the one on the mantel. For good measure he snatched a container of kerosene standing by the door.

He didn't want light, Tucker knew, as he watched the quartet back out onto the veranda. Buford meant to set fire to the house, with the rest of them in it.

Tucker turned to Christopher. "Help your father," he told the boy as he led him back to the hallway. "Get him outside. Now."

"You're going after them? But he said—"

"He's going to kill Jude anyway. I can't let that happen."

For once the boy didn't argue. Nodding solemnly, he turned to his father.

Tucker raced out the front door, reaching the side of the house in time to watch Rooster step from the bushes, taking aim with the shotgun. Before Tucker could warn him not to risk hitting Jude, the boy let off a blast.

Claiborne dropped to the ground, clutching his leg, his lamp flying through the air to land near Buford's feet. Kerosene went splashing, igniting the leaf-strewn ground. In the glow of the sudden fire, Tucker watched Jude scramble away toward the back of the house.

He turned his attention to Buford. Though momentarily distracted by the flames near his legs, the man now faced Rooster, pointing his gun in the boy's direction. One shot, Tucker thought, as he aimed his revolver, aware that it had to be perfect. Setting his sights on the bastard's black heart, he thought of that long-ago day when he'd been forced to put down his dog. This, too, would be a mercy killing, he decided, his way of putting Jude and her family out of their misery.

But the instant he squeezed the trigger, Buford moved to sidestep the flame creeping toward him, and Tucker hit the kerosene container instead.

Shouting an oath, Buford let go of Guin as he spun around to assess this latest threat. The volatile liquid sprayed his trousers. Buford had time enough to raise his gun again and mutter, "Damn you, Boone," before the tenacious flame caught up with him, licking hungrily at his fume-soaked clothing, transforming him into a raging ball of fire.

Tucker ran to push Guin out of the way, beating down the flames attacking her skirt. "Do something," she cried to him, staring at the terrible specter of Buford running about the yard, his ungodly howls splitting the night.

He hesitated, tempted to let the man suffer the same fate Buford had given his mother, but Guin's pressure on his arm pricked his conscience. Noticing Jude and Rooster, carting pails of water to douse the flames near the house, he went to them, clenching his jaw. He took Rooster's bucket and flung water at Buford, now reduced to a whimpering wretch, twitching on the ground.

Sending Rooster to refill his pail, Tucker reached for Jude's, but she held tight, eyeing him coldly. "I've got no love for the man, either," he told her, "but as your mother reminded me, we can't stoop to his level."

Guin stepped up to place a hand on his arm. "It's too late, Mr. Boone. He's dead now and beyond feeling." She shuddered, looking back at Buford. "Thank you for trying though. I might despise Lance for what he did, but no one should die so horribly."

Jude tossed her pail of water on the piles of leaves, and after a slight hiss, the night went eerily silent. Renny Claiborne had taken off, Tucker noticed. Given his wound, he must have crawled away in the confusion.

With a sigh, Guin turned to Jude. "As long as you're all right, I think I'll go inside to tend to your father."

"He's out in front with Christopher," Tucker told her, eyeing what was left of Buford. "Unlike him they're both fine."

Looking from him to Jude, Guin gave him a feeble smile. As she walked away, the silence deepened.

Turning to Jude, seeing her bruises and scrapes, those badges of her strength and courage, Tucker struggled for the right opening. He ached to cradle her in his arms, to reassure her that her family was safe, yet the stiff manner in which she held herself warned that she'd only push him away.

He stared at her, memorizing every feature, struck anew by how much his hopes and dreams were tangled up with this woman. "I'm glad it's over," he said inanely.

"Yes, I suppose it is." Her tone was flat, her gaze riveted on the house.

"I want to explain. What I said in there, that nonsense with Buford—"

"Please, no more." He could hear the strain in her voice, as if she feared that with one more word, she'd break apart. "It doesn't matter anyway."

He took a step closer. "Of course it matters. How else will we know how to go from here."

"From where, Boone?" she asked sharply, stepping back. *"To* where?"

He didn't know which emotion had the greater grip on him, anger or dread. "Damnit Jude, you can't think—"

"I don't know what to think anymore," she cried out. "You lied to me, and kept lying, even when you had no real need. And you're so good at it, so glib and charming. How am I ever again supposed to know if you're telling the truth?"

Anger won over. "You could at least look me in the eye," he growled at her. "What happened to trusting me?"

"What happened? You look me in the eye, Boone, and tell me you didn't know what those men planned to do with Rafe, that all along you weren't in this for the money. Tell me that honestly, and then we can talk about trust."

How cold she sounded, how remote. What could he say now that wouldn't make it worse? Whatever his motives, he'd done all that she'd accused. No sense adding to it with another lie.

She sighed heavily. "I hear a boat coming. Most likely it's my brothers, bringing the law. You'll want to be heading out, before anyone starts looking too deeply into your past."

"I don't need anyone protecting me."

"It's not for you," she said coldly, still refusing to look his way. "It's for your brothers, so they can have that farm." She wrapped her arms around her, as if suddenly cold. "Like I said earlier, they can stay here. You can send for them once you've taken care of matters in Missouri."

He tried to reach for her, to warm her. "Jude—"

She wrenched away. "If you'll excuse me, I want to see that Rafe is okay."

She pushed past and Tucker saw no reason to stop her, or even remind her that he'd already said that Latour was fine. She'd only point out yet again how little she could trust him.

"Jude don't mean half what she says," Rooster said, stepping up beside him. "Give her time to cool down, and she'll come around."

"She meant it, all right." Taking the bucket from the boy, he tossed its contents on the smoking leaves, just to be certain the fire wouldn't threaten the house. From downriver, he could hear the boat edging closer. "It's time I left anyway."

"If you say so." Rooster cast a longing glance at the house. "Give me a half hour, and I'll go collect the twins."

Tucker, too, gazed at the house, knowing full well what

EVERY DREAM COME TRUE 327

he'd be leaving behind. "I can't take my brothers with me this trip, Rooster. Jude said they could stay here until I get things settled, so I was hoping maybe you'd stay and help out with them."

"You and me, I thought we were a team."

Setting a hand on the boy's bony shoulder, Tucker felt his throat tighten again. "We are a team, son, and I'm going to need your help once I get the deed for the farm, but right now, Jude needs you more. I want you to watch out for her, keep her happy and smiling. Can you do that for me?"

Rooster still looked rebellious, but he nodded all the same.

"I'll send for you," Tucker told him, gently squeezing his shoulder. "I swear it, just as soon as I am able."

"Yeah."

He winced at Rooster's flat tone. Not even the boy believed him. "I'd appreciate it if you'd saddle up some horses and take me to Roseland, so I can explain to the twins what I'm going to do."

"They won't understand it any better than me. Don't you get it, Boone? We're all supposed to stay together."

"The horses, Rooster. I'll meet you in the drive."

The boy stomped off, clearly upset. Not feeling much happier himself, Tucker went to the front of the house, meaning to take one last opportunity to explain, but the Latours had already gone inside. "Jude went upstairs with Guin and Rafe," Christopher explained, standing guard at the door. "Your friend Brady took off running when he heard the shotgun blast. From his shouts, I imagine he convinced the others to flee with him. You might want to do the same, Boone."

Everybody seemed anxious to see the last of him. "I need to talk to Jude first," he said anyway.

Christopher planted his feet stubbornly. "She don't want

to talk to you. Haven't you hurt her enough? You just go on and leave her to her family."

She'd sent her brother to get rid of him—couldn't make the message any clearer than that. Watching Christopher turn to climb the stairs, Tucker felt like another door had been slammed in his face. Open up and let us help you, she'd once said to him. Now maybe she could see why he kept to himself.

Gazing up the empty stairway, Tucker reached inside his shirt for the locket. No real reason to wear it now. Cupping it in his hand, he realized how much strength he'd gained from that silly piece of silver. How much hope.

He set the locket down firmly on the hallway table. What was it Billy had said about fate? That no matter how hard we tried to change things, we always ended up right back where we belonged.

No, nothing had changed, he thought, as he turned to stride out the door. Even with all that had happened, he was still Tucker Boone, the loner. Always was and always would be.

Twenty-four

Jude stared out the window, clutching the locket, half wishing—half dreading—she'd see Boone walk up the drive. Not much chance of that, though. Nearly a week had passed since she'd sent him away—a grueling week of fixing the legal blame on Lance Buford—and it had begun to sink in that she might never see Tucker Boone again.

I don't know what to think, she'd told him, and she still didn't, despite spending both night and day pondering each detail of their time together. Logic insisted that she condemn Boone for lying to her, yet she'd seen his face that day at the farm, had held him in her arms, and she wanted to believe he'd had his reasons. She, too, would have sacrificed everything to avenge her mother's death, her heart argued, only to have her brain point out that if he were so noble, why had he left with the carpetbag full of money? If he'd taken it to buy back the farm, as she hoped, then why had he yet to send for his brothers?

On and on it went, her mind a battlefield of conflicting emotions, pride leveled against yearning, hope warring with heartbreak. She kept telling herself to be glad that she'd been strong, that she'd spared herself a lifetime of pain and sorrow—but deep down, forever after, she'd be haunted by the look on his face when she called him a liar. *Some folks aren't worth saving,* he'd once told her, and by walking away that night she'd pretty well told him he was one of those people.

Tears pooled in her eyes as she clutched the locket. "Why, Boone?" she whispered out the window. "Why couldn't we build that farm together?"

But that was dumb. To share a life, they had to talk, to find some way around the ever-widening gap between them—but each day that slipped by with no word from him made it clear that Boone would rather confront the future the same way he'd met the past—alone and unfettered.

"I remember when I gave you that locket," Guin said from the doorway. "What happened?" she asked gently, gliding over to sit beside Jude on the window seat. "What has you so sad?"

"I don't know what you're talking about."

Guin smiled, well aware that they'd played this game of conversational hide-and-seek too often in the past. "I remember your swearing that you'd keep that locket until you could give it to your own little girl. Tucker Boone must have been pretty special to you if you'd trust it in his care."

"You knew I'd given it to him?"

"I'm your mother. Of course I'd notice where my girl gives her heart."

All at once it was too much: Guin's caring, the worry and loneliness, the fear that she'd never see Boone again. "Oh, Guin, I love him so much," she cried, falling into her mother's arms. "Why did he have to be the wrong man?"

Saying nothing, stroking her hair, Guin let her pour out her heart. Starting from the first day she'd met Boone, carefully omitting how intimate they'd been, Jude told her mother what had happened between them. It felt good to get it all out, but she felt sad and depleted when she was done. "And now," she added with a sniff, pulling away, "I don't know what to believe. You heard him that night. You heard Lance. I don't want to think Boone could care more about the money than us, but what choice has he left me?"

Guin shook her head. "There's always a choice. The choice that you make in here," she said, pointing at Jude's chest.

"Funny, Boone always told me to think with my head, not my heart."

"Of course he would—he's a man." Guin chuckled. "What male ever trusts his true feelings?"

"Rafe seems to."

Guin shook her head, no doubt thinking about how her stubborn husband had insisted upon traveling to New Orleans to see the lawyer today, for all that he still limped with a cane. "He's gotten better about expressing himself, but I'm still working on him." She reached out to pat Jude's hands. "Even at his worst, Rafe would agree that you should trust in your own feelings. Nobody is more perceptive about others than you."

Jude grinned sheepishly. "Except maybe Rooster."

"And who is most vocal about going to Missouri?"

Not a day went by that Rooster didn't campaign to go after Boone, claiming he was suffering terribly without them. "Rooster already has the twins nagging me night and day. Don't tell me he's recruited you, too?"

"Does he need to? We both know you want to go." Guin smiled. "Ah, honey, I know it seems a big risk, but sometimes that's what love is. It wasn't easy for Rafe and I, either, but we wouldn't be here, living out our dream, if we hadn't taken that leap of faith."

"How can I trust him? He lied to me."

"Shouldn't you at least give him the chance to explain? Your family and those who love you know you must have picked Boone for a reason. Forget trusting him. Maybe it's time you had a little faith in yourself."

Jude gazed at the locket in her hand. Trust, that's what it came down to. Guin was right—she had picked him for a reason, one that had nothing to do with logic or accusations. It was that streak of decency she'd glimpsed from the start, and the knowledge that Tucker Boone needed her. That she needed him.

She looked around the bedroom she'd known for so

much of her life, at the mother who'd pulled her through many a crisis. "But, Guin, how can I leave Camelot?"

Guin looked away, a little misty-eyed herself. "It won't be the same without you here to keep us going—but, honey, all Rafe and I ever wanted was to see you kids happily settled. If Missouri is where you need to go to start pursuing your own dreams, well, at least it's not so far away we can't visit."

"So are we going or not?" Rooster asked impatiently from the doorway. "Cob and Germy is just about busting a gut, waiting to hear."

Scrubbing at her eyes, Jude tried to speak sternly. "For heaven's sake, Rooster, those boys have names. Why don't you ever use them?"

"We don't mind," Jacob said, poking his head in the room. "Ain't nobody ever bothered to give us a nickname before. Huh, Germy?"

The younger boy appeared next to Jacob with an ear-to-ear grin. "Nope. I think it's kinda nice. Done made us one big happy family."

Stifling a grin, Jude decided she had to spend more time with the twins, if for no other reason than to repair the damage Rooster had done to their grammar.

"Then maybe you'd better find a nickname for me, too." Christopher loomed behind the three boys. "You don't think I'll let Jude go alone?"

"But I thought you hated Boone," she said, surprised by his grudging offer. "You told me you didn't trust him."

Christopher shrugged, looking at his feet. "It's not easy to admit, but I think I was jealous. Like with Rooster, I wanted to jump to conclusions, to think the worst." He looked up then, staring her straight in the eye. "The thing is, I watched his face that night with Buford. Everything Boone did, he did to protect you. I reckon if he can be that concerned with my sister's welfare, the least I owe him is the chance to explain."

"Oh, Christopher, do you mean it?" She stood, hard put to hide her happiness. "You'll really come with me to Missouri?"

"For a time. Somebody's got to protect you from Rooster."

Seeing the younger boy was ready to snap back at him, Jude clapped her hands at all four boys. "Then what are you guys doing standing here gaping at me? Shouldn't you start packing?"

Giving a series of war whoops, the quartet turned back into the hallway.

"Kip"—she could hear Rooster jeering at her brother as they walked off—"that's what I'm gonna call you."

"Over my dead body. Want me calling you Mikey?"

"Want me showing you my fist?"

Rolling her eyes, Jude turned to Guin with a wide, spreading grin. "Pray for me, will you? It looks like I'm off to Missouri with my big, happy family."

Boone stepped into the empty lawyer's office, sick at heart. He had less than half the amount he needed to pay off the taxes, and no real hope that anyone would listen to his plea, but he'd run out of options. Unless he could convince the court to grant him more time, in less than six hours the family farm would slip out of his grasp forever.

He thought of his brothers and Rooster, waiting in Louisiana. They must be scared, wondering what had become of him, but he couldn't contact, or even send for them, when every last cent had to go to saving their future. Lilah and her greed had left him all but destitute.

It still made him furious that she'd cleaned out his bank account, and only the fact that she, too, had been ruined, both financially and physically, had stopped him from taking out his rage on her hide. Badly burned, Lilah wouldn't have much of a life from now on. She'd be going straight from the hospital to a jail cell, until the folks of Salvation had their savings repaid.

Someday Tucker might see his money, but by then it would be too late, unless he could convince this lawyer to argue his case.

With added frustration, he thought of Buford's carpetbag, knowing now that it must have been his money inside it. Picturing Billy's grin when he'd last seen him, Tucker could well imagine his old friend out west somewhere, living it up with his savings, laughing all the way to the bank.

Clasping his hat in his hands, Tucker stared out the window, wondering where the lawyer was and what could be keeping him. It drove him crazy, this waiting and standing still. That was when the thoughts got hold of him: the yearnings, the wondering about what might have been. For the past two weeks, he'd tried convincing himself it was better this way, but late each night, facing yet another empty day ahead, he knew it wasn't better, not by a long shot.

Funny, the things he found himself missing—Rooster's offbeat humor, Jacob's solemn logic, Jeremy's unswerving devotion. Yet what he missed most, what he ached for with startling intensity, was a smile—Jude's smile as she bullied him into doing what they both knew was best.

He clasped his hat tighter. Life just wasn't the same without Jude, would never be the same again. Somewhere along the way, she'd taught him that Tucker Boone wasn't so much a loner as a man alone.

Damn, he had to find some way to get her back into his future.

It was why he was here, when his natural inclination might have been to give up the fight. For the first time in his life, he'd found a cause worth the battle. One way or another, he was going to get back the farm and make it a home to be proud of. Not just for his brothers but to convince Jude she belonged there with them. He'd win her back, damnit, or he'd die trying.

"Tucker Boone?" a voice called from the doorway, and turning, Tucker felt as if the air had been sucked from his lungs. The man in the doorway wasn't the lawyer he'd expected, but rather Congressman Curtis Holland, his father.

It had been some time since he'd seen him, so Tucker should have expected the graying hair and lined features, but he hadn't. No more than he'd anticipated the man to be here. The last thing he needed right now was this ghost from his past. "I'm Boone," he said coldly.

Clearing his throat, Holland stepped into the room, looking everywhere but at Tucker's face. "You're probably wondering what I'm doing here," he started, then let an awkward silence fall between them.

"I've got a good idea." Having neither time nor patience for games, Tucker decided to get it all out in the open. "You want the farm back. You see an opportunity to get it cheap, and you aim to take it. Let me warn you, though, I'm not a helpless young boy this time. My mother charged me to take care of the twins, so I'm honor bound to do whatever I must to stop you. And quite frankly, after what you did to their mama, I'd think even you would see it's time to do right by them."

"Indeed?" Holland faced him now, his steel-gray brows raised in surprise.

Tucker braced himself, knowing he could be one sentence away from being hauled off by Holland's good buddy, the sheriff, but nonetheless determined to have his say. "All these years we never asked a thing from you, never traded on our kinship, going about our business and letting you go about yours. My mother sung your praises to the grave, Congressman. For her sake, if nothing else, I'm asking you not to take this last chance at a future away from my brothers."

Holland's only answer was a sigh so deep, it left another uncomfortable silence blanketing the room. "I hadn't remembered your being quite so blunt, Jesse," he said after a while.

Tucker bristled. "Begging your pardon, sir, but I can't see how you could remember much of anything about me. And it's Tucker, now. Tucker Boone."

"Yes, well, why don't we start with your reading this?" Suddenly brisk and businesslike, Holland held out a piece of paper embossed with a government seal.

"What is it?"

Holland smiled faintly. "Ah, yes, I do remember your skepticism. In short, what you're looking at is a pardon for all crimes committed during the course of the war. But I'm afraid it's been made out in the name of Jesse Holland."

"A pardon?" Stunned, Tucker couldn't keep the amazement out of his tone.

"I suppose I've come to agree with you. Something does need to be done about the twins, and you stand a much better chance of keeping them—and that farm—if you can use your own name."

"Why?"

"I assume you mean, why the change of heart?" Holland smiled sadly. "Let's just say I've recently been forced to take a good long look at myself, and I haven't much enjoyed what I've seen. What I did to your mother . . ."

His voice trailed off, his face contorted with pain. He walked across the room to gaze out the window, as if he felt more comfortable addressing it than Tucker. "Your mother was the finest woman I've ever known. A stronger man would have stayed at her side and been far richer for it, but I was young and ambitious and weak—and too readily influenced by what my family expected of me. All these years later, what do I have? A career I despise and a life that brings no satisfaction, and the sad knowledge that I could have had three fine sons to take pride in—had I once had the courage to acknowledge them."

Tucker shifted uneasily, trying to summon up the old

hatred and suspicion but instead found himself almost pitying the man.

"I know it's too late to make amends for what I did to your mother, but I do plan to do right by you and your brothers. I'm done hiding from my past, Jesse."

"I told you, the name's Tucker."

Holland turned to face him, smiling grimly. "I suppose I can't blame you for taking on a new name when your daddy's done little to make you want the one he gave you, but don't let that stubborn pride of yours stand in the way of your future. Please, take the pardon, son, and for the same reason, I want you taking this, too." He stepped forward, handing Tucker a second paper.

"What's this?" Tucker asked warily as he took them from this stranger who suddenly expected to be his father.

"The deed to the farm, with all taxes paid until the end of the year. Call it my stake—hell, call it my faith—in your future."

Tucker stared at the papers, unable to read, to see anything at all in his shock. "I can't take this," he said automatically. "I can't accept your charity."

"You know, that's exactly what your young lady warned me you'd say."

Tucker raised his gaze from the papers to focus on the man's face. "What young lady?"

Curtis Holland chuckled softly. "That's quite a little tigress you have there, son. Darned near chewed my head off, making me see what I should have realized years ago. She says it's not too late, that it's never too late to show someone you love them."

He clenched the papers. It was all coming at him too fast to absorb. "Wait, are you talking about Jude?"

"I don't know. Am I, young lady?"

Tucker whirled to find Jude waiting quietly in the doorway.

Without thinking, he took a step forward, invitation

enough for her to come flying into his arms. Lifting her up, kissing her, savoring the sweet miracle of holding her in his arms, he forgot all about the man behind them until Curtis Holland audibly cleared his throat.

"I think I'll leave Jude to convince you," he said, striding for the door. "It would appear she can do so far more eloquently than I."

"We'll come talk with you later," Jude assured Holland.

"Don't you think that was my decision to make?" Tucker asked her when his father had left the room. "I'm the one who has the history with that bastard."

"Oh, Boone, please don't be difficult about this. He's giving you the farm."

"If you think that after a lifetime of neglect, I'm going to let that man just stroll in and take over, you have—"

Grinning, she placed a gentle finger over his lips. "The last thing I want to do now is argue. For one thing I've had enough of it on the trip up here with my brother and Rooster, but I really need to hear you say you're glad to see me."

"Glad?" He took her face in his hands, running his thumbs over the soft, warm skin of her cheeks. "Don't you know it's been hell without you? God help me, but I've felt like one of your strays, cut off from the herd. All I could think about was finding my way back to you. I'd have sold my soul just to see your smile."

She obliged him by beaming ear to ear. "Oh, Boone, I know just what you mean. There's so much I want to say to you, so much to get straight between us—but all I can think of at the moment is how good it is to see your face. I can't help it. I think I'm always gonna love you."

Crushing her to him, he kissed her long and hard, celebrating inside like a man who'd just been reprieved from a hanging. Thinking of how she'd come all this way—how she'd gone to his father on his behalf—he knew he would indeed sell his soul for this woman. "Then there's hope?"

he asked huskily when they at last broke apart. "You think—one day—you can forgive me?"

"If you can forgive me. I guess we're both what life has made us, and sometimes that'll mean bending our rules if we want to stay together." With a shy smile, she reached up to place her locket over his head. "I once promised that I'd believe in you, that I'd stay fighting in your corner—and as long as you'll have me, that's what I aim to do."

Feeling the locket against his chest, Tucker knew a keen sense of rightness, all the pieces falling into place. "I have to know," he told her with a catch in his voice. "Does this mean you're proposing to me, woman?"

She looked away, suddenly shy. "I wasn't trying to trap you into marriage, Boone, I was just—"

"Because if you're not," he said, holding her arms so that she had to look at him, "you should know I expect nothing less. I want to make good and certain that you are my woman and nobody else's, until death do us part."

Moisture pooled in her eyes as she stared up at him. "Oh, Boone, are you serious? You really want to get married?"

"Put plain and simple, I love you, Jude. You are my life. I just can't imagine living it without you."

She bit her lip, as if afraid to hope. "You sure you want the commitment? All that added responsibility?"

He had never loved her more than in that moment. "Somebody's got to help you take care of all the strays you've collected," he told her gruffly.

"Oh, Boone," she said in a rush, raining kisses on his face. "Then I guess this means we truly will be one big, happy family."

The family part he still wasn't all that convinced about, but kissing her long and hard, he was pretty damned sure of the happy part.

Epilogue

Three Years Later

Jude gazed out the kitchen window at the glittering river in the distance, feeling a rush of excitement. Christopher should be here soon, returning from a year-long journey to the mine fields in Montana, and with his arrival, her family would be complete. The rest of the Latours had descended on them the day before, to celebrate the new baby's christening.

Glancing back at the cradle, Jude found Guin reaching down for the six-week-old Sarah, unable to resist cuddling the baby in her arms again. It had been this way with little Tucker two years ago, when he was the infant. Jude smiled indulgently, understanding that her mother couldn't stop herself from spoiling her grandchildren. And Lord knew, her son refused to go anywhere his Grammy Guin didn't go.

Jude turned back to the window in time to notice Amanda run by with Jeremy, whispering and plotting as they always did when the families got together. They'd all better brace themselves for some mischief, she thought. Jeremy had proven to have a remarkable sense of humor, and with Amanda to egg him on, there was no telling what might be waiting in anyone's bed tonight.

Jacob, on the other hand, considered himself far too mature for such nonsense, choosing instead to stay with

Rooster, who tended to follow her brothers around on their visits. Now that he could read, Rooster had become insatiably curious about the rest of the world and ruthlessly pumped Peter and Paul for information about their trips out west, or Patrick about his travels abroad. Nowadays he even managed to talk to Christopher without arguing, though neither could resist the occasional taunt.

Anxious for her brother to arrive, Jude looked again at the river, only to have her gaze snared by the two men in the pasture—her husband and father—as they watched the new foal test its legs. From their smiles, it would seem last night's vigil in the barn had been well worth the effort, that this latest addition to the Holland stables would prove profitable as well.

Jude still found it hard to get used to her last name, though it had been at her urging that they adopt her husband's given one. She maintained that it made sense businesswise to use the influence her father-in-law offered, but unlike everyone around her, she'd never quite gotten around to calling him Jesse. In her mind, and in her heart, he would always be just plain Boone.

With a rush of emotion, she gazed at her husband of three years, marveling at the change in him. Gone was the Colt at his hips, and with it the bitterness that had hardened his clear blue eyes. He stood tall, proud, and confident—the breeze rippling through the golden strands of his hair as he surveyed the dream he had worked so hard to build. Raising horses had meant taking out a loan, money hard come by in the early days after the war. It wasn't until much later that they'd learned the cash had been advanced by his father. And while at first, the thought had enraged Boone, becoming a father himself had mellowed the man enough to see past his pride to the relative practicality. Being Boone, though, and no stranger to hard work, he'd vowed to slave day and night until he paid back every penny. His dream, after all, was to call the ranch their own.

Lord, but she loved that man.

"You're going to burn a hole in that glass the way you're staring through it," Guin teased gently. "Just go on outside and be with Jesse as you're clearly dying to do."

Torn, Jude stared from her husband to her mother. Her time with Guin was brief and all too precious, but, oh, how she longed to be at Boone's side as he watched the foal run, sharing their hope for the future.

"Go on," Guin encouraged, understanding as she always did. "You worked just as hard bringing that horse into the world. Go out and savor the moment with your husband. We'll be only too happy to take care of the little ones."

Sparing a glance at John, keeping Tucker busy with his new blocks on the floor, and Jeanie, waiting impatiently for her turn to hold the baby, Jude untied her apron and tossed it onto the table. "I'll be right back," she promised, dashing out the door.

Making her way to the pasture, she realized a third man had joined Boone and Rafe. Though his back was to her, his distinguished air and expensive clothing told her their latest guest must be Curtis Holland. Now that he'd retired from politics, Boone's father was forever showing up for a visit, and he especially liked to be here to trade views with Rafe.

She felt another fierce rush of pride as she thought of how over the years, Boone had found a way to reconcile his differences with both men. Once they'd sat down and talked, he and Rafe had discovered they had much in common, making it natural that they become friends. The process had been harder with his father, and things were still a bit strained between the two—but as she'd pointed out, a man couldn't go forward until he resolved his past. She hadn't told Boone yet, but she'd already decided that they would name their next boy Curtis.

Boone turned then, spotting her, his handsome face breaking into a wide, beaming smile. Hurrying to close the distance between them, he reached out for her and lifted her high in the air. "We've got us a winner, sweetheart," he told Jude as he set her back down on her feet. "Even the congressman thinks so."

She had to do something about getting him to call the man *father*, she thought, though clearly this was not the moment to chide him. Boone was already going on about the next mare ready to foal, and his hopes for that addition to the stables. Holding his arms, staring at his sun-bronzed face, she could feel the excitement running through his veins. "What is it?" she asked when he paused for breath. "Something's happened, hasn't it?"

"Never could hide anything from you." He grinned down at her. "The congressman came to tell me that he just received a wire from Billy Cochran. It would seem my old buddy does have a conscience. He's sent the exact amount Lilah stole from me, with instructions that it be deposited in my account."

"Oh, Boone, that's wonderful."

His grin became more a grimace. "I should warn, the gift has strings attached. It seems he's planning on coming for a visit."

Jude did her best to hide her misgivings. She still didn't know what to make of Billy, and she wasn't sure Boone did, either, but the two nonetheless had a bond between them, and as long as he was her husband's friend, she'd do her best to make Billy welcome. Though before he came, she'd make sure to lock up the silver.

Boone grinned suddenly, no doubt following her thoughts. "That might be a good time to let the congressman take the twins and Rooster on that trip he's promised. That should avoid Billy exerting any bad influence on them."

"He might have changed," she offered, though in truth she held little hope of that.

Boone nodded. "Time and a shift in circumstance can

do a lot for a man. Look at me. All Billy really needs is a purpose in life. And with it, the love of a good woman."

Feeling his hand brush her cheek, Jude melted inside. He didn't have to say more for her to know what he was thinking. She, too, said a silent prayer of thanks each night for the miracle of their marriage.

"Which reminds me," he said suddenly, removing his hand to reach into his pocket. "According to our agreement, I should be returning this."

With confusion she stared at the locket he placed into her hand.

"Guin tells me you're supposed to be handing it down to our daughter," he explained gently.

"Yes, but—"

"You offered it as collateral, Jude. As I remember, I was only supposed to hold on to it until I had this place bought and paid for."

"The money from Billy?" she asked, searching his eyes. "It's enough to pay off that loan to your father?"

His smile seemed to engulf her. "That it is, and there's enough left over to pay for the mare I've been eyeing down in Tennessee. Ah, Jude, it's really happening. The farm, the stables, our children. All our dreams are coming true."

Reaching up to pull his head down to hers, Jude kissed him with all the love in her, unaware that anyone else in the world existed.

Until Rooster's shout pierced their self-absorption: "Listen, a steamboat. It must be Christopher at last."

Latours came from everywhere, joining with Hollands as they made their way to the dock. Smiling at her husband, linking arms with him, Jude joined the rest of her family as they hurried to greet her brother.

It wouldn't always be like this, she knew—all her loved ones gathered for such a happy occasion—but all in all, she had to agree with Boone. Squeezing his arm, so happy

EVERY DREAM COME TRUE

she felt ready to burst, she realized that her wishes for the future had indeed come true.

Every dream and more.

Author's Note

Every now and then, a cast of characters comes alive and won't go away. For me, that's how it was after writing *Always*. The Latours of Louisiana, especially Jude, apparently had yet another story in them, one so many of you urged me to tell. Thank you for those encouraging letters—I really enjoyed researching and writing *Every Dream Come True*.

For the record, as far as I've been able to discover, there never was a Gray Ghost Gang or a town in Missouri called Salvation. The strife along the Kansas-Missouri border was only too real, I'm afraid, as was General Order Eleven, allowing Union troops to turn the area into what many called "The Burnt District." The government hoped the ordinance would discourage the local guerrilla fighters and their sympathizers, but the destruction and bitterness caused by the torching of civilian property led many of those irregular soldiers to take to a life of crime like Billy Cochoran did—most notably, the Younger brothers and the notorious James Gang.

If you enjoyed *Every Dream Come True*, as always, I'd love to hear from you. Please write to:

> Barbara Benedict
> PO Box 4024
> Tustin, CA
> 92780-4024

ROMANCE FROM ROSANNE BITTNER

CARESS (0-8217-3791-0, $5.99)

FULL CIRCLE (0-8217-4711-8, $5.99)

SHAMELESS (0-8217-4056-3, $5.99)

SIOUX SPLENDOR (0-8217-5157-3, $4.99)

UNFORGETTABLE (0-8217-4423-2, $5.50)

TEXAS EMBRACE (0-8217-5625-7, $5.99)

UNTIL TOMORROW (0-8217-5064-X, $5.99)

Available wherever paperbacks are sold, or order direct from the Publisher. Send cover price plus 50¢ per copy for mailing and handling to Penguin USA, P.O. Box 999, c/o Dept. 17109, Bergenfield, NJ 07621. Residents of New York and Tennessee must include sales tax. DO NOT SEND CASH.

ROMANCE FROM HANNAH HOWELL

MY VALIANT KNIGHT   (0-8217-5186-7, $5.50)

ONLY FOR YOU   (0-8217-4993-5, $4.99)

UNCONQUERED   (0-8217-5417-3, $5.99)

WILD ROSES   (0-8217-5677-X, $5.99)

Available wherever paperbacks are sold, or order direct from the Publisher. Send cover price plus 50¢ per copy for mailing and handling to Penguin USA, P.O. Box 999, c/o Dept. 17109, Bergenfield, NJ 07621. Residents of New York and Tennessee must include sales tax. DO NOT SEND CASH.

FROM ROSANNE BITTNER:
ZEBRA SAVAGE DESTINY ROMANCE!

#1: SWEET PRAIRIE PASSION   (0-8217-5342-8, $5.99)

#2: RIDE THE FREE WIND   (0-8217-5343-6, $5.99)

#3: RIVER OF LOVE   (0-8217-5344-4, $5.99)

#4: EMBRACE THE
    WILD WIND   (0-8217-5413-0, $5.99)

#7: EAGLE'S SONG   (0-8217-5326-6, $5.99)

Available wherever paperbacks are sold, or order direct from the Publisher. Send cover price plus 50¢ per copy for mailing and handling to Penguin USA, P.O. Box 999, c/o Dept. 17109, Bergenfield, NJ 07621. Residents of New York and Tennessee must include sales tax. DO NOT SEND CASH.

SPINE TINGLING ROMANCE
FROM STELLA CAMERON!

PURE DELIGHTS			(0-8217-4798-3, $5.99)

SHEER PLEASURES		(0-8217-5093-3, $5.99)

TRUE BLISS			(0-8217-5369-X, $5.99)

Available wherever paperbacks are sold, or order direct from the Publisher. Send cover price plus 50¢ per copy for mailing and handling to Penguin USA, P.O. Box 999, c/o Dept. 17109, Bergenfield, NJ 07621. Residents of New York and Tennessee must include sales tax. DO NOT SEND CASH.

PASSIONATE ROMANCE FROM BETINA KRAHN!

HIDDEN FIRES	(0-8217-4953-6, $4.99)
LOVE'S BRAZEN FIRE	(0-8217-5691-5, $5.99)
MIDNIGHT MAGIC	(0-8217-4994-3, $4.99)
PASSION'S RANSOM	(0-8217-5130-1, $5.99)
REBEL PASSION	(0-8217-5526-9, $5.99)

Available wherever paperbacks are sold, or order direct from the Publisher. Send cover price plus 50¢ per copy for mailing and handling to Penguin USA, P.O. Box 999, c/o Dept. 17109, Bergenfield, NJ 07621. Residents of New York and Tennessee must include sales tax. DO NOT SEND CASH.